PRAISE FO

Miss Moriarty, I

"Tense and atmospherically rich, particularly in the Cornwall chapters, the novel is interspersed with brief scenes of Charlotte and Ingram's new intimacy, including some chuckle-inducing letters. . . . An enjoyable jigsaw puzzle in the Holmes tradition, with gothic thrills and a dash of romance." —*Kirkus Reviews* (starred review)

"Readers will revel in seeing Charlotte and her dearest companions at the top of their game in this eventful and pivotal entry in the formidable series." —*BookPage*

"*Miss Moriarty, I Presume?* is a complex story, full of twists and unexpected turns. Settle in for a delightful read, full of red herrings and memorable set pieces, and above all, let the talented Sherry Thomas dazzle you as she performs literary sleights of hand at every turn. Brava!" —Criminal Element

PRAISE FOR

The Lady Sherlock Series

"These books, which recast Sherlock Holmes as Charlotte Holmes, are perfect for those who adore layered stories. Unignorable questions of gender, expectation, and privilege lurk beneath complex mysteries and a slowly scorching romance." —*The Washington Post*

"Loaded with suspense . . . a riveting and absorbing read . . . a beautifully written novel; you'll savor the unraveling of the mystery and the brilliance of its heroine." —NPR

"Sherry Thomas has done the impossible and crafted a fresh, exciting new version of Sherlock Holmes."
—Deanna Raybourn, *New York Times* bestselling author of
A Perilous Undertaking

"Sherry Thomas is a master of her craft, and *A Study in Scarlet Women* is an unqualified success: brilliantly executed, beautifully written, and magnificently original—I want the next volume now!"

—Tasha Alexander, *New York Times* bestselling author

"Readers will wait with bated breath to discover how Thomas will skillfully weave in each aspect of the Sherlockian canon and devour the pages to learn how the mystery unfolds."

—Anna Lee Huber, national bestselling author of the Lady Darby Mysteries

"Clever historical details and a top-shelf mystery add to the winning appeal of this first volume in the Lady Sherlock series. A must-read for fans of historical mysteries." —*Library Journal* (starred review)

"A completely new, brilliantly conceived take on the iconic detective.... A plot worthy of [Sir Arthur Conan Doyle] at his best." —*Booklist*

"Fast-paced storytelling and witty prose add further appeal for those who like their historical mysteries playful."

—*Publishers Weekly* on *The Art of Theft*

"Quick-witted and swashbuckling, Thomas's novel is a feminist Victorian delight. Perfect for fans of Deanna Raybourn, Elizabeth Peters, or C. S. Harris, *The Art of Theft* is an excellent entry in a wonderful historical series. Its deft pacing, quirky heroine, and intriguing cast of characters make it a mysterious tour de force."

—Shelf Awareness on *The Art of Theft*

"With an increasingly beloved detective crew, this Victorian mystery offers thrills and sharp insights into human behavior."

—*Kirkus Reviews* (starred review) on *Murder on Cold Street*

A
TEMPEST
AT SEA

SHERRY THOMAS

BERKLEY
New York

BERKLEY
An imprint of Penguin Random House LLC
penguinrandomhouse.com

Copyright © 2023 by Sherry Thomas
Penguin Random House supports copyright. Copyright fuels creativity, encourages
diverse voices, promotes free speech, and creates a vibrant culture. Thank you for buying
an authorized edition of this book and for complying with copyright laws by not
reproducing, scanning, or distributing any part of it in any form without permission.
You are supporting writers and allowing Penguin Random House to continue
to publish books for every reader.

BERKLEY and the BERKLEY & B colophon are registered trademarks of
Penguin Random House LLC.

Library of Congress Cataloging-in-Publication Data

Names: Thomas, Sherry (Sherry M.) author.
Title: A tempest at sea / Sherry Thomas.
Description: First Edition. | New York: Berkley, 2023. |
Series: The Lady Sherlock series
Identifiers: LCCN 2022031846 (print) | LCCN 2022031847 (ebook) |
ISBN 9780593200605 (trade paperback) | ISBN 9780593200612 (ebook)
Subjects: LCGFT: Novels.
Classification: LCC PS3620.H6426 T46 2023 (print) |
LCC PS3620.H6426 (ebook) | DDC 813/.6—dc23/eng/20220711
LC record available at https://lccn.loc.gov/2022031846
LC ebook record available at https://lccn.loc.gov/2022031847

First Edition: March 2023

Printed in the United States of America
1st Printing

*To my wonderful, kind, and beautiful mother,
with whom I love going on ocean voyages*

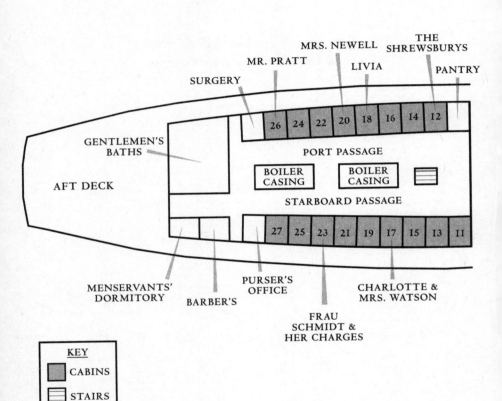

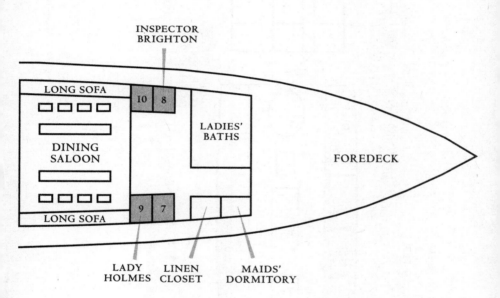

INSPECTOR
BRIGHTON

LONG SOFA

DINING
SALOON

10 | 8

LADIES'
BATHS

FOREDECK

9 | 7

LONG SOFA

LADY
HOLMES

LINEN
CLOSET

MAIDS'
DORMITORY

Saloon Deck (main deck)

Not drawn to scale. Some structures have been omitted.

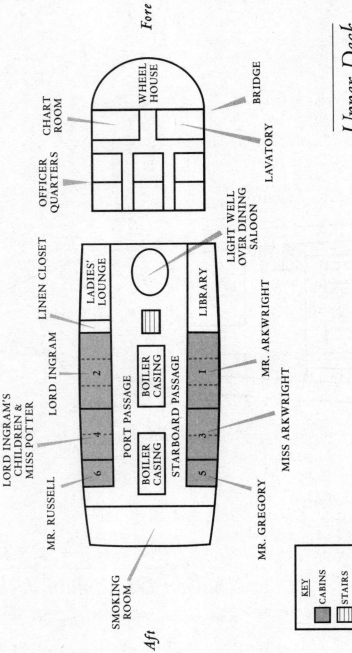

Upper Deck

Not drawn to scale. Some structures have been omitted.

Fore

CHART ROOM

WHEEL HOUSE

BRIDGE

OFFICER QUARTERS

LAVATORY

LINEN CLOSET

LADIES' LOUNGE

LORD INGRAM'S CHILDREN & MISS POTTER

LORD INGRAM

MR. ARKWRIGHT

LIGHT WELL OVER DINING SALOON

LIBRARY

MR. RUSSELL

PORT PASSAGE

2

BOILER CASING

1

MISS ARKWRIGHT

BOILER CASING

4

STARBOARD PASSAGE

3

MR. GREGORY

6

5

SMOKING ROOM

Aft

KEY

CABINS

STAIRS

INTERIOR PARTITION

One

"There's something you're not telling me, Ash," said Charlotte Holmes.

The night was starless, the sky low and heavy. But spring was beginning to make itself felt as a certain fullness in the air, the swelling of blackthorn buds on the cusp of flowering.

Charlotte was warmly wrapped in an Inverness cape, a deerstalker cap on her head. No one who saw her in her masculine attire now—if anyone could see in the pitch-blackness—would have mistaken her for the pink silk-clad vixen who had successfully ambushed Lord Ingram Ashburton earlier in the evening.

It had been their first meeting since her terribly inauspicious "death" in Cornwall, where her body was said to have been dissolved in a vat of perchloric acid. Her closest associates had "mourned" in a manner befitting those who could not publicly acknowledge their grief. But they had also worried in truth as weeks wore on with no news from her.

Charlotte, even before she had been advised to stay away from her usual haunts following that spectacle on the Cornish coast, had decided on a safe haven: none other than Eastleigh Park, the country seat of the Duke of Wycliffe, Lord Ingram's eldest brother. The estate's hunting lodge had proved a peaceful abode for her and, of course, an excellent location in which to lie in wait for Lord Ingram to turn up for his annual Easter visit.

And now, after a few highly pleasurable hours becoming reacquainted in his bedroom in the main residence, he was escorting her back to the hunting lodge, as she could not be seen in his quarters come morning, whether as a man or a woman. The night was thick as a wall. She walked nearly blindly, but he had grown up on this estate and ambled along, guiding her with an occasional touch on her elbow or the small of her back.

"I'll tell you when we're inside," he said, in response to her earlier comment, his tone deliberately light.

But when they'd entered the hunting lodge and lit a few sconces, he did not divulge what he'd kept from her. Instead, he left with a hand candle to make sure that the structure, bigger than her ancestral home, was free from hidden intruders. Charlotte removed her caped coat and prosthetic paunch, strolled into the drawing room, and stretched out on a settee, the gold brocade upholstery of which was visibly fraying— the hunting lodge, an opulent addition to the estate a hundred and fifty years ago, had not been improved in at least two generations.

He returned, handed a biscuit tin to her, crossed the room to a padded chair upholstered in the same worn brocade, and leaned against its rounded armrest, one leg straight, the other half-bent. He was rarely so informal in his posture. But even so, his shoulders remained open, his weight evenly distributed. He lifted his head and seemed about to speak—but didn't.

A single lamp bronzed the antlers mounted above the door and delineated shadows in the hollow of his cheeks. Charlotte opened the tin, nibbled on an almond macaroon, and waited, though she had already guessed what he was about to tell her.

It was not about Moriarty—her lover was distracted, but not yet alarmed. Still the matter had made him concerned for her safety. A task that required her to leave Eastleigh Park then—a task for Sherlock Holmes? And who could make such a request and be sure that he would, in fact, relay it to her?

When she'd polished off the slightly too sweet macaroon and he still hadn't spoken, she flicked crumbs from her fingertips and said, "What does my lord Remington want, exactly? And is he not aware that the estimable consulting detective of 18 Upper Baker Street is not currently offering 'his' services to the public?"

Lord Remington, Lord Ingram's brother, was responsible for much of the intelligence gathering in the far-flung corners of the empire. But in recent months, he had taken a greater interest in the domestic side of things.

Lord Ingram expelled a breath. "Oh, Remington is more than aware of your absence from London. I believe he is of the view that rather than rusticating, you might as well lend him a helping hand."

No one who had attracted Moriarty as an enemy could afford to merely rusticate. Charlotte had been busy. "Is my lord Remington dangling safety from Moriarty as a lure?"

She had no plans to venture abroad on someone else's behalf for a lesser prize.

Her lover looked grumpy, very nearly irate. "At this moment, I'm not sure even the power of the crown—let alone Remington, merely a servant of the crown—could keep anyone safe from Moriarty."

"Surely that's too pessimistic an outlook?"

"Surely you're right, madam. All the same, I find it difficult to be pleased about anything that involves risk to you."

She smiled to herself, opened the biscuit tin again, and took out a jam tart. "What exactly is Lord Remington offering me?"

"More or less what Moriarty thought he might: When you decide to reemerge into the world, Remington will let it be known that to harm you would be to injure him."

A magical amulet it wasn't, but neither was it something to sneeze at.

"And in exchange," continued Lord Ingram, "he wants you to find a dossier that has gone missing—Remington has judged you very good at finding things."

"He is not wrong about that." Ever since her toddlerhood, Charlotte had always known not only where everything was located in the house but also if any items had been misplaced. "However, I imagine that what he wants found would not be as easy to locate as Mrs. Watson's reading glasses."

"No. Not only does Remington not know where it is, he cannot even be sure who has it."

Apparently, Lord Remington's underlings had been cultivating in secret a Prussian embassy attaché. But perhaps their practice of secrecy left something to be desired, for Herr Klein, the attaché, was abruptly recalled to the fatherland. Lord Remington's underlings, however, were convinced that before Herr Klein's hasty departure, he'd left them something.

But Herr Klein had not stepped out of his hired house in the days immediately preceding his removal. Moreover, his house had been watched by parties both British and Prussian. So, to whom had he entrusted this dossier?

The Kleins—husband, wife, and two young children—were no longer in Britain and would not have been available for questioning even if Herr Klein had remained at his post. Their servants, relying on delivery for foodstuff and laundered garments, had also not left the place during the period of greatest interest.

By the time Charlotte officially took on the commission, the house—and the servants—would have been searched multiple times by agents of the German Empire.

Moreover, while she would be furnished with a list of names, individuals who had entered and departed the consular assistant's household during the most critical span of time, she would not be permitted to question anyone on the list for their connection to the Kleins or their reasons for visiting the Klein household. She was only to observe and search—while keeping her involvement an absolute secret, naturally.

Two

Livia Holmes stepped out of her hotel room, feeling as if she were in a dream.

All her life, she had longed to travel. And not just to London, or Cowes, or someone's country house for a fortnight, but far, far away, a voyage for no other reason than to comprehend the height and breadth of the known world.

And now that the moment was here, now that she had but to walk down the stairs, exit the hotel, and head for the Port of Southampton, she was desperately afraid that she might wake up after all and find that everything was but a dream.

Like all those dreams she'd had as a child, running away from home, just Charlotte and her. And all those dreams she'd had of late, of holding her Mr. Marbleton by the hand and sprinting toward a carriage, a train, a ship, and once, even a hot air balloon, which only needed its ballast removed to float into the sky.

She tightened her fingers around the handle of her satchel. Perhaps she was all the more anxious because it had already been such a lovely trip.

According to Lord Ingram, who had arrived first, he and his children had spent a few wet, chilly days in the port city. But as soon as Livia and Mrs. Newell reached Southampton, the weather had turned sunny and mild. Together, everyone had driven out to nearby New Forest and visited the ruins of a thirteenth-century abbey. They had made a tour of Southampton's stretches of medieval town walls. And yesterday afternoon they had strolled along the sinuous River Itchen, then flown kites in a nearby park. Livia, who had only intended to watch, had found herself with a spool in hand, running on bright new grass, laughing as her butterfly kite caught the current and shot straight up.

On the way back to their hotel, young Master Carlisle, Lord Ingram's son, had leaned against his father in the carriage, and Lord Ingram had pulled the boy closer. And Livia had felt almost as warm and safely ensconced.

"Are you ready, my dear?" asked Mrs. Newell, stepping into the passage after Livia. She was both Livia's second cousin and her official sponsor for this trip.

Livia took Mrs. Newell's arm and felt steadier. She loved the dear old lady, and it was her very great fortune to set out with someone who had always watched out for her. "Yes, ma'am. I'm ready."

With a smile, Mrs. Newell patted Livia's hand. They walked down the passage in the direction of the stairs. *May I stride ever closer to the journey of a lifetime,* Livia silently petitioned the universe. *May I begin a new life altogether.*

They reached the stair landing. A man and a woman descended from above, the woman clad in the most beautiful traveling costume Livia had ever beheld.

The cut of the dress was impeccable, the construction precise, the material understated yet luxurious. It moved with the smoothness of cream pouring from a pitcher, but more sumptuously—the simple-looking grey skirt was lined with several layers of tissue-thin blush pink silk chiffon. Together the pink and grey were delicate and evocative, reminiscent of a cherry sprig in blossom just visible in a spring mist.

The only imperfection, Livia was sorry to note, was the wearer of this sartorial sorcery.

She was about Livia's age, twenty-eight or so. Her figure served the dress well, but her features were more prominent than pretty. Had she evinced some vivacity or a steeliness of character, she might have made for an unconventional beauty. But she was simply . . . *there*. To say the dress overwhelmed her would be too generous. The dress, in all its splendor, existed independently of her.

Her companion was a tall, broad man whose day coat nearly burst at the seams to accommodate his shoulders and upper arms. His features, like hers, were oversized. On some men, that translated into a brooding handsomeness. But this man's countenance seemed only ferocious—and vaguely misaligned, as if God had been in a hurry on the day of his creation.

Livia and Mrs. Newell emerged onto the stair landing as the man and the woman reached the bottom of their flight of steps. Everyone hesitated. Then the man motioned toward the next flight, indicating that Livia and Mrs. Newell should proceed. A courteous gesture, but it came across to Livia—who, granted, was wildly sensitive about such things—as tinged with a trace of impatience.

She nodded and walked down beside Mrs. Newell—and nearly stumbled at the sight of the man who stood at the foot of the steps, looking up.

Roger Shrewsbury.

As Livia saw it, Charlotte had made only two unwise decisions in her entire life: trusting Sir Henry, their father, to sponsor her to an education; and after he'd reneged, ridding herself of her maidenhead to blackmail him for funds necessary for that education. The instrument of her lunacy had been none other than Roger Shrewsbury, a childhood chum who was married enough and pliant enough to be almost perfect for her purposes.

Charlotte had failed, however, to account for Shrewsbury's monumental uselessness. How incompetent must a man be to turn a simple hymen breaching into one of the biggest Society scandals in years?

Livia lifted her satchel two inches higher, gauging its weight. Her steamer trunk had gone to the docks directly from the train. Even her smaller cabin luggage had been collected this morning. And she, not entirely trustful that all her belongings would make their way onto the ship, had overstuffed the satchel.

It was heavy. So heavy. Perfect for coshing Roger Shrewsbury on the head.

"I wouldn't, my dear," whispered Mrs. Newell.

Livia gritted her teeth. She'd lacerate him with her eyes then and, when he took note, give him the cut direct.

But he didn't notice her at all; he gawked somewhere above and behind her. She glanced back.

There is no excellent beauty that hath not some strangeness in the proportion, Francis Bacon had said. And it was Livia's experience that some faces that at first struck one as irregular could, with greater familiarity, become ravishing. But even with a second look, the woman in the lovely traveling costume still failed to fascinate.

Not that Shrewsbury appeared enraptured, only incredulous, dismayed, and agog.

The man perceived this stranger's undisguised scrutiny of his companion. He glared at Shrewsbury, such a menacing look that Livia, nowhere near its trajectory, flinched.

Roger Shrewsbury, on the other hand, failed to register the man's displeasure. The woman looked bewildered and clung to the man.

Livia gave Shrewsbury another pointed stare as she walked past him. He remained oblivious.

As Livia and Mrs. Newell arrived in the hotel's dark-paneled foyer, Lord Ingram came through the entrance. "Ladies, good morning. I have sent the children off with Miss Potter. Shall we also make our way to the quay?"

Livia lowered her voice. "My lord, I just saw Roger Shrewsbury. You don't suppose that he is also traveling on the *Provence?*"

Lord Ingram did not appear as surprised as Livia felt. His gaze swept the foyer and returned to Livia. "I have not paid much attention to Mr. Shrewsbury's doings of late."

Livia was absurdly pleased. Of course he felt as she did, that Shrewsbury was a blundering ass who did not deserve to show his face in civilized society.

"My goodness," hissed Mrs. Newell, "but what *is* that boy doing?"

Livia had stood with her back to the rest of the foyer, determined to give Roger Shrewsbury the cold shoulder whether he knew it or not. But at the alarm in Mrs. Newell's tone, she turned to look.

Indeed, what in the world was Roger Shrewsbury doing?

The large man they had encountered on the stair landing had business to transact at the reception; his companion stood by meekly, her face lowered. And Roger Shrewsbury, the arrant fool, set himself barely three steps to the side and stared at the woman as if she were the first living, breathing female he'd ever witnessed.

Or perhaps it would be more accurate to say that he gaped at this otherwise ordinary woman as if she had two heads and three arms.

Lord Ingram sucked in a breath. "I think I'd better——"

He was too late.

The man spun around. He towered over Shrewsbury. "Sir, what is the meaning of this? Why do you persist in staring at my sister?"

He spoke with barely leashed anger, his Liverpudlian accent overlaid with the expansive vowels of . . . Australia?

Roger Shrewsbury blinked. His Adam's apple bobbed up and down as he took in the size of the man before him. "I——I'm sure I don't know what you mean."

"Maybe you don't. I scowled at you the entire way down the steps, but you goggled at her so hard you didn't even notice."

"There's——there's a very good explanation for it, sir, I assure you. And you need not worry that I will approach your sister. I wouldn't. I really wouldn't."

"Then what possible explanation could there be?"

The man took a step forward. He was nearly nose to nose with

Shrewsbury—or rather, Shrewsbury's nose was level with the second button of the man's shirt.

His sister caught him by the arm. "Jacob, please, please don't make a scene. Let's just go."

"No, this man hasn't expressed the least contrition."

"It doesn't matter, Jacob. I—"

"It does matter, Willa. You should never tolerate such disrespect."

"But it's not disrespect," mewled Roger Shrewsbury. "I was just bowled over, that was all. You understand, right, miss?"

Livia, who had craved for the brother to bury his fist in Roger Shrewsbury's face, was now torn between a desire to kick Shrewsbury in the head—why not simply apologize and bring the matter to an end?—and a wild curiosity.

Shrewsbury took half a step backward, even as his hand stretched out in a beseeching gesture. "I don't know whether you recognize me, miss, but last I saw you, you were—you wore only hors d'oeuvres and a bunch of grapes."

The siblings froze. Livia, too, could not believe what she was hearing. She looked around. She hadn't noticed earlier how crowded the foyer was, how many astonished and scandalized faces swiveled between Shrewsbury and the woman against whom he'd leveled a charge of indecency, at the very least.

"How dare you!" roared the brother. "How dare you cast aspersions on my sister!"

His meaty hand gripped Shrewsbury by the neck.

"I swear I'm telling the truth," squealed Shrewsbury. "Please, miss, please don't let him kill me. It was autumn before last, at that house party in the Kentish countryside. Surely you remember? You were the centerpiece on one of the tables. I gave you a glass of water when you told me you were thirsty!"

Livia gasped. The worst was Shrewsbury's desperate sincerity. He really believed he was helping himself in relating the specific details of an act of *public* indecency.

The brother's gaze swung to his sister. Her hands hovered, trembling, before her lips. And then she turned, picked up her skirts, and ran, her heels clacking loudly on the floor.

Livia was convinced that she would trip and injure herself. But the woman named Willa, though she stumbled and nearly mowed down a porter, shot out of the foyer at an impressive speed.

Her brother, like Livia, stared at the door through which his sister had disappeared.

He turned around and plowed his fist into Shrewsbury's face. Ladies screamed. Porters screamed. Livia would have screamed, too, if any sounds could have emerged from her throat.

Roger Shrewsbury staggered backward, teetered over someone's luggage, and crashed to the floor. Porters came rushing and attempted to hold the man back from further assault.

"No, Mr. Arkwright, you mustn't! Please! No more!"

But Mr. Arkwright shook them loose, yanked Roger Shrewsbury up by the collar, and administered another awful-sounding punch. Shrewsbury spun and fell face-first into reception, landing with a loud *ding* upon the bell.

Amid another fusillade of screams, Mr. Arkwright marched out of the hotel.

The RMS *Provence*, berthed quayside, shone in the sun, its steel hull a gleaming black, its upper levels blazing white. Four masts, each with three sets of crossbeams, rose fifty feet from the weather deck. Though they had the full complement of rigging, no sails had been unfurled to flap in the breeze. A platoon of seagulls squatted on the crossbeams; one strutted across as if on parade.

The masts were only auxiliary features. The *Provence*'s propulsion depended on a triple-expansion steam engine that drove a single screw propeller. Two stubby and rather incongruous-looking funnels rose between the masts to conduct exhaust from the great boilers below up and away from the vessel.

"Are you sure that one over there is not . . . *her*?" asked Mrs. Watson, her voice low and anxious.

Charlotte, standing with her back to the bulwark, her face tilted up to admire the *Provence*—so as not to appear too interested in the passengers—glanced toward "that one over there" referred to by Mrs. Watson, a woman of about thirty who had her hand on the shoulder of a young girl, the girl just tall enough to peer down at the bustling quay that smelled of coal smoke, grease, and a hint of rubbish.

"No," she murmured, telling Mrs. Watson what the latter already knew. "The one we're looking for would be traveling with a boy. Two boys, in fact."

Three weeks had passed since Charlotte and Lord Remington's emissary had agreed to terms. Her search since had been thorough, systematic, and fruitless. As fate would have it, her final possibility, a German governess, was scheduled to board the *Provence* on the exact sailing as that taken by Livia, Mrs. Newell, and Lord Ingram.

The ship had a maximum passenger capacity of seventy and sold only first-class passages, so everyone boarded on the same gangplank. Charlotte was sure she'd missed no one, but noon was drawing nigh and Frau Schmidt and her charges still hadn't appeared.

She turned around. The *Provence* measured 440 feet in length and 44 feet across at the beam, but other than the towering masts that dwarfed the funnels, it was not a terribly tall ship. With a hull full of coal and cargo, and the quay a good six feet above water, Charlotte did not loom much higher above the quay than she would have had she been standing at the bow window of her office, looking down on Upper Baker Street below.

Burly stevedores surrounded wagons of luggage and provisions. Enormous slabs of ice covered in straw mats were crane-lifted into the hold to keep those provisions fresh. Farther away, a mail wagon jostled toward them, eager to entrust its contents to a Royal Mail ship headed for the distant outposts of the empire.

Wait—the man coming up the gangplank, early middle age, tall, slightly portly, with a deep-featured face and a cordial expression, was he . . .

Yes, he was. Inspector Brighton of Scotland Yard.

Charlotte glanced down at the water; it was low tide in the estuary, and a band of green growth clung to the side of the quay. She did not look at Inspector Brighton again, not even when he must have disappeared inside. There had been a Brighton on the passenger list, but she and Lord Ingram had not considered that it might be their former adversary.

What was he doing here?

Ah, here came the Shrewsburys.

Because she had seen the passenger list, she had not worried earlier when Livia had embarked looking troubled. One of Livia's great regrets in life was not being able to bludgeon Roger Shrewsbury daily. To be confined shipboard with him must strike her as abhorrent and intolerable.

Shrewsbury had lowered the brim of his hat almost past his eyes, but when he glanced up at the small forest of bare masts atop the ship, Charlotte spotted the beginnings of a black eye—as well as a cut cheek, swelling up shiny and purple.

This was odd. To know that he'd sail on the *Provence*, Livia had to have seen him. But if she'd seen him like this, she should have appeared delighted, rather than disturbed.

Come to think of it, her dear Ash, when he'd come aboard, had also appeared somber. She'd attributed it to his concerns for her safety, but there could have been more than one cause for his gravity of mood.

The Shrewsburys did not embark by themselves but followed closely in the wake of a man in his early thirties, who strolled up the gangplank swishing his walking stick. Yet for all his air of jaunty superiority, his jacket was not new but had been remade to follow the most current dictates of fashion. Cutting the collar sharper likely presented no great difficulty, but the lengthening of the hem . . . As he sauntered past Charlotte and Mrs. Watson, stationed near the top of the gangplank, a strong breeze flapped up the center front of the jacket and revealed that the inside lining was short by three quarters of an inch.

A man of appearances.

Roger Shrewsbury, upon setting foot on the *Provence*, emitted a moan halfway between relief and anguish. He turned, as if he wanted to remain on deck for a while and look around.

His wife, her face stony, tugged on his arm. "Come."

When they'd gone past, Mrs. Watson leaned into Charlotte. "What did the wife see in him?"

Yet another luggage wagon drew up quayside; stevedores hoisted cabin trunks to their shoulders and deployed handcarts for the bulkier steamer trunks.

"His older brother, the baron, was childless after ten years of marriage," Charlotte whispered into Mrs. Watson's ear. "She's a minor heiress, some fortune but not enough to tempt a titleholder. Her parents thought they ought to take a chance on a younger son, and Mr. Shrewsbury was the younger son they settled on, since he seemed to have a decent chance of coming into a title. But after they married, the baroness gave birth to two boys in two and a half years."

"Ah . . ." said Mrs. Watson. Then, after a pause. "Do the children look like the baron?"

Charlotte had always enjoyed Mrs. Watson's earthy and mischievous bent of mind. This separation from her—Mrs. Watson had been in France since the events at Cornwall—had been long indeed. "Before Livia and I made our debut, Mrs. Newell told us, *Never comment on likeness*. But I will venture to say here, between friends, that yes, the boys resemble their father greatly."

Down below, three carriages pulled up to the quay almost simultaneously. A large man descended from the first and handed down a beautifully dressed woman—the man, too, was handsomely attired, but his physique was such that theoretically well-fitted garments ended up bunching and straining with the least movement.

The next carriage disgorged a medium-size man of about thirty. He glanced at the man and the woman from the first carriage, who were clearly related, and made a move as if to approach. But in the end, he only followed them, seven or eight paces behind, as the pair threaded their way toward the gangplank.

The occupants of the third carriage were slower to emerge. Charlotte held her breath. *Let it be Frau Schmidt and her charges. Let it be them.*

This was not how she had envisioned joining her friends and her sister on this trip: Spending so much time near her closest associates would make it easier for Moriarty to find her; nor could she use Lord Remington as a shield against this heightened danger, since she hadn't yet completed her task. But now that she was here, on the verge of a grand reunion, she was loath to leave in the event that her quarry did not show up.

Besides, where else would she find Frau Schmidt, if not here?

A woman alit from the third carriage. She was too young and too fashionable to be Frau Schmidt. An older, amply proportioned woman in a puce overcoat stuck out her head and studied the ship with a skeptical look.

Charlotte was astonished enough to raise a brow. Mrs. Watson gasped. "But that's—that's—"

That was none other than Lady Holmes, Charlotte and Livia's not particularly beloved mother. And her name had *not* been on the passenger list.

Lady Holmes stomped forward; the other woman, who must be her new maid, hurried after her.

Halfway up the gangplank, the beautifully dressed woman stopped and tugged at her skirt—it had snagged on the fibers of the rope railing. Her brother, who had been walking ahead, turned back and crouched down by her side.

The woman spoke. Snippets floated up to Charlotte.

". . . won't come loose."

". . . that'll tear."

". . . so frightfully costly."

Her tone was much too distraught for a mere snagged hem.

The man from the second carriage stopped a few paces away. He looked eager to help and, at the same time, afraid to go near.

Lady Holmes, her path blocked, turned down the corners of her lips. She tapped him on the shoulder and gestured for him to yield. The gangplank was narrow, and Lady Holmes not. The man turned sideways. The ropes behind him bowed outward as Lady Holmes shoved past.

"It was not *that* expensive, Willa," said the brother, sounding exasperated. "Really, I promise you it wasn't."

"I don't think you remember how much things cost anymore, Jacob."

The woman was still trying to untangle her skirt, but her gloved fingers were no help.

"Let me," said the man.

"You'll just tear it," answered the woman with such despair that Charlotte and Mrs. Watson glanced at each other.

"They'll weigh anchor any minute now and some of us are in a hurry," said Lady Holmes, her voice loud and peevish. "Step aside, will you?"

The sister's head whipped around. Her brother didn't move at all. "I will, when I'm asked nicely."

Lady Holmes looked as if someone had shoved a fly into her mouth. She'd heard his rough origins in his accent and she would never ask anything nicely of *him*.

Her finger jabbed out. "Listen, you common blackguard, when a lady tells you to step aside, you step aside."

The man remained unbothered. "And where is this lady? All I hear is some old fishwife barking for no reason."

Lady Holmes stood agape. Her husband had said a great many unkind things to her over the years, but Charlotte didn't believe she'd ever been spoken to with such disregard by a stranger.

The man's sister, who had tried so hard to avoid damaging her hem, now freed her skirt with a hard yank. She straightened. "Let's go, Jacob. Let's *go*."

She sounded desperately weary, yet pulled at her brother with a fierce strength.

It was not until they'd boarded that Lady Holmes managed a half-strangled, "How dare you!"

Her maid murmured some soothing words and persuaded her to resume her progress.

But Charlotte's attention was no longer on her. Down below, a woman was being tugged in opposite directions by two young boys. One jumped up and down and tried to run up the gangplank—she could hardly hold him back. The other, whom she was attempting to guide forward, drooped down as if he were asleep; she could not move a single step without dragging him along the not-so-pristine quay.

Finally. Frau Schmidt, in the flesh.

With great effort Frau Schmidt restrained the overexcited boy and rebuked him. The boy lowered his head and stood penitently to the side. She next sank to her haunches, set her hands on the other boy's arms, and spoke to him softly and seemingly not in English.

The governess had only one charge in the Pennington household, the boy she was able to discipline with a few words. And this other boy, listed as G. Bittner, must be a temporary charge—it was not an uncommon practice for parents of unaccompanied children to retain someone else's governess for the duration of a voyage.

Charlotte tapped Mrs. Watson, whose gaze had followed the combatants of a minute ago, and gestured with a push of her lips toward the quay. "Madam, we have work to do."

Three

"Have I ever told you, my dear, that the late Mr. Newell once sailed on the *Great Eastern*?" said Mrs. Newell with a twinkle in her eye.

She and Livia were undertaking a small tour of the ship's upper level public rooms, crossing the short distance from the library to the ladies' lounge.

"The largest ship ever built?" Livia marveled, as she opened the door of the lounge for Mrs. Newell.

If the *Great Eastern* were a nineteen-hand Shire horse, the *Provence* would be but a Shetland pony next to it. But of course, one of the *Great Eastern*'s many problems had been that it was too large and could never have fitted through the Suez Canal.

"He was determined to sail on the largest ship ever built at least once. And what a sailing he chose." Mrs. Newell chortled. "Two days out of Liverpool, she ran headlong into a hurricane that sheared off her paddle wheels, ripped away her sails, and bent her rudder two hundred degrees. She barely managed to limp into Queenstown, and the local authority kept her out for a good long while, afraid she'd damage their harbor."

"Was Mr. Newell not afraid?" Livia could scarcely imagine his ordeal.

The ladies' lounge was on the port side of the *Provence*'s upper level, its wallpaper printed with cheerful seashells, several large-paned windows open to the unseasonably warm day.

"Terrified," answered Mrs. Newell dryly. "They were caught in the hurricane for three days, and he said he was never so sure of impending death. But once he was on land again, it became one of the greatest and most beloved adventures of his life. And if he told the story after he'd had a few drinks, you'd think he personally jury-rigged the propeller that got the ship back into port."

Livia laughed. A soft breeze meandered in, bringing with it the scent of water and grass. She'd been feeling glum earlier, after what she'd witnessed at the hotel, and forgotten that she was still headed out to sea, to adventure.

She leaned on a windowsill. Outside, sunlight poured down, unimpeded by a single cloud. The *Provence* drifted southeast along the tidal estuary below Southampton. Green banks glided by; water fowls took flight before the prow of the oceangoing steamer.

What a lovely beginning to the greatest adventure of her life.

The three rows of gilded pendant lights in the *Provence*'s dining saloon, each containing two electric bulbs, were not lit—it was one o'clock in the afternoon and the saloon was bright from banks of windows *and* a light well overhead. Still, both Livia and Mrs. Newell craned their necks to look.

A few years ago, the *Tuscany*, the *Provence*'s sister ship, had docked in London for a time before its maiden voyage. There its brilliant electric lights had been displayed nightly, a flashy spectacle of the very latest in maritime technology: not the availability of electric lights in and of itself but the sheer abundance on a single vessel.

"Ah, modernity," murmured Mrs. Newell. "I remember reading about Mr. Franklin's kite experiment when I was a little girl. I did not think, in those distant days, that someday I would dine under the glow of bottled lightning."

Blue velvet sofas had been set into the port and starboard perimeters of the saloon, running their entire length. Along the sofas, eight tables had been placed, four on each side. In addition, two long tables occupied the center of the saloon.

They sat down at the port sofa table closest to the aft entrance. Livia removed her gloves and ran her fingertips lightly over the tufted upholstery.

So soft, so smooth, so new.

Her parents' home had been built more than two hundred years ago and its maintenance, in recent decades at least, had not been stellar. Everything sagged and creaked. Everything had tarnished over time. And even when all the rooms had been thoroughly cleaned, an odor of age lingered, of unseen decay in the walls and perhaps the foundation itself rotting away.

The *Provence*, on the other hand, had entered service only the year before and was disorientingly bright and shiny, albeit in a nice way. Livia laughed inwardly at her desire to lie down on the long sofa and wallow in its springy newness.

A stewardess filled their water goblets and inquired whether they wished to have consommé or mulligatawny soup. As she departed, an elderly woman in a russet day dress entered the dining saloon. She trudged forward with small steps, leaning on a cane. There were ravines—no, gorges and canyons—carved into her face. Against all those wrinkles, her blue-lensed spectacles appeared incongruous, like a bicycle parked next to a monolith at Stonehenge.

The old woman's gaze came to rest on Mrs. Newell. She blinked— and advanced toward their table, moving a little faster than earlier.

"Forgive me, ma'am," she said, her voice low and scratchy. "I don't mean to be rude, but you bear a great resemblance to a very old friend of mine. Her name is Adelia Reeve."

Livia recognized Mrs. Newell's maiden name. Mrs. Newell shifted, evidently as surprised as Livia.

Her reaction gratified the woman. "Yes, it really is you, isn't it?"

Mrs. Newell had a sharp mind. Livia expected that she would quickly identify the woman. But Mrs. Newell stared blankly at her, then looked toward Livia—not in appeal, exactly, but as if she herself couldn't believe she had no recollection of this stranger who obviously knew her well enough.

"Oh, I suppose I haven't been eighteen for a while," said the woman, sounding crestfallen. The lines on her face burrowed even deeper. "But you must at least remember my name. I was Sybelle Henderson when we were at Miss Ridgewood's school together. You were lucky—you were there for only six months. I had to endure the place for four years."

Her tone perked up. "We had a little fête when you were leaving. Lizzie Lumley, God rest her soul, smuggled in cake and sausages. Pauline Archibald played her pocket violin under the blanket. And I predicted that you'd meet with great fortune in your life."

Like images from a magic lantern spinning round the walls of a darkened room, wonder and disbelief chased across Mrs. Newell's features. Clearly, she recalled the details described by the former Sybelle Henderson, but still couldn't connect the latter's ancient face to her own memories of that bygone era.

The former Sybelle Henderson gave her tinted glasses a self-conscious adjustment. "I haven't slept well of late and fatigue makes me look a bit older. But surely you can still see my bone structure?"

Livia tried, but given the depth and multitude of the woman's wrinkles, she felt as if she were guessing at the shape of the original landscape beneath a wildly serrated Hindu Kush.

Mrs. Newell gave a small cackle. "I'm sure you haven't changed, but my eyes aren't what they used to be, and of course I'm much too vain to wear glasses in public."

"Oh ho ho!" Her erstwhile schoolmate hooted with laughter. "That does *not* sound like you. I was always the vain one, determined to net myself a wealthy husband. You, on the other hand, were busy plotting an independent spinsterhood."

Mrs. Newell chortled—not as awkwardly this time. "Alas, I wasn't able to achieve that laudable goal. But my late husband was a good man. I've been Mrs. Newell for most of my life now, by the way. And this is my dear young cousin, Miss Holmes."

The woman introduced herself as Mrs. Ramsay. She shook Livia's hand with surprising force and readily agreed when Mrs. Newell invited her to join them for luncheon. Livia, often uneasy with strangers, was, for once, more curious than discomfited.

And Mrs. Newell did not disappoint her. "So you did net a wealthy man?" she asked, as soon as soup was served to Mrs. Ramsay.

"Why, yes," answered Mrs. Ramsay proudly.

She'd seated herself opposite Mrs. Newell. Behind her tinted lenses, her eyes gleamed a dark, mysterious cobalt. "I insisted that I would only work in the household of a widower who was both virtuous and prosperous—almost came to blows with my aunt over that because she was too impatient to get rid of me and didn't want to wait. But just such a posting came up in a few months' time, and three years later I was Mrs. Archer."

Mrs. Ramsay raised one finger, as if counting. "After Mr. Archer went to his eternal rest, my own dear second cousin Mr. Henderson confessed that he'd always secretly admired me from afar. And now that he was a successful printer, he asked, could he aspire to my hand?"

She raised a second finger. "Mr. Henderson and I had eight good years. When he passed on, along came Mr. Archer's old friend Mr. Ramsay, who'd lost his wife some time ago."

Mrs. Ramsay waved three fingers in demonstration of the final tally. "I enjoyed a happy twelve years with dear Mr. Ramsay. Now I'm at last settled into widowhood. But if the Good Lord sees fit to set another excellent man in my path, who am I to say no?"

She winked in bubbly cheer; Livia felt the corners of her own lips lifting. It wasn't every day that she met someone who so evidently enjoyed life.

Her dear Mr. Marbleton did. And she could only pray that in captivity he still managed to find enough small pleasures to make his days bearable.

Mrs. Newell raised her glass. "I always did think it would be a lucky man who obtained your hand. How very kind of you to anoint not one but three such men."

Sybelle Henderson Archer Henderson Ramsay laughed and clinked Mrs. Newell's glass with her own.

The dining saloon was now two-thirds full and hummed with conversation. Stewards and stewardesses crisscrossed the space with unobtrusive swiftness. The aroma of grilled lamb chops wafted over from a nearby table, whetting Livia's appetite.

"I apologize for the intrusion, ladies, but is that you, Mrs. Newell?"

Livia's field of vision brightened at the sight of a silver-haired man.

When ladies vowed "'til death do us part," they were probably too busy with other thoughts to imagine their sprightly bridegrooms as actual older men. But if they did, they likely hoped that their new husbands would, after a few decades, look like *this*.

He wore the passage of time lightly. There were grooves across his forehead, and webs of lines at the corners of his eyes, but his features remained distinct and chiseled, his countenance alert, his gaze keen.

His bearing was straight but not stiff. His frock coat, while a little formal and old-fashioned for a mere shipboard luncheon, was of good quality and attested to a well-kept physique. And his entire person emanated a competence and rectitude that inspired trust.

"My goodness, Mr. Gregory, how—how do you do?" blurted Mrs. Newell.

The recognition came swiftly this time, and Mrs. Newell smiled with, if not genuine pleasure, then at least a great deal of amusement.

"Excellent memory, my dear lady!" exclaimed the newcomer. "What a delightful surprise to find you here."

Introductions were performed all around. "Mrs. Newell and I were at school together, sometime in the Dark Ages," said Mrs. Ramsay, her eyes alive with curiosity. "How do you two know each other?"

Mr. Gregory grinned. "Well, Mr. Newell was an enthusiastic philatelist, and I as well. He wrote me about a rare misprinted stamp in my collection, and that was how our acquaintance began."

Livia had heard tales of Mr. Newell's pursuit of a rare stamp all over the Continent, the kind of stories that had firmly affixed the late Mr. Newell in her mind as an exuberant and mischievous figure who did what he damn well pleased.

Mrs. Ramsay wished to know the year the stamp was issued and whether the mistake had been an overprint, a case of imperforation, or whatnot. Together Mrs. Newell and Mr. Gregory explained that the stamp had been issued in India some thirty years ago and had the queen's face upside down.

Livia relaxed. She was beginning to hope that Mr. Gregory, too, would be invited to sit down.

"Why, dear cousin! I thought you'd be here!"

Livia's heart stopped. Her mind stopped, too. She was caught in a hailstorm, bullets of ice striking everywhere.

She recognized that voice. How could she not?

The voice of her mother.

She didn't trust in luck—not her own, at least: The universe she knew was never content unless it had caught her dress in a door.

In a way, her sense of doom had been appeased by learning, in the aftermath of the debacle at the hotel, that the Shrewsburys, too, had booked tickets on this passage: Yes, the ants had arrived at the picnic. But Lady Holmes was too much. Lady Holmes turning up on the *Provence* was a visitation of infected rats, the vanguard of the plague.

She was coming ever closer, waving with one hand and with her other hand picking up her skirts to walk faster.

"My dear Mrs. N—ah!"

She tripped over her own feet. Mr. Gregory, still standing by the table, reached out and caught her.

"Thank you!" said Lady Holmes, steadying herself. And then, after she had a good look at her rescuer, "Why, my knight in shining armor, thank you, indeed, Mr. . . ."

For a moment, Livia's astonishment outpaced her dismay.

If she were to use one word to describe her mother, it would be *glum*. If she were to use a few more, *glum, self-important, with a tendency to anger.* She'd seen Lady Holmes in countless outbursts, big and small. She'd seen her look down her nose at most everyone. And she'd seen her sunk in her chair, radiating bitterness and regret, eyes intent yet unseeing, lost in the imaginary life she might have led had she made different choices.

But Livia had never, not once, seen her mother flirt.

Mr. Gregory, taken aback by Lady Holmes's abrupt attempt at coquetry, let go of her in a hurry.

It was Mrs. Newell who said calmly, "Lady Holmes, allow me to present Mr. Gregory, a friend of the late Mr. Newell. Mr. Gregory, Lady Holmes."

Without allowing for Lady Holmes to respond, Mrs. Newell went on to introduce Mrs. Ramsay.

Lady Holmes barely nodded at Mrs. Ramsay. "You will join us for luncheon, won't you, Mr. Gregory?"

Mr. Gregory glanced at Mrs. Newell. "I don't wish to intrude . . ."

"But of course you will not be intruding," said Mrs. Newell, smiling rather . . . apologetically? "Please take a seat. You, too, Lady Holmes."

Lady Holmes preened as Mr. Gregory handed her to the spot on the sofa next to Livia, thanking him profusely and reacting not at all to Livia's murmured greeting of "Mamma." Livia would have been embarrassed by her fawning behavior if she wasn't so relieved that Lady Holmes was too busy to pick faults with *her*.

Mr. Gregory sat down beside Mrs. Ramsay, directly across from Livia and only indirectly across from Lady Holmes. But that was good enough for Lady Holmes. She quickly set about extracting the facts of his life. He lived in Surrey, sang in the village choir, and, besides philately, enjoyed the collection of antiquarian books. And no, his lady wife had not come with him on the trip—she had departed the earth many moons ago.

He was in the middle of describing, per Lady Holmes's request, repairs to an old book's binding, when Lady Holmes sprang to her feet, jostling the contents of the table. Plates rattled. Livia shot out a hand to protect her water goblet.

"What is *that woman* doing on this steamer?" Lady Holmes hissed at Livia.

That woman was Mrs. Shrewsbury, entering the dining saloon beside a man who was not her husband.

"I am as bewildered as you are, Mamma," Livia answered from behind gritted teeth.

Roger Shrewsbury was useless, but his wife had been the one who had gathered a battalion of other women to witness Charlotte's disgrace. *She* had made sure that the matter could not be hushed up, that Charlotte would be expelled from Society.

"How dare she flaunt her respectability before my eyes," seethed Lady Holmes. "I will never forgive her for what she—"

Recalling herself, she refrained from publicly alluding to her youngest daughter's scandal. She plunked down and smiled at Mr. Gregory, her jaw clenched tight. "Please do not mind me, sir. I spied a disagreeable former acquaintance, that is all."

The others at the table wisely moved on to a different subject. For a while, Livia worried that Mrs. Ramsay might compete with Lady Holmes for Mr. Gregory's attention. But Mrs. Ramsay, in spite of her avowed receptiveness to a fourth husband, was less interested in Mr. Gregory than in Lady Holmes. To be sure, Lady Holmes's heavy-handed flirtation was fascinating in a horrifying way, a ship about to capsize, but in Mrs. Ramsay's wrinkle-hemmed, blue-lens-occluded eyes, there was no ridicule, only a pure curiosity.

Toward the end of the meal, a stewardess placed Nesselrode pudding molded in shapes of seashells and nautiluses on the table. Mrs. Ramsay, who barely glanced at the pretty array, asked, "If I understand correctly, Lady Holmes, you and Miss Holmes are related?"

"That is correct. She is my daughter," answered Lady Holmes, sniffing. She had judged Mrs. Ramsay as someone whose station in life was beneath her own. Mrs. Ramsay's attire might attest to comfortable finances, but Lady Holmes would precede her into any dining room in London, and she saw no reason not to feel and act superior.

"But if I'm not mistaken, Lady Holmes, Miss Holmes was surprised to see you. Were you not, Miss Holmes?" asked Mrs. Ramsay brightly.

Livia exhaled. Thank goodness someone was taking it upon herself to inquire into Lady Holmes's sudden appearance. If Livia had asked, her question would have been swatted aside, whether in private or before others.

"I was indeed astonished to see you, Mamma. When Mrs. Newell invited you to come along with us earlier, you said no."

Lady Holmes puffed out her mighty chest. "True, Mrs. Newell did beg me time and again to join her on this trip. But I've never been one for outlandish places."

Livia gripped her dessert spoon. Mrs. Newell had politely extended an invitation to Lady Holmes without offering to pay for the trip. And Lady Holmes, true to her distaste for foreign lands and customs—and her thorough emptiness of pocketbook—had declined.

And yet here she was.

"I entrusted my Olivia to Mrs. Newell and thought I'd amuse myself in London," continued Lady Holmes. "But in London, I thought again of the *Provence* and my friends aboard. In the end, I couldn't help myself."

She beamed at a shrinking Mr. Gregory. "And I must say I am absolutely delighted with my choice."

Except for confirming to Mr. Gregory that he would have no peace on this voyage, Lady Holmes's answer had proved useless—even Livia could deduce that she'd changed her mind. But what had caused it?

Not to mention, at home Sir Henry controlled the purse strings. Lady Holmes had received some money from Charlotte earlier, but she had already squandered it. How had she been able to afford a passage on the *Provence*? No, two passages—she never went anywhere without her maid in tow.

Livia needed Mrs. Ramsay to ask more questions, even if that would be prying. Alas, Mrs. Ramsay only raised her glass. "We are elated to have you among us, my lady."

Lady Holmes batted her lashes at Mr. Gregory. "And what a pleasure this journey has already been."

Four

L ord Ingram hurried down the stairs toward the dining saloon.
The note that had been shoved under his cabin door read
Lady Holmes and maid aboard. How was that possible?

The *Provence* had sold its last remaining cabins to Charlotte
Holmes and company days ago. The passenger list he'd furnished
Holmes he'd copied from the duty room, when he'd sneaked aboard
last night under cover of darkness, as the ship, quiet and empty,
bobbed quayside. And Lady Holmes's name had not been on the list.

How, then, had she obtained her tickets? Who had made it possible, and why?

He stepped into the dining saloon. A well-dressed woman coming from the opposite direction reached Mrs. Newell's table ahead
of him.

"M'lady, here's the shawl you asked for earlier."

Lady Holmes's maid?

The maid blocked his view of Lady Holmes, but the latter did not
sound pleased. "When did I ask for a shawl?"

"When we were on the train, m'lady," said the maid, her head
bowed in deference. "You said that you wished to have a shawl with
you at luncheon, so that you could take a stroll on deck afterwards.
But you forgot to take it."

Lady Holmes's brows knitted in concentration. Miss Olivia, on the other hand, appeared resigned, as if it were normal for her mother not to remember what she herself had said only hours ago.

"Well, fine, leave the shawl and go," said a grumpy Lady Holmes. But the next instant she was all smiles. "Well, Mr. Gregory, can I persuade you to join me for a stroll?"

"Ah, I'd dearly love to, but I have not yet unpacked my things," said a man sitting with his back to Lord Ingram, shaking his head with exaggerated regret.

Before Lady Holmes's lips could turn down in displeasure, Lord Ingram stepped forward. "My lady, I should be honored to escort you."

Relief rose all around the table, as thick as steam in a Turkish bath. Mrs. Newell unclenched visibly. Miss Olivia mouthed *Thank you, thank you*. Mr. Gregory shook Lord Ingram's hand as if they were old friends reunited after decades.

And as if he had no idea who Lord Ingram was.

The only person more curious than happy to see him was an exceedingly elderly lady introduced as Mrs. Ramsay, who sported blue glasses and a russet turban that matched her dress. When he inquired whether anyone else at the table cared to join the promenade, Mrs. Newell and Miss Olivia turned him down with alacrity, but Mrs. Ramsay hesitated.

She toyed with a ring on a silver chain around her neck. Occasionally widows carried their wedding rings thus, to commemorate their departed husbands. But surely, this ring's circumference rendered it much too loose for any human hand. Indeed, one would need fingers the size of great big sausages—

It was no wedding band but a ring to encircle the base of a man's shaft. Holmes had pranked him by making him rescue one like it, perhaps this very one, from the Garden of Hermopolis in Cornwall. And he'd had to give a convincing portrayal of grief while he'd held the infernal device.

He'd never come so close to actually choking.

He should have realized that this was no time for games and that

Holmes would leave him a clue as to her identity. But this clue—he bit the inside of his cheek so he wouldn't burst out laughing.

"Ah, it's no use," said Holmes in an old woman's age-roughened voice. "The idea of a walk is tempting, but these days I need a good nap after luncheon."

Her face moved a little stiffly, but unless one stared hard—and out of politeness most people wouldn't—that slight unnaturalness would go unnoticed and one would come away with an impression of age and blue glasses and not much else.

He prayed that this excellent disguise would keep her safe. His and Miss Olivia's whereabouts were no secret. If Moriarty should think to install someone on the *Provence* . . .

"I wish you a good rest, madam." He turned to her mother. "Lady Holmes, shall we?"

※

Lady Holmes stomped, as if the planks underfoot offended her. It astonished Lord Ingram anew that this woman had given birth to Holmes.

Her blood flowed in Holmes's veins. Her nose and cheeks were replicated almost exactly on Holmes's face. Her blond hair—although hers was turning grey—used to bounce in ringlets atop Holmes's head, before the latter had shorn hers short to don wigs more easily.

But despite their physical resemblance, the two women could not be more different: Instead of forging kinship, God had but plucked a random womb for Holmes to make her way into the world.

"Oh, but it's becoming chilly," moaned Lady Holmes, when they were three minutes into their walk.

Her youngest daughter would have stated outright if she wished to seek warmer surroundings. Lady Holmes, on the other hand, gazed at Lord Ingram and left it to him to read her mind.

Which, given her lack of subtlety, was at least easy to interpret. He promptly guided her to the library on the upper deck and ordered her a glass of wine.

Lady Holmes, revived by the wine, launched into a fresh stream of grievances, this time against London dressmakers who were not appreciative enough of the honor her patronage bestowed upon them. "Therefore, when my late cousin's estate wired me the money he'd left me, I resolved not to spend any of it on those snobbish couturiers— though I made an exception for this shawl."

She ran her fingers lovingly over the black shawl that her maid had brought her earlier, the scalloped edge of which called to mind the mantillas of Spanish grandes dames.

Lord Ingram had been watching for an opening to ask why she'd come aboard. "Is it a mourning shawl for your esteemed cousin?"

He had his doubts about this alleged cousin. Even if such a cousin had existed, Lady Holmes would have been overlooked in the writing of his will: One did not bequeath her anything out of affection because she did not inspire affection; and one did not need to leave a gift of pity, as she was not in true penury.

Lady Holmes waved her hand. "Oh, no, he died a while ago, but only recently was everything sorted out and the funds dispensed. Shall we drink a toast to him?"

If she was telling the truth, then the timing was suspect. And if she wasn't . . . He raised his glass. "To your cousin."

She took a long draught and sighed with appreciation. "Very good claret, this is. Very good."

"And very fortunate for us that you decided to catch the *Provence* in time. If you don't mind my curiosity, my lady—"

The door of the library opened to admit Mrs. Shrewsbury and a man who looked familiar. In the aftermath of the Punching, while Lord Ingram tapped a supine Roger Shrewsbury on the cheek and instructed a stunned hotel clerk to have a physician fetched and some whisky brought to hand, Mrs. Shrewsbury had come running, and this man had been somewhere behind her. And later, with the physician examining Roger Shrewsbury and everyone else holding their breath, the man had stage-whispered to a distracted Mrs. Shrewsbury about "that beast Arkwright—you don't know the half of it."

Lady Holmes's expression hardened. She stared at Mrs. Shrewsbury as if she could flay her with nothing more than the force of her anger.

Mrs. Shrewsbury bit her lower lip and murmured something to the man. He immediately held open the door for her again.

"I hope you weren't intending to speak to that woman, my lord," huffed Lady Holmes after they had left.

"No, indeed. After what she and her husband did to Miss Charlotte, it would matter little to me if I never saw them again."

Lady Holmes's eyes shone with a rare spark. She leaned in closer and lowered her voice. "My lord, I am greatly heartened that your affection for my youngest daughter has not waned with time and . . . events."

With time and events, his affection for Holmes had only redoubled. "I should hope I am not a friend only in fair weather."

"No one could possibly believe so of you," said Lady Holmes ardently. "But when I think of how my poor child has suffered, far from our protection and without the shield of a lady's reputation . . . It breaks a mother's heart."

Lady Holmes was not a monstrous parent, per se, merely a selfish one who measured her children's worth by what they could bring her. Her agony might have been sincere following Holmes's exile, but that had been occasioned not so much by anxiety over her daughter's fate as by her own loss of prestige.

Not to mention the deprivation of that lucrative future son-in-law she could have had if only Holmes had said yes to any number of proposals.

"It was indeed a great plight," he murmured. "You have all my sympathy."

Lady Holmes passed her hand before her face in theatrical lament. "If only Shrewsbury had been a free man, we would have made sure that he did the right thing. But the despicable cad was already married and what could we do?"

"No, there was nothing anyone could have done."

He knew. He'd tried.

"But things are different now—with you, at least, my lord," said Lady Holmes eagerly, her hands laid together above her bosom. "You are no longer encumbered. And I'm sure my Charlotte, were she to learn of the constancy of your affection, would be deeply moved."

"I, like all her friends, pray daily for her safety and well-being," he said primly.

But that did not make his statement any less true.

"Perhaps the time has come for more than prayers. We, her family, cannot bring her back from the wild. But—with a bridegroom by her side, she could regain some of her lost respectability."

He had to admire Lady Holmes's restraint in not naming him outright as that potential bridegroom.

"She could have had that last year, when my brother proposed after . . . those events involving Mr. Shrewsbury. But she turned down my lord Bancroft."

To be sure, she hadn't exactly turned Bancroft down but backed him into a corner and forced him to withdraw his proposal. Lord Ingram, however, didn't believe Lady Holmes would be invested in the details.

"Oh, that thoughtless girl," Lady Holmes moaned. "She is my despair!"

But after another fortifying gulp of good claret, her despair retreated sufficiently for her to say, "That was last summer. By now, surely Charlotte would have had enough of this prolonged banishment."

"But I understand, from speaking to Miss Olivia, that Miss Charlotte has sent home a number of cheques since December of last year. She must be all right, if she can spare funds for the family's upkeep."

Lady Holmes chortled awkwardly. "Mere pittances, those were, mere pittances. And if you don't mind my saying so, my lord, I rather thought that the amount she forwarded was from the . . . assistance that *you* offered her."

Ah, coming just short of saying that he must have been keeping her daughter as his mistress all along.

"My lady, I'm afraid you're mistaken. Miss Charlotte has never appealed to me for assistance, and I have not offered her a sou."

He had paid the invoice for three hundred pounds she had sent for saving his neck from the hangman's noose, but that was different.

Lady Holmes blinked rapidly, her expression changing from disbelief to dismay, and then to outright horror.

She had never understood her youngest daughter's unusual gifts. Therefore, unlike Mrs. Newell, who had guessed on her own that Sherlock Holmes was none other than Charlotte Holmes, Lady Holmes did not suppose her child to have any means of support except dependence on a man.

And now, with Lord Ingram stating plainly that he had never extended such patronage, she was mortified that she had more or less asked him to marry a girl who must be sleeping with someone else.

Her flight—after she'd downed the rest of her wine—was swift. Lord Ingram took a slow sip from his own glass.

Under police questioning the year before, he'd said that he had no intention of ever proposing to Charlotte Holmes. One, he was disenchanted with the institution of marriage as a whole, and two, he wasn't audacious enough to marry her even if she were on her knees begging for his hand.

He had not lied. Marriage to Holmes had always been unthinkable, and not only because he had already been married. To the man he had been then, it had resembled crossing the Niagara on a high wire while juggling a few burning torches: a thousand ways for the enterprise to plunge into disaster, and only the slenderest chance of making it to the other side unscathed.

He had changed. The man he was today still found marriage to Holmes unthinkable, but for very different reasons.

The protection of his name and the prospect of his future fortune had seemed to him, as a younger man, the greatest gifts he'd had to offer. But Holmes had never needed such gifts, and he had found her frank disregard of his most evident assets unnerving.

Now he at last understood what Holmes had grasped from the very beginning: that many of the things he'd clung to with all his might, things he'd believed to be fundamental to his dignity and his manhood, had, in the end, mattered very little.

He did not need to be husband to the woman he loved, not if becoming his wife would diminish her freedom and choices. Moreover, when he'd been a boy of twenty, laying everything he had at the feet of his then beloved, what he had really yearned for was to be loved for himself.

By taking marriage out of consideration, by spending time with him only because she enjoyed his company, wasn't Holmes giving him exactly what he'd always wanted?

———❖———

The *Provence* featured two passenger levels, the upper deck and the main, or saloon, deck. The maids' dormitory was one of the forward-most dwellings on the saloon deck, immediately next to the ladies' baths.

A woman in her mid-thirties answered Livia's knock.

"Yes, miss?" she asked tentatively.

Livia squared her shoulders. "Is Norbert here?"

Lord Ingram would try to find out how and why Lady Holmes had come aboard. But since Lady Holmes could be quite averse to truth-telling, Livia had decided to speak to Norbert, Lady Holmes's new maid.

"Miss Holmes?" Norbert emerged from behind the other woman. The dormitory, with two sets of top-and-bottom bunks squeezed in, had barely enough room for its occupants to turn around. Norbert wasted no time in coming out to the passage.

She was in her early thirties, clad in an eggshell-colored dress printed with small stylized birds in light grey. The dress would have been the height of fashion several years ago—ladies' maids often had the first pick of their mistresses' castoffs—and served as further evidence that Norbert's previous employer had been a woman of both deeper pockets and better taste than Lady Holmes.

"Is everything all right, miss?" asked Norbert, her attitude one of dignity and neutral respect.

She could not be more different from the timid, retiring Abbotts, who had served Lady Holmes for seven years, an eternity in the Holmes household, where servants came and went as frequently as the seasons changed. But even an institution like Abbotts couldn't last forever. She had retired earlier this year, and Norbert had been her replacement.

The ship sailed perfectly smoothly, yet Livia felt as if it had hit an iceberg, the impact jarring her entire body.

It had seemed natural that Abbotts should resign at some point—even the most long-suffering servants could put up with only so much inconsideration and ungenerosity. After Abbotts left, Livia resigned herself to helping with her mother's toilette; it would not be easy to find a satisfactory replacement for Abbotts.

But Norbert had come after only a week and suited Lady Holmes's requirements perfectly. She was hardworking and organized, could remove any stain from a hem, *and* possessed a great flair for dressing hair. She was also presentable, yet not so pretty or lively that she risked catching Sir Henry's perpetually roving eye. Lady Holmes was, for once, pleased with her choice.

Considering Abbotts's departure and Norbert's arrival from a different perspective, however, did those events not dovetail too neatly with Charlotte's feigned death in Cornwall? If Moriarty wanted a minion to keep a close eye on Livia, in case she had news from Charlotte, he could not find a better perch than from inside the Holmes household.

"Miss Holmes?" Norbert peered at her.

Livia started. "Everything is fine," she blurted. "I came to find you because I forgot to ask my mother for her cabin number."

"Her ladyship's cabin is right there, miss. Number 9."

Norbert pointed. The dining saloon had two entrances, one forward, one aft. To either side of the forward entrance stood a partition about three feet wide and six feet tall, covered with a dark blue velvet similar to that which upholstered the dining saloon sofas. Lady Holmes's cabin was behind one such partition.

Livia's heart kicked against her ribcage. Should she leave right away? Or should she question Norbert as if she had no suspicion that Norbert was a Moriarty agent lying in wait?

What if Charlotte, thinking she was safe enough, decided to meet them at a port of call, only to be ambushed?

"Number 9." Livia pushed the words past her suddenly dry throat. "I'll remember that. Thank you. And will you come with me, Norbert? I have some more questions I'd like to ask you."

She had to continue with her original plan. It would appear strange if she *didn't* corner Norbert to get some answers after Lady Holmes materialized without a word to anyone. Norbert expressed little surprise at Livia's request and allowed herself to be led into the dining saloon, where a dozen or so passengers had gathered at the two long central tables to play cards over glasses of lemonade.

Livia headed for one of the peripheral tables out of earshot of the other passengers. She took a seat and motioned Norbert to do the same, but Norbert shook her head and remained standing.

"Norbert, can you tell me how my mother came by the wherewithal to pay for this trip?" Livia asked bluntly. Before she'd knocked on the door of the maids' dormitory, she'd turned it over and over in her head, how to approach the matter in a subtle, oblique manner. But now she only wanted to be done as soon as possible. "I don't wish to speak ill of her, but she can be gullible and shortsighted. I hope that in obtaining the funds she hasn't somehow become beholden to unsavory characters."

Norbert blinked at Livia's declaration that fraud and villainy had played a part in Lady Holmes's presence aboard the *Provence*. "I'm— I'm sure it couldn't have been anything of the sort."

Then what could it have been? "Will you tell me how she decided that she must go to—"

In her earlier disorientation, Livia hadn't even thought to ask her mother about her destination.

"Bombay, miss. And to be sure it came to me as a great surprise, too. We were in London, visiting Harrod's and some couturiers. Then yesterday evening, out of the blue, her ladyship informed me that I was to have everything packed so we could make for the railway station in the morning to catch a sailing out of Southampton."

"And you didn't think that was strange?"

Because you arranged for the whole thing?

"I was astonished, to be sure, but also overjoyed," said Norbert earnestly. "I haven't been abroad in years, and I've always longed to go on a grand voyage again. So I leaped to the packing and didn't question her ladyship's decision—in fact, I was afraid to ask anything in case she changed her mind."

Come to think of it, at home Livia had once overheard Norbert speak to a maid of all work about having sailed far and wide alongside a previous mistress. *You step on a boat and lo and behold you're in Wellington. Before long you've also visited Hong Kong and Yokohama. And then the next thing you know you've crossed the Pacific Ocean all the way to San Francisco.*

About being a seasoned traveler, Norbert was at least consistent in her account.

Livia rubbed her temple. "So the first you knew that you'd be sailing on the *Provence* was when you were told to pack?"

"Yes, miss."

"My mother didn't take you with her to visit the ticket agent?"

"No, miss."

If true, this was extraordinary: Lady Holmes did not like to do herself what could be done for her by others.

Livia tapped her fingers against the seat of the sofa. "Did she arrange for the tickets via the hotel?"

"Perhaps she did, miss, but I didn't know anything about it."

"And she produced the tickets when you reached Southampton," murmured Livia.

"That she did, miss," answered Norbert. Her eyes were clear, her gaze candid, her posture straight but not stiff.

Whenever Lady Holmes did anything, it was with constant complaints on what a difficult time she was having. For her to be silent and efficient? Livia could not imagine such a thing.

And yet according to Norbert, this was exactly what had happened.

Or was it?

Abbotts was very decent, but Norbert concocted a marvelous hair tonic and made old lace look practically new again. She gave Sir Henry's boots such a brilliant shine that he talked about it for two days.

The Holmes's finances were too depleted to afford an indoor manservant, especially not one dedicated to Sir Henry's personal upkeep. Lady Holmes's maid, nominally her own lady's maid, in fact had to look after everyone's wardrobe.

Norbert, with her abundant skills and her even temperament, could have found a post that came with a better mistress, greater remuneration, and fewer duties. Livia once asked Lady Holmes why Norbert had come to work for them. Lady Holmes, not perceiving the subtext of the question, had answered that of course it was because the employment agency dispatched her, the same employment agency that had dispatched Abbotts years ago.

The urge stole upon Livia to demand answers directly from Norbert. *Why did you come to us? Who sent you? And what do they want?*

But she only said, after a minute, "Thank you, Norbert. You may return to your duties."

Five

Mrs. Ramsay was tireless.

Lord Ingram narrowly held his mirth in check as she scampered about. Yes, scampered. She stooped and complained frequently of age and aching limbs; nevertheless, she was as busy as a spinning top, playing with his children and Frau Schmidt's charges, distributing brightly wrapped Parisian bonbons, and greeting all the passengers who came by.

The chalky cliffs of the Isle of Wright were receding in the distance. The air that streamed over the *Provence* held a bare hint of salt. Elsewhere, white deck chairs had been arranged on teak planks stained a warm ocher, but here on the aft deck the space had been left open to allow for games of deck quoits and deck billiards.

Mrs. Ramsay, leaning on her folded-up umbrella, tossed a rope ring directly into the center of a set of concentric circles. She hooted. A quartet of disappointed children moaned in defeat—this old lady was not the kind to let them win uncontested.

Mrs. Ramsay chortled, so delighted that her eyes disappeared behind her wrinkles. "All right, all right. I won't play anymore. One of you young people will win the next game."

The tip of her parasol thudding, she galumphed to stand beside Frau Schmidt near the port bulwark. Before giving out bonbons to Rupert Pennington and Georg Bittner, she had asked their governess for permission. The two women had struck up a friendly conversation; now they were once again talking and laughing together.

Holmes, as Lord Ingram remembered her best, was still and silent. Her energetic and gregarious role as Mrs. Ramsay amused him, but he hoped it wouldn't drain her.

"Why, hullo, Mr. Gregory, lovely to see you again." She raised her raspy voice and waved. "Come here and keep us wallflowers company for a minute."

Mr. Gregory, just then arrived on the aft deck, went to pay his respects to the ladies.

Dannell, Remington's emissary, had not trusted Holmes to take charge of the search. To hear her tell it, she'd been deployed more as a human camera, told to go to such and such place and conduct a thorough search, then to draw from memory the entire interior arrangement with every single item labeled.

While she'd been away from London, sneaking into dwellings specified by Dannell, it was discovered that Frau Schmidt had left London well before she was scheduled to and that they might not be able to intercept her before she boarded the *Provence*. Still not trusting Holmes to handle the matter on her own, Dannell had brought out the mostly retired Mr. Gregory, whose seductive powers over both sexes had proved highly advantageous to the crown over the years, to charm the German governess.

Lord Ingram had looked askance at the scheme. But at Mr. Gregory's approach, a light of wonder came over Frau Schmidt's face. And with the presentation of this legendary—in certain circles—lover, her smile bloomed like the first flowers of spring.

Perhaps the clichéd old tactic might work after all.

A few minutes after she'd beckoned him over, Mrs. Ramsay left Mr. Gregory and Frau Schmidt to strike up a conversation with a man standing at the aft rail, but the man bowed and left shortly thereafter.

"Who was the fool who didn't want your company?" asked Lord Ingram when she finally reached him. She'd asked him for permission before giving his children sweets, and then, not another word. Given the way she'd been the soul of amiability with everyone else, if she stayed away much longer, it would appear as if she were deliberately avoiding him.

But, of course, all that socializing was to make sure that she hadn't singled out anyone for attention.

"The fool is Mr. Pratt, headed for Sydney. I'm not sure what he plans to do there—he seems to have decided on the trip in a hurry. But yes, it's true he wanted no company." She grinned. "That's why I talked to him, so that he'd leave."

And they could at last speak without anyone nearby.

"Are you all right?" she asked. "Not too tired?"

"I am. I'm getting old."

He'd stolen aboard the *Provence* last night to practice his extremely rusty skills at electrical wiring and would have appreciated a nap after luncheon, but Lady Holmes's inexplicable presence had jolted him awake. Even now his nerves jangled. "Who's Mrs. Ramsay, by the way? Lady Holmes said she's some sort of old acquaintance of Mrs. Newell's?"

"She is. Mr. Dannell sent me all the way to Norfolk. On my way back to London, Mrs. Ramsay and her companion came into my railway compartment and we fell into conversation. I realized after a while that she was the Sybelle Henderson of Mrs. Newell's reminiscences. I must have made a good impression on her because by and by she confessed that she wasn't headed to Egypt, as she had told me at first, but to London to have some procedures done."

"What procedures?"

"Beautifying surgical procedures, one to lift the skin under her chin and another to make her bosom sit up more pertly."

Lord Ingram winced. He'd heard of such surgeries, but after enduring a great deal of pain and discomfort, one could just as well look no better than before, or worse.

"She's a lively lady, very personable, but rather saddened by the decay wrought by age." Holmes tapped her face. "This is, of course, exaggerated so the true contours of my features cannot be discerned, but she does have a great many wrinkles and wore several scarves around her neck to conceal what she called her wattle, which she did not show me. And even her blue spectacles aren't for a sensitivity to light, as I first thought, but merely to distract from the rest of her face.

"As soon as I got off the train, I thought that I could perhaps use her identity. She'd hired a place near Ilfracombe for her recuperation and planned to be out of sight for at least several months, if not half a year, while telling everyone that she'd gone on a long trip abroad. So even if someone should doubt my disguise later, they would only learn that Mrs. Ramsay had indeed been out of the country at the time. And that she had been acquainted with Mrs. Newell would give me an excuse to approach you and Livia."

He shook his head. As with all such things, even the very good was less than perfect.

"Don't worry too much," she said. "Tell me what you've found out about my mother's presence."

He and Miss Olivia had met to discuss their findings—or the lack thereof. He repeated to Holmes what little they'd learned, adding, "Cabin 9 had a Mrs. Emery listed. It's Miss Olivia's opinion that Lady Holmes, who is extraordinarily proud to be *Lady* Holmes, would never have put herself down as a plain missus. Someone else bought her ticket, and that ticket somehow landed in her lap."

From the center of the aft deck rose a cry of "Good toss!" Georg Bittner, Frau Schmidt's temporary charge, had landed a rope ring exactly on the bull's-eye and Lucinda, Lord Ingram's daughter, had exclaimed in praise.

Frau Schmidt had stopped speaking to watch Herr Bittner, now she said something to Mr. Gregory, perhaps about her charges. Mr. Gregory listened, his attention fully engaged, yet not so fixed as to make its recipient uncomfortable.

Beside Lord Ingram, Holmes loosened and rebuttoned a strap around her parasol. "I agree that my mother made up the bit about the generous late cousin. As for Norbert as Moriarty's minion—that is an elegant hypothesis. It would explain much, wouldn't it? She needs to be here so she managed to drag my mother here, too, while making her believe it was her own idea."

"But you don't think so?" he asked with a leap of hope.

It was terrifying to think of Moriarty striking deep inside the Holmes household. He prayed that was not the case.

"I don't know enough about Norbert to make any firm pronouncements. The only thing I can say is that she probably *is* a seasoned traveler." She touched a pearl button on her bodice. "When she came to the table at luncheon, I noticed her buttons, which resembled ivory but had a grain to them. They were made from tagua nuts— vegetable ivory.

"And vegetable ivory, being neither native to Britain nor generally used to fabricate buttons, suggests that she obtained them abroad, possibly close to their source in Oceania or South America.

"If Norbert had claimed an insular existence, if she'd said that she'd never been outside of London or Shropshire until she came to work for my mother, that would have made her suspect. But now it's the other way round. Now there's nothing incongruous about those buttons. It doesn't eliminate her from suspicion, but it behooves us to wait and see."

A peal of laughter rang out—Frau Schmidt, laughing so hard that she'd fallen back against the bulwark. Mr. Gregory appeared just as delighted, if less raucously so.

Shipboard society operated by rules quite distinct from those of society proper. That reduced stricture worked to their advantage. On land, Frau Schmidt would have never comported so with a gentleman, for fear of being perceived as too forward. Here she was clearly more relaxed.

Still, it would have been infinitely preferable to burgle Frau Schmidt on land. But Dannell refused to wait until she reached Madras, where her employer had taken a new post, so it was on the *Provence* that Holmes must make her attempts.

The children's game of deck quoits produced a champion, Lucinda. The girl waved, her smile ebullient. "Papa, did you see me win? And Mrs. Ramsay, may I have the extra bonbon you promised the winner? I promise I won't eat it today."

"It would seem that the story of Hansel and Gretel has failed to instill in her a commensurate wariness of old women bearing sweets," said Lord Ingram in a low voice, for Mrs. Ramsay's ear alone.

She cackled and sallied forth, well on her way to becoming the most popular old woman on this voyage. Then she came back. "I forgot to tell you, I've been out and about hoping to run into Inspector Brighton—yes, he is that Brighton on the passenger list. I wonder why he's on this sailing."

The sun still shone, yet a chill spread from Lord Ingram's nape. The gamboling children and happily chatting adults on the aft deck, too, appeared as if in a haze.

In the aftermath of the Cold Street case, he and Holmes had both wondered whether Inspector Brighton hadn't been too fervent in his desire to pin not one but two murders on their friend Inspector Treadles. Had he been entrusted by Moriarty to see to that particular outcome?

They'd decided at the time that they had more urgent matters to worry about—and that they were unlikely to run into him in the future. Yet here he was, on a ship with a number of Sherlock Holmes's known associates.

What did he want?

—— ✦ ——

Lord Ingram's chance to speak to Inspector Brighton came within hours.

Upon entering the dining saloon, redolent with the aroma of butter-poached lobsters, he first saw Mrs. Ramsay. She presided, with a cheeky majesty, over the same table she'd occupied at luncheon, but this time sitting where Mrs. Newell had been, on the sofa, the entire saloon under her purview. A pair of young army officers shared her table, the three engaged in animated conversation.

Well, he'd always known that even when Holmes became a lady of many decades, she would not lack for masculine companionship if she but wished for it.

Of her dining partners from luncheon, Mrs. Newell, Miss Olivia, and Mr. Gregory were absent, all three avoiding Lady Holmes, perhaps, who occupied a starboard table by herself, sawing at a beefsteak with sullen determination. It occurred to him, and not for the first time, that her presence could interfere with Mr. Gregory's wooing of Frau Schmidt. But the voyage was long, and Mr. Gregory might well prove adept at handling ladies competing for his attention.

Lord Ingram's pulse quickened—there was Inspector Brighton, sitting at a port table near the forward entrance. Also at the table was a stout man of about fifty in a crisp navy blue uniform, its two rows of gold buttons sparkling. That must be Captain Pritchard, who had invited Lord Ingram to dinner.

At his approach, the captain rose, beaming. "My lord, welcome to the *Provence*, a pleasure to have you aboard!"

"But of course," answered Lord Ingram, "it's my privilege to travel on this magnificent vessel. And my pleasure to meet the man in charge."

Captain Pritchard, pleased at the compliment to his ship, shook Lord Ingram's hand heartily and said, "I believe, sir, that you are already acquainted with Inspector Brighton of Scotland Yard?"

He shook Inspector Brighton's hand. "We have indeed met."

The policeman's trustworthy-looking face made it difficult to imagine his ruthlessness. But Lord Ingram and Holmes knew better, and forewarned was forearmed.

He took a seat beside Inspector Brighton. "Captain, you take an interest in the policing of crimes?"

He had wondered at his invitation to the captain's table. He had not bought his passage as lord anything, merely Mr. I. Ashburton. And most steamship captains, as far as he knew, did not make it a point to study *Debrett's Peerage* in their spare time. But with Inspector Brighton having also been invited, he was beginning to see why. Was the captain fascinated by murders?

"You are only about one-quarter correct, my lord," said Inspector Brighton wryly. "Captain Pritchard here takes great interest in your friend, the consulting detective Sherlock Holmes."

Lord Ingram started. With the exception of the search for Miss Moriarty, Holmes had not taken on any major cases since December of last year. Had the great consulting detective's celebrity already become widespread and affixed in the mind of the public?

He managed not to glance at Holmes, only a few tables away. "A shame that my friend could not be here himself—I'm sure he would have been delighted to discuss his methods with you, Captain."

"Yes, I've heard that Mr. Holmes has taken a long leave of absence from London. More's the pity," said the captain, signaling a nearby steward for wine. "Do please convey my most sincere wishes for his health and well-being."

"I will, when I write to him next," Lord Ingram promised. "Alas that you should have only us, Captain. Nothing compares to sitting before Sherlock Holmes himself."

The captain's eyes shone with anticipation. "That may be, but I am nevertheless overjoyed to meet you gentlemen who have worked with him on actual life-and-death investigations."

Lord Ingram was sorely tempted to point out that Inspector Brighton would have charged his colleague Inspector Treadles with two murders the latter did not commit were it not for Holmes's timely interference. But now that Inspector Brighton was required to listen to him wax poetic about Holmes's brilliance while Captain Pritchard all but levitated in rapture—

He accepted a glass of wine and proffered, with relish, Sherlockian anecdotes by the dozen. Of course, he brought up nothing that had a connection to Moriarty or would place too much attention on Miss Holmes, the sister who received clients and performed much of the legwork of the investigations.

It was not until coffee was served, its rich, heady aroma enveloping the table, that Captain Pritchard, with some reluctance, changed the subject and inquired into his guests' purposes in traveling.

"A friend from the French School at Athens has invited me to join him on the island of Delos, in the Cyclades, for ongoing excavations," answered Lord Ingram. "I have not made up my mind whether to take him up on his offer, but it certainly makes for an interesting trip, for myself and my children, to see one of the birthplaces of classical antiquity."

He told his dinner companions a little more about the long-abandoned island and its still rich but much plundered archaeological treasures—there had been a stark lack of preservation at most ancient sites. Then he turned to the policeman. "And you, Inspector, what brought you on the *Provence?*"

"Ah, I wish it were a trip to the Greek isles," began Inspector Brighton, who had not spoken much during the meal. "But alas, it is only that—"

"Captain Pritchard, how do you do?"

Lord Ingram turned around and saw Mrs. Shrewsbury first. Next to her stood the man who'd addressed the captain—the same man who had accompanied her to the library earlier and the hotel foyer this morning.

The captain looked at the man blankly for a moment. "Ah, Mr. Russell, how do you do?"

"Wonderful memory, Captain—I don't know how you remember everyone," said Mr. Russell.

He did not sound as impressed as he claimed—perhaps because the captain had needed an effort to recall him?

"Anne," he continued, "may I present the most excellent Captain Pritchard? Last year I had the pleasure of traveling on the *Provence* under his capable stewardship and I am delighted to repeat the experience. Captain, my cousin Mrs. Shrewsbury."

Captain Pritchard rose and paid his respects to the lady, as did Lord Ingram and Inspector Brighton. Introductions were barely finished when Mr. Russell gushed, "And you must allow me to thank you, my lord, on both my own and my dear cousin's behalf, for coming to her husband's assistance this morning, after the dastardly assault upon him by Mr. Arkwright."

"Mr. Arkwright?" exclaimed Captain Pritchard. "Surely you do not mean our passenger Mr. Arkwright."

"Goodness, is Mr. Arkwright also sailing on the *Provence*?" said Mr. Russell with a look of great innocence.

"Yes. In fact, I invited him to dinner tonight—he is acquainted with the directors of the company. But, alas, he is seasick and could not come."

"Ah," said Mr. Russell, drawing out the syllable into a sound of deep innuendo. "While I have no particular insight into Mr. Arkwright's health, I am willing to lay a large wager that his absence tonight is instead caused by certain revelations made this day."

"Oh?" murmured the captain, his brows drawn together.

"More than that I cannot divulge, I'm afraid, at least not in mixed company. Safe to say that the matter will turn vexing for Mr. Arkwright when he reaches Sydney, and perhaps even before," said Mr. Russell, the keen light in his eyes that of a man who planned to *make* the matter a problem for Mr. Arkwright, if it didn't become one on its own.

After Mr. Russell and Mrs. Shrewsbury left, the three men at the table sat down again. Captain Pritchard, shaking his head, was the first to speak. "I hope this enmity won't make for a fractious sailing."

"I am a complete stranger to the situation and ought not to venture opinions," said Inspector Brighton gravely. "Yet I cannot help but feel that Mr. Russell did not conduct himself in a gentlemanly manner just now. He seems intent on sowing disharmony. And if the matter has to do with a lady, then that renders his effort that much more scurrilous."

His pronouncement surprised Lord Ingram. Inspector Brighton had not struck him, during his investigation of Inspector Treadles, as being either gentle or gentlemanly. But perhaps he was ruthless only in the course of his investigations, and more forgiving elsewhere.

Captain Pritchard strung together a few sentences that sought to cast the matter as a misunderstanding. "And what were we speaking of before we were interrupted? Ah, Inspector, you were saying?"

"Only that I've been sent to train the Malta constabulary in modern detecting methods."

Lord Ingram had heard about this training program. But when Inspector Treadles had mentioned it, not long ago, Chief Inspector Fowler, not Inspector Brighton, had been the one appointed for it.

"Molding a new generation of police officers for the empire is an admirable task," he murmured.

"Provided I survive the trip." Inspector Brighton exhaled with overt trepidation. "I've never done particularly well on trains. Sometimes I suffer from vertigo for days afterwards. This first day on the *Provence* has been surprisingly pleasant, but goodness only knows how I will react when we meet rougher seas."

"We shall endeavor to keep you as comfortable as possible, Inspector," the captain promised gallantly. "Why, we could have fair winds all the way to Malta."

Of that, Lord Ingram wasn't so sure. He'd checked the barometer outside the bridge when he'd boarded and again before dinner. The pressure had dropped noticeably.

Somewhere beyond the horizon, a storm brewed.

Six

The cabin shared by Mrs. Watson and Miss Charlotte, with its white walls and double bunks, was decent, if bare, not badly cramped, but also far from roomy—it had been the last remaining cabin on the saloon deck and it simply had to do.

The door opened and in stepped Miss Charlotte. Her face, still made up as Mrs. Ramsay, was oddly dewy. Mrs. Watson rose from the sling stool on which she'd been sitting. "How was your bath, my dear?"

Miss Charlotte whipped off her turban to reveal a head of still-damp short curls, dyed grey to match Mrs. Ramsay's age. "Marble tubs, gilded fixtures, soap tablets already provided—I approve."

Mrs. Watson chortled. She sat the girl down on the sling stool and rubbed her hair with a towel. Miss Charlotte busied herself peeling her "face," which came off in irregular strips, their underside embedded with whitish lumps.

Mrs. Watson was proud of these disgusting-looking pieces of detritus. The previous autumn, she was experimenting with various aging methods when she realized that small bits of crumpled-up tissue paper, when painted over in flesh color, bore a remarkable resemblance to wrinkles. But it wasn't until the beginning of this year that Miss Charlotte thought to contact Miss Longstead, a well-trained and inventive chemist they'd met during an investigation. Miss Longstead, at Miss Charlotte's request, had come up with a formulation that adhered securely to the face as it dried, appeared a decent facsimile of skin, and did *not* flake or crumble with the movement of facial muscles in speech or laughter.

Mrs. Watson leaned down. "Let me see."

The formulation, for all its merits, irritated the skin and could not be worn day after day. As expected, Miss Holmes's face was red and splotchy. Still, Mrs. Watson sucked in a breath. She set aside the towel and fetched the girl a puff of cotton soaked in witch hazel water.

Miss Charlotte accepted the cotton puff and wiped it over her face. "I'm all right. I saw Mr. Gregory outside. He was standing at Frau Schmidt's window and they were talking."

Mrs. Watson felt her professional interest piquing. She'd been lucky—in her youth, the men she'd wanted to become her protectors had happened to be ones she would have allowed in her bed anyway. But Mr. Gregory had no such luxury: He was appointed the ones he must seduce. How did he do it?

"What were they talking about?"

"He asked, 'You mentioned that there are vineyards in the valley where you grew up?' In fact, while I stood there, it was the only question he asked. And she told him about the vineyards, the wines they produced, local cheeses, the practice of mountain pasture in summer, and how a cousin of her mother's quit his law practice to live in a hut high in the Alps," said Miss Holmes, in her usual dispassionate tone. "In the end, it would not be that he seduced her but that she seduced herself with her reminiscences."

Mrs. Watson laughed, then sighed. "Now there's true seduction for you—he sensed that what she wanted was a rapt audience, and he gave it to her."

Miss Charlotte, who needed no understanding from others, rose from the sling stool. "I think I'll put on my stewardess uniform. In case there is a summons at night."

Mrs. Watson's thoughts left romances true and false and returned to the task at hand. She'd always liked Remington, but that emissary of his, Dannell, was overcautious and overinterfering. It should not be difficult for Miss Charlotte to devise a way to search Frau Schmidt's cabin. But Dannell had been convinced the children would be seasick the entire time and never leave their cabin and that, even otherwise, any daytime attempt to pick the lock would surely be seen. As a result, now their entire effort must be molded around The Seduction.

Each cabin aboard the *Provence* boasted an electric summons button. Mr. Gregory was to persuade Frau Schmidt to summon a stewardess in the evening to keep an eye on her sleeping charges so that she herself could escape to meet with Mr. Gregory in his cabin, saying that she needed to take a bath or that she was feeling a little unwell and must take some air on deck.

To make sure that it was Miss Charlotte who answered these summonses and went to Frau Schmidt's cabin, the night before the *Provence* sailed, Lord Ingram had ventured aboard and rearranged the wiring behind the summons panel in the duty room so that should Frau Schmidt's summons button be pressed, the indicator light for Miss Charlotte and Mrs. Watson's cabin would glow instead and a stewardess would knock on their door soon thereafter.

This was a cumbersome solution: The occasion of Frau Schmidt's seduction might not be the only one for which she'd request help. It was decided that Mrs. Ramsay's companion Miss Fenwick would remain in their cabin most of the time, so as not to leave any summons from Frau Schmidt unattended, leading the latter to suspect that something might be the matter with her electric button.

Today Mrs. Watson was Miss Fenwick and received not a single summons. Tomorrow Miss Charlotte would be stuck in this cabin all day.

The girl climbed up to the upper bunk and plumped the pillow. The redness on her face had faded somewhat from earlier but still showed in welts and splotches. "Let's see," she said, slipping under the cover. "Mrs. Ramsay met a number of people today."

Mrs. Watson listened carefully. She'd already studied the passenger list and was familiar with the names. If she ventured out tomorrow as Mrs. Ramsay, she would need to recognize at least the young lieutenants with whom Mrs. Ramsay had dinner—everyone else she could ask to reintroduce themselves, citing her advanced age as an excuse.

"Before I went to the baths tonight, I also saw Lord Ingram on deck, and finally learned how Roger Shrewsbury got his black eye," continued Miss Charlotte.

As she related the story of Miss Arkwright's public disgrace, Mrs. Watson felt at once hot and cold, assailed by her own shame and fear from a different era. She sank down into the sling stool that Miss Charlotte had vacated. "My God, that poor woman."

Miss Charlotte lay with one cheek on her pillow. Against her dyed-grey hair, her face, with those large eyes and soft cheeks, appeared almost childlike. "Apparently, Mr. Arkwright went to Australia to make his fortune when he was still a boy, and in Sydney, no one knew that he had a sister. He might have found her only on this trip."

How bittersweet the reunion must have been, how miraculous. Miss Arkwright, her vast relief at no longer needing to debase herself for survival. And then . . .

"Have I ever told you, Miss Charlotte, that one time, when I was traveling with Dr. Watson and Penelope, I thought I saw a loutish relative of a former protector? The man used to leer at me and tell me that I'd better be nice to him because who knew how much longer I'd have his cousin's patronage. I almost suffered an apoplectic attack, imagining my past brought up before my family by this odious man—not that Dr. Watson wasn't fully aware of it, but the thought of being subject to that kind of leering vitriol again . . ."

"But you were not as unfortunate as Miss Arkwright," said Miss Charlotte softly.

Mrs. Watson went to the fold-up washstand and splashed water on her face, feeling a little calmer as the cool liquid struck her skin. "He turned out to be a stranger in a hurry who barely glanced my way. But that feeling of absolute panic was seared into my head, and for weeks on end I had nightmares about what could have been."

She sighed and turned around. "I'm at a different point in my life now. Penelope has grown up. She knows that I'm not her aunt but her mother, and she has cheerfully accepted that and everything that goes along with it. Miss Arkwright, on the other hand . . . For her, I'm afraid the stigma will never go away."

———— ✳ ————

Livia stood outside the bridge, huddled against a deep penetrating chill. She'd awakened hoping for another warm and sunny day, but it was as if the weather, too, had felt her mother's deadening presence and deteriorated accordingly.

In the distance she could descry patches of blue sky where streaks of sunlight poured down to dye the sea a matching shade of bright cobalt. But nearer the ship, everything was a drab, dispiriting grey, the very hue of the English winter she thought she'd left far behind.

A large black board, painted with a map of the world, hung outside the bridge. On this board the vessel's progress would be recorded at noon every day, its most recently measured position marked. For now, the board was still blank, but at Livia's inquiry a junior officer nearby informed her that they'd already exited the shallow waters of the English Channel to steam along where the Bay of Biscay met the Atlantic.

The sea had become choppy; moving across the deck made Livia feel halfway drunk, liable to zigzag if she didn't forcibly hold herself to a straight path. Yesterday the RMS *Provence* had seemed to her everything that was great and mighty. But before the fathomless power of the sea, it resembled more a paper boat floating down the Thames, blithely unaware of the soggy fate that awaited it downstream.

Not many passengers were out and about in the less-than-pretty, less-than-inspiring conditions. On the fore deck, a group of gentlemen played deck billiards with much ribbing and teasing. A pair of ladies, who seemed to be mother and daughter, stood on the port promenade and gazed toward the horizon.

Livia had just rounded to the empty starboard promenade

when Lady Holmes's voice boomed. "Olivia Augusta Holmes, there you are!"

Livia recoiled by habit, before she realized that her mother didn't sound as irascible as she usually did. In fact, her tone was almost chirpy.

"You are up rather early, Mamma," Livia ventured. "I thought I'd let you sleep a bit longer before looking in on you."

Lady Holmes's laudanum habit usually kept her asleep until mid-morning. Then, in her grogginess, she often remained abed another hour.

"Oh, no, I already had a little stroll with Mr. Gregory."

That would explain her good mood. Poor Mr. Gregory.

From the aft deck came peals of laughter—Lord Ingram's children?

"Shall we go say good morning to his lordship?" Livia immediately suggested.

Lady Holmes in a better mood was still Lady Holmes. Livia didn't want to be alone with her any more than necessary. But Lady Holmes took Livia by the arm and dragged her forward—in the opposite direction.

"What—what's the matter, Mamma?"

"No, no, nothing." Lady Holmes stopped. She panted, two patches of color on her cheeks. "Well, I guess you might as well know. I asked him to marry Charlotte, and he said that he has not supported her financially."

So her mother had interpreted Lord Ingram's answer to mean that Charlotte was now the plaything of some other man? Livia coughed, which Lady Holmes took as a sign of communal embarrassment. "That sister of yours. One of these days she'll be sorry, if she isn't already bathing in daily regrets."

Livia tamped down her frustration. Why couldn't her mother wish Charlotte well? Why couldn't she see that Charlotte had never needed anyone else's good opinion to prosper?

Then she wondered, what if Lady Holmes *could*? What if she instead *feared* the possibility that her youngest child was living life happily on her own terms?

"Anyway, don't waste your time on Lord Ingram—he's for Charlotte."

Livia would have sputtered if that would have been any use. Of course he was for Charlotte. That they both loved Charlotte was the foundation of their friendship.

"Have you met any gentlemen aboard?" continued Lady Holmes in the same breath.

She had met Mr. Gregory, but she didn't think that was what Lady Holmes wanted to hear. "Not yet, Mamma."

"Never quick to act, are you?" Lady Holmes patted her own coiffure with a complacent superiority, forgetting that when she'd acted quickly and married Sir Henry, she'd regretted her choice bitterly. "But never mind, I've come up with a brilliant idea."

"Oh?" Livia's stomach tightened.

"You know about the boor and his streetwalking sister, do you not?"

Livia nearly clamped a hand over her mother's mouth. She looked around in a sudden sweat. Thankfully, the nearest windows were all closed and no one was in their immediate vicinity. "Mamma, please, not so loud. And where did you hear about the Arkwrights?"

"Norbert bunks with Mrs. Shrewsbury's maid, who was there that morning at the hotel. She said you were there, too—and you didn't tell me a thing."

Lady Holmes glared at Livia in accusation and then, "Well, never mind, it isn't exactly suitable for a young lady to witness such things, let alone speak of them. Did I tell you the boor was rude to me when I embarked? I was running late and told his sister to get out of my way. You'd think it would be an honor for someone born in the gutter to yield to a lady, but no, he had the gall to take umbrage. Now what does that tell you?"

That Lady Holmes was one of the least gracious people to ever walk the face of the earth?

Livia's silence earned her a stinging slap on the arm. "Stupid girl. That tells you the boor can be yours."

At Lady Holmes's leap of logic—no, plunge of irrationality— Livia's lips flapped. She felt like a fish trying to speak underwater. "Mamma, you cannot possibly be thinking—"

"Oh, no. Of course I wouldn't set you to court that boor—you haven't got the skills or the looks for it. But the sister, now there's a pariah. And you're the foolishly softhearted kind. I say women who lure men from the straight and narrow ought to be tarred and feathered, but I'll bet you feel sorry for the creature. So why don't you take that confounded sympathy and do something with it?"

The ship swayed. A great plume of spray shot up against the hull. Livia stumbled. Her mother tottered in the opposite direction, gripped the gunwale, and raised her voice. "Her dream of respectability lies in shards. And on a ship like this, she's all alone. No woman would speak to her, and any man who does must have designs. So here's your chance, Olivia. Go knock on her cabin. Befriend her. Be the shoulder for her to cry on. Need I say more?"

Livia opened and closed her mouth a few more times.

Were she the sort of woman who could successfully execute such a plan, she would not have needed reminders to exploit Miss Arkwright's plight. Not to mention she hadn't the least interest in pursuing Mr. Arkwright.

"Mamma, your idea, I'm sure, is exceptional. But I'm not very good at approaching strangers. Miss Arkwright might be grateful, but Mr. Arkwright would take one look at me and guess my true purpose."

"What if he does?" Lady Holmes made her usual dismissive hand-wave. "He ought to be pleased as punch that a lady such as yourself would condescend to make an effort for him."

"But if he is not, then I will no longer have any association with

Miss Arkwright either. Don't you think that would be cruel to her, to have someone extend friendship, only to find out that it was false and full of ulterior motives?"

Lady Holmes rolled her eyes. "Why do you care about that strumpet?"

"Because she is a decent person, which is more than I can say for you," came a hard voice above them.

Mr. Arkwright, looming before the open window of his upper-deck cabin, looked down directly at Livia. "I apologize that I cannot marry you, miss. I would rather shoot myself than be related to your mother. But I'm sure my sister would appreciate your kind company, if that is still at all possible."

⁕

The sea, choppy at sunrise, had become only choppier at one o'clock in the afternoon. It wasn't so egregious yet that special frames needed to be set on the dining tables to hold food and cutlery in place, but the water in Lord Ingram's glass did tremble, ripple, and occasionally even leap, a microcosmic tempest that mirrored the unrest without.

"The barometric pressure has dropped by another quarter inch since morning," he said. "We could be in for a rough night."

Mr. Gregory turned to the boy of about six seated next to him. "Do you like storms, Herr Bittner?"

Georg Bittner, who had reddish brown hair, a beaky nose, and thin lips, thought for a moment and nodded.

He was the only child in the dining saloon. Not many children were aboard the *Provence*, and all the others were being fed in their own cabins, much in the same way that at home, children—children born to parents who could afford first-class passages, in any case—ate in the nursery and not at the dining table with their parents.

Had Frau Schmidt brought her charges to the saloon, she might have heard an earful from scandalized passengers. But who was going to tell a handsome gentleman do-gooder that he had perhaps not followed all the rules?

"Do you suppose that—" Georg Bittner paused, as if he needed to reorganize the sentence in his head. His English was correct, but somewhat lacking in fluency. "Do you suppose, Mr. Gregory, that Mrs. Ramsay will have bonbons for us after the storm?"

Mrs. Ramsay had opted to have luncheon sent to her cabin. If two women must share one false identity, that of Mrs. Ramsay's was not a terrible candidate. But still, Mrs. Watson's Mrs. Ramsay would not resemble Holmes's Mrs. Ramsay in every detail, nor would they sound identical, and the more Mrs. Watson's Mrs. Ramsay ventured abroad, the more differences might be noticed.

Mr. Gregory smiled kindly. "I'm sure that Mrs. Ramsay, if she has any bonbons left, would be happy to share them with young passengers." He rose. "Now come, Herr Bittner, since we're finished with our meal, let's take a look at Frau Schmidt and Rupert Pennington from the window and then perhaps we can play a game of deck billiards."

Young Herr Bittner, a born sailor, barely wobbled as he made his way out of the dining saloon. Frau Schmidt's other charge had been seasick since morning, trapping his governess in the cabin. Mr. Gregory, however, had turned the situation to his advantage, taking Georg Bittner in hand and, from time to time, keeping Frau Schmidt company via her window.

They were lucky that Lady Holmes had not been abroad much—she would hardly be pleased to discover Mr. Gregory paying court to someone else. Lord Ingram did not mind Lady Holmes's absence, but he worried that he'd seen little of Miss Olivia since luncheon the day before. She did not enjoy being cooped up, and he hoped that having her mother around would not turn her into a hermit against her will.

He was about to leave, too, when Mr. Arkwright entered the dining saloon, his gait slow, his gaze sweeping back and forth over the diners. Such was his force of personality, like that of an engine of war arriving outside a besieged castle, the rather sparse collection of diners fell silent at his approach.

As he passed by Mrs. Shrewsbury and Mr. Russell's table, the latter said suddenly and loudly, "And speaking of centerpieces . . ."

Mrs. Shrewsbury dropped her fork. It clanged against her plate, the sharp impact reverberating from the walls.

Arkwright halted.

Russell turned around and gave a grin that was all teeth. "Why, hullo, Arkwright. Fancy seeing you here."

Arkwright acknowledged him with a curt, "Russell."

Russell turned back to Mrs. Shrewsbury and said, at a much more normal volume, "And speaking of centerpieces, dear cousin, do you remember the grapevine that grew out of Mrs. Broadbent's dining table at her country estate?"

Jacob Arkwright stared at the back of Russell's head, then he walked on.

— ❧ —

Lord Ingram spent much of the afternoon on deck with his children. Lucinda thrilled to darkening skies and growing waves. Carlisle, who thrilled instead to well-built block towers and neatly organized bookshelves, nevertheless realized that it frightened him less to see the *Provence* cutting through the waves, rather than to huddle in his cabin with his eyes closed, imagining, each time the ship tottered, that its sinking was imminent.

Lord Ingram explained how the ship was ballasted deep down in the hull so it could recover its balance. The children hung from grab lines on the side of a lifeboat and learned about the items it carried— oars, a sea anchor, bailers, towropes, boat hooks, a compass, and a lantern, many of which were not stowed in the lifeboats themselves but in locked boxes along the deck.

The rain had started when they went back inside, weaving their way up to the upper deck, hanging on to the stair balustrade for the entire climb.

The children's parlor cabin, which they shared with their governess, was immediately next door to Lord Ingram's suite. In fact, they shared a private bath. But Lucinda, who adored the idea of having her own lodging, preferred for her father to come and leave via the front door like a proper visitor.

To that end, he shook hands with both children, and was shown out with all pomp and circumstance. He stood a moment with his hand on their door and wished, for the hundredth time since their mother's departure, that they needed never to grow up. That they would always be so happy with so little.

The *Provence* lurched. He slid across the passage and just stopped himself from ramming into a boiler casing. Somewhere forward, on the staircase, perhaps, someone did bang into something. There was a yowl, followed by a stream of curses.

Jacob Arkwright.

Arkwright had a starboard suite of cabins on the upper deck. The space between port and starboard cabins was bisected lengthwise by two large boiler casings, the bases of the ship's funnels, which obstructed much of what Lord Ingram, standing in what on the deck plan was marked as the port passage, could see of the opposite side, or even of the stairwell.

But when Arkwright's voice came again, this time from the starboard passage, probably in the vicinity of his own front door, it was audible enough despite the rough sea and the pouring rain, thanks to the gap between the boiler casings.

His tone was rough. "What are you doing here, Pratt?"

There had been a Pratt the afternoon before who hadn't wanted to talk to Mrs. Ramsay, but he wished to speak to Arkwright?

"Good evening, Mr. Arkwright," answered Pratt with great deference—*and* great urgency. "Are you aware that a certain Mr. Russell, who has his domicile in Sydney, is going around telling everyone the rumors regarding Miss Arkwright?"

"And what of Russell's unseemly speech regarding my sister?" Arkwright did not sound surprised.

"It means that you have no more hope of keeping Miss Arkwright's past a secret."

"Australia is different," said Arkwright. Lord Ingram could almost see him shrug. "It's less fussy. It's got hundreds of thousands of ex-convicts, for heaven's sake."

"But solicitation was not a transportable offense," pointed out Pratt.

A tense silence.

"I—of course I did not mean to imply that Miss Arkwright might have practiced anything of the sort. What I intended to say is that she will not be living among ex-convicts—or at least I hope not. How will your friends treat her? More importantly, how will your friends' wives and sisters treat her? Have you no idea?"

Arkwright did not answer.

"I know, to someone like you, sir, that I'm utterly useless," Pratt went on, sounding encouraged. "But perhaps I'm exactly what Miss Arkwright needs—now more than ever. I will not use her to curry favors with you. And I'm not so ambitious that I'll thrust her into the sort of company she fears. With me she doesn't ever need to set foot in Australia, where her notoriety would have already spread. We can go on to America or back to Britain and live quietly."

"And you think I'll entrust my sister to a stranger to live far away from my reach? I've seen 'em all, Pratt, and you don't fool me. You're a fortune hunter. The only reason you want her is because she's my sister and I'm a very rich man."

"I am no such thing!" Pratt's voice rose. "Is human affection of no value to you then? Or do you think that no man can love her because of her past?"

"That is not what I said," growled Arkwright. "I did not say no one would love her; I said I don't trust *you*. And she doesn't trust you either, or she'd have let me know that she wants you."

"How can you be so obtuse?" cried Pratt. "She couldn't give her heart to anyone earlier because she couldn't trust anyone to stay if they knew the truth. But I know the truth and I'm still here. Why can't you at least give me a chance to prove myself?"

"I have nothing else to say to you."

"Or is it really something that has nothing to do with me?"

Pratt lowered his voice, but syllables still drifted to Lord Ingram, standing right next to the gap between the boiler casings. ". . . accidentally slept with . . . before you recognized . . ."

The next sound was the bone-crushing impact of a fist—and Pratt's shriek of pain.

"Shut your mouth. And if I ever hear you mention anything of the sort again—"

Another sickening crunch of knuckles on skull, followed by another cry of distress from Pratt.

"Stay away from my sister, you sorry little man." Arkwright spat. "And this is your final warning."

Seven

"M y dear, have you thought of the future?" asked Mrs. Watson. In some ways, the recent weeks and months in Paris had been a lovely interlude for her. She adored spring in the City of Lights. She saw a great deal of her marvelous Penelope. And Miss Bernadine Holmes—Miss Charlotte's elder sister who required looking after—grew healthier and happier under her care.

And yet, faced with a resolute lack of news from Miss Charlotte, even though she knew the girl to be safe, she'd fretted about her safety, everyone's safety, and their collective future.

"Yes," said Miss Charlotte.

She still wore her cabin stewardess uniform, a white blouse over a black skirt, a sandwich plate in her lap. On her head sat a brunette wig, the same kind as worn by the real-life Mrs. Ramsay. The sling stool on which she sat, not exactly a sturdy piece of furniture, scraped as her weight shifted with the slanting of the floor, the sound barely audible against the percussion of rain outside.

Her answer came so swiftly that Mrs. Watson, who had hesitated a long time before speaking her question out loud, took a moment to react. "You have? I mean, of course you would have thought of the future. Have—have you a plan then?"

"Many," said Miss Charlotte, biting into the remainder of her sandwich.

"Many?" echoed Mrs. Watson.

She was suddenly nervous.

The electric lamp cast a sharp-edged silhouette on the wall behind Miss Charlotte. She did not speak again until she'd set aside her plate and taken a sip of water. "Yes, many, most of which will be rejected along the way. And some of the rest will fail, no doubt."

Mrs. Watson swallowed. "I see you've been busy in your seclusion."

"Yes," said the girl. Her face, with its serenity and detachment, could have served as a model for Titian's *Madonna*. "Being in seclusion made me realize that I would not care to be forced into seclusion again."

Mrs. Watson almost pitied Moriarty, before she remembered that they were David and he Goliath.

Yet David had defeated Goliath in the end.

Her heart pounded. "Has anything been set into motion?"

"Yes, things have been set into motion. And more things will be set into motion once I regain my freedom to move about."

"And M—Moriarty?"

"Reduced to insignificance, if all goes well. But then again, all could go ill for us, too."

Mrs. Watson's fingertips shook. Her imagination had been far too timid. She had not dared orchestrate, even in her mind, Moriarty's complete annihilation.

"And don't worry, I have not forgotten Mr. Marbleton."

No, of course she wouldn't have.

Mrs. Watson breathed hard. "What should I do?"

"What you have always done, ma'am. You are the senior partner in the enterprise of Sherlock Holmes."

Miss Charlotte's tone was unexceptional, one she would have used to advise Mrs. Watson to stick to her usual breakfast. Yet Mrs. Watson shot up from the lower bunk, where she'd been sitting, barely avoiding cracking her head on the edge of the upper bunk. A strange energy surged everywhere inside her and she could not remain still another moment.

"I—I could use a walk."

Out in the passage, it felt as if the *Provence* were a horse in a steeplechase—that is, if the horse, after leaping over an obstacle, fell into a ditch directly on its flank.

The rolling of the ship made it hazardous to advance, but it also kept passengers in their cabins, and she saw no one on her way to the upper level. However, two women occupied the ladies' lounge, praying earnestly with their eyes closed.

She entered the empty library instead and pushed the chairs to the bookshelves, which had been equipped with narrow horizontal bars across the front. As the ship rose and plunged, books slid and rattled against the bars but did not fall out.

She lurched, teetered, and staggered, yet managed to pace along the path she'd cleared. It hadn't been all that long ago that she first met Miss Charlotte. Such a halcyon moment, no danger at all and only the happiness of trying something that had never been done before.

But she, who had first put the idea to Miss Charlotte to hang out shingles as Sherlock Holmes, consulting detective, ought to have known that the simple act of helping people and finding out the truth could never be so simple. One person helped was another's path blocked. And society ran on appearances, not truths. Unearthed facts revealed everything that had been buried with them, everything that those with appearances to keep, profits to turn, and powers to accumulate did not wish to see laid bare, dirt, blood, and all.

It was always going to be a dangerous career.

And now Miss Charlotte wished to take the danger head-on.

Mrs. Watson was afraid, so afraid she was barely aware of the more imminent menace of the storm. And yet she was also—feverish. The ship skidded to port and threw her into the chairs, and she leaped up to pace some more.

The lamps went out.

She stilled, gripping on to the top of a bolted-down sofa. In the darkness, wind shrieked, rain pummeled, waves battered the hull. No, it wasn't altogether pitch-black. The glimmer from mast lights atop the ship shone on an explosive plume of spray. Water whipped the windows. Mrs. Watson, standing two feet away, flinched.

Electric light returned with an abrupt brilliance that made her squint. At the same time, the library's door burst open. Mrs. Watson spun around. A tall man with a harsh face and the shoulder of a bull stood in the doorway.

Mr. Arkwright. She had seen him—and his sister—come up the gangplank the day before, but had not known then who they were or what had happened to Miss Arkwright.

He stared at her in disbelief—and consternation. Belatedly, Mrs. Watson remembered her beauty mask.

By the time she'd had her talk with Miss Charlotte, she'd already taken off her Mrs. Ramsay face. Despite the restlessness that prickled hot and cold all over her body, she hadn't rushed out of the cabin at once, but had first glued on a false nose, then donned a beauty mask, and finished by throwing on a shawl so that the mask would attract as little attention as possible.

The beauty mask, made of chalk white India rubber, covered the entire face except for holes cut out for the eyes, the nostrils, and the mouth. And with her black dress and the black shawl wrapped around her head, she must appear a phantom from a second-rate gothic novel.

But Mr. Arkwright said nothing. In fact, he wasted not another second on her. From the door, which was situated near the aft wall, he took two steps into the library and leaned starboard, peering around her at the space beyond the far end of the bookshelves.

The library was the size of an ordinary drawing room, albeit narrow in proportion. Mr. Arkwright satisfied himself with one look and left as abruptly as he'd come.

Mrs. Watson stared at the once-again closed door. Had he been looking for someone? His sister?

What if the girl had gone missing? What if the unkindness of the world had become too much? A splash over the side of the ship on a stormy night and who would notice?

She sank into the sofa. The ship buckled and swerved. The door reopened, this time admitting a young woman in a dark blue dress, a cream-colored shawl wrapped around her shoulders.

Miss Arkwright—and she was all right! Mrs. Watson sprang to her feet. Miss Arkwright stumbled backward and held out a hand, as if to ward off an evil spirit.

The blasted mask again!

"I apologize!" Mrs. Watson threw aside her shawl and yanked at the beauty mask's elastic straps, tied around her head. "It was most thoughtless of me to wear this mask where I could alarm other passengers."

"Oh, no, no, it's quite all right," said Miss Arkwright, shuffling in place.

Only to stare at Mrs. Watson even harder when the latter, after disentangling the straps, at last had the mask in her hands.

"I apologize again," Mrs. Watson rushed to add, recalling her face in the mirror earlier in the evening, all red and angry from a day under disguise. "I must look a fright—and it's all on this pernicious mask. I was told that it would confer myriad benefits if I would but apply a battery of emollients, wear it overnight, and let my face perspire.

"But the exercise has always seemed contradictory to me. Far be it from me to fault something as laudable as perspiration, but to sweat all night long under an impermeable layer, especially if one had smeared on, beforehand, all types of vegetable and animal grease—isn't it less a regimen to relieve the pores, and more one to clog them to death?"

Miss Arkwright giggled a little—perhaps more out of astonishment than anything else.

"As you can see, my skin has not prospered under this particular treatment, but I was too vain to leave my cabin looking like that . . ."

Mrs. Watson thanked the inventor of the mask for giving her an easy scapegoat. She and Miss Charlotte had brought several such masks aboard, not to use as intended but for answering knocks in the middle of the night when neither had any disguises on, or in case Frau Schmidt summoned a steward to fetch a doctor for a feverish child.

"You are quite all right, ma'am," said Miss Arkwright softly. "I am the one who should apologize for intruding on your privacy. Good night."

She turned to leave.

"Why don't you join me, Miss Arkwright?" Mrs. Watson heard herself say. "The storm would seem less threatening with someone else by my side."

Miss Arkwright turned back, her expression halfway between in-credulity and an incredulous hope. "You—you know who I am, ma'am?"

"If you are wondering whether I've heard certain rumors aboard this ship, then yes, I have."

"And it does not bother you, ah . . ."

"Miss Fenwick," said Mrs. Watson. "I serve as companion to Mrs. Ramsay, and no, the rumors do not bother me."

"But—what about Mrs. Ramsay?"

"She might be curious, but I don't believe she would mind."

Miss Arkwright stiffened, and Mrs. Watson could have slapped herself. "Please do not think, Miss Arkwright, that I've asked you to join me to satisfy anyone's curiosity, tawdry or benign. I only wish you to know that not everyone will turn their back on you because of what a stupid, irresponsible man shouldn't have said."

The ship dipped as if it had taken up alpine skiing. Mrs. Watson grabbed anew at the top of the sofa. Miss Arkwright hung on to the door.

"Will you come in then?" Mrs. Watson extended the invitation again, after she'd steadied herself.

Miss Arkwright's hand opened and closed a few times around the door handle. "Yes. Yes, I will. Thank you, Miss Fenwick."

Relief washed over Mrs. Watson—she was probably being an interfering old biddy again, but she very much wanted to make sure that Miss Arkwright would be all right. "Will you have a seat?"

They sat down on the long sofa, several feet apart. But now that she had convinced Miss Arkwright to stay, Mrs. Watson wasn't sure how to proceed next. "Shall I ring for something?" she asked, her words sounding both too loud and too bubbly.

"Oh, no, please don't take the trouble."

But a cup of tea or a glass of wine wasn't there merely to assuage a guest's thirst. A beverage gave both host and guest something to do, to better negotiate the trickiest bits of a meeting of strangers.

Miss Arkwright bit her lower lip. Mrs. Watson had the abrupt sensation that she regretted accepting Mrs. Watson's offer of friendship and that when she spoke next she would take her leave after all.

"Oh, actually, I've a few biscuits."

Before she'd left their cabin, Miss Charlotte had given her a handful of biscuits wrapped in a clean handkerchief, in case she became hungry. Hurriedly Mrs. Watson took the biscuits from her reticule and set them on the sofa, with the handkerchief now spread open as a plate. She took one and gestured at Miss Arkwright to do the same.

Miss Arkwright watched her for a moment before picking up a biscuit and biting into it. "Oh, it's a butter biscuit."

Mrs. Watson seized the opening. "Many years ago, I lived for a while with my grandfather and he would buy me butter biscuits. Frankly, the ones he bought didn't have much butter. But I loved them—I was younger and hungrier in those days."

Miss Arkwright smiled shyly—her face softened remarkably when she smiled—and took another nibble at her biscuit. "My brother worked for six months as a baker's apprentice. Sometimes he was given a few biscuits—or so he said—and he always gave them to me."

Her brother's accent marked his place and class of origin as soon as he spoke; hers did not. Their features attested to a shared parentage, but their speech pointed to very different paths in life.

A tiny crumb fell onto Miss Arkwright's lap. She exclaimed softly, picked off the crumb, and smoothed her skirt with the back of her hand, her touches light and reverent, as if the dress were a holy relic. Mrs. Watson hadn't paid close attention to the dress earlier. Now she saw that what she'd believed to be merely a severe expanse of dark blue was in fact the kind of understated elegance that could be arrived at only with a great deal of forethought and even more money.

The main structure of the skirt was brocade of a less intense blue, intricately embroidered in a pattern of peacock feathers and sprinkled with an abundance of beads and seed pearls—then covered by a near transparent top layer of midnight blue Persian silk, so that only those privileged to come near the dress and remain awhile in its vicinity could discern the craftsmanship and sartorial flair that went into its construction.

"My, what a marvelous dress."

"Yes, now my brother can give me things besides biscuits . . ." She smiled, but the corners of her lips did not turn up. "I hardly dare recall how much this dress cost—and it's nowhere near as ruinously expensive as some of the truly extravagant items in my wardrobe. The lace on my pantalets—which nobody would see—is finer than what most women can afford for their wedding gowns."

Her free hand balled into a fist. Her voice dropped into a lower, darker register. "My heart burns when I think of how people must be laughing at him, because of me."

She was an unusual-looking woman, Miss Arkwright. Even if she wasn't beautiful, she should have been eye-catching. Yet it was only now, with the intense, angry unhappiness in her voice, that she became slightly less forgettable.

"I see someone who is trying to make up for his long absence," said Mrs. Watson quietly. "The only things he can give you now are what he can buy—because to prove his love would take much longer. And you must not think only of the inconveniences you might have caused him, when the opposite is truer. By taking you out of your own familiar milieu, he was the one who brought you into the orbit of that fool Mr. Shrewsbury, and he was the one who confronted Mr. Shrewsbury, precipitating an incident that was far more consequential to you than it could ever be for any of the men involved."

Miss Arkwright closed her hand over her biscuit. When she opened it again, there were only broken pieces on her palm. Crumbs trickled down to her dress, and this time, she seemed not to notice at all. "I hate to be disloyal, but I must admit that at times my thoughts have gone in a similar direction. I wish desperately that Jacob had left that man alone. But in the end, the fault is mine."

And what could Mrs. Watson tell her? Unless and until the world changed, Miss Arkwright *would* be held at fault.

Her voice became distant, almost disembodied. "Should I have expected this? Would the universe have allowed a woman like me to prosper? Perhaps it's telling me I should have submitted more meekly to the fate of girls left without fathers and brothers. Perhaps I shouldn't have bothered to try so hard."

As if to underscore her words, a web of lightning ignited. The crack of thunder that followed was so deafening that Mrs. Watson's heartbeat sped up to a hard staccato, a mallet knocking on her ribs.

Before she could reply, the door of the library opened yet again. Mr. Arkwright loomed, his face hard, his bulk filling the doorway.

"I've been looking for you, Willa," he said. "Come."

———❖———

The knock came while Charlotte was on her knees, thinking about Lord Ingram.

Or rather, she knelt on the small sofa by the window and watched the storm in the dark, while thoughts of her lover swarmed inside her head.

During the years of his marriage, she had dwelt on him as little as possible. After Lady Ingram's departure, the situation remained complicated and she went about her daily business without spending too much time wondering what he might be doing or when they would see each other again.

But now . . .

Was he standing guard over his children, reassuring them that they would be safe through the night, or were the children already asleep and he back in his own suite? Could she conceivably steal upstairs for a visit? To be sure, she'd spent time with him only the day before, extremely recent for two people more accustomed to being apart than being together.

But the way he'd looked yesterday afternoon in that perfectly fitted pewter grey lounge suit. And his serious, respectful mien, so utterly appropriate for interacting with an elderly lady of slight acquaintance. And then, as he spoke of wariness regarding old women bearing sweets, the glance he had slanted her, his gaze very slightly hooded, his true inclination visible for a fraction of a second . . .

She would call it a promise of delights to come except he never promised. He only delivered.

The knock yanked her back to the present. She scrambled off the sofa, turned on the lamp, and answered in Mrs. Ramsay's voice. "Yes?"

"Stewardess, ma'am. You called for service?"

She hadn't, but Frau Schmidt must have.

Charlotte had already prepared a beauty mask; she slipped it on. "Thank you for coming so quickly, my dear," she said through the door, pulling at the mask to make sure that its elastic strips held fast. "Let me warn you that I've got my night mask on, so don't be apprehensive."

She fastened a tentlike dressing gown over her stewardess uniform, opened the door, and smiled at the stewardess. Goodness knew what her smile looked like through the mask's cut-out holes. The stewardess, despite her warning, took half a step back.

"I'd have taken it off, my dear," Charlotte explained kindly, "but the turmeric unguent I've got underneath looks even worse, I'm afraid."

"Not at all, ma'am, not at all," replied the stewardess gamely. "How can I be of help?"

Every time Frau Schmidt summoned service, Charlotte and Mrs. Watson must come up with a reason for needing assistance. Thankfully, tonight's task was ready-made.

"Won't you be so kind as to find Miss Fenwick, my companion? She might be in one of the public rooms, or walking about. Perhaps she will have a mask like mine, perhaps not, but she will be in a black frock."

The stewardess remained stoic at being told that there might be another masked woman roving about. "Certainly, ma'am. Should I just tell Miss Fenwick that you are looking for her?"

"Yes, that would be quite good of you." Charlotte slipped a coin into the stewardess's hand.

The stewardess smiled and curtsied. "I'll send her to you, ma'am. Good night, ma'am."

Charlotte wasted no time in tossing both the beauty mask and the dressing gown to the side. She put on wire-framed spectacles and an orthodontic device—one of her least favorite things about disguises—that subtly yet substantially altered the shape of her face.

Her cabin was starboard on the saloon deck. Frau Schmidt's, in the same stretch, was only three doors further aft.

When Frau Schmidt answered her knock, Charlotte was all smiles. "Good evening, Frau. How may I help you?"

"Oh, it's you again."

Charlotte had already shown up at her door three times today, once to bring a bucket for poor Rupert Pennington, once to change bedding, and a third time with broth and plain toast for the boy. Fortunately, those needs hadn't been too difficult to anticipate—their first day aboard, Charlotte had already asked for two buckets and two sets of extra bedding. Today when a stewardess had come to Charlotte's cabin a little before tea time, Charlotte had ordered broth and toast, in expectation that Frau Schmidt would want Rupert Pennington to eat something, even if he remained seasick—and she had guessed correctly.

Charlotte kept smiling. "Yes, it's still me, ma'am. I'm taking an extra shift for my friend who is unwell."

"That is very wonderful of you. I do apologize for troubling you so much today."

Inwardly, Charlotte raised a brow. Earlier, Frau Schmidt had been harried, looking after her seasick charge, and had not bothered to chitchat. She had also not looked as presentable as she did now: Since Charlotte last saw her, she'd changed her dress and recoiffed her hair.

Was it possible?

"It is a privilege to serve, ma'am," Charlotte declared. "How may I be of assistance tonight?"

"You really are too kind. If you don't mind, will you stay with the children for some time? After a day like this, I'm desperately in need of a bath. My poor charge is fast asleep—he took a bit of laudanum and should sleep through the night. Young Herr Bittner is still awake, but he shouldn't give you any trouble at all."

No doubt Frau Schmidt was trying to speak with every ounce of austerity she could muster, but her hand rubbed against the side of her dress, her ears were a bright red, and she did most of her talking looking not at Charlotte but back at her charges.

"Of course, Frau Schmidt," Charlotte said as reassuringly as she could. "Will you allow me to return to the duty room to let my workmate know that I will be up here for some time?"

After making sure that Frau Schmidt's door had closed behind her, Charlotte returned to her own cabin. Mrs. Watson arrived on her heel, looking both tense and tensely excited. "Well, my dear?"

"Frau Schmidt says she wishes to take a bath." And that had been exactly what Mr. Gregory would have persuaded her to say. Except Charlotte hadn't thought she'd attempt it so soon. "Will you go to the ladies' baths, Mrs. Watson, in case she actually heads there? If she isn't there in a quarter hour . . ."

Mrs. Watson exhaled. The two women clasped hands. They did not need to speak any more on the significance of the moment. If they found what Lord Remington sought, they would be in a much better position to take on Moriarty.

Enough time had passed for a trip to the duty room and back. Charlotte left to knock on Frau Schmidt's door again.

She was quickly admitted to a cabin that was white paneled like her own, and about the same dimensions.

"I will be back soon," promised Frau Schmidt.

Charlotte inclined her head. "It will be an uneven trip to the baths, Frau Schmidt. Please use care."

Frau Schmidt, who had her satchel in hand and stood as stiffly as figures in Egyptian tomb paintings, swallowed. "*Ja*, I will be most mindful of the danger of slipping and falling. But I am also determined to be as clean as the day I was born, in case this is my last night on earth."

Charlotte wished her a pleasant bath and closed the door.

It was her understanding that many cabins on the *Provence* featured iron bedsteads instead of berths. Her cabin, booked last minute, had two stacked bunks. Frau Schmidt's cabin combined these features: It had been provided with a bedstead that was just wide enough for two people to squeeze onto, and there was also a swinging berth above that could be pulled down.

The odor of vomit that had been inescapable the first three times Charlotte had been summoned had largely dissipated. Frau Schmidt must have kept the window open until it had started to rain—and sprinkled drops of essential oil in the cabin: The strongest note in the air wasn't that of either saltwater or stomach acid, but that of peppermint.

A muffler had been wrapped around the electric lantern and dimmed its light. This muted glow shone on Rupert Pennington slumbering soundly on the bedstead, drooling a little. On the pull-down berth, Georg Bittner was nearly hidden under a mound of blankets.

"Are you still awake, Herr Bittner?" asked Charlotte softly.

The boys lay with their heads toward the door, where Charlotte stood. At her question, Georg Bittner craned his neck until his face was nearly parallel with the shorter edge of the pull-down bunk. "How did you know I was awake?"

"You were moving a little."

"Was I?" The boy sighed. "I didn't know."

Charlotte laughed softly. "You wanted me to think you were sleeping?"

Young Herr Bittner did not answer. He was not a beautiful child, his nose much too big for his pale, freckled face, but he did have nice eyes, thickly fringed with slightly reddish eyelashes.

After a while, when it became clear that his silence was his answer, Charlotte asked, "How is it that you didn't take some laudanum to go to sleep? You don't like the taste?"

Pure laudanum, opium dissolved in alcohol, was bitter. But Lady Holmes's favorite preparation, laden with syrup and licorice, tasted more like an overzealous liqueur.

"The taste is all right, but when I wake up, I can hardly remember who I am."

"That would be a good reason to stay away from laudanum. But aren't you afraid to remain awake on a night like this?"

If the child didn't go to sleep, the night would be a lamentable waste. Charlotte glanced at the pocket watch pinned to the cuff of her blouse. Almost nine o'clock. How long would Frau Schmidt take at her "bath"? Three quarters of an hour? The boy, with his wide-open eyes and alert expression—not to mention the vapors of peppermint oil in the cabin acting as a stimulant—seemed unlikely to fall asleep in that time.

Could she come up with a legitimate excuse to search the cabin while he looked on? "Since you are awake anyway, do you wish to play games?"

Georg Bittner put one arm around his pillow. "Are we going to drown if the ship sinks?"

So he was afraid after all—she adored a good storm, and even she could not wait for this one to subside.

"The ship is unlikely to sink," she replied. "And if it does, there are lifeboats. The crew will try to get passengers, especially children, onto lifeboats."

"But why put children on lifeboats?" asked the boy gravely, with perfect logic. "Do children know how to handle lifeboats?"

"I suppose it's because grown-ups think it's only fair to let children live, since children haven't been on earth very long."

Young Herr Bittner thought for a moment. "Maybe they don't want children to die yet because children would take up all the places in heaven, since they haven't had time to be really bad."

Charlotte raised a brow. "A theological bent of mind, I see."

This time it was the boy who waited. And when it became apparent Charlotte had nothing to add on why children deserved to live longer, he lifted himself up on one elbow. "Can we really play games this late at night?"

"When you're at sea and there's a storm and your governess has had to leave for some reason."

This made Georg Bittner smile a little, revealing two missing front teeth.

"I suppose, with your permission, I can have a look around, and see if there's anything we can play?"

Charlotte kept her words casual; she did not want the boy to sense any unusual excitement on her part.

"But there are no toys here," answered Georg Bittner with rather a great deal of resignation for a child his age. "Rupert said his parents told Frau Schmidt that he's too old for toys, since he'll be in preparatory school next year."

"What about books? You've any books?"

"Only Frau Schmidt's Bible."

Charlotte didn't know whom she ought to pity more, two children on a long voyage with no books and no toys, or the governess who had to keep them contained and well behaved until they reached their destination.

"You'll be amazed at what you can make games out of, when there are no 'toys' as such on hand. I have a friend who has devised a number of games that can be played with sticks, pebbles, and a handful of dirt."

Hope shone in the boy's face for a brief moment. "But where will we find dirt?"

"A very trenchant question." Charlotte pretended to think for a moment. "Did Frau Schmidt bring a slate board and some chalk? Surely she must still teach Master Rupert his lessons during this sailing? I know games we can play on a slate board."

Georg Bittner bolted upright—he was small enough that he had no need to worry about bumping his head on the ceiling. "Yes, we have one. She keeps it in the secretary."

Frau Schmidt's travel secretary, a lap-size wooden case with a hinged cover that slanted gently to function as a writing surface, was stowed at the foot of the bed. As she lifted the cover, Charlotte angled her body: She would hide the chalk—and any other writing implement—and use its absence to search elsewhere in the cabin.

"Hmm, we seem to have a minor problem. I found the slate board—but there is no chalk. Not even pencils."

Georg Bittner scrambled off the pull-down bunk. But by the time he arrived, besides the slate, there were only neatly arranged notebooks and exercise books in the secretary. "Oh no! Maybe Rupert really did throw the pencils overboard. He said if she couldn't find pencils, then she couldn't make him do his lessons."

"But she probably knows him well enough to know that he might do something of the sort. Do you think she'd have chalk and pencils stashed away elsewhere, where he wouldn't suspect?"

The boy looked amazed that anyone could think that far ahead. "Maybe you can look in her cabin trunk? It's under the bed."

Charlotte smiled. It was the invitation she had been waiting for.

❋

Lord Ingram had worried that Carlisle would have trouble falling asleep. But the boy's eyelids drooped within minutes. Lucinda, as usual, chattered on, excited to tour the innards of the ship in the near future, after the storm had passed.

Sometimes, as Lord Ingram listened to her, he thought of her mother, the woman he had divorced. Had the former Lady Ingram ever been so lively as a little girl, so full of interest in life and its many adventures? And if so, who and what had doused her inner flame and degraded it to that secret but all-consuming smolder of anger?

When Lucinda, too, fell asleep, he spoke for a minute with Miss Potter, then thanked her and wished her good night.

"Good night, my lord," said Miss Potter, who had looked after him when he'd been a child. "And my dear, you do not need to thank me so often."

"Perhaps not," he said, smiling at her. "But I wish to."

The betrayal of his wife and one of his brothers had not made him more misanthropic, only more grateful for those who had treasured and safeguarded his trust.

He tottered back to his own suite of cabins, where a note awaited him on the floor just inside the door, written in Holmes's own version of shorthand, but not by her.

C in Frau S's cabin. Frau S headed to baths, supposedly, but no trace of her there.

He exhaled slowly. The hunt was underway.

Earlier he had meant to while away the evening in his parlor, or perhaps his sleeping cabin—he could see Holmes knocking on his door in a stewardess's uniform, asking cheekily whether he'd summoned her and how she could be of service to milord. But now that she was otherwise engaged . . .

He took himself to the smoking room, where if he sat in one particular chair, he had a view of Mr. Gregory's starboard cabin.

Should Frau Schmidt leave too soon, perhaps he could find some means to detain her a little longer, so that Holmes would have more time to complete her search.

The particular chair he wanted, however, was occupied by one of the young lieutenants who had dined with Mrs. Ramsay the night before. He and his fellow soldier, each with a glass of port in one hand and a cigar in the other, seemed settled in.

Lord Ingram nodded in greeting, went to the windows, and opened one. Cold air rushed in, but very little rain, only a sensation of moisture on his face: The ship had tilted up and this bank of windows, at the very rear of the smoking room, which was located aftmost on the upper level, was temporarily shielded from the elements.

And then the ship plunged and he hurriedly shut the window. Still, rain landed on the back of his hand and dampened a section of his sleeve.

He turned around. The ship scudded a good ten feet starboard before listing nearly forty-five degrees. The man who entered the smoking room just then stumbled. He gripped the handle of the door and barely righted himself before the ship plunged again, flattening him against the door.

Roger Shrewsbury.

He grinned at Lord Ingram. But when Lord Ingram failed to respond, the light in his face faded. "Um, my lord. How—how do you do, my lord?"

They had once addressed each other in much less formal terms. But after Shrewsbury's fecklessness had cost Holmes her reputation, Lord Ingram had stopped treating him with the indulgent affection one reserved for a childhood friend, even if a rather hopeless one. Lord Ingram leaned against the wall, took out his cigarette case and a box of matches.

"My lord, a word with you?" asked Shrewsbury, looking down at his feet. "Please."

Lord Ingram expelled a breath. "Let's speak in the passage."

In the *port* passage, of course, right next to a boiler casing, which completely blocked the view to Mr. Gregory's starboard cabin—God forbid that Shrewsbury should see Frau Schmidt emerge from a man's door and ruin her life, too.

But now that they were alone, Shrewsbury only scuffed his heels—or was he trying to find better purchase against the floor? Thunder cracked. Waves lashed. This close to a boiler casing, Lord Ingram felt the vibration of the ship's mighty engines, valiantly propelling her forward.

On the level below, had Holmes found anything? How much more time would she have? The lamps had gone out earlier for a few seconds. What if they were to go out again in the midst of—

"My lord, I haven't thanked you for coming to my aid yesterday morning," Shrewsbury piped up at last.

"Pray speak nothing of it. I was more concerned that chaos at the hotel would prevent my own timely departure."

Shrewsbury flinched. "Do you—my lord, do you also think that I behaved badly?"

Lord Ingram raised a brow. "You do *not* think so, Mr. Shrewsbury?"

His old schoolmate reddened. "But I didn't do anything wrong. If a woman you last saw covered in hors d'oeuvres appears in an expensive dress on the arm of an obviously wealthy man, wouldn't you take a second or a third look? I wasn't planning to bother her. Can't I even look at a woman in public now? And if a man is to defend a woman's honor, shouldn't he be sure that there is some honor to defend?"

Lord Ingram turned over his cigarette case in his hand, when he would have preferred to throw the sharp-cornered object at someone's very thick skull. "Unlike you, Mr. Shrewsbury, I would not so easily convince myself that I should follow a woman from one side of a hotel to the other merely to gratify my curiosity.

"Did you do anything wrong? If you believe, as you seem to, that a woman who was once dressed only in hors d'oeuvres has no right to complain however she is stared at in public, then I can't persuade you otherwise. But perhaps you ought to ask a different question.

"Did you do anything right? Did you conduct yourself in a manner that would make anyone applaud, or at least rise to your defense, or are you reduced to such inquiries as 'Do you think I behaved badly?'"

Shrewsbury bit his lower lip. "Mr. Russell applauded me."

"And no doubt he is a great friend of yours who only wants the best for you. No doubt you trust and admire him in equal measure."

"But to who else can I ask such things? You—you no longer advise me."

"Mrs. Newell was there. She is well known to have a good head on her shoulders. She would have advised you had you been humble enough to seek counsel."

Shrewsbury didn't speak for some time. His throat moved. "Are you still angry at me because of Miss Charlotte Holmes?"

Lord Ingram flicked open the cigarette case, took out a cigarette, and dropped the case back into his pocket. "Yes, I am. And are you going to again defend yourself by saying that you didn't do anything wrong?"

Shrewsbury opened his mouth, and closed it again.

Lord Ingram gave him a long look. "Maybe you didn't do anything wrong, per se. But as with so many other decisions in your life, Mr. Shrewsbury, you should have known better."

※

Nothing.

At Georg Bittner's urging, Charlotte searched every square inch of the cabin—and everyone's cabin trunks twice—before she declared that the chalk had rolled into a deep recess under the bed and that, oh dear, the pencils had in fact been in the secretary all along but underneath the notebooks, causing them to be overlooked earlier.

They played games of noughts and crosses for some time, moved on to charades, and then made a small bundle of two handkerchiefs wrapped around the "hard-won" piece of chalk and tossed it back and forth, while the boy asked Charlotte about the faraway places she'd visited.

Charlotte, having spoken to a stewardess or two in Southampton, answered that she seldom had opportunity to go ashore in foreign ports. But then, recollecting from the many travelogues she'd read, she presented various details that she remembered, details that could ostensibly have been seen by a curious stewardess from aboard the ship, such as the artificial breakwaters, called moles, constructed in Gibraltar harbor, which cradled the Royal Navy Dockyard.

Georg Bittner fell asleep approximately forty minutes after Frau Schmidt had left. Charlotte stood in the center of the cabin and scanned her surroundings, but did not pull out any trunks to rifle through them again—Frau Schmidt could return any moment.

Nothing. She'd once again unearthed nothing.

To be sure, her official duty was only to list everything in every locale she was tasked to visit, and she would do it here, too. But *that* was not going to gain her what she needed from Lord Remington.

Dannell, Lord Remington's emissary, was convinced that the information they sought must be contained in a palm-size booklet on German language and culture, commissioned and printed by the embassy to distribute free of charge to the general English public. His reason? Herr Klein, the Prussian attaché whom they had been cultivating, had left the embassy with a box of twenty such booklets, but only nineteen had been found in his house after his departure.

Also, since Herr Klein already knew that his position had become exposed and that he needed to entrust the information meant for the British to a random stranger, he would have chosen something not only small but nice. Something that this random stranger, upon discovering it among her possessions, would not toss out but continue to keep.

Charlotte stumbled forward and gripped the bedstead to steady herself—the *Provence* seemed to have dropped from a great height. She glanced at the boys. Rupert Pennington remained fast asleep. Georg Bittner jerked, but he, too, slept on uneasily.

She teetered across the cabin and sat down with a sigh on the small sofa under the window.

Dannell had been just as convinced that a traveling salesman who had called on the Klein household had been given the missing copy of the booklet. So convinced that Charlotte had been sent to the homes of this man's mother and sister in Norfolk, because he'd visited them in the days since.

Charlotte, on the other hand, had always doubted the only-nineteen-booklets-found orthodoxy. Who had passed on this piece of information to the British? Did they have another someone inside the embassy? If so, shouldn't that person be lying low, as the saying went, rather than taking a sizable risk in an atmosphere of suspicion and mistrust, just to nudge the British search in a particular direction?

The *Provence* banked hard. Foghorns blared, several long, shrill blasts. Charlotte rose to her knees on the sofa, pulled aside the curtain, and looked out of the window.

A ship almost as large as the *Provence*, mast lights barely visible in the pouring rain, silhouette dark and ghostly, shot past a mere fifty feet away.

The *Provence* shuddered as it encountered the wake generated by the other vessel. Charlotte let out a breath. A near miss, that was. A very near miss. Any closer and nothing else would have mattered.

She sank back down on the sofa.

Dannell had also been under the impression that the dossier they wanted had been microphotographed and that Herr Klein had pilfered one copy of the miniaturized result. *This* Charlotte thought more probable—she'd encountered microphotography of late and it was indeed an excellent method of conveying a great deal of information in secret, provided the recipient knew what to look for.

But—

The cabin went dark.

Electricity had failed earlier in the evening—and been restored almost immediately. Charlotte waited for the lamp to flash back on. But that did not happen.

Was it possible that the near miss *hadn't* been a near miss? What if instead the two ships had scraped each other as they passed and the

Provence was now taking on water, the operation of its dynamos already abandoned, the entire ship to be relinquished very soon?

No, too unlikely. If the *Provence* had developed a leak somewhere, that was one thing. But a collision, she doubted it could have gone unnoticed.

Sounds of speech came in the passage. She went to the door and opened it a crack.

". . . disruption will be temporary. I assure you, ladies and gentlemen, your lamps will be shining brightly again in approximately one quarter of an hour," announced a man—a junior officer, she would guess—at the top of his lungs.

He must have brought an old-fashioned lantern, for a bit of light also came through the opening of the door. Charlotte dared not go out into the passage, but other passengers did.

"What caused the malfunction?" a woman asked, her voice teary.

The man who spoke next sounded just as worried. "Are you sure we'll be all right? This is a terrible storm."

"I've sailed through worse storms than this and the captain is far more experienced than I am. Now, ladies and gentlemen, if you don't mind, I must inform the passengers on the upper deck and then return to my duties on the bridge. I bid you all a good night."

The junior officer's reassurances would have been more convincing if he didn't sound as if he were running away from further questions.

Charlotte might be the only person at least somewhat glad of his hasty departure: The passage was dark again and she was able to stick her head out of the cabin. Up and down, passengers who had heard the message were relaying it to those who had opened their doors too late.

Briefly, a cacophony of troubled voices drowned out the storm. Some aired fearful conjectures. Some tried to calm others down. And then an authoritative female voice—Mrs. Newell's—reminded everyone that they ought to return to their cabins lest they should fall down in the dark and hurt themselves.

When a quarter of an hour had passed, the electric lamp in Frau

Schmidt's cabin indeed blazed back to life. Frau Schmidt herself arrived a few minutes after that, full of apologies for how long it took her in the baths. Her hair had been put under a turban-like wrap—so she had given thought to her appearance post-"bath" and did not come in with obviously dry hair—and she looked appropriately flushed, as befitting someone who had been in a warm, steamy environment.

Charlotte assured Frau Schmidt that really not that much time had elapsed, accepted a coin, and left.

—❈—

Frau Schmidt remained in Mr. Gregory's cabin a good bit longer than Lord Ingram had dared hope.

Twenty minutes after he dismissed Shrewsbury and returned to the smoking room, the young lieutenants departed and he at last obtained the chair he wanted—the one with the clear line of sight to Mr. Gregory's door. By the time Mr. Arkwright came in to light a cigarette, however, Lord Ingram was beginning to be on edge. Had too much time passed? Had Frau Schmidt already slipped out and returned to her own cabin and he'd simply not seen her?

But he remained in place, watching. Mr. Arkwright smoked in brooding silence and left. The ship nearly collided with another vessel and Lord Ingram did not budge. But when the lamps went dark, he knocked on his children's door and stayed with Miss Potter until a ship's officer announced that electricity would be restored soon. To his incredulity and delight, after he went back to the smoking room, after illumination returned as if by magic, Frau Schmidt, looking only slightly disheveled and wholly rejuvenated, left Mr. Gregory's cabin.

Now *that* had to be time enough for Holmes to search to her heart's content.

He expelled several long breaths, returned to his own cabin, and turned on the light. Thunder rolled. Rain drummed thickly. His reflection shone in the window before he pulled the curtain shut.

A familiar sequence of knocks came at his door. Holmes. He opened the door, yanked her inside, and glanced up and down the passage before closing the door again. She was barely disguised—she'd taken out the orthodontic device—and too many people on this ship could recognize her. But he didn't have the heart to lecture her on the danger she faced—she understood it better than anyone.

Not to mention, one look and he knew that Frau Schmidt's cabin had not yielded what she sought. "No?"

"No."

She didn't appear disappointed or grim, merely resigned.

He sighed. "I have cake."

She brightened. "You do?"

"Yes, in case Mrs. Ramsay decided to pay me a visit."

She tutted. "Mrs. Ramsay is far too careful about her figure to consume cake. I, on the other hand, can be tempted anytime."

"Well, then, come and face your temptation."

He showed her into his sleeping cabin. A plate of pound cake sat on his bed, the lemon-colored slices studded with currants and candied peel.

"Hmm, is the cake here because you were afraid it would slide off your desk in this storm—or because you wished to lead me to your bed?"

Mrs. Ramsay's liveliness had made him forget how impassive the real Holmes was. She'd asked her question in an uninflected voice and without any flicker to her smooth, blank countenance.

"My concern was mostly for the cake," he said.

Mostly, but not all.

"Ah." She sat down at the edge of the bed, set the plate of cake on her lap, and took a bite. Her expression became one of fierce concentration—and equally fierce enjoyment. "Good cake."

His heartbeat quickened. He sat down beside her. "So, what do we do next—about Frau Schmidt?"

"Let's discuss that tomorrow. In any case, there's nothing more we can do tonight."

Heat spiked into his abdomen. "I thought you came to discuss that," he murmured.

Her attention entirely on the cake, she said, "No, I came because I missed you."

He was on his feet before he'd quite understood what he'd heard. His ears rang. "Don't say things like that."

She glanced up, her large blue eyes at once transparent and unreadable. "Why not?"

Because I've made my peace with the fact that you might never say—or feel—such things.

He heard himself chortle. "You're right. What was I thinking? By all means, feel free to say it as often as you'd like."

She took another forkful of cake. "Since our last meeting in Eastleigh Park—no, since before that—I've been thinking of you at a rather unnecessary frequency."

The floor dropped—he took a step back so as not to lose his balance. Her words made sense individually, but together they were only a roar in his head.

She looked—and sounded—as if she were talking about some outlandish gadget she'd read about in the Patent Office catalogues. That was familiar. Her aloofness from her own emotions was also familiar. But what she was telling him—was she saying anything remotely similar to what he *thought* she meant?

The floor tilted again. He found himself with his back against the wall. She set aside the cake, rose, and closed the distance between them. She peered at him, as if she'd never seen him before.

Her hand cupped his cheek, the touch a jolt down his spine. "Have I always liked you this much?"

Urgent knocks came at his front door. His heart thumped in alarm. He gripped her by the arms and listened.

The knocks came again, louder, more insistent. "My lord! My lord! Are you at home?"

Shrewsbury. The idiot. What did he want *now?*

Eight

The sound of knocking.

Charlotte opened her sore eyes and squinted at the travel alarm clock next to her pillow. Not yet eight o'clock. How inconsiderate—she'd hardly slept.

The knock came again, soft and timid-sounding.

She slid off the upper bunk. Fortunately, her makeup as Mrs. Ramsay was already in place and she did not need to bother with the beauty mask.

"Yes?" she croaked, standing in her stockinged feet on the cold floor.

She swayed a little. No glass-smooth sea yet. But compared to the chaotic buckling of the night before, the *Provence*'s current progress felt as triumphant and unimpeded as the advance of a hot iron across an expanse of starched linen.

"Is that you, Miss Fenwick? This is Willa Arkwright. I'm sorry to bother you but I need your help!"

Her voice was even softer than her knocks, barely above a whisper.

On the lower bunk, Mrs. Watson stirred. "Is that—"

"Yes. You stay put. I'll answer."

Last night, before Charlotte had sallied forth to call on Lord Ingram, she'd returned to her cabin to speak to Mrs. Watson, and Mrs.

Watson had confessed that she'd befriended Miss Arkwright. She did not regret that on its own, but had become anxious about an over-sight: She'd failed to consider that Miss Fenwick was a real person, and that the real Miss Fenwick might have wanted nothing to do with someone of Miss Arkwright's notoriety.

Charlotte put on Mrs. Ramsay's blue spectacles and set Mrs. Ram-say's wig on her head. The wig was already coiffed and ready to don. And since no one was under the illusion that Mrs. Ramsay came by her head of luxuriant chestnut hair naturally, there was no need to glue the wig on with spirit gum. Charlotte secured it with a pair of pins.

She opened the door to Miss Arkwright, standing in a much-creased dress. She seemed to have slept in it—and not very peaceful slumber, judging by the shadows under her eyes.

At Mrs. Ramsay's appearance, she took a step back. "Oh, I'm sorry. I was looking for Miss Fenwick."

Charlotte came out of the cabin and closed the door behind her. "Miss Fenwick is still resting. May I help you, young lady? Miss Ark-wright, you said?"

"Yes. And you must be Mrs. Ramsay?" Miss Arkwright hesitated. "Miss Fenwick mentioned you last night, and I hope I have not of-fended by—"

"You said you needed help, Miss Arkwright?"

Charlotte was certain that the real Mrs. Ramsay, if she had a caller this early in the morning, would get to the point.

At her brusque question, Miss Arkwright swallowed. "We—well, you see, ma'am, my brother isn't answering his door, and we also can't find him in any of the public rooms. His valet has gone to locate someone to open the door, but the stewards who come might want to speak to me first. And I was hoping that—that perhaps Miss Fen-wick could . . ."

Her voice trailed off.

"I see," said Charlotte. "You worry that you'll be treated in a less-than-respectful manner."

Miss Arkwright colored but did not say anything.

"No need for such unnecessary concerns. You are not only a paying customer, Miss Arkwright, you and your brother have taken some of the most expensive accommodation on this passage," continued Charlotte briskly. "But, that said, I will come with you. One moment."

She retreated back into the cabin. Mrs. Watson was up and waiting just inside the door. "Is everything all right?" she asked in Miss Fenwick's voice, her jaw tight, her voice low. "Is Miss Arkwright all right?"

"The girl seems fine," replied Charlotte. "We are about to go see whether everything is all right."

She brushed her teeth and flung aside her fortress-like dressing gown. She, too, had gone to bed fully dressed. Mrs. Watson helped shake out the wrinkles in her dress, then set a small hat on Charlotte's head.

Charlotte picked up Mrs. Ramsay's walking stick, nodded at Mrs. Watson, and was out of the door again.

Miss Arkwright gave her a grateful but uneasy smile. "This way, please, Mrs. Ramsay."

They walked forward and climbed up the stairs, which were located just aft of the dining saloon.

On the upper deck, Charlotte rapped imperiously at Mr. Arkwright's door with the head of her cane, three times in rapid succession, and then again two knocks.

No response.

She looked sideways at Miss Arkwright. "I don't suppose your brother accumulated his wealth by staying abed past eight in the morning."

"No. Even when we were children, he always got up at first light." Miss Arkwright worried a corner of her handkerchief. "These days he's up before half past six to read the papers and look through his correspondence—on land, that is. Maybe he allows himself more sleep at sea, but I don't think so.

"It was quarter to eight when his man came to me. He said he'd first knocked on my brother's door at seven—later than usual, since he thought this morning of all mornings his master wouldn't have minded a bit longer in bed. At quarter past seven, when he still hadn't had a response, he checked everywhere on both passenger decks. And then he knocked on my door and told me his concern. There's a connecting door between my brother's en-suite bath and my sleeping cabin. Usually it's not locked and I only need to knock before entering. But this morning, that also wouldn't open."

Charlotte knocked again, this time with the ferrule of her cane, producing a sharper, more metallic sound. "Is it possible that Mr. Arkwright is in the midst of a tour of the engines? And there is always a chance, isn't there, that he has been invited to a private breakfast by the captain?"

Miss Arkwright twisted her handkerchief and managed a smile. "Of course, there is every chance."

Footsteps mounted the stairs. A small, nervous-looking man arrived with a steward. The steward maintained a polite look on his face, but it was clear that he didn't think much of the valet's anxiety.

"This is Mr. Arkwright's sister. She also believes it best to check his cabin," said the valet, his voice squeaking with his need to justify his position against the steward's skepticism.

Miss Arkwright stiffened. But contrary to her fear, the steward was no lecher; he only nodded at her and went to the door. After knocking loudly, he produced a key.

"Frankly, miss, I don't expect to see your brother in there," he said to Miss Arkwright without quite looking at her. "That is not to say I think he's fallen into the sea or any of that nonsense—not at all! Most likely he's found . . . agreeable companionship, let's say. He spent the night in a different cabin and is late to rise this morning. It happens more often than you think on a long voyage."

Charlotte tutted. "Young people these days. So impatient. They should limit themselves to flirtations—until Gibraltar, at least. But then again, what could flavor a passionate encounter more memorably than the danger of shipwreck?"

Everyone stared at her, especially Miss Arkwright.

Charlotte shrugged. Ah, but it was liberating to be an old lady of independent means. One could say almost anything—the real Mrs. Ramsay certainly did.

The key turned.

The steward opened the door fully and switched on the electric lamp. Charlotte had the impression that he meant to perform a dramatic sweep of the arm, and perhaps even utter a triumphant "ta-da." But his arm, half-raised, fell limply. He emitted a strangled yelp and leaped back, thumping into the boiler casing.

The valet, with a frightened glance at the steward, stepped into the doorway.

"No!" he whispered.

"What happened?" cried Miss Arkwright at the same time. "And what are those things on the wall?"

She stood opposite the opening of the door; Charlotte, on the other hand, had her view into the parlor blocked by both the valet's back and the door itself.

Again, taking advantage of—or perhaps lightly abusing—the privileges of respectable elderly ladyhood, Charlotte took the valet by the arm and steered him back into the passage. And then, before a frozen-looking Miss Arkwright could move, Charlotte entered her brother's parlor.

A man's body lay facedown in a puddle of blood. He was situated halfway into the cabin, near the right-hand or aft wall. The puddle had dried in its outer periphery, but at the center it still wobbled a little, darkly, with the ship's movement.

The man, who seemed to have suffered a bullet wound to the head, was quietly and resolutely dead, no different from other murder victims Charlotte had witnessed. The left-hand wall of the parlor, however, had been garishly scrawled over with three words, each letter the size of a platter.

Or rather, two and a half words.

COMMON, VULGAR, and BASEB, which, had the scribbler

finished it, would probably have been BASEBORN, a charge that could, perhaps, have been leveled at the self-made Mr. Arkwright.

Underneath the letters, a revolver gleamed on the floor. Beside it, a walking stick lolled at a drunken angle.

Charlotte, unlike the valet before her, did not block the doorway but walked in and moved two steps to the side, clearing the line of sight from Miss Arkwright to the body.

Miss Arkwright clasped her hands over her mouth, her eyes open so wide they showed a rim of white both above and below the irises.

"Jacob?" emerged her muffled voice. Then, a little louder, "Jacob, is that you?"

"Would you care to come closer to identify him?" asked Charlotte. "I don't believe the gentleman on the floor can answer you."

Someone whimpered—not Miss Arkwright but the valet, who had again crowded into the doorway. "No, this can't be. This cannot be."

"Will one of you step forward?" Charlotte injected a trace of impatience into her voice. "I am an aged lady, and it cannot be salubrious for me to remain in this parlor much longer."

Miss Arkwright rushed past Charlotte, but not in her brother's direction. Instead, she ran toward the interior of the suite of cabins, opening doors loudly and hastily. Soon, sounds of retching erupted.

"Young people of today! It is only a body—and not even all that gruesome!" Charlotte gestured at the valet with her cane. "You, what is your name?"

The valet pointed tentatively at himself. "Me, ma'am? Fuller, ma'am."

"All right, Mr. Fuller, you come inside and you tell me if this gentleman is your employer."

Fuller stumbled nearer, as if the ship still thrashed uncontrollably in a turbulent sea. "Should—should I not go take a look at Miss Arkwright, ma'am?"

"Are you her maid?"

"No, ma'am."

"Then what business do you have when she is in the bath?"

Fuller flushed scarlet.

A commode glugged. Running water fell into a basin. Miss Arkwright reemerged pale and hollow, a shadow of her already uncertain former self.

Charlotte tapped her cane against the floor. "You can see very well, Mr. Fuller, that Miss Arkwright needs to be led away from this place. Will you identify the victim so she doesn't have to?"

Fuller yielded to Mrs. Ramsay's authority. "Yes, yes, of course."

He carefully stepped around the puddle, squeezed himself in the space between the body and the wall, and crouched low.

The sight that met him made him close his eyes for a long moment. "My condolences, Miss Arkwright."

Miss Arkwright gripped Charlotte's arm and made a sound like a small wounded animal trying to hide.

Charlotte glanced at Miss Arkwright and sighed. "I suppose that can't be helped now. And you over there"—she pointed with her cane at the hapless steward outside the door—"inform the captain that his presence is needed here. And be discreet about it, Mr. . . ."

The man didn't even hear his name being asked for. "Yes, the captain," he muttered. "That's right, the captain."

He ran off.

Charlotte took another look around the parlor and ushered everyone out. "Come, come, especially you, Miss Arkwright. No need for you to stay here."

"But Jacob—my brother—shouldn't we at least clean him up or something?"

"In good time, my child, in good time. This is now a crime scene. I may not know what Scotland Yard would do in such a situation, but I do know we civilians mustn't muck about too much until the professionals have had a look."

In the starboard passage, with the cabin door now closed behind them, Charlotte asked Miss Arkwright, "Shall we return you to your room, my child, and ring for some whisky?"

Before Miss Arkwright could answer, Miss Fenwick rushed up. "Mrs. Ramsay, Miss Arkwright, is everything all right?"

Mrs. Watson was a very beautiful woman. Miss Fenwick, with her altered nose and jaw, the latter thanks to an orthodontic device, barely passed for handsome. And yet she gave off a most appealing aura—behind her owlish-looking spectacles, her eyes still shone with Mrs. Watson's great kindness.

She held out her hands toward Miss Arkwright—worries of how the real Miss Fenwick would and would not act were now secondary to Miss Arkwright's palpable distress. Miss Arkwright gripped Mrs. Watson's hands as if she'd been tossed a lifeline in a storm. "Oh, Miss Fenwick, I'm so glad to see you. And no, I'm afraid everything has gone wrong. *Everything.*"

"Ah, the mythical Miss Arkwright, is it?" interjected a man's voice, dripping with sarcasm.

Mr. Russell emerged from the space between boiler casings, several paces aft. Miss Arkwright did not appear to recognize him on sight, yet she was instantly on guard. She let go of Mrs. Watson's hands but turned her body more toward the two women. "Yes?"

"George Russell, at your service." Mr. Russell smiled with a sneering. contempt that conveyed exactly what kind of man he was and exactly what sort of things he was about to say. "I am a friend of your brother's in Sydney. I think I speak for the entire city when I say we are all looking forward to . . . seeing a great deal of you, my dear Miss Arkwright."

Miss Arkwright froze. Mrs. Watson opened her mouth and forcibly closed it again. Fuller, standing farther away, clenched his fists.

An even smugger smile spread across Mr. Russell's face.

Charlotte studied him. She'd heard about the incident in the dining saloon the day before, during which Mr. Russell deliberately brought up the word "centerpieces" as Mr. Arkwright walked by. Obviously, he didn't mind antagonizing Mr. Arkwright to his face. Was he but doing more of the same here, or was he feeling particularly emboldened because he already knew Mr. Arkwright to be dead?

Mr. Russell's jeering expression faded, replaced by one of irate uncertainty—perhaps he hadn't expected an old woman's flat, impersonal scrutiny in response to his inflammatory remarks. He glanced at Mr. Arkwright's door. His lips flattened. Then he said, in a tone of belabored insouciance, "Such an excellent day. I bid you all good morning, ladies."

After his departure, Miss Arkwright glanced toward Fuller. The valet did not seem to notice her. He only stared at his dead master's door and murmured, "Such an excellent day *for whom*?"

"My dear Miss Fenwick," said Charlotte, "why don't you take Miss Arkwright to her own cabin? There is nothing she or any of us can do for Mr. Arkwright right now, and the process of inquiry will only distress her further."

Mrs. Watson guided Miss Arkwright away. Fuller went on staring at the cabin door, as if he were one of those faithful dogs who kept bringing their dead owner's slippers day after day, year after year. Charlotte rubbed the top of her cane and mulled over her situation. The last thing she needed, as a woman traveling under an assumed identity and in the middle of an elaborate scheme of her own, was a murder investigation.

Yet a murder investigation was about to take place.

Before his breakfast, Lord Ingram took a brief walk outside.

The last vestiges of the storm had disappeared and the *Provence* sailed under a blue sky in which drifted puffs of fat, white clouds. The wind remained fierce, whipping waves across the surface of the sea. But he, for one, could waltz about the deck, its pitch and yaw notwithstanding.

The dining saloon, lit brilliantly by the morning sun, was only one-third full—a number of passengers must have decided to sleep in. Captain Pritchard, however, was on hand, speaking amiably to the diners and commending them on their composure during the tempest.

He saw Lord Ingram and immediately came forward. "My lord, good morning! I am about to sit down for a bite. May I persuade you to join me?"

He had large bags under his eyes, and his jowl, too, seemed looser than Lord Ingram remembered, but he was in good spirits, smiling broadly, his eyes twinkling.

"It would be my pleasure," said Lord Ingram.

They touched briefly on the prevailing conditions—no troubles anticipated for the next twenty-four hours, at least—before Captain Pritchard took a sip of his tea and said, "This morning I was thinking again, my lord, of the cases you told me about, the lesser-known investigations of Sherlock Holmes. And I marveled anew at his mind. It is as if the rest of us only travel along the circumference of a circle, but he cuts along tangents and arrives much more swiftly on the other side."

In honor of Holmes, Lord Ingram buttered his toast rather extravagantly—for him, that is. She would not limit herself to such a paltry allotment unless she were approaching Maximum Tolerable Chins. "Ah, but Holmes's ability isn't the only remarkable thing about him," he said to the captain. "My friend has always possessed the most even of temperaments and a great willingness to learn. I still remember vividly how out of the blue I received a letter in shorthand, which he'd taught himself because he thought it would be useful."

"And what did you do?" asked Captain Pritchard, his eyes alive with interest.

"Not wanting to be outdone, I learned shorthand to write back to him," said Lord Ingram, laughing. "Funnily enough, on excavations, familiarity with shorthand has enabled me to record much more detailed daily logs than I would have setting everything down in longhand."

"This furthers my belief that a man must surround himself with only men of great caliber. Your association with Sherlock Holmes, my lord, what a boon it has proven to be!"

But what about surrounding oneself with women of great caliber?

It had been a bit of sly fun for Holmes to use her made-up nom de guerre to help Inspector Treadles solve a few puzzling cases, with Lord Ingram as their intermediary. But with Sherlock Holmes's fame growing and, should they survive Moriarty's tender mercies, likely to grow even more, Lord Ingram was beginning to be troubled by the thought that she might never be able to claim the credit that was rightfully hers.

Not only because she was a woman, but because she was a fallen woman. If he knew the truth, her admirer Captain Pritchard would need to steer clear of her, for the sake of his own reputation.

If he was a good man, that is.

Were he a lesser man in the mold of George Russell, who knew what might become of his erstwhile esteem?

"I have indeed derived incalculable benefits from my association with Holmes," murmured Lord Ingram.

The captain cut into his omelet. "Have you other such examples of—"

A steward rushed up to him. "Sir, sir, may I approach?"

The captain, startled, gave him permission.

The steward leaned down and whispered in the captain's ear.

"Are you absolutely certain, Johnson?" demanded the captain, his eyes bulging with disbelief.

"I saw everything myself, sir."

The captain abandoned his cutlery and shot to his feet. "My lord, forgive me. There is a matter that needs my urgent attention."

"Of course, Captain. Let me not keep you from your duties."

But the captain took no more than ten steps before he doubled back. "My lord, may I trouble you to come with me? In this matter I may very well require your assistance."

Lord Ingram glanced at his plate. He usually consumed a modest breakfast. Today, however, he was famished. And today it appeared that he would remain famished for a while longer.

He left his seat. "Certainly. Shall we?"

The second officer, who was also in the dining saloon to greet passengers after their distressing night, was bidden to come along. As they cleared the dining saloon and started up the stairs, Captain Pritchard informed the company in a low voice that something unfortunate might have befallen Mr. Arkwright.

A chill rose from Lord Ingram's feet. "How can that be?"

He remembered Arkwright from the night before, consuming two cigarettes in quick succession and then leaving the smoking room just as swiftly. He might have been silent and broody, but he'd also radiated a hunter's ferocity and ruthlessness—and he couldn't have been more alive.

"I ask myself the same," answered the captain in a barely audible voice. "I can only hope Johnson's eyes have cheated him sorely."

The chill spread to Lord Ingram's fingertips.

If Arkwright had died of unnatural causes, there would be an inquiry. And since there happened to be a Criminal Investigation Department inspector on hand, the matter would be handled in a professional, methodical manner.

Should Inspector Brighton identify the culprit easily, that would be one thing. But should the case prove puzzling or drawn out, a murder investigation had every potential to become a maelstrom, towing under anything or anyone unfortunate enough to be caught in its vicinity.

A detailed, thorough account of where every passenger was the night before could reveal that Frau Schmidt had not been in her cabin during those hours most relevant to the investigation. And if Inspector Brighton were to dig further, it might come to light that no stewardess aboard had answered any summons to look after Frau Schmidt's charges during her absence. Worse, that the duty room never recorded any request emanating from her cabin since the beginning of the voyage.

That, in and of itself, would constitute only a conundrum for the investigator. But Lord Ingram and Holmes had to worry about more than Inspector Brighton. What if someone aboard was indeed working for Moriarty? That someone might learn of the discrepancies and wonder whether Charlotte Holmes was involved.

Whether she was a passenger among them.

The company arrived outside Mr. Arkwright's suite of cabins. Lord Ingram was somehow unsurprised to see Holmes as Mrs. Ramsay, waiting alongside a stricken-looking man who appeared to be a servant.

After the briefest of greetings, the captain and the second officer entered the suite.

"Dare I assume you have already seen the inside, Mrs. Ramsay?" Lord Ingram asked.

"I have indeed," she answered quietly.

"And are you all right?"

What he wanted was to hear her assessment of the situation. If she wished, she could ask him to escort her to the nearby library, giving them some privacy to discuss the matter at hand.

But she appeared not to have any such plans in mind. "Oh, it was terrible. But worry not, my dear boy, I have reached an age where nothing dismays me anymore—not for long, in any case."

She turned her attention to the manservant. "Mr. Fuller, how are you faring?"

The valet gave a laugh that sounded more like a wail. "Better than Mr. Arkwright, I suppose. Very kind of you to ask, ma'am."

"And you, Mr.——?"

The question was for the steward, who stretched his quivering lips in an attempt to smile. "Johnson, ma'am. Frankly, I can't hold a single thought in my head right now, ma'am, but otherwise I'm all right."

She patted him on the shoulder and turned to Lord Ingram. "My lord, will you escort me to Miss Arkwright's cabin? I wish to take a look at her. She did not seem so well earlier."

He offered her his arm. She took slow steps, hunched over, her cane striking heavily against the floor, giving the impression of an old woman who, despite her valiant demeanor, had been overtaxed by the events of the morning.

He knew it was feigned and the result of excellent acting; still, his heart ached—the woman underneath the makeup had to be tired, too.

"Thank you, my dear," she said. And then, in a low voice, "You will be my eyes and ears now, sir."

"Madam," he murmured, "at most I will be your stenographer."

She chuckled and patted him on the shoulder as she had Johnson the steward.

It was only a few steps between the Arkwright siblings' cabins. Soon he was back before Mr. Arkwright's door. The ship's officers emerged. They had gone into the suite looking apprehensive, but with a flicker of hope that perhaps there had been a horrible misunderstanding. They reemerged with that hope extinguished. The captain, in particular, had to brace his hand on the doorjamb.

When he spoke, his voice croaked, that of a desert traveler who hadn't had any water in two days. "Johnson, inform Dr. Bhattacharya that he is needed—and then inform the master-at-arms. And Mr. Spalding, kindly knock on Inspector Brighton's door."

The hairs on Lord Ingram's nape stood on ends. What if Inspector Brighton was working for Moriarty? And what if he were to use the murder investigation to sniff out Holmes's presence . . .

Johnson and Mr. Spalding left. Captain Pritchard slowly straightened. He looked around; his gaze settled on the valet. "Mr. Fuller, is it? I understand your devotion, but there is no point waiting here. Go have some breakfast at least, young man. Soon enough you'll be needed for questioning."

He had to repeat himself before the valet understood and, with a numb nod, complied. Fuller first knocked on Miss Arkwright's door and inquired after her, and only then left.

When he had disappeared from view, the captain said, as if to himself, "More than once I have wondered how I would conduct myself if a murder happened on my watch. I have thought of the words I would speak to calm the passengers, the details I would notice that had been overlooked by everyone else, and even the triumph that would be mine when I, through a system of ruthlessly logical deductions, arrived at the identity of the culprit."

He smiled ruefully at Lord Ingram. "But now that it has happened, I feel—I feel as if someone had smashed all the windows on the *Provence*, snapped her masts, and detonated her boilers."

"I understand, Captain." Lord Ingram sighed. "A murder shatters the safeguards we believe to be in place. Without those safeguards, the world is a perilous place indeed."

Captain Pritchard took off his cap, ran his hand through his thinning hair, and replaced the cap with an agitated downward tug. "Perhaps I ought not to have been so enthusiastic in the discussion of crimes."

"You did not bring it about any more than farmers praying for rain are responsible for floods."

The captain rubbed his hand over his eyes. "Am I correct in thinking, my lord, that in the normal course of an investigation, a police inspector would not work alone but would have a second on hand to take note?"

"That seems to be the case, in my experience," answered Lord Ingram.

But he had also known instances in which a police inspector met one-on-one with a suspect or a witness, taking notes for himself. Or perhaps not taking notes at all, because he was not questioning the other party but browbeating.

"Given your proficiency in shorthand, my lord, may I volunteer you to be Inspector Brighton's amanuensis? I'm afraid that among the crew we've none with that skill, and from what I remember, no passenger has brought along a secretary for this voyage."

Cold pricked Lord Ingram all over, his neck, his spine, the back of his knees. He flexed his right hand, as if he anticipated nothing worse than cramped fingers. "I am more than willing to do my part, Captain."

Not for the captain, and certainly not for Inspector Brighton, but for Holmes, who had charged him to be her eyes and ears.

He would watch Inspector Brighton for her.

He would do what he could to keep her safe.

Taking notes for Inspector Brighton gave Lord Ingram little control over the direction of the investigation but promised to devour a great deal of his time. He spoke to his children and Miss Potter, letting them know that he would be busy in the coming days. Then he returned to his suite and took out his camera case.

In the passage outside his suite, a steward now stood guard—probably not just any ordinary steward, but one who'd had some special training under the master-at-arms. When he crossed the stair landing to reach the starboard passage, he encountered another steward who had been set in place. At his arrival, this steward moved forward to block his progress.

"That's quite all right," said the captain. "Lord Ingram may come through, but no one else for now."

Next to the captain stood Inspector Brighton and a man of Subcontinental origin who was presumably Dr. Bhattacharya, the ship's surgeon. Inspector Brighton, to Lord Ingram's surprise, leaned against the side of the passage.

"Are you all right, Inspector?" Lord Ingram dimly recalled what the policeman had said at dinner the first night about not traveling well and not looking forward to rougher seas.

They'd had nothing but rougher seas since.

"A bit of vertigo, nothing too serious. When I can sit down, I'll feel better," replied Inspector Brighton, sounding less than vigorous. His gaze slid to the case Lord Ingram carried. "Is that photographic equipment you bring, my lord? *Most* helpful. I was just bemoaning the lack of a camera."

"I'm afraid we won't have access to actual photographs until we reach Gibraltar, at the earliest, as I haven't any fixers on hand for developing the negatives."

"Still, much better than nothing."

After Dr. Bhattacharya was presented to Lord Ingram, Inspector Brighton said, "Well, shall we go in, gentlemen?"

"I will leave the work of the investigation to you, Inspector," said Captain Pritchard. "I will only be in your way."

Inspector Brighton pushed off the wall and stood straighter. "But I thought you were highly interested in such criminal matters, Captain."

Despite his weathered skin, the captain appeared ashen, with little of his former air of haleness. "I thought so, too, until it happened on my ship. And now I only wish that the serenity of this great vessel had never been disturbed by so inhumane an act."

"I understand," said Inspector Brighton gravely.

Captain Pritchard inclined his head, grateful for the sympathy. "What you have already asked for, Inspector, I will have delivered to you. You must send word should you require anything else. Any steward will know how to pass on your message to me."

He left, his steps heavy. Inspector Brighton regarded his departing back for a while, then opened the door to Mr. Arkwright's parlor. Lord Ingram and Dr. Bhattacharya filed in behind him.

A potent, coppery odor stung Lord Ingram's nostrils. No one spoke as they took in the sight of the body, the blood, and the firearm some distance away.

The parlor, with its window currently facing west, would have been relatively dim at this hour of the day but for the electric lamp that shone with a steady luminosity. In furnishing and arrangement, it was nearly identical to Lord Ingram's suite. Near the door, a writing desk. Under the window, a large sofa upholstered in midnight blue brocade, with brass studs along the base and the armrests. On the white-paneled wall, a large painting. In Lord Ingram's parlor, the painting depicted the Taj Mahal. Here it was more difficult to make out the subject because of the words that had been scrawled over the image, blood-bright letters that screamed their contempt and loathing.

"Common. Vulgar. Baseborn. Do people kill one another over such opinions these days?" muttered Inspector Brighton, shaking his head.

Lord Ingram stared, at once repulsed and transfixed. This violent hatred for what someone could not help being—since when had people *not* killed because of it?

"Why am I not allowed to pass?" A voice rose outside in the starboard passage. "Has Arkwright bought the whole ship now? Or has that sister of his become such a holy relic that no one is allowed to come within fifteen feet of her? Where's the captain? Does he know about this?"

Inspector Brighton and Lord Ingram turned. Dr. Bhattacharya, who was closest to the door, opened it a crack.

"It's the captain himself that has us standing here, Mr. Russell," said a steward. "If you want to use the smoking room, you'd best take the port passage."

"I will," said Russell, unmollified. "And I will take this up with the captain when I see him next."

It became quiet again on the upper deck. The physician closed the door. Inspector Brighton rubbed his temple and murmured, "Mr. Russell seems highly interested in Mr. Arkwright. One wonders whether that interest was reciprocated."

With a thud of his heart, Lord Ingram realized that the policeman had commented on Russell as a suspect. Everyone remotely connected with Arkwright would now be a suspect.

Inspector Brighton proceeded to study the victim. At his direction, Lord Ingram took photographs of the body in its original position and then, with Dr. Bhattacharya's assistance, turned it over.

There was a collective intake of breath.

A bullet had entered Arkwright's head via his left eye, leaving behind a hideous hole. Another had struck him in the shoulder. With a frown, Inspector Brighton sank to his knees to look over the dead man, especially his hands, and examined his pockets, which turned out to be empty.

He rose again and yielded the spot so Lord Ingram could take photographs of Arkwright's front. The parlor was spacious for that of a seagoing vessel, but with three grown men inside, a large body on the floor, and a blood puddle that should not be trampled underfoot, there was not a great deal of room to maneuver.

When Lord Ingram was done, Dr. Bhattacharya, who had gone near the window to be out of the way, approached the body at the policeman's instruction. Inspector Brighton himself tiptoed across the cabin to where the firearm had fallen near the vandalized wall.

After Lord Ingram took pictures of the revolver—and the walking stick next to it—Inspector Brighton picked up the revolver with a handkerchief. He tilted out the cylinder. Three chambers were empty.

Mr. Arkwright had been shot twice. Where was the third bullet?

"There," said Inspector Brighton, and pointed at the door.

A bullet had been embedded near the door, at approximately shoulder height.

"Interesting," said the policeman next, scrutinizing the ebony walking stick. "There is a filament of light-colored hair, approximately ten inches in length, stuck near the end of the cane."

A woman's hair? But the Arkwright siblings were both dark in coloring.

Inspector Brighton gave the revolver and the cane to Lord Ingram to place on the writing desk and at last turned his full attention to the vandalized wall. "Does it not strike you as extremely odd, my lord, the juxtaposition of these words and this rather bloody scene?"

To Lord Ingram, the writing and the crime seemed very much of a piece, but he said, as he crossed to the window to take a panoramic photograph of the graffiti, "If you refer to the words themselves, then true, they are incongruous."

"Their color is aggressive and ominous. But someone who would use *common* and *vulgar* as epithets strikes me less as a crazed killer and more as a person who would strip off his glove and slap his adversary across the face with it," mused Inspector Brighton. "I might expect a duel at dawn at twenty paces, blood shed, lives lost, and whatnot— something far more . . . ceremonious than this *execution*. Unless—"

He turned around. "Doctor, is there any chance the words were scrawled in blood?"

"Unlikely," said the physician without looking up. He spoke with a light Bengali accent. "Blood doesn't dry to such a brilliant scarlet."

"Then our paradox remains." Inspector Brighton put his nose close to the wall. "It does not smell of dried blood either."

"What does it smell of?" asked Lord Ingram.

"It gives off a pleasant odor. Like something ladies might use."

That color . . . "Something—along the lines of rouge?"

Inspector Brighton searched in his pocket. Lord Ingram, who had finished photographing the wall, offered his own handkerchief—Inspector Brighton's was on the desk, under the revolver. The policeman murmured his gratitude and dabbed the handkerchief on the crossbar of the A in VULGAR, a red slash through what appeared to be a white gazebo on the painting. He then rubbed the handkerchief against itself and took another sniff. "I'm not terribly familiar with rouge, but this very much resembles it. Which makes the whole affair even odder."

"You suspect the participation of a woman, Inspector?"

"Possibly. But it is also possible—perhaps more likely—that a man did this to throw suspicion on a woman. Certainly the height of the letters suggests that a woman of average height could only have written them by stretching her arm while standing on tiptoes."

"But for a man to perform such a sleight of hand would require him to have access to rouge, which can't be so easily found on a vessel at sea," said Dr. Bhattacharya, rising from his crouch by the body.

"True, though there must be a number of couples traveling together . . ." mused Inspector Brighton.

Lord Ingram could confirm nearly the exact opposite.

He'd counted two army officers, four missionaries, a professor of Sanskrit bound for Delhi, and a smattering of civil servants going to new posts—and none had brought along a spouse. There were the wife and daughter of a civil servant headed to India to join him, and Frau Schmidt, escorting her two charges.

They, alongside Lord Ingram's party, Holmes, Mrs. Watson, Miss Olivia, Mrs. Newell, Mr. Gregory, Lady Holmes, the Arkwright siblings, Mr. Pratt, Mr. Russell, the Shrewsburys, Inspector Brighton, and a small assortment of servants, constituted everyone aboard.

The Shrewsburys were, in fact, the only married couple traveling together.

Lord Ingram felt a stab of foreboding.

"I have already asked for a detailed passenger list, as well as deck plans with everyone's cabins labeled—we shall know soon enough those married couples who are aboard," said Inspector Brighton.

He passed the red-soiled handkerchief back to Lord Ingram and indicated that he should place it on the desk, alongside the revolver. "Any pronouncement on the time of death, Doctor?"

Dr. Bhattacharya glanced at the body. "I am no pathologist, Inspector, and have seldom been called upon to determine the time of death. But given the relatively normal ambient conditions inside this chamber, I think death occurred between eight o'clock and midnight last night. And if I were pressed for greater accuracy, I would say between nine and eleven."

Inspector Brighton placed a hand on a spot on the wall free of rouge marks. "I'm no physician at all, but having worked with pathologists and witnessed how they establish times of death, I would concur."

Lord Ingram felt as if he stood on a carpet of needles in his bare feet. "I was in the smoking room last night. Mr. Arkwright came and stayed ten minutes or so. I can't be sure of the exact time he left, but it couldn't have been too long before the electric lamps went out the second time."

He estimated that electricity failed the second time around five minutes to ten. Having scratched a match in the dark to look at his pocket watch, he was certain of his information, but asked that the policeman verify it with the ship's officers.

Inspector Brighton looked grave. "If so, we have a narrow window of time during which the murder could have taken place."

Dr. Bhattacharya rubbed one hand on his other arm—Lord Ingram, too, would have been apprehensive if the first time he estimated the time of death in a murder investigation, the time frame was suddenly compressed to only an hour.

As for himself, he might as well have been set on a unicycle, the seat of which was twenty feet in the air. What if he was the last person to see Arkwright alive?

Inspector Brighton went on to make a thorough study of the parlor. Lord Ingram, directed to record a puddle of water near the window, touched the arm of the sofa. It was still damp.

"I spy something," said Dr. Bhattacharya, crouched low on the floor and getting into the spirit of evidence-gathering. "See there, under the writing desk?"

Inspector Brighton knelt down and extracted the item from the corner it had rolled into. It was a small spherical glass container, still one quarter filled with a reddish substance.

A rouge pot.

"Speak of the devil," murmured Inspector Brighton, peering into the lidless jar. "Was the culprit caught in the act? There is enough rouge left to finish the last word."

Lord Ingram photographed the rouge pot. Inspector Brighton made another search of the parlor without unearthing anything further. He opened the door into the sleeping cabin and performed a similar inspection there. Mr. Arkwright's luggage, as well as his brief bag that contained letters, papers, and a fair amount of currency, British and Australian, appeared not to have been disturbed.

In the bath the policeman's attention was drawn to the still wet basin. "This was used more recently than midnight."

"I spoke to Mrs. Ramsay earlier," said Lord Ingram. "She mentioned that Miss Arkwright had felt unwell."

"But the bath does not stink of vomit, does it?" asked Inspector Brighton.

"No, indeed," concurred Dr. Bhattacharya. "It does not smell of recent regurgitation."

Lord Ingram remembered Miss Arkwright's stricken expression in that hotel foyer. Her desperate dash to get away. The last thing she needed was to become a suspect in her brother's murder.

Inspector Brighton sighed. He sounded as if he, too, was reluctant to turn his thoughts in that direction. "Doctor, I thank you for your assistance this morning. Before I let you return to your regular duties, dare I hope you've something for seasickness that would not impede my work on this investigation?"

The ship's surgeon shook his head. "I'm afraid not, Inspector. The only substances I can prescribe would also make you drowsy."

"I thought so," said Inspector Brighton stoically. "In which case, I had best bring this case to a satisfactory conclusion as swiftly as possible."

Nine

Inspector Brighton had been given the library to conduct his investigation. The room had large rectangular windows on two sides, two forward-facing—giving onto the bridge—and three overhanging the starboard promenade on the saloon deck below.

One long sofa stretched—and bent—along the windows. Of the half-dozen padded armchairs that had also been provided for the passengers, two had been set facing each other in the center, the rest moved out of the way against the bookshelves. A cream-colored cloth that hadn't been there before was now tacked to the door, blocking its etched glass panels so that no one could peer in on the proceedings.

But instead of their first witness, it was Captain Pritchard who entered, an anxious hope on his face. He handed the passenger list and pages of deck plan to Inspector Brighton. "I apologize for my impatience, gentlemen. But have you come to any insights with regard to the crime?"

"I do have some ideas," said Inspector Brighton. "Though it is very early in the case, a few things appear to be beyond dispute."

The captain brightened. "Oh?"

Inspector Brighton took out the small glass container from his pocket. "We found this in the cabin."

Captain Pritchard's expression changed, as if Inspector Brighton cradled a scorpion in his palm. "The substance inside—is it what was used to write those words on the wall?"

"The rouge? Yes, most likely."

The captain peered harder. "Rouge? A woman committed the crime?"

"That conclusion would be premature. Though I'll admit that the presence of the rouge pot does make me less suspicious of men without easy access to a woman's personal items."

The only man aboard who officially enjoyed such access was Roger Shrewsbury.

Lord Ingram would be lying if he said that, in the wake of Holmes's scandal, he hadn't wanted Shrewsbury to be struck by lightning. But a longing for divine wrath was one thing; the very real possibility of the hangman's noose was quite another.

"There is also the matter of what we *didn't* find in Mr. Arkwright's cabin," continued Inspector Brighton. "Both his doors were locked: the connecting door in the bath latched from inside, the front door locked with the key. Had his key been left behind in the cabin, the case would be much more perplexing. But the key isn't anywhere inside, and I'm inclined to think that our culprit left with it, locking the door on his or her way out."

"Why?"

"For fear of a prompt discovery?" mused Inspector Brighton. "A plan to return to finish writing the word *baseborn* later? At this point, Captain, your guess is as good as mine."

The bags under the captain's eyes, already prominent, drooped even further. "Would you say that this is a puzzling case, Inspector?"

"Puzzling?" Inspector Brighton frowned. "I suppose it is somewhat mystifying at the moment. But it could very well become clearcut when we discover the owner of the rouge pot."

"Does it have—"

"No, there are no initials or other identifying marks on the jar. But I wouldn't worry, Captain. We are in the middle of the Bay of Biscay. The murderer has not escaped."

Captain Pritchard's jaw moved. "*That* is exactly what concerns me the most."

———❈———

A chill inched down between Lord Ingram's shoulder blades. Most of his apprehension had centered around Holmes's safety and continued anonymity, but the captain was right: A murderer loose on the *Provence* was no small matter.

A discussion followed on when and how to inform the passengers—Mr. Arkwright's death could not be kept a secret forever, or even for much longer. By and by, the captain shook hands with both men, wished them luck, and left.

Inspector Brighton lowered himself into a padded chair with a grimace. "It dismays you, too, does it not, my lord, the presence of a murderer at large?"

It dismayed Lord Ingram more that his thoughts could so easily be read by a potential enemy. He sat down to the policeman's left, on the long sofa, and placed a travel secretary on his lap, getting ready to take notes. "The isolation of shipboard society heightens the sense of danger. Every single person one encounters could be Mr. Arkwright's murderer."

Inspector Brighton stroked his chin. "I do not share your fear to the same degree, my lord. It's true that in theory everyone is capable of killing, but to the vast majority, murder does not even occur as an idea, let alone a plan to be carried out.

"Had Mr. Arkwright died elsewhere, I might have been more inclined to suspect a greater number of the passengers. But he died in his own cabin. Unless it was a steward or stewardess with a secret grudge and a spare key, the killer must be someone Mr. Arkwright would admit to his quarters late at night."

It would indeed narrow the scope of the investigation if one eliminated everyone who would *not* have been let in by Arkwright himself.

The next moment, the policeman said, "But tell me of *your* encounter with Mr. Arkwright, my lord. I'm curious as to how it had come about."

His tone was amiable, yet Lord Ingram had the sensation that he himself was trekking across tall grass and just heard a peculiar rattling sound.

"It came about because I was in the smoking room and Mr. Arkwright walked in. We'd never been introduced so he did not greet me, nor I him. He smoked and left. I thought nothing of it—he was a man with a great deal on his mind and it seemed most natural that he should want a cigarette or two at the end of his day."

"Did you see, by any chance, where he went when he left?"

"He went toward the starboard passage."

He'd disappeared behind the bulk of a boiler casing, presumably passing before Mr. Gregory's door on his way to his own suite.

Inspector Brighton had been perfectly still, listening to Lord Ingram. But now the fingers of his left hand lifted and tapped once, twice against the armrest of his chair. Lord Ingram had no reason to be nervous—he hadn't even known Arkwright. All the same, his heart hammered, a hard percussion.

The policeman's hand stilled again. "A pity the two of you did *not* strike up a conversation. Are you ready to discover what happened to Mr. Arkwright, my lord?"

———※———

Despite Inspector Brighton's assertion that the killer was most likely on close terms with Mr. Arkwright, the first person he questioned was not one of those privileged individuals but Johnson the steward, who arrived pushing a laden food trolley.

He served tea and refreshments. "Inspector, my lord, Captain Pritchard said I ought to speak to you first, so that I can return to my duties as soon as possible."

"And indeed we do not want to keep you from your duties, Mr. Johnson," answered Inspector Brighton, indicating the chair opposite his. "Take a seat, my good man."

"Oh, no, Inspector, I can't possibly," said Johnson, his eyes wide. "We aren't to sit in the presence of passengers."

Inspector Brighton did not insist. "Very well, Mr. Johnson. Give us your account however you'd like."

On his feet, and with keen attention to the contents of everyone's teacups, Johnson chronicled his morning.

His shift in the duty room began at six o'clock sharp. At seven forty, the summons from Miss Arkwright's cabin came. When he arrived outside her cabin, Fuller told him that he and Miss Arkwright were anxious to enter Mr. Arkwright's room, as the latter was nowhere to be found.

Johnson, unable to convince Fuller that his employer had found pleasanter ways of passing time than sleeping alone in his own bed, brought the valet to the duty room to speak to the head steward, who dispensed the spare key. Johnson and Fuller returned to the upper deck and opened the locked cabin.

At this point Johnson paused and gulped. "It was a terrible sight, it was—Mr. Arkwright's body, the blood on the floor, and the walls scribbled all over with those awful words. She is a most respectable ship, the *Provence*. Things like this aren't supposed to happen on her."

Inspector Brighton made sympathetic noises.

Johnson described Miss Arkwright's rush to the bath to retch, Mrs. Ramsay's command to him to report to the captain, and his subsequent trip, at the captain's instruction, to find Dr. Bhattacharya.

Inspector Brighton questioned him on the operation of the duty room. Lord Ingram made himself breathe slowly and evenly. But Johnson's answers revealed not only pride in a well-functioning system but an absolute lack of any suspicion that said system might have been tampered with.

In contrast to Johnson, who offered to serve another round of biscuits and sandwiches to his interrogators before he left, Fuller entered looking drained. He sank heavily into the proffered chair.

"My condolences, Mr. Fuller, on your employer's passing," said Inspector Brighton, with a slight faltering to his voice. Perhaps it was only seasickness and not sympathy, but his commiseration sounded genuine.

The valet gripped his hands together in his lap, his red-rimmed eyes on the policeman. "You will find the villain, won't you, Inspector?"

Inspector Brighton met his gaze. "I will do my utmost, Mr. Fuller."

His promise failed to fortify Fuller. The valet looked down and shrank further into himself. "Thank you, Inspector."

Undaunted, Inspector Brighton asked, "Can you tell me something of Mr. Arkwright's life, Mr. Fuller, as well as the reason for his visit to Britain? I understand that he was on his way back to Australia."

"That is correct. But I can't tell you much of Mr. Arkwright's early life, Inspector, other than that he arrived in Australia nineteen years ago—as a stowaway, legend has it. He himself has—had never mentioned how or why he emigrated. Or anything else about his past."

Fuller spoke loudly and clearly enough, but there was an . . . illiquid quality to his speech, reminiscent of crystallized honey that poured most reluctantly, refusing to leave the jar except in clumps.

"In fact," the valet went on, "until he brought Miss Cor—Miss Arkwright home, I had no idea that he had any family members still living."

Inspector Brighton did not fail to catch that slip of the tongue. "Miss Cor—? Who is that?"

Fuller, who had been staring at his hands in his lap, did not look up. "My apologies, Inspector. I'm still much more accustomed to speaking of Miss Corwin when it comes to Mr. Arkwright. She's a young lady in Sydney that for a while I thought might become Mrs. Arkwright."

Inspector Brighton gave him a hard look, but did not pursue the matter further. "I have heard something—an incomplete as well as inaccurate account, I'm sure—about Mr. Arkwright finding his sister only recently. I'd assumed that a family reunion had been the reason for his trip. Did he not tell you of it?"

"Perhaps it was, but he said nothing to me about it."

"What purpose did he mention then?"

"Visiting the shipyards in Belfast. He has—had been thinking of expanding into transpacific shipping and wanted to see the ship-building process before making up his mind as to whether to invest in new ships or to acquire older vessels."

"Is that all?"

The valet hesitated. "That's all he ever told me—or anyone, as far as I know. But he had me arrange a fitting for him in Savile Row, and he went there the day after we reached London, well before his visit to Belfast.

"It was a gentleman's wardrobe. Not to say that he didn't already have a gentleman's wardrobe. But the wardrobe he ordered had everything a man could possibly need for a London Season, and yachting and grouse shooting come August."

On the subject of clothes, the Season, and the merrymaking that continued even afterward, Fuller's speech became more eager, as if that solidifying honey had been warmed up and now flowed freely.

Inspector Brighton had declined Johnson the steward's parting offers of more refreshments, but had requested that the latter move a large terrestrial globe, which had been banished to a corner, to the side of his armchair. He'd been sitting with his left hand atop its meridian ring. At Fuller's dissertation on his employer's wardrobe, his fingertip leaped to the pointer atop the hour circle. "Are you implying that Mr. Arkwright intended to browse the Marriage Mart?"

"That's what I was coming to believe. He was a successful man, Mr. Arkwright. There would have been many ladies happy to be his wife."

Fuller raised his head. A light had come into his eyes. Was he imagining the welcome his late employer would have received at Society events across London?

"Did you ask him?" demanded Inspector Brighton.

Fuller slumped, and became small and desolate again. "I didn't. Mr. Arkwright was not in the habit of confiding in his staff. I thought time would tell, but a week before the *Provence* sailed, he suddenly told me that he'd already acquired passages, without telling me why."

"And again, you didn't ask?"

"He hired us to follow instructions, not to demand explanations. I did ask Miss Arkwright—she was the one who bought the tickets—and she said she had no idea either."

Inspector Brighton tapped the conical tip of the globe's pointer with the pad of his index finger. "You believed her?"

The question surprised Fuller. It surprised Lord Ingram, too—not that it was asked but that it was asked so early.

"I haven't known Miss Arkwright long but she seems an obliging sort. I'm sure that if she'd known, she'd have told me."

"But she didn't tell anyone anything of her past, did she?"

The valet blinked at Inspector Brighton's bald approach. "Well, that's not the same thing at all, is it?"

It was not so much an answer as a rejection of that line of inquiry.

Inspector Brighton said nothing. He stroked the meridian ring of the globe, the vertical circle of bright brass reflecting the motion of his palm and wrist. Seconds ticked by, then minutes. Fuller swallowed and fidgeted in his chair.

Lord Ingram, when he'd been a suspect in a murder investigation, had been subjected to a similar silence, one intended to establish dominance. He'd had the inimitable Sherrinford Holmes, one of Charlotte Holmes's more remarkable alter egos, to casually break the silence. But here he could not do the same for the valet.

Inspector Brighton, satisfied that the intransigent Fuller had been suitably cowed, at last went on. "Tell me something of yourself, Mr. Fuller. You seem familiar with the Season, more so than your late employer."

Fuller cleared his throat. "Yes, Inspector. I did for a younger son of a noble family for four years—he unfortunately passed away. I answered an advertisement put up by a gentleman who was inspired by *Around the World in Eighty Days* and wanted to make a similar trip.

"He took me to be his Passepartout, but he was no Phileas Fogg. His money ran out in Sydney. His family wired funds for his passage home, but I was stranded. So I advertised in the local papers, promising to turn any man into a gentleman, and Mr. Arkwright's house-keeper engaged me on his behalf."

A voluble answer. He was trying to ingratiate himself back into Inspector Brighton's good graces.

The policeman gave no hint that he'd heard anything beyond facts and particulars. "Would you characterize his household as harmonious?"

"Yes, simple and quiet. Mrs. Lambert, the housekeeper, runs a tight ship."

"And how would you characterize Mr. Arkwright's rapport with his sister?"

Fuller took out a handkerchief and held it, still folded, between his hands. Did his palms perspire? A less fastidious man might have wiped them on his trousers.

"They hadn't seen each other for nearly twenty years," Fuller said slowly, picking his words with care. "There was also a significant age difference. To me it seemed that they were very courteous to each other. I think they understood that, after such a prolonged separation, they must proceed as well-intentioned strangers, and not rush anything."

"Did Mr. Arkwright have a will?"

Another expected question that still landed like an artillery shell. But this time Fuller answered immediately. "I don't know whether he left a will. I don't know that he'd ever thought of dying. Mr. Arkwright wasn't that kind of man—he was far too busy with the here and now."

Inspector Brighton looked him up and down. "Very well. Now that you have given us a rough background for Mr. Arkwright, furnish an account of Mr. Arkwright's movements aboard the *Provence*."

"I can give you only a general idea, Inspector. I've done for gentlemen who preferred their gentleman's gentleman close by, but Mr. Arkwright was never like that. I was to look after his toilette and dress in the morning and at night, but he didn't need me to wait on him in between."

Again, the valet exhibited penitence, explaining his limitations in detail.

Inspector Brighton gave the globe a slight spin and stopped it with a fingertip. "Very well. Proceed."

Mr. Arkwright, it seemed, had stayed in either his own cabin or his sister's on the first day of the voyage. That evening, he had chosen not to dress for dinner in the dining saloon, but had his supper sent to the upper deck.

The next morning, on the last day of his life, he had an early breakfast in his parlor. Fuller did not see him again until evening, and not for a lack of trying. The valet knocked on his door at luncheon and at tea time. He had not been at home, nor at Miss Arkwright's either time.

"I arrived to help him dress for dinner. He let me put him into a dinner jacket but told me that he would not need me again. Said that the storm would only get worse and there was no need for me to run up and down to check on him, best stay put."

The globe spun nearly an entire turn. Inspector Brighton, who had seemed fascinated by its smooth, leisurely revolution, turned his gaze to Fuller. "And I take it that you did not follow his instruction on that account?"

The valet reddened. "He left for dinner a little after seven. I knocked on his door again not long after eight—it didn't seem the sort of night for lingering over dinner—but he was not in his cabin. Or at least he didn't answer my knock. So I left to spend an uneventful, if uncomfortable, night."

Inspector Brighton's attention returned to the globe. "And this morning?"

In a flat tone, Mr. Fuller gave an account. His incredulity at his knock going unanswered. His growing alarm. And then, his horror at the sight that greeted him when the steward opened the door.

"Have you given some thought, Mr. Fuller, as to who on this ship could have done such a thing?"

The policeman's voice had turned softer, but not gentler. His words skimmed across Lord Ingram's skin with the icy edge of a razor blade.

The valet, his eyes full of anguish, seemed not to have heard the menace in the question. "I've thought of nothing else since, but I don't know. I don't know. Mr. Arkwright spoke his mind. Being that he came from the lower class, that didn't sit right with some people. But that couldn't have been reason enough to kill a man, could it?"

"It shouldn't have been, yet Mr. Arkwright lies dead. Therefore, I'd like to know about recent disagreements Mr. Arkwright might have had."

Fuller grimaced. "Well, there's Mr. Shrewsbury, I suppose—Mr. Arkwright punched him because he was disrespectful toward Miss Arkwright. There's Mr. Russell, who is, if you will excuse me, gentlemen, a rotter and bounder through and through. And then there's Mr. Pratt. He wants to marry Miss Arkwright, but Mr. Arkwright would have none of it."

At least he hadn't singled out Roger Shrewsbury.

"Of those men, whom do you most suspect?" asked Inspector Brighton.

"Mr. Russell," said Fuller without a moment's hesitation. "He and his rotten character are known in Sydney. Not to mention he's hovering on the edge of bankruptcy and Mr. Arkwright could easily have finished him off."

"Why didn't Mr. Arkwright?"

Fuller sat up straight. "Mr. Arkwright didn't give a ha'penny about Mr. Russell. Mr. Russell is the one preoccupied with Mr. Arkwright, not the other way around—and he knows it."

The valet radiated pride. Perhaps a little too much of it?

Inspector Brighton cast him a narrow-eyed glance and asked him to submit a written record of his own movements aboard the *Provence*. Fuller complied with his request, scribbling away.

The police officer turned to Lord Ingram. "I believe we should also each submit such a document."

And so it begins, the unmasking of Sherlock Holmes.

Lord Ingram took out a fresh sheaf of paper. "Certainly, Inspector."

⁂

"Mr. Fuller, about Miss Arkwright, I'm sure rumors have reached your ears?"

Another softly uttered question with claws.

Lord Ingram paused in the middle of his statement. He'd thought Inspector Brighton had finished questioning Fuller for the time being.

Fuller's jaw clenched. "Yes, I understand that there have been rumors, which I'm sure are entirely false."

His tone was nowhere as emphatic as his words.

"And you may be right about their lack of veracity," said Inspector Brighton breezily. "But the fact remains that these rumors now exist. They may even reach Australia before you do. Did you not have any concerns about them?"

Fuller jotted down a few more words in his time statement. "Does what I think about these rumors have anything to do with Mr. Arkwright's murder?"

"Frankly, Mr. Fuller, I do not know. What I do know is that one can never guess, at the onset, which line of inquiry or which particular morsel of information holds the key to a case. Therefore, I must ask every question and follow every thread, even if they seem to everyone, even myself, not to matter in the grand scheme of things."

Broadly, Lord Ingram agreed: Sometimes a single, easily overlooked detail could make all the difference. But was that Inspector Brighton's only purpose in asking the question? Or was he trying to drive a wedge between Fuller and Miss Arkwright?

"Very well," said Fuller. "I did worry that the rumors might affect Mr. Arkwright's reputation. As such, there have been unkind whispers in Australia about him having perhaps been an escaped convict—which is absolutely not true at all, by the way. Having a sister said to have practiced the oldest profession, well, that wouldn't have helped, would it?"

And there they were, seeds of disunity and discord.

For the first time since the investigation began, Inspector Brighton smiled. "I understand entirely, Mr. Fuller."

According to Inspector Brighton's own criteria, Fuller and Miss Arkwright, by virtue of having easy access to Mr. Arkwright's cabin, ranked as the two passengers most likely to have committed the murder. Perhaps Lord Ingram should feel relieved that Inspector Brighton was concentrating on the case, priming his two chief suspects to turn on each other. But the depth and deftness of his calculation only made Lord Ingram more fearful for Holmes: This was a man who could conduct a murder investigation *and* use it for his own ends.

Moriarty's ends.

Lord Ingram finished his time statement first, Fuller shortly thereafter. Inspector Brighton looked through both before dismissing Fuller, who left with an expression of obvious relief.

Miss Arkwright had already been summoned. Murmurs arose outside the library, greetings between the valet and the sister. Lord Ingram wondered whether Fuller looked Miss Arkwright in the eye—and vice versa.

Miss Arkwright entered, clad in a black silk dress. Among her belongings, the dress might be the closest approximation to mourning attire, but the luster of the material and the profusion of jet beads in swirling arabesque patterns marked it as an extremely fashionable item—one that made her look like a housemaid secretly trying on one of her mistress's new purchases.

The men rose. Inspector Brighton swayed: Standing up and sitting down were clearly chores for a man suffering from vertigo. Lord Ingram was grateful. The police officer could have remained seated, claiming unwellness. But it would have been a crushing blow to Miss Arkwright for a man not to rise to greet her so soon after the rumors had begun, even if he had a legitimate excuse.

"My condolences, Miss Arkwright, on your devastating loss," said Inspector Brighton, once everyone was seated. "Thank you for speaking with us."

Miss Arkwright smiled, but the muscles of her cheeks were too rigid to permit more than a symbolic stretching of her lips. "Of course, Inspector."

A steward brought in a fresh pot of tea, but Miss Arkwright declined both tea and refreshments.

"I understand, Miss Arkwright, that you and Mr. Arkwright reunited only recently?" asked the inspector after the steward had left.

"That is correct, Inspector," answered Miss Arkwright in a small voice.

Her Liverpudlian accent was much lighter than her brother's. In fact, it was almost undetectable, if one didn't listen for it. And whereas his had retained the rough edges of the waterfront, hers had become rounded and polished. Not so much that she could pass for someone to the manor born, but if she were to claim that her family had operated an apothecary or that her grandfather had sold stationery and her father had gone on to acquire a paper mill, those claims would not be subject to strenuous doubt.

"How did you and your brother meet again? From what Mr. Fuller said, Mr. Arkwright did not travel to England with a reunion in mind."

Lord Ingram tensed. What Mr. Pratt had said earlier and got himself punched for . . . Was it really possible that the siblings had come upon each other in a . . . transactional situation of physical intimacy?

"I own a sewing shop that specializes in gentlemen's handkerchiefs."

Exactly what her accent was perfect for, that of a respectable shopkeeper.

"I'm proud to say that our quality is superb and our prices very reasonable. In recent years, even the shops on Savile Row have come to place orders with us. We'd received an especially large order in anticipation of a busy Jubilee Season and I'd decided to deliver the order in person. On that day, my assistants and I had just arrived before the shop when a man approached to ask for directions."

Miss Arkwright smiled again, a smile that almost brightened her eyes, before grief overshadowed the pleasure of her recollection. "I recognized him right away. He was sixteen when he left, but he was already tall and grown up, and his face hadn't changed that much. So he was there, asking me for directions, and I simply said, 'Jacob?'

"It startled him. He stared and stared at me, only to say, in the end, 'It can't be you. It can't be you, Willa.'"

Tears pooled in her eyes. She dabbed at them with a handkerchief that had shadow-stitched flowers and bobbin-lace edges. It had probably not been produced by her shop, but purchased for her by her brother, along with the rest of her costly wardrobe.

"And that was how we met. I am overwhelmed, thinking of it now. But at the time it was hardly an emotional experience. If anything, our reunion presented a problem.

"We'd each assumed we were the sole survivor of our family, made peace with that mundane tragedy, and lived our lives accordingly. To suddenly discover that no, the long-lost sibling was not dead after all—I, for one, had no idea how to react, whether I ought to be glad or angry, and whether he deserved a place in my life after abandoning me all those years ago to fend for myself."

Inspector Brighton traced a finger on the globe—the direct path between Australia and Britain? "But you sorted that out."

"We . . . were curious about each other," said Miss Arkwright slowly. "And we realized, after we met again and caught up for a bit, that now it wouldn't be as easy to walk away as it could have been that day on Savile Row. We had no other family. And we remembered things about each other that no one else did."

"How much time elapsed between your reunion and your departure on the *Provence*?"

"Three weeks."

The policeman frowned—in concentration, it seemed to Lord Ingram. He did not appear displeased. "That is not a very long time at all."

"No, indeed, a much shorter time than I'd anticipated. I thought he'd be in England for half a year or more. But one day he suddenly said that he was needed in Australia and would I come with him. I was rattled and at first said no. He didn't try to persuade me but settled a large sum on me instead."

"How large a sum?"

Miss Arkwright hesitated. Then, very quietly, "Ten thousand pounds."

Lord Ingram raised a brow. He had given the former Lady Ingram fifteen thousand pounds' worth of jewelry to take with her on the run; it was meant to last her for decades.

Inspector Brighton set the globe spinning. "A considerable sum."

"Indeed. With only a tiny portion of it, I was able to pay my chief assistant to take over the supervision of my shop, the welfare of which had been my main concern about leaving England."

"Did you ask your brother what caused him to abruptly change his plans?"

The globe, in slowing down, creaked once. Miss Arkwright flicked it a glance, then quickly looked down at her ornate handkerchief. "I did ask him, but he said only that it was complicated."

"And that was answer enough for you?"

"We were barely reacquainted. It didn't feel right to press when he clearly didn't wish to speak further on the subject."

Inspector Brighton gave the globe a baleful look, as if he, too, had been disturbed by that small squeak that had nevertheless been disproportionately loud. "Was your brother equally respectful when *you* didn't wish to speak on certain subjects?"

Lord Ingram winced—and did not bother to hide it.

Miss Arkwright's fingers clamped over the lace borders of the handkerchief, but she retained her composure. "Are you referring, Inspector, to the rumors Mr. Shrewsbury spread?"

"Yes."

"I told my brother the truth. I've never spent a day of my life selling my person."

Inspector Brighton met her declaration with undiluted skepticism. "Why did you not tell Mr. Shrewsbury that?"

She smiled bitterly. "I'm not sure I can adequately explain the unhappy stupefaction I experienced. An attack on a woman's reputation is not akin to a thrust of a rapier that can be parried, resulting in no harm to the defender. It's much more like throwing a bucket of ink on a bride leaving church. No matter how she shouts, no matter how much everyone else tries to shield her, some ink will invariably splatter on her beautiful gown, and that gown will never be pristine again.

"Such was my mental state that morning: I could not believe the words coming out of Mr. Shrewsbury's mouth. Somewhere inside I was screaming, but no retort pushed its way past my lips. All I could think of were the years of endless work, and the hunger and deprivation I'd endured in order not to sell my favors to any man.

"In a few minutes Mr. Shrewsbury demolished everything I'd built. My proudest achievement—that coming from nothing I had attained independence without resorting to prostitution—was now as destroyed as that ink-splattered wedding gown."

Her despair clawed at Lord Ingram. He could barely imagine the ferocity of will that had lifted her out of the squalor of her childhood, only to have all that fierce pride crash into the abyss of a blackened name . . .

"My brother was angry when he caught up with me, after he'd punched Mr. Shrewsbury. He asked the same question you ask now. Why didn't I mount a vigorous defense on my own behalf? And when I explained to him that it was already too late the moment those reckless words left Mr. Shrewsbury's lips, he became angrier still. An impotent rage, because even if he found Mr. Shrewsbury again and pounded him to a pulp, it would do nothing to repair the damage that had already been done."

Unlike Lord Ingram, Inspector Brighton evinced not the least sign of being moved by her story. "Did he believe you?"

"I was unsure until last night, when we spoke again on the matter. He said that he did believe me, because he himself had been the target of rumors that labeled him a runaway convict."

Tears rolled down her cheeks. "And that was the last time I saw him alive."

Inspector Brighton had the decency to wait until she had wiped away her tears before posing his next question. "Do you know, Miss Arkwright, who stands to benefit from your brother's death?"

She did not take umbrage at his pointed tone. Or perhaps she seethed but managed not to show it. "I do not," she answered, once again stoic. "I do not know what will happen to his estate."

"Do you have any idea who on the *Provence* would wish to see him dead?"

"I don't know who would want him dead, but I do know whom he took care to warn me about."

Inspector Brighton leaned forward an inch. "Really? Who is that?"

Miss Arkwright put away her handkerchief. "Mr. Pratt. I was surprised by Jacob's warning, to say the least. I found Mr. Pratt a decent fellow. I didn't want to marry him, but I wouldn't have thought to beware him."

The list of passengers and the deck plans, which had all the cabins labeled with their occupants, had been set on a small collapsible table to the right of Inspector Brighton's chair. He studied them. "And why, Miss Arkwright, do you not wish to marry this perfectly decent Mr. Pratt?"

"I don't object to Mr. Pratt so much as I have no plans to ever marry. I find it difficult to trust that a husband wouldn't at some point seek to defraud me. Given that is how I think, I believe I did Mr. Pratt a favor by not marrying him. Why make a nice man miserable?

"But my brother declared that I was wrong about Mr. Pratt. He said that he'd seen men like Mr. Pratt before, and that a dark, rotten heart beats beneath his pleasant, everyman demeanor. He said that he would rather deal with ten bounders like Mr. Russell rather than one treacherous snake of Mr. Pratt's caliber."

She spoke haltingly, her expression that of someone eating a new food that tasted of strange ingredients. "I've known Mr. Pratt for some time. It feels terrible to voice such judgment against him, even if it's not my own. But as much as I hate to bring adverse attention upon Mr. Pratt, I cannot let my brother's words disappear with him into the grave."

Inspector Brighton frowned at this new information. "When did you speak to your brother yesterday evening, Miss Arkwright? And for how long?"

"It must have been around quarter to nine or a little later that we sat down in my parlor. And we spoke for a half an hour, perhaps even forty minutes."

"And that was the last you saw him?"

She looked down and swallowed. "Yes. The last time I saw him alive."

"Can you give me an account of this morning?"

The account Miss Arkwright provided dovetailed neatly with Fuller's narrative, then split off with her hurrying to knock on Miss Fenwick's door.

"Miss Fenwick?" Inspector Brighton consulted the deck plans again.

"It upset me, the thought of perhaps being stared at by members of the crew who'd heard the rumors. I felt in need of an ally—and Miss Fenwick had been sympathetic to my plight. But in the end, it was her employer, Mrs. Ramsay, who came with me for moral support."

"And is Mrs. Ramsay also sympathetic to your plight?"

Miss Arkwright smoothed the lustrous jet bead-laden folds of her skirt. "I—I'm not sure, but she has been very helpful."

Inspector Brighton set aside the deck plans and spun the globe again. Lord Ingram held his breath until the globe had creaked and come to a slightly wobbly stop.

"I see," said the policeman. "I understand that you felt unwell after seeing the crime scene, Miss Arkwright?"

"A rather violent bout of nausea." Her hand settled over her abdomen, as if the same sensations assailed her again. "I've never been delicate, never had a fit of vapors or anything of the sort, but at that moment I was overwhelmed. And yet, possibly because I hadn't eaten anything the night before, when I reached the bath, despite my nausea, I did not sicken."

Inspector Brighton's features, as ever, appeared steady and trustworthy, but his eyes were devoid of warmth: He had no sympathy for her, not for her physical suffering, her grief, nor the general upheaval in her life caused by Roger Shrewsbury's carelessness.

Lord Ingram had thought him overzealous in the pursuit of Inspector Treadles—at Moriarty's behest, perhaps. But it now appeared just as likely that Inspector Brighton simply became machinelike in the grip of investigative fervor and no one, once his suspicion fell on them, escaped unscathed.

Not a comforting thought either, that.

"Let me not keep you for much longer, Miss Arkwright," said the policeman. "It has been a terrible day, and I hope you can find solace in your brother's memory."

"I shall endeavor to," said Miss Arkwright, with yet another attempt at a smile. "I shall endeavor to."

Ten

When the door closed behind Miss Arkwright, the library turned darker.

Lord Ingram glanced out of the window. A cloud must have drifted in front of the sun. The sky was still blue, but the sea had turned a denser, heavier shade.

It occurred to him that the library was, in fact, immediately next to Mr. Arkwright's suite of cabins—on the other side of the library's aft wall was written *common, vulgar,* and part of *baseborn* in someone's rouge.

By now the body should have been removed to the hold to be preserved on ice until a proper autopsy could be performed in Gibraltar. And perhaps diligent cabin stewards were at work, scrubbing away all the residues of the killing.

At the thought of that puddle of blood on the floor, however, even the air in the library seemed to take on a faintly metallic bite.

"She was very unhesitating in throwing this Mr. Pratt to the wolves, our Miss Arkwright," murmured Inspector Brighton. "I wonder what he would think of it."

He rang the bell and instructed the steward who entered to open a window. A cool breeze charged into the library. The sun reemerged, the world brightened, and Lord Ingram's attention shifted from sensory recollections to the perils facing Miss Arkwright.

"I overheard a conversation between Mr. Arkwright and Mr. Pratt yesterday," he said, when the steward had left. "It was not a friendly exchange, and Mr. Arkwright was indeed highly hostile to the idea of Mr. Pratt marrying his sister."

He recounted everything he'd gleaned from his accidental eavesdropping except the exact words that had occasioned Arkwright's violent blows.

"I wonder whether Mr. Arkwright's antipathy toward Mr. Pratt was a result of his own observation or a reflection of Miss Arkwright's ill will," said Inspector Brighton, biting into a small triangular sandwich.

Refreshments sat aplenty in the library, but time to eat had been scarce. Lord Ingram remembered the plate that Steward Johnson had set down beside him on the sofa.

"Then again," Inspector Brighton went on, "a man in love is liable to become less rational—he begins to see only what he wishes to see and hear only what he wishes to hear. In the face of a brother's open enmity, he might very well interpret the sister's softer, more ladylike demurral as having been performed under duress to please the brother. If only he could remove that brother permanently . . ."

Lord Ingram's heart skipped several beats. The lobster salad in his sandwich tasted of the very essence of the sea, briny-sweet and succulent. Was it possible that Inspector Brighton's gaze would land—and remain—on Pratt, thereby leaving Holmes alone?

"Will you summon Mr. Pratt for questioning?" he asked, keeping his tone neutral.

"Perhaps, in good time. But now I wish to speak to Miss Fenwick."

"Miss Fenwick?" Lord Ingram echoed—and hoped he sounded only moderately puzzled, as if he couldn't put a face to the name, and not like a steam siren blaring off.

"Yes, Miss Fenwick indeed. I am curious about the woman who had the audacity to befriend Miss Arkwright."

Fuller and Miss Arkwright had each been waiting outside the library when the previous interview finished, but Miss Fenwick had to be found. Inspector Brighton expressed his satisfaction with that particular state of affairs. "This means we have time for more refreshments, my lord."

The lobster salad sandwich, so delicious a moment ago, now stuck to Lord Ingram's throat. Why would Inspector Brighton choose to first question Miss Fenwick, who had little to do with anything, ahead of Pratt—or Mrs. Ramsay, who was at least an eyewitness to the discovery of Mr. Arkwright's body?

A steward knocked and reported that Miss Fenwick had arrived. Inspector Brighton and Lord Ingram both rose at her entrance.

Lord Ingram had always marveled at Mrs. Watson's ability to appear as convincing as a woman of thirty-five as she did as a woman of sixty. Yes, there was the application of cosmetics, of course, but it had just as much to do with her posture, her bearing, and the timbre of her voice, which became grainier as the age of her character increased.

But then, she'd been a professional onstage, after all.

Miss Fenwick was in her forties, a few years younger than Mrs. Watson's actual age. Her distinguishing characteristic was a beak of a nose, which dominated her face and prevented one from noticing anything else for a while.

Her demeanor, however, displayed not a whiff of self-consciousness, at least not about her features. With great reserve she nodded at the men inside the library and, at Inspector Brighton's indication, took the chair opposite his. The steward who'd shown her in closed the open window, but one last flurry of fresh air rushed in. The ends of the discreet bow on her small felt hat fluttered and only emphasized the stillness of the woman.

"Thank you for speaking with me, Miss Fenwick," said Inspector Brighton after the steward had left.

"Of course, Inspector."

He offered tea. She declined. From behind her round-rimmed glasses, she gazed at him with undisguised incomprehension, unable to fathom why he wished to speak to her, of all people, at this critical juncture.

An incomprehension Lord Ingram well shared.

"You travel as companion to Mrs. Ramsay of Cambridgeshire, Miss Fenwick?" Inspector Brighton began.

"That is correct, Inspector."

"Where in Cambridgeshire do you ladies reside, if I may inquire?"

"About ten miles outside Cambridge itself."

"In a residence left to Mrs. Ramsay by her late husband?"

Miss Fenwick's apparent puzzlement only grew, as did Lord Ingram's agitation. It was an effort not to bunch up his shoulders, and to keep his shorthand notations uniform and legible. At least Inspector Brighton left the globe alone, for now.

"No, Mrs. Ramsay sold her dower property. She bought Ambrose House because she wished to settle closer to her natal village in her old age, having lived elsewhere most of her life," explained Miss Fenwick patiently, as one would to a nosy neighbor.

"And how do you and Mrs. Ramsay find Ambrose House?"

"I find it admirable in every regard—Mrs. Ramsay had the plumbing modernized and radiators installed for heating."

A trace of confusion had crept into Miss Fenwick's voice but she was, of course, too well-mannered to demand a reason for why she was being questioned on things that had nothing to do with Mr. Arkwright's murder. "Mrs. Ramsay, I believe, is largely satisfied, but occasionally she does grumble that the garden does not seem to respond very well to her ministrations."

"What manner of woman would you say your employer is, Miss Fenwick?"

Despite Miss Fenwick's general restraint, she gave Inspector Brighton a look that plainly said, *Is Mrs. Ramsay that relevant to the case?* She also glanced inquiringly toward Lord Ingram, as if some part of the answer could be found in the sight of his rapidly moving pen.

Lord Ingram willed himself not to breathe too heavily. Why was Inspector Brighton so interested in Mrs. Ramsay? Did he already know that Mrs. Ramsay was Charlotte Holmes and was merely playing games?

"Mrs. Ramsay?" Miss Fenwick murmured eventually. "She is one of the most generous souls I've ever had the pleasure of knowing."

Inspector Brighton rested a fingertip on the horizontal ring of the globe; Lord Ingram's heart leaped into his mouth.

"Generous enough to tolerate your friendship with Miss Arkwright?"

Miss Fenwick sat up straighter. "Inspector, I barely know Miss Arkwright. I'm not sure that there is anything for Mrs. Ramsay to disapprove of."

"And yet Miss Arkwright went to you for succor this morning."

"The poor woman. I can only imagine how alone and isolated she must have felt, that our small chat counted for so much in her books."

"Would you describe the contents and the circumstances of this small chat for me, Miss Fenwick?"

"Certainly. I'd been unwell for most of yesterday, but toward the evening, despite the storm worsening, I was beginning to find my sea legs. Mrs. Ramsay suggested that I not remain cooped up in our cabin, but go for a walk."

The buckets and the soiled beddings brought out from Frau Schmidt's cabin had been subsequently passed off as Miss Fenwick's. Therefore, Miss Fenwick had been incontrovertibly seasick.

"I would have preferred the ladies' lounge, but there were two ladies already inside, so I came in here, to the library. After a while, Miss Arkwright opened the door, although at the time I didn't know it was her. She saw me and was about to leave when I told her that there was no reason she couldn't stay.

"She clarified her identity and asked me to reconsider. I'd heard the rumors from Mrs. Ramsay, but I was hardly going to expel her for that when none of us might outlast the night. I said so and she stayed until her brother came for her again."

Inspector Brighton had been listening expressionlessly. Now a sharp interest lit his countenance. "What time was that? And what do you mean by 'again'?"

"He'd entered briefly earlier—I was alone then. He came again quarter to nine or thereabouts and told Miss Arkwright that he'd been looking for her."

"Did you remain in the library after they left?"

"No, Inspector. Very soon after their departure a stewardess sent by Mrs. Ramsay came to fetch me."

"And why did Mrs. Ramsay want you, Miss Fenwick? Surely it was not because she learned that you were conversing with Miss Arkwright?"

"No, indeed. She simply wanted to make sure that I was all right. When I returned to our cabin, I told her about my encounter with Miss Arkwright."

Inspector Brighton raised a brow. "And she, too, was unconcerned about Miss Arkwright's potentially scandalous past?"

"She said only that life shouldn't be so hard for a woman," answered Miss Fenwick.

She'd calibrated her tone so that it was quiet and uninflected, as if she were reading aloud an article on the latest development in steam laundries. But her words could be construed as a rebuke to Inspector Brighton.

To that, the policeman gave a noncommittal "Hmm." "Mr. Arkwright fetching his sister from the library—was that the last you saw of him?"

"No, it wasn't. I saw him once more after that."

"Oh?" Inspector Brighton's gaze again became keener. "When was this?"

"About an hour or so after I parted ways from Miss Arkwright—perhaps around twenty minutes to ten."

Shortly before Arkwright marched into the smoking room, then.

"And where did you see him?"

"Near the ladies' baths—I was coming out from the baths, and he stood in that space between the ladies' baths and the dining saloon."

The ladies' baths were situated foremost on the saloon deck, next to the maids' dormitory. The dining saloon was not exactly amidships, but farther forward. As a result of that, between the ladies' baths and the forward entrance of the dining saloon, there were only four passenger cabins, two on either side of a short corridor.

"What was Mr. Arkwright doing there?"

"He asked me—very politely, I must say—whether the menservants' dormitory was in the vicinity, and I told him that he was in the wrong part of the ship. That he would find the menservants' dormitory all the way aft, next to the gentlemen's baths."

Inspector Brighton's forehead creased. With concentration—or displeasure? Fuller, at least, had not mentioned that his employer was looking for him. "I see. And then?"

"Then I left to go back to my cabin."

"And was *that* the last time you saw him?"

"Yes, Inspector."

"Miss Arkwright—did you see her again last night?"

"No, Inspector."

"Did you see other passengers out and about on that trip to the ladies' bath?"

"No, Inspector."

At the end of this series of rapid questions, Miss Fenwick braced her hands on the armrests of her chair. Her shoulders sagged a little, her chin drooped, even the small bow on her hat seemed to have wilted.

Lord Ingram could only imagine how trying it must be for Mrs. Watson to pretend to be someone else at this moment, to channel all her fear and anxiety into her performance so as not to attract further notice from her interrogator.

Inspector Brighton looked Mrs. Watson over, as he'd looked over Fuller and Miss Arkwright—as if she were a peddler of "antiques" outside the Roman Colosseum and he a wary tourist who'd been defrauded one time too many. "Miss Fenwick, do you have any idea who might have wished Mr. Arkwright harm?"

Miss Fenwick shook her head wearily. "I never saw Mr. Arkwright before the final hours of his life. I have no idea who would have wished to kill him. How could I?"

───── ❊ ─────

"A sensible woman," said Inspector Brighton after Miss Fenwick's departure. "A little too kindhearted, perhaps, but sensible nevertheless."

"Indeed," murmured Lord Ingram—and breathed past the dread that blocked his airway.

"It occurs to me, my lord, that of late you have landed in proximity to murders rather frequently," said the policeman, with a measure of both amusement and sympathy. "Three in the past six months, including this one."

And two of those three cases had been solved by Sherlock Holmes. Was that Inspector Brighton's point?

He approximated a rueful smile. "Yes, now that you mention it . . ."

"I hope you at least slept well last night," said Inspector Brighton with seeming solicitude.

Lord Ingram had not slept well at all, and it froze his lungs that the man might have any interest in *his* whereabouts during those critical hours. "Alas, much tossing and turning for most of the night for me."

Inspector Brighton looked as if he was about to say something else but thankfully, at that moment, Mrs. Ramsay was shown in.

The men rose.

She had changed out of the rumpled grey frock she'd worn earlier in the morning. By Holmes's standards, Mrs. Ramsay dressed with restraint—certainly no one would compare her attire to an embroidered footstool. But for a woman who looked old enough to have given birth to the queen, her new day dress of blue-and-green plaid was positively jaunty.

She leaned on her cane but advanced with surprising speed. Before Inspector Brighton had finished his "Good morning," she had already taken her seat. Then, with a small motion of her fingers, she indicated that they could also sit.

Inspector Brighton, nonplussed at having been upstaged, took a moment to comply. "Ah, thank you for coming so quickly, Mrs. Ramsay."

"I was already waiting for Miss Fenwick in the ladies' lounge just across. It would have been rude for me to have taken much longer." She set her gloved hands atop the handle of her walking stick. Her blue-spectacled eyes bored into Inspector Brighton. "I hope you are not using this investigation for your own personal purposes, Inspector?"

Lord Ingram nearly dropped his pen. The question had been foremost on his mind, but to hear it put forward not only directly but from a position of authority—what was Holmes planning to do?

Inspector Brighton blinked. "My dear Mrs. Ramsay, this voyage has not agreed with me. I assure you I would much rather sleep the day away than shoulder the heavy burden of a murder investigation. May I ask why you have levied such a charge, even if in jest?"

"I do not jest, Inspector." Mrs. Ramsay wagged a finger. "There was no need for you to question my dear Miss Fenwick before you saw me, young man. Did you contrive it so that you might speak sooner to a handsome young lady?"

Inspector Brighton's jaw unhinged. "I assure you, Mrs. Ramsay, that nothing could be further from the truth!"

His voice had risen half an octave.

Lord Ingram clamped his lips together. He could not have imagined this when Mrs. Ramsay first walked into the library, that within two minutes he'd be trying not to laugh.

Mrs. Ramsay tutted. "Maybe you speak the truth, Inspector, and maybe not. But Miss Fenwick is an unmarried young lady of my household, and I will make sure that no man approaches her heedlessly."

Inspector Brighton sent a brief glance heavenward, a prayer for strength. "That will not happen here, ma'am. You have my word of honor."

"Oh? Then how do you explain the many questions you asked of her that had nothing to do with Mr. Arkwright's death? Are you married, Inspector?"

"No, I am not," answered Inspector Brighton, his tone that of a boy despairing over how he could possibly explain to the headmaster the cache of contraband found under his bed.

Lord Ingram bit his lower lip so as not to grin from ear to ear.

"Then allow me to give you a piece of advice, Inspector. Well, two pieces. First"—the ferrule of her cane thudded against the floor—"do not ask a young lady questions that are beyond the scope of your acquaintance—even a woman who knows nothing of murder investigations can sense irrelevant inquiries. And two"—the point was emphasized by another solid thud—"have the courage to declare your intentions, sir. Put into proper context, your curiosity will appear not so much bizarre as reasonably romantic."

"Reasonably—" Inspector Brighton's dismay was now palpable.

Mrs. Ramsay, having said her piece, leaned back into her chair. "Now, Inspector, how may I be of help?"

Her strategy was sound, her execution even better. Her accusation was no tongue-in-cheek banter, nor was it remotely overwrought. She'd caught the inspector precisely where he'd overstepped a little, and leaned on her age and respectability to magnify that deviation from norm.

A fresh pot of tea arrived. Mrs. Ramsay took a cup to drink black.

Inspector Brighton used the opportunity to collect himself. He cleared his throat. "Mrs. Ramsay, may I inquire into the purpose of your trip?"

"Purpose?" Mrs. Ramsay raised a brow. "Well, since you seem to consider it relevant, I will render you a full account."

There is a hint of glee to her tone. Inspector Brighton gripped his saucer. Lord Ingram, once again, had to stop himself from grinning.

"I believe Miss Fenwick told you that I returned to Cambridgeshire after the death of my dear Mr. Ramsay. But she, being a discreet young lady, would have said only that I wished to be nearer to my natal village.

"I've always liked the Cambridgeshire landscape, but I had a difficult upbringing there. Other than the horrible school to which my uncle and aunt sent me, I've been much happier everywhere else I've lived.

"I returned to Cambridgeshire, therefore, not for the merits of my natal village but to be among those surviving cousins who had not been kind to me in my youth and to flaunt before them my subsequent good fortune."

She looked around at the men, defying them to pass judgment. Inspector Brighton kept his expression neutral. Lord Ingram only wished he could leap to his feet and applaud.

Mrs. Ramsay, satisfied, took a sip of her tea. "Alas, as gratifying as petty vengeance can be, it does lose its charm after a while. I've been mulling a move to the coast, perhaps somewhere near Dartmouth. But before I quit Cambridgeshire entirely, I wanted to give my relations something else to envy me for: a grand voyage. Ergo, the *Provence*."

"I see."

"I understand you were also interested in my house, Inspector?"

Inspector Brighton opened his mouth, possibly to notify Mrs. Ramsay that he had been sufficiently informed about her place of domicile, but she raised a hand to forestall him.

"It is a nice property, Ambrose House, not terribly impressive, but comfortable and appealing. When I decamp to south Devon, I will put it up for let. I also have some properties in Bath and Bristol that generate income—nothing too extravagant, but very decent for an old woman.

"I'm not sure how much Scotland Yard pays its estimable inspectors, but unless you have other sources of income, Inspector, you cannot hope to maintain Miss Fenwick in the style she is accustomed to, with servants to do everything and holidays both domestic and abroad."

Inspector Brighton reddened. "Please, Mrs. Ramsay, if I may iterate again, I was not attempting to deepen my acquaintance with Miss Fenwick under false pretenses."

"Then you should not have interviewed her before more important witnesses, not when there is a murderer among us."

Mrs. Ramsay's statement was delivered quietly, and without any percussion of ferrule upon the floor. But Inspector Brighton swallowed and bowed his head. "You are correct, ma'am. I was overcome with personal curiosity. I should not have let that guide my professional choices."

"Good," said Mrs. Ramsay with a twirl of her cane. Lord Ingram noticed for the first time that its head was a silver lioness, a quartet of knifelike cuspids in her open maw. "Now, have you any proper questions for me, Inspector, ones that are not motivated by undue interest in my companion?"

Inspector Brighton set his hands flat on his lap, in the manner of a chastised schoolboy. "You may not think this question passes muster, Mrs. Ramsay, but I am curious as to why, when Miss Arkwright came to your cabin in search of Miss Fenwick, you were the one who went with her?"

Mrs. Ramsay nodded—the question did pass muster, then. "I applaud Miss Fenwick for her kindness toward Miss Arkwright last night, in the relative solitude afforded them by the storm. But this morning Miss Arkwright knocked on our door in the glaring light of day. Miss Fenwick has never been married and is still young enough that for her to keep company with Miss Arkwright would make her subject to gossip, too. I, on the other hand, am beyond idle speculation. The choice was easy."

"You did not *need* to go with Miss Arkwright," pointed out Inspector Brighton.

"I see why you are still unmarried at your age, Inspector. You lack gallantry."

Inspector Brighton, who'd just taken a sip of tea, choked on it. It led not to a quick cough or two, but a loud, wheezing fit. He shot up and stumbled toward the windows, all the while hacking violently, his body bent over, his hand clutching at his chest.

Lord Ingram, too, had to cough in order not to laugh out loud.

Ah, Holmes.

A curious lightness of being unfurled in his chest.

Ever since he had first been forced to admit, aloud, that he was in love with Charlotte Holmes, a part of him—at times, all of him—had treated the matter with the gravity one reserved for deluges and earthquakes.

After all, if one fell in love with lightning, cyclones, or other such elemental phenomena, wouldn't one need to be on guard against one's own destruction?

Now, for the first time, he was simply and completely delighted to be in love.

With a glance at her—as solemn and immovable upon her seat as a stone carving of a pharaoh—he rose and struck the policeman between the shoulder blades.

It took a full minute before Inspector Brighton returned to his chair, red-faced, his eyes glimmering with involuntary tears brought on by his bout of prolonged coughing.

"Do"—he wheezed—"do forgive me."

"I've heard of a just word landing hard, Inspector, but I've never seen it land quite this hard," said Mrs. Ramsay breezily. "And to answer you properly, Inspector, to turn away in her hour of need a young lady who has never done me any harm—I suppose I could have done that, but I would have been ashamed to call myself a lady afterwards."

Inspector Brighton cast a wary glance at his tea before he drank from it again. "I'm sure you are right, Mrs. Ramsay. I'm sure."

He asked her to give an account of the finding of Mr. Arkwright's body and she did, finishing a cup of black tea and touching the biscuits not at all. Lord Ingram was impressed.

"Did you not go with Miss Arkwright to the bath, when she was feeling unwell?" asked Inspector Brighton, at the end of Mrs. Ramsay's delineation of events.

She gave him an incredulous look. "I am not Miss Arkwright's nursemaid, Inspector. I am not even her friend. I am the shield of respectability that she temporarily borrowed, and my obligations to her do not extend to the water closet."

Inspector Brighton, once again, appeared suitably chastised. "No doubt you are correct, ma'am. May I ask one last question?"

"Certainly. And then I shall at last take a long walk on deck and enjoy this glorious day."

"Do you have any idea who might have wished to kill Mr. Arkwright?"

"Not at all, Inspector, and that's why I'm glad we have you on board. You will safeguard us from this hardened criminal, will you not?"

Inspector Brighton inclined his head and was in the middle of reassurances when loud knocks came at the door.

"Inspector Brighton! Inspector Brighton!" Johnson's voice. "Inspector, you must come and see this!"

Eleven

So storms do pass, Livia thought to herself.

The air outside her window was cool but hinted of warmth to come. Sunlight danced silver upon the deep blue sea. After a very long night, the day promised to be—

Rapid knocks came at her door. "Miss Holmes? Are you there, Miss Holmes? Are you awake?"

Livia's contemplative mood shattered. *Norbert.*

As soon as she opened the door, Norbert said, "Miss, will you please come and take a look at her ladyship's door? I could explain, but it would be better for you to see it for yourself."

She led the way at a blistering pace; Livia was both alarmed and confused. Lady Holmes was often foolish, but her foolishness led to the alienation of those around her, not outright trouble. Yet Norbert's haste indicated that something far more serious was afoot.

They crossed the dining saloon. It was past breakfast hours, but a number of passengers still lingered over their cups of tea. Mr. Gregory, sitting alone but looking perfectly chipper, raised his hand in salute.

After the bright and sunny dining saloon, the passage beyond, despite its electric lamps, felt dim—and, once the saloon door had closed, isolated. Norbert had already rounded one of the partitions that flanked the saloon entrance.

"I didn't expect her ladyship to be up yet, but I thought I'd check anyway." Norbert spoke so fast, her syllables collided with one another. "Only to see *this*. I couldn't believe my own eyes and—Miss Holmes?"

The maid poked her head out. Livia realized belatedly that she'd stopped next to the partition that concealed Lady Holmes's door from view and gone no farther. She picked up her skirts and hurried on.

A thin reddish-brown streak, a few inches long, smeared the white door at eye level. A more brilliant smudge marred the door handle. Hammers banged away in Livia's head as she inched closer. She grazed the higher mark with a corner of her handkerchief; it did not budge.

Blood?

She took a deep breath and bent down to examine the door handle, which looked too scarlet to have been soiled with either fresh or dried blood.

"I think that's rouge," said Norbert. "I sniffed it earlier, and it smells just like the batch I made for her ladyship recently."

"Rouge?" Livia repeated blankly. The din in her head faded—all the hammers, too, had become dumbfounded. Lady Holmes used rouge? Lady Holmes, who had always emphasized that rouge was for actresses and harlots?

And why would anyone apply rouge to a door handle?

Livia knocked. "Mamma? Are you in there, Mamma? Are you all right?"

No answer.

"When I knocked earlier, I didn't receive an answer either," said Norbert, still speaking at near twice her normal speed. "What should we do, Miss Holmes?"

Livia bit the inside of her cheek. Had there been only rouge, everything could have been reasoned away as a prank. But the presence of blood . . .

"We'd better summon someone to open the door," she said.

"There's a summons button inside the dormitory," offered Norbert, "but I'm not sure how fast anyone would come, since they know we're only servants."

"Use it anyway," Livia told her.

It should still be faster than her going back to her cabin and using the button there.

A steward arrived rather speedily. The two women were already waiting by the dining saloon door. As soon as he emerged, Norbert hailed him. "Are you here to answer the summons from the maids' dormitory, good sir?"

"Yes, indeed. How may I be of help, ladies?"

"I'm maid to Lady Holmes, who is in Cabin 9, and this is her daughter Miss Holmes, in Cabin 18. I'm sorry to trouble you but we will need Lady Holmes's door opened."

The steward's expression changed instantly. "Is anything the matter?"

"We certainly hope not," answered Norbert. "But she isn't responding to our knocks, and there might be a small smear of blood and a smear of something else red on the door. Would you—"

The steward squealed and leaped back. "I—I shall speak to the head steward right away."

He ran off. *Through* the dining saloon, an act of carelessness that surely must be frowned upon, and perhaps might even lead to a reprimand.

Norbert stared at the closing saloon door. "I was prepared to go to some lengths to convince him," she murmured, as if to herself, "but he didn't even need to take a look at her ladyship's door."

Livia's stomach clenched. She went behind the partition and knocked again. "Mamma, are you there?"

Still no answer.

Barely two minutes later, a different steward arrived, not running but still breathing fast. He introduced himself as Durbin, the head steward; peered closely at the door; and unlocked it.

But instead of opening it, he stood back and yielded the place to Livia. Livia, the inside of her head clamoring again, thanked the man and wrapped a handkerchief around her hand.

Air had turned into glue—or at least aspic—and she could move only at the speed of glaciers. It took a geological era for her hand to clasp the door handle, and then all of recorded history before she saw the darkened interior of the cabin.

Less than forty-eight hours had passed since they set sail, and the cabin already smelled like Lady Holmes's boudoir at home: the heavy aroma of laudanum, the even more ponderous sweetness of lilac perfume, and underneath, a just-perceptible note of sourness, that of someone who perspired heavily during the night.

Livia switched on the electric lamp. A harsh light flooded the cabin.

Norbert gasped. "Oh no! But I'd left this place so neat last night."

The cabin did not seem to Livia any messier than her mother's room usually was, before someone came around to tidy up. A pale gold cape had been dropped in a careless heap on the floor. A nightgown and a buttercup-hued dressing gown sprawled on top of a pile of magazines on the sofa. Two more magazines had fallen to the floor, as well as a silver travel cup, with only its rim peeking out from underneath the bed.

Upon the bed, Lady Holmes, fully dressed in a gown of fuchsia satin, slept facedown, one arm thrown over the side. She snored lightly but not peacefully: Her breaths hitched at frequent but unpredictable intervals, eerie silences that lasted from a moment to several seconds.

Several seconds had constituted an eternity to the young girl Livia had once been, horrified by the possibility that her mother might have stopped breathing. But these days she'd find it strange if Lady Holmes's snores weren't punctuated by these patchy absences of sound.

Normally, faced with a slumbering Lady Holmes, Livia would have quietly withdrawn from the cabin. Today, however, she had to at least make sure that her mother hadn't suffered an injury. She moved closer to the bed—and sucked in a breath.

Which was echoed by Norbert's gasp. "There is—there is—"

Norbert held up the gold cape. The front of the cape had an uneven scarlet streak, the same color as the substance that coated the door handle. One white swansdown-trimmed cuff was red-smudged, and the swansdown trimming near the closure, too, was similarly blotched.

"I think it's because of this," said Livia, lifting Lady Holmes's heavy, limp arm, draped over the edge of the bed, to show her scarlet-stained hand.

They stared at each other. Lady Holmes snorted, breaking the sudden pall. Norbert rushed to the bed, knelt down, took Lady Holmes's hand, and sniffed.

"Bitter almond oil," she declared. "I'm sure this is the rouge I made her."

"Bitter almond oil?" Livia knew very little about the concoction of creams and pastes.

"Yes, the recipe called for sweet almond oil, otherwise the vermilion and gum tragacanth mixture would dry into brittle chunks. But I also added a drop of bitter almond oil, so that it would smell nice, like marzipan."

"But why in the world would she use that much rouge?"

And in the middle of a terrifying storm, no less?

"Maybe she was looking for something else and accidentally dipped her hand into it?" suggested Norbert. "The lamps didn't work for some time."

Livia sank down to her haunches and examined her mother's hand, which did smell like something Charlotte would enjoy eating. The red substance was smooth, not the slightly gritty texture of blood left behind. When she slid her finger across Lady Holmes's palm, her skin came away colored faintly but evenly.

Yes, rouge, most likely.

But if the scarlet smudge on the door handle was left by the rouge on Lady Holmes's hand, what of the other stain?

Lady Holmes slept without a cap. Her hair, which had not been brushed out and plaited for bed, remained in an evening coiffure, now lopsided and disheveled. Strands that had come loose from her chignon hid her face, which was buried in the pillow.

"Let's see if we can roll her over," said Norbert.

"One second," said Livia.

There was something in her mother's other hand: her laudanum bottle, miraculously upright. Norbert took the bottle and put it out of the way.

They strained and heaved. Lady Holmes's back fell onto the mattress with a flop. Her head, too, rolled with the motion, revealing a blood-streaked cheek.

Norbert whimpered.

Dried blood also matted Lady Holmes's hair, a splotch of red so dark that it looked black on blond locks turning white with age.

Livia shivered. Had her mother left her bed at night and, in all the turbulence and abrupt darkness, hit her head on something? It was all too likely.

She leaped up and found the head steward outside. "Mr. Durbin, we'll need the ship's surgeon to come as soon as possible."

The head steward stumbled back a step. "Is her ladyship—is she also"—he swallowed—"also no more?"

"What? No! She's perfectly alive. But she's sustained an injury to the head and must have medical attention right away."

"I see. I see. Wonderful. What a relief." Mr. Durbin shook himself. "Yes, of course you'll need Dr. Bhattacharya. Let me fetch him for you."

Livia stared after the head steward. Only when he'd disappeared into the dining saloon did it register on her what he'd said. He hadn't asked whether Lady Holmes was no more but whether she was *also* no more.

Had someone died on the *Provence*?

Livia was standing before the fold-up washstand, wetting a towel, when a knock came. Norbert rushed to open the door, but it was Mrs. Newell, not the ship's surgeon.

Livia hurriedly shut off the spigot and gave Mrs. Newell a highly condensed version of events.

Her dear cousin leaned down and gingerly touched the dried blood on Lady Holmes's hair. "Even with her usual dosage of laudanum, she should be awake enough to complain about the comings and goings—and a bright light in her face, no less. I wonder whether she has suffered a concussion."

"I was beginning to—"

Loud, hasty footsteps reverberated in the corridor, coming to an abrupt halt outside the door.

But no one knocked.

Surely, as startled and fascinated as the physician must be by the sight of blood and rouge on the door, his first priority should be the patient inside who needed his ministrations.

At a nod from Mrs. Newell, Livia opened the door and nearly bumped into a tall, stout man in his forties.

"Miss Holmes? I am Inspector Brighton of the Metropolitan Police."

Livia's eyes widened. *Scotland Yard* was aboard? It was only the next moment that she recognized Inspector Brighton's name: the officer who had *not* managed to put Inspector Treadles away, much to her disappointment at the time.

But what did he want? And was that not Lord Ingram standing behind him, looking gravely apprehensive?

Mrs. Newell came up to the door and set a hand on Livia's back. "Good morning to you, Inspector, my lord," she said with the sort of calm authority that Lady Holmes had aspired to her entire life but never achieved. "Is something the matter? My cousin is in need of attention, but only the medical kind, and not the constabulary variety, as far as we are aware."

"There is no need to be alarmed, ladies," Inspector Brighton reassured them. "Ah, here comes Dr. Bhattacharya. May we enter? I'm sure you would wish for the good doctor to see to the patient as soon as possible, and the matter I am about to discuss is not yet public knowledge."

The involvement of the police, the question from the head steward about whether Lady Holmes was *also* no more—there had indeed been a death aboard, and perhaps not of the natural variety.

Livia swallowed and stepped back. "Of course. Do please come in."

The cabin was now packed as tight as a London omnibus, with Lady Holmes on the bed, Norbert by her side, Livia, Mrs. Newell, and the three men all clustered together. Indeed, Lord Ingram stood with his back pressed against the door.

"Norbert, will you see to tea for our callers?" said Livia.

Inspector Brighton declined tea on behalf of all the gentlemen, but Norbert, reading Livia's intention correctly, said that she would find some fresh beddings.

When Norbert had left, Dr. Bhattacharya washed his hands and approached Lady Holmes. He examined her head and neck, tapped her on the cheek, and then poked her on the shoulder.

Lady Holmes, lying solidly on her back, grunted.

"We rolled her from her stomach to her back earlier, her maid and I," Livia explained, "because there is blood on the door and we wanted to see her face, at least."

"It does not appear that she has suffered any injury to the neck or the spine," said the doctor, "so no great harm done, most likely."

He lifted Lady Holmes's hand, exhaled, and asked, "And what is this red substance?"

"Rouge, we think."

Dr. Bhattacharya glanced back at Inspector Brighton. "That is rather odd."

Inspector Brighton, however, raised a brow. "Rouge. I thought ladies did not use rouge?"

Livia found that she didn't know how to answer this seemingly innocuous inquiry. Until a short while ago, she'd thought the same.

"The use of rouge is considered a bit vulgar, to be sure," said Mrs. Newell to Inspector Brighton, again coming to Livia's aid. "But with skill—and a little addition of glycerol—the result need not be conspicuous splotches. One can achieve a natural, healthy glow."

"So ladies do use rouge but do not admit to it?" asked Inspector Brighton. He did not sound shocked, only curious.

"When a lady is assured of both her stature and her virtue," replied Mrs. Newell primly, "and sees nothing untoward in a little cosmetic enhancement once in a while."

Huh, thought Livia.

She glanced at Inspector Brighton to gauge his reaction, but saw only Lord Ingram's expression of barely controlled horror.

He had never looked like that, not even when he himself had stood accused of murder. Unease buffeted her. She felt like the *Provence* of the night before, a little tin toy, storm lashed and wave tossed.

Dr. Bhattacharya let go of Lady Holmes's hand. He doused a cloth with peroxide of hydrogen and dabbed it at the edge of her head wound. Lady Holmes grunted but slept on.

"Is the lady in the habit of taking something to help her sleep?" he asked.

Livia collected herself. "She usually has a supply of laudanum."

"May I see it?"

Livia found the bottle. A scratch came at the door. Norbert entered. "I've some fresh linens for the bed, Miss Holmes. If you don't have anything else for me, miss, I'll wait outside."

"Thank you, Norbert. Before you go, do you know how many drops of laudanum my mother took last night?"

"I'm afraid I don't, miss. I didn't measure it out for her last night."

"Can you look at the bottle and make an estimate?" asked Dr. Bhattacharya. He took out another container from his bag and poured the solution inside on a different cloth. The abrupt sweetness of carbolic acid prickled Livia's nostrils.

Norbert came near the bottle of laudanum Livia held out, squinted, and said, "At least fifteen drops?"

The ship's surgeon, picking up a roll of bandaging, frowned. "Is that normal for Lady Holmes?"

Norbert took two steps back. "I haven't worked for her ladyship for very long, Doctor, but I don't believe so. Usually she takes about seven or eight drops at night. When she's feeling agitated or unwell, ten."

Livia, too, frowned. Fifteen drops, that was too much. But maybe, after taking this overlarge dose, Lady Holmes's trip to the water closet had turned disastrous, thereby explaining her injury—and her subsequent tussle with the rouge pot?

She cast a surreptitious glance at Lord Ingram. He had by now schooled his expression into a tight blankness. But the strain at the corners of his lips—

No, whatever had happened to her mother could not be so simple. It could not be inconsequential.

Dr. Bhattacharya finished cleaning and bandaging Lady Holmes's head wound and proceeded to check her airway. "It is possible she is still under the effect of laudanum, if she has consumed twice her usual amount. It is also possible that she has suffered a light concussion. Let me see if I can wake her up."

He tapped Lady Holmes on the shoulder again, then poked in the same spot with some force. When he still didn't get enough of a reaction, he pinched the skin above Lady Holmes's wrist, whereupon Lady Holmes groaned unhappily and opened her eyes a bare sliver.

"Mamma? Are you all right?" Livia cried.

"Your ladyship?" called the doctor. "Your ladyship, can you hear me?"

"Not so loud. Oh, my head hurts. Give me some water, Norbert. And good gracious, why are there men in my chamber?"

"It's the doctor, your ladyship," said Norbert. "You've been injured, and he's here to make sure you're all right."

Lady Holmes stared at the brown-skinned man seated beside her on the bed, her dull expression beginning to sharpen with disbelief.

"Miss Norbert," said Inspector Brighton, "kindly escort Lady Holmes to the ladies' baths. I'm sure she would appreciate an opportunity for her morning ablutions. In any case, her bedding will need to be changed, unless she wants to return to these same bloodied sheets."

"Should she be——" Livia began.

"A little ambulation never hurts anyone," said the doctor, rising. "And the ladies' baths are very near."

Livia thought Lady Holmes would object to being told what to do, but she slowly lifted a hand. Livia pulled her to a sitting position. Norbert packed a few items and helped Lady Holmes lumber off the bed. Briefly it registered on Livia that her mother's skirt looked strangely deflated.

Mistress and maid left the cabin. Inspector Brighton gazed another moment at the door through which they'd disappeared, then turned around and addressed the ship's surgeon. "What do you think is the cause of her wound, Doctor?"

"Blunt force trauma. An encounter—or more likely several encounters—at considerable momentum with a heavy object that has a smooth, round shape, I would say."

"Do you spy such an item in this room?"

Dr. Bhattacharya paused in the packing of his bag and looked about. Lady Holmes's was a single-berth cabin. The furnishing consisted of a fold-up washbasin with a mirror above, a long narrow sofa, and a bed. Livia was reminded again of how new everything was, all keen edges and acute corners. The finials on the bedstead were sharp as spikes.

"I do not," concluded the physician.

"Do you, ladies?" The question was directed at Mrs. Newell and Livia.

Mrs. Newell frowned but shook her head. Livia would have suggested the edge of the washbasin, but why would Lady Holmes have had *several* encounters with it?

"Will you permit me to conduct a search, then, for the object that injured Lady Holmes?"

The uneasiness Livia felt chilled into fear. "Is it very important,

Inspector? Once my mother returns from the baths, she'll be able to tell us what she banged her head on, won't she?"

"I'm afraid it is indeed very important. Most passengers have not been informed yet, but earlier this morning Dr. Bhattacharya and I attended the site of a highly unnatural death."

Livia had already come to that conclusion; still, she had trouble drawing her next breath. "On the *Provence*?"

"Yes, on the *Provence*. It happened last night, a shocking act of violence. In fact, the steward who answered your summons was one of those who discovered the body.

"When he saw blood on Lady Holmes's door, he informed me immediately. I, of course, assumed the worst. I am unspeakably glad that the worst did not happen here and that Lady Holmes's wound, while alarming, does not seem to be life-threatening. But you understand, Miss Holmes, why I cannot regard her injury as a mere accident?"

"But surely you cannot imply that my mother was attacked by some unknown assailant?"

"No one knows what happened. But I can tell you this, Miss Holmes, there is a dangerous and ruthless individual aboard. I cannot eliminate the possibility that Lady Holmes also encountered this person last night."

In that case, thought Livia wildly, shouldn't Inspector Brighton be turning the entire vessel inside out for this evildoer, rather than displaying so much interest in the contents of Lady Holmes's cabin?

But Inspector Brighton had already begun his search.

He was thoroughly impersonal about it. But the sight of a man methodically going through a woman's things . . . Livia was pummeled by embarrassment.

Which was nothing compared to the fear that was beginning to choke her.

"May I have a word with you outside, my lord?" she heard herself ask.

She didn't *want* to know what Lord Ingram dreaded about the situation, but she needed to know.

"Not yet, Miss Holmes," said Inspector Brighton. "This is not the best time—I need his lordship's assistance."

Livia noticed only then that Lord Ingram had brought a case with him and was taking out a camera.

His gaze met hers. "It will be all right, Miss Holmes."

He carried the camera outside. Through the half open door, Livia heard the clicking of the shutter.

The act of photography, almost more than Inspector Brighton's search, made her heart plummet: Her mother's cabin was being treated as a scene of crime.

It should be. *There is a dangerous and ruthless individual aboard*, the policeman had said. Therefore, he ought to take Lady Holmes's injury seriously and investigate the matter, with attention paid to every detail. Exactly as he appeared to be doing.

Yet she grew more afraid with each second he spent digging through Lady Holmes's belongings.

Inspector Brighton closed Lady Holmes's cabin trunks and frowned.

A soft knock came at the door. It was Norbert again, holding an armful of Lady Holmes's clothes. "Beg your pardon, ladies, my lord, Inspector, but I forgot to take her ladyship's combs to the baths."

She propped open a sling stool and set the clothes on top of it. But before she could retrieve what she'd come for, Inspector Brighton said, "Miss Norbert, I do not see a rouge pot among Lady Holmes's possessions. Are you certain she brought one with her?"

Something in Inspector Brighton's tone made Livia tense even more. Norbert glanced at her, as if she'd sensed the same.

"I . . . um . . ."

"Speak the truth, Miss Norbert. You have nothing to fear by speaking the truth."

"We did bring one aboard, Inspector."

"Does it resemble these jars?"

The jars Inspector Brighton held up were of porcelain, semitranslucent, with tight-fitting lids.

"Ah, no." Norbert hesitated another second. "Those are her ladyship's face creams. The rouge pot is round and made of glass, with an etched silver lid."

"Hmm," mused Inspector Brighton. "Of course, there is one item I have not searched yet. Among the items you brought back just now, Miss Norbert, do I spy the dress Lady Holmes was wearing earlier?"

Norbert glanced again at Livia. Livia found herself edging closer to Mrs. Newell, needing the dear old lady's fortitude to shield her from what was to come.

"Yes," answered Norbert quietly.

"Are there pockets to the dress?" Inspector Brighton pressed on.

"Yes, Inspector. There are hidden pockets."

"Kindly extract their contents, please."

As Norbert picked up the fuchsia satin frock, Dr. Bhattacharya took half a step forward. Livia's heart thundered. Inspector Brighton's confident proceeding had made her wonder whether he knew exactly what to look for. Now it appeared that even the physician anticipated something.

The first item Norbert found was Lady Holmes's cabin key, red smeared around the bow and the small metal tag that gave the cabin number. The next item, some sort of a round disk, resolved itself to be a silver lid.

Inspector Brighton, a gleam in his eye, took the lid from Norbert's hand. "Are those Lady Holmes's initials embossed on the lid?"

"Yes, Inspector."

"Anything else in those pockets?"

Norbert reached into a different pocket. Her expression changed as she drew out a second cabin key. It, too, was red-smudged.

"And what, pray tell, is *that*?" asked Inspector Brighton.

Livia's nails dug into the center of her palm.

Norbert stared at the tag, as if she'd forgotten how to read Arabic numerals. After a long moment, she murmured, "It's the key to Cabin Number 1."

Twelve

The cream churned in the tea, making everything clouded, murky. Livia's stomach churned, too. She wasn't sure how she'd arrived on the upper deck, in the library, but here she was, seated opposite Inspector Brighton, a cup of tea in hand.

She'd protested that her mother needed her but Inspector Brighton had pointed out, very reasonably, that Lady Holmes, upon returning from the baths, would have Norbert, Mrs. Newell, *and* Dr. Bhattacharya to see to her comfort and well-being. Besides, he only needed to impose on Livia for a few minutes. Would she kindly come this way?

She might have objected more strenuously had Lord Ingram not signaled, with a subtle tilt of his head, for her to comply.

"Thank you most kindly, Miss Holmes," said Inspector Brighton, "for agreeing to answer my questions."

"Of course," she muttered, barely able to sound sincere.

She glanced at Lord Ingram, who had a notebook open and a pen at the ready. She had been interviewed by the police before, as part of a murder investigation. It was a different investigator today and a different note-taker, yet the tableau felt eerily familiar. But who had died? And who was the person Inspector Brighton believed to have committed the crime? Should Livia help convict or exonerate this person?

If only Charlotte were here to tell her what she needed to do!

"Miss Holmes, may I inquire where you and Lady Holmes are headed?"

Ought she to lie? "I am headed to Port Said, Inspector," she said. "And my mother, Bombay."

She couldn't lie about destinations. The policeman could easily discover those from the ship's purser.

"Your journeys end in different places?" He sounded genuinely surprised.

"Indeed. I am accompanying our cousin Mrs. Newell to see the pyramids of Giza and the great temple at Abu Simbel. Mrs. Newell issued the same invitation to my mother, but my mother declined, as she felt herself unequal to the rigors of the journey."

"And yet Lady Holmes is here on the *Provence*."

Livia felt the pounding of her heart in the back of her head, a frenzied throbbing just on the threshold of pain. Why had Inspector Brighton been so pleased to see the rouge lid in Lady Holmes's pocket? And what did it signify that she had someone else's key in her possession?

"Her presence came as a surprise to us as well." This was again something Livia couldn't lie about; her shock at seeing Lady Holmes had been witnessed by too many. "She said that she changed her mind."

Inspector Brighton perused the globe next to him, measuring with his gaze. "It's a much longer trip to Bombay, is it not? Twice the distance as that to Port Said. Did Lady Holmes give any reason for her change of heart?"

"Only that she came to believe the trip to be a good idea."

"Has Lady Holmes traveled extensively in her life?"

The gears in Livia's brain spun frantically. Could she say yes? Lord Ingram would not contradict her. Mrs. Newell, too, could be counted on to substantiate her statement. But her mother—when had Lady Holmes ever corroborated with Livia? And how could someone with so much disdain for other lands and other peoples pass herself off as a seasoned traveler?

"I—I believe she journeyed to Paris for her honeymoon. But subsequently, no. I'm not aware of any great voyages."

"Did you not find it a bit . . . inconsistent that Lady Holmes suddenly undertook a journey of such length?"

Yes, and how I wish she'd stayed home!

"I did make further inquiries, but my mother considered the matter sufficiently discussed."

"I see." Inspector Brighton tapped a finger against his temple. "When was the last time you saw your mother before you had her door opened this morning?"

"Around midmorning yesterday."

"And you didn't speak to her again afterwards?"

Perhaps she had Mr. Arkwright to thank for that. "Inspector, even at home there are times when I do not see my mother for a day or two, when she chooses to stay in her room and have her meals sent up."

"You do not visit her on such occasions?"

She managed a thin smile. "My mother prefers sons or, failing that, married daughters. I am neither, Inspector. I try not to remind her too often of my existence."

Inspector Brighton studied her. She pretended to be interested in the plate of biscuits that had been set beside her—even selected one and took a bite. She wanted to give the impression that she had nothing to hide, but she hated his razor-sharp attention, the sense that he could see through all her meager defenses and even shabbier machinations.

The silence was broken only by the scratch of Lord Ingram's pen. And then, even that stopped.

Livia drank some tea to wash down the lump of biscuit in her mouth. At the arrival of unwanted food, her stomach churned harder. She yearned to look to Lord Ingram for reassurance, but bit into the biscuit again and held herself back.

Something made her think that his position, too, might be precarious.

Inspector Brighton still regarded her with that same piercing skepticism in his eyes. Had she lied after all—and lied badly enough to brand herself as fundamentally deceitful?

"Very well, Miss Holmes," he said. "What manner of woman would you say your mother is?"

Livia let out a breath and took another swallow of tea. "She is— she cares greatly about being a ladyship."

The policeman looked thoughtful at the assessment. "Does she know many people on the *Provence*? Has she made friends?"

"She has long been acquainted with Mrs. Newell, Lord Ingram, and the Shrewsburys. As for whether she has made friends, she seems to approve of Mr. Gregory, who was a friend to the late Mr. Newell."

"Has she made any enemies?"

The tea in her hand rippled. The image of the formidable Mr. Arkwright rose to mind. "I do not believe so."

"Are there any passengers aboard that she dislikes?"

"My mother dislikes most people she comes across." And Livia was grateful for it for the first time in her life.

Inspector Brighton raised a brow. "In that case, are there any passengers that she dislikes intensely?"

She did not hesitate. "The Shrewsburys."

Did she sense a glance from Lord Ingram?

"Why?"

"It's a matter of some delicacy with regard to my younger sister."

At her closed tone, Inspector Brighton looked toward Lord Ingram. Livia took the opportunity to do the same, but her friend was busy writing, his head bent.

Inspector Brighton's attention returned to Livia. "Anyone else?"

Her heart raced. She was loath to bring up Mr. Arkwright, and not only because of her mother's animosity toward the man. Cabin I. She hadn't been able to think clearly earlier, but wasn't Cabin I on the upper deck? Lord Ingram and his children had cabins on the upper deck. So did the Arkwrights, Mr. Arkwright having so memorably eavesdropped on Lady Holmes from directly overhead.

"Perhaps people do not care for my mother's company, but I'm sure no one on this boat would wish to injure her."

Lady Holmes was foolish, yet she was not without some native cunning. She browbeat Livia and the servants freely. But as much as she would have liked to dress down her husband in a similar manner, she had never said or done anything to cause Sir Henry's perpetual irritation with her to erupt into rage or violence.

Outside the household, she walked a similar line, sniffing at her social inferiors but containing herself before those of a greater stature. It seemed unlikely to Livia that the instinct that had served Lady Holmes well enough all these decades would suddenly abandon her here, on the *Provence*.

She raised her head and stated her position more firmly. "People go out of their way to avoid my mother, yes, but they do not seek to do her bodily harm."

"And yet bodily harm has been visited upon her, Miss Holmes," Inspector Brighton reminded her coolly. "And yet."

———※———

Miss Olivia departed pale but dignified. Lord Ingram wondered whether he looked similarly perturbed. She'd acquitted herself well enough, had stopped the chaos from engulfing her. But he felt that chaos rising, like water on the deck of a sinking ship, ankle deep and ice-cold.

Inspector Brighton turned to Lord Ingram. "My lord, may I inquire as to the nature of Lady Holmes's grudge against the Shrewsburys?"

"Mr. Shrewsbury compromised Lady Holmes's youngest daughter," he answered. "Mrs. Shrewsbury made it public."

At moments like this, he wondered whether he ought to wish that Holmes's scandal had never taken place. They lived in a perilous present that led into an unpredictable, possibly deadly future. And yet, could any of them truly go back to that oppressive past, when they had all struggled to breathe, whether they realized it or not?

Inspector Brighton appeared contemplative, as if he, too, were preoccupied with existential inquiries. "Has Lady Holmes ever taken retaliatory measures against the Shrewsburys?"

"No."

"I suppose nothing she could have done would have made any difference to her daughter's fate. A man is not greatly punished for such transgressions—and his wife is considered to have already suffered enough."

Had Anne Shrewsbury not been directly responsible for Holmes's downfall, Lord Ingram would have agreed that she had suffered enough. But his sympathy for her was in short supply.

He said only, "Do I need to record our exchange, Inspector?"

Inspector Brighton waved a hand and summoned Norbert.

Norbert at a police interview gave the same impression she had on the day the *Provence* sailed, that of a pleasant, helpful demeanor wrapped in a dress that was stylish without being attention-grabbing. What she told of herself accorded with what Lord Ingram already knew: that she'd worked elsewhere and joined the Holmes household only recently. What she told of Lady Holmes also accorded: the sojourn in London, the sudden change of mind, the rush to catch the *Provence* before she sailed.

"You didn't ask her ladyship about her volte-face?"

"It was not my place to question her, Inspector," said Norbert respectfully.

"I thought a lady's maid also functioned as an advisor to her mistress."

"On matters of style, perhaps. And of course some maids become confidantes to their mistresses. But I'm too recently in Lady Holmes's employment to make such presumptions. And in any case, her ladyship prefers to make up her own mind."

Inspector Brighton nodded. He must have understood what both Miss Olivia and Norbert had been trying to say, that Lady Holmes was stupid and obdurate and could not be reasoned with.

His focus turned to Lady Holmes's doings aboard the *Provence*. Norbert, with great sincerity, pleaded ignorance. "Her ladyship hasn't needed me except in the morning to see to her toilette, in the evening to help her dress for dinner, and at night to ready her for bed. Other than taking her shawl to her at luncheon the day we sailed, I haven't seen her ladyship except in her cabin."

"And where are you the rest of the time?"

"In my dormitory, sir. Lady Holmes wouldn't wish to see me gallivant about."

She said it with such graceful forbearance that Lord Ingram, who had been feeling vaguely uneasy about her, abruptly understood what it was that bothered him: It did not disturb her at all to appear before Inspector Brighton.

And not only that. Even Holmes, with her tremendous presence of mind and a ready strategy, had taken her encounter with Inspector Brighton seriously. Norbert, on the other hand, viewed herself entirely as a spectator.

"And that is normal for the two of you?" the policeman went on.

"In town she takes me with her when she ventures abroad, and in the country, too, if she looks in on high street or such. But here there are no shops or high streets."

Yes, now that he was listening for it, he heard the blitheness in Norbert's voice, despite her prompt and respectful answers.

"Still, she didn't have you accompany her when she took turns on the deck?"

"No, Inspector."

Lord Ingram remembered Holmes telling him, long ago, that while her father sniffed at every passing skirt, he would be furious if his wife ever attempted anything similar. Lady Holmes possessed enough canny instincts not to display her fondness for the very handsome Mr. Gregory in front of Norbert, but not enough to avoid enmeshing herself into the unfolding of a murder.

Norbert's testimony continued. Before this morning, she had last seen Lady Holmes after dinner the evening before. At home, Lady Holmes preferred to change into her nightgown as soon as she rose from the dining table, so that she would be more comfortable, but last night she had dismissed Norbert without allowing the woman to help her change or brush out her hair.

Who had Lady Holmes gone to visit, still all dressed up? And how had her rouge come to be smeared in crimson letters on Mr. Arkwright's wall?

"And did you retire after you were dismissed, Miss Norbert?" asked Inspector Brighton.

"I was in my dormitory the remainder of the night, except for a trip to the baths for bathing."

Lord Ingram's fingers clenched around his notebook. When had Norbert been in the baths? Would she tell Inspector Brighton that no one else had been there?

"In the middle of the storm?" asked Inspector Brighton with a perfectly reasonable degree of incredulity. "Or had the storm already abated by then?"

"No, indeed, Inspector, the storm didn't abate for hours afterwards. You see, sir, some regular passengers don't care to see us servants using the same facilities." Norbert maintained her deferential manner. "So we must find times when the baths are emptier. And what better time than last night? But if you are asking, sir, whether I saw Lady Holmes at any point after I said good night to her, no, I didn't."

Inspector Brighton went on to ask the usual questions about the events of the morning and Lady Holmes's potential enemies. Norbert gave straightforward answers to the former and pleaded ignorance on the rest.

Lord Ingram made himself look no more concerned than any other secretary keeping up with dictation.

Norbert had done very well at her interview. She'd established herself as someone caught on the periphery of trouble, forced to deal with the disarray left behind by others. But he could not forget what she'd said about taking a bath in the middle of the storm. And he could not remotely believe it.

Had she been signaling something—not to Inspector Brighton, but to him? What was she trying to say? What did she know? And what did she *want*?

Thirteen

Sunlight rained down from an aquamarine sky. The breeze was brisk, yet left a tantalizing hint of warmth on the skin. Stewards and stewardesses circulated about, serving jam biscuits and potato fritters to passengers on deck chairs. The dining saloon, too, had remained open after breakfast, with lemonade and hot cocoa on hand, and games of chess, backgammon, and dominos made available for the amusement of those who preferred to remain inside.

It was an artificial peacefulness, made possible only by the ignorance of the majority. But Charlotte enjoyed it nevertheless, the whooshing of wind in her ear, the slight bumps underfoot as the *Provence* cleared larger waves, the musing of a pair of civil servants as to whether their current latitude echoed that of Biarritz's, or whether the ship had traveled farther south and was now parallel with the top of the Iberian Peninsula.

She enjoyed even more the sight of Mrs. Watson as the world's kindest, most considerate interrogator. Charlotte, as Mrs. Ramsay, had just introduced Miss Fenwick to Frau Schmidt. The two, both women of a certain age, both not exactly servants yet not exactly equals of their household employers, quickly found much in common.

Charlotte herself had been expressly forbidden from questioning anyone directly on how they had entered the Kleins' sphere. Mrs. Watson hadn't, and she would perform the rule-breaking for Charlotte.

There was no telling what Inspector Brighton would unearth. Charlotte intended to discover the culprit as soon as possible—that should stop the murder investigation. But she also couldn't abandon her original task. Her future plans depended on it.

And she had very little time. 'Til Gibraltar, at most.

At the center of the aft deck, Rupert Pennington, hale and happy once again, was at another game of deck quoits with Georg Bittner.

"They play well together," observed Mrs. Watson from the starboard bulwark, where all three women stood.

"Yes, thank goodness," agreed Frau Schmidt. Her attire was as appropriate as ever, but she'd tied a scarf printed with pink peonies around her hat, and the ends of the scarf fluttered prettily in the cross-current.

"The one you are escorting only temporarily—you say his father is in Port Said? I hope the parting will not be too difficult for the boys," said Mrs. Watson.

Frau Schmidt, looking in the direction of Mr. Gregory's window on the upper deck, answered belatedly, "Oh, the parting will be all right. I do hope young Herr Bittner and his father will get along—they've hardly ever set eyes on each other."

She went on to recount the short and rather unhappy life of poor Georg Bittner, who had lost his mother at birth and had grown up alternately with relations of his Scottish mother and those of his German father. But now his father had at last decided that the boy ought to join him.

"They wanted a German-speaking governess, so that he would remember his German before he met his father. When I went to Edinburgh to get him, I thought I would have to teach a wee Highlander how to speak German. But they needn't have worried—his German is better than his English."

So Edinburgh was where Frau Schmidt had gone, when they couldn't find her.

Georg Bittner was a good springboard to ease the topic to Frau Schmidt's own Germanness. Mrs. Watson, with both skill and empathy, inquired into the governess's experience living and working in a foreign country. After a while, the subject moved naturally to her interaction with other native German speakers in London, most of whom she'd met via the German-language Sunday service she attended.

One of her friends in London was a fellow governess. Sometimes after church they would walk in the park together. The woman was a distant relation to the wife of an attaché at the embassy. The Kleins had to leave suddenly when this fellow governess was sick, and Frau Schmidt had returned a few books to them on her behalf.

"I thought I would leave the books with a servant, but Frau Klein received me in person and was very kind."

"Oh, I've never been inside an embassy," enthused Mrs. Watson. "What was it like?"

Frau Schmidt explained that the Kleins did not live inside the embassy, which was not large enough to function as a place of both work and accommodation for the entire staff. "But they had a nice little house. And Frau Klein even gave me a batch of *vanillekipferl* that she'd made."

She patted her satchel. "I left with my handbag bulging."

Was that how the dossier had made it into Frau Schmidt's possession, along with a great many crescent-shaped shortbread biscuits? "And is Frau Klein a good baker?"

"She . . ."

The governess's voice trailed off. Her gaze landed somewhere behind Charlotte. The very sightly Mr. Gregory had arrived.

". . . is a very decent baker, I would say," Frau Schmidt managed to finish her sentence.

Mr. Gregory smiled in greeting and offered his hand to all the ladies to shake. After a minute of chitchat, Charlotte and Mrs. Watson took their leave. Charlotte, as Mrs. Ramsay, was greeted by passengers all along the starboard promenade, some stretched out on deck chairs, others taking in the view along the bulwarks. She returned the greetings and introduced Miss Fenwick, who hadn't been seen much on the *Provence*.

It was only as they headed inside that Mrs. Watson handed a folded message to Charlotte. "From Mr. Gregory," she whispered. "He passed it to me when we shook hands."

Charlotte opened the piece of paper. *Norbert claims to have been in the baths last night.*

The arrival of an agitated Steward Johnson at the end of Charlotte's interview had led to apologies and hurried departures on the part of Inspector Brighton and Lord Ingram. It had not been difficult for Charlotte to ascertain, standing atop the staircase, that the men had gone forward.

Mrs. Watson, dispatched on a reconnaissance trip, had brought back intelligence that Lady Holmes, her head bandaged, had entered the ladies' baths supported by Norbert. Mrs. Watson, as she left the baths, had also witnessed Lord Ingram taking photographs of Lady Holmes's door.

It was hardly surprising, then, that Norbert should have been interviewed by Inspector Brighton. But her presence in the baths last night . . .

Steward Johnson flew out of the dining saloon and skidded to a hard stop to avoid slamming into Mr. Russell and Mr. Pratt, who were about to walk up the steps. When had those two become acquainted with each other?

"Young man, walk, do not run," admonished Charlotte, just then approaching the stairs herself.

Johnson stopped, reddening. "You're right, ma'am. It's just that I've another message for the—the library, and then I've got to get to the galley quick, too."

He went around Mr. Russell and Mr. Pratt with care but still climbed the rest of the steps two at a time.

Another message? Charlotte glanced in the direction from which he'd come. Had Lady Holmes's condition worsened?

Livia and Norbert stared at Lady Holmes. They glanced at each other, and then stared at Lady Holmes some more.

Washed and powdered, clad in her voluminous white nightgown and an equally voluminous yellow dressing gown, Lady Holmes reclined on her bed, a cover pulled up to her chest, a mound of pillows behind her back.

Despite the half-worrisome-looking, half-comical bandaging around her head, she appeared comfortable and smug, a cat who'd eaten the canary.

A very foolish cat who'd swallowed a time bomb made to look like a canary and had no idea that she was about to be blown up.

It had happened in an instant. Norbert had summoned a steward to request broth and plain toast for Lady Holmes. The steward who had come was the very one who had answered their summons earlier and been so startled. Just before he left, Lady Holmes had added in a booming voice, "And tell that inspector I wish to speak to him!"

A full minute after the steward's departure, Livia at last managed to croak, "Mamma, why did you ask for Inspector Brighton?"

The police would speak to her eventually. There was no reason to hasten the arrival of that moment.

"Well, what do you think?" retorted Lady Holmes, full of her usual testiness. "I endured a dastardly assault last night. I am making a report, of course."

Despair lashed at Livia. She wobbled. They should have let Lady Holmes sleep and never woken her up. They should have begged Mrs. Newell not to depart to her own interview. And they should have prevented Dr. Bhattacharya from using an effective topical analgesic. If Lady Holmes's wound still hurt badly, maybe she wouldn't be in such a mood, champing at the bit to make someone else suffer.

"Mamma, do you not realize that the inspector would ask about your rouge? Your clothes were covered in it!"

Lady Holmes's gaze turned shifty for a second, but only a second. "What rouge? Norbert put away my rouge last night. Ask her."

Norbert shrank into a corner of the cabin, her eyes on the floor, clearly having chosen the route of the ostrich with her head in the sand.

Livia gritted her teeth. "And you had someone else's key in your pocket, Mamma."

"Nonsense, why would I have had anyone else's key in my pocket?"

"Mamma—"

"Olivia, if you cannot remain quiet, then go to your own cabin. If I desired your counsel, I'd have sought it."

Livia wished she could stop talking. She wished words weren't spurting out of her like blood from a severed artery. "But Mamma, have you ever spoken to the police? They'll want to know everything. Are you sure you want to tell Inspector Brighton *everything* about what happened?"

Lady Holmes all but rolled her eyes. "Of course I have spoken to the police. They are a useless lot, by and large, but they are respectful enough. I will tell this copper what he needs to know and nothing more."

Country constables were usually amiable, and hardly likely to speak harsh words to the mistress of a house reporting on a servant who absconded with a few silver spoons. But Criminal Investigation Department inspectors were blood-hardened hunters shooting to kill.

Livia opened her mouth to reason with her mother one last time. A knock came at the door. She felt a surge of relief, seeing only a stewardess with a tray of broth and toast. Then that relief evaporated: Inspector Brighton stood behind the stewardess, his eyes keen as lances.

Lord Ingram came, too. This time he didn't appear so much as if he'd been caught in a sudden apocalypse. But he still looked grim, a man facing a drawn-out disaster who'd had time to acclimatize himself to that dismal reality.

Norbert bustled about, bringing the bowl of broth to Lady Holmes. Livia retreated a few steps from her mother's bedside. Did she serve any purpose here other than to make the cabin more crowded?

Inspector Brighton braced a hand on the wall. "You wished to speak to me, Lady Holmes?"

The expression on his face reminded Livia of nothing so much as the anticipation Charlotte evinced before a slice of good cake. The man was about to *dine*.

Lady Holmes, oblivious to her peril, scanned the policeman's informal pose with disdain. "Yes, I wish to report an assault upon my person last night by that man Arkwright."

Livia felt as if someone had stuffed a large boulder in her stomach. There had been stewards stationed in the upper-level passages, and she had not been at liberty to verify the location of Cabin I. Now she was certain that the key had belonged to Mr. Arkwright and that he was the one who had perished overnight.

With a tilt of his head, Lord Ingram gestured at Livia to join him on the sofa, where he'd made ready to take notes. She hesitated only briefly before doing so. As she sat down beside him, a sigh of relief left her lips.

Without realizing it, she'd come to think of him as a brother. Someone she could always rely on.

"Your charge of assault would have been better brought up to the *Provence*'s master-at-arms, Lady Holmes," said Inspector Brighton. "I've been tasked by the captain to investigate one matter and one matter only. But since I'm already here, I'll be happy to hear your account. When and where did this incident take place?"

Lady Holmes took a sip of her broth. "It wasn't long after I'd dismissed Norbert for the night. A knock came at my door. I thought perhaps Norbert needed to tell me something—or maybe it was my daughter."

"Did you not ask who it was?"

"I did, but I heard no answers, only the door knocking again, so I opened it. And why should I have suspected anything untoward? This is a civilized ship with only first-class passengers, is it not?" huffed Lady Holmes. "But regardless, when I opened the door, it was Mr. Arkwright. And before I could ask him what he was about, he hit me with his walking stick!"

Inspector Brighton tutted. Livia hardly dared peek at Lord Ingram for his reaction. What kind of rubbish was this? Why in the world would Mr. Arkwright knock on Lady Holmes's door and then strike her? Simply because she was intolerable?

The muted response to her claim failed to gratify Lady Holmes. She screwed up her face. "After I was struck, I did not come to until the ship's surgeon awakened me. But now that I am better, I demand that justice be done!"

"Sooner or later, justice is always done—or so I am convinced, my lady," said Inspector Brighton smoothly. "Were there eyewitnesses? Others who can corroborate your account?"

"No. The word of a lady ought to suffice," said Lady Holmes emphatically.

"You are certain that it was Mr. Arkwright, Lady Holmes?"

"Of course I am."

"And that he struck you without giving any reasons as to why?"

"That is correct."

Livia tried to set her face in a mask of impassivity. Lady Holmes's story might explain her wound, but what about the rouge all over her clothes and her hands? What about that other cabin key in her pocket?

"Where did you fall down after he struck you, Lady Holmes?"

"On—" Lady Holmes's eyes became unfocused. Had she realized, for the first time, that according to her tale, she should have collapsed on the floor? Yet she'd awakened in bed. "What does it matter? Are you going to doubt my story because I had the fortitude to raise myself to my berth?"

"Oh, it will take more than that to make me doubt your story, my lady."

The muscles of Lady Holmes's cheeks relaxed; she was somewhat mollified. Livia gripped the edge of the sofa. Why did her mother not hear the deep mockery in the policeman's words?

"When you moved from the floor to the bedstead, Lady Holmes, did you not think to summon Dr. Bhattacharya? Surely your head must have disturbed you greatly at the time?"

"Well, I was suffering at the time, wasn't I?" snapped Lady Holmes. "People who are suffering can't be expected to think clearly."

She took one more sip of her broth and shoved the bowl at Norbert.

"Very well," said Inspector Brighton. "Miss Norbert, what time were you dismissed last night from her ladyship's cabin?"

Norbert offered a slice of toast to Lady Holmes, who waved it away in irritation. Norbert, unperturbed by her mistress's ungraciousness, set the food tray aside on a sling stool. "It couldn't have been later than twenty to nine."

"And when did Mr. Arkwright arrive to make trouble, Lady Holmes?"

"At nine o'clock."

Inspector Brighton pitched a brow. "You are certain about that, Lady Holmes?"

"Yes, I am. Very certain. Norbert wound my travel clock before she left and she said that it kept time, the clock."

Inspector Brighton paused, clearly savoring the moment. "That is odd, Lady Holmes, as I've been trying to ascertain Mr. Arkwright's whereabouts the night before for other reasons. And from what I understand, shortly before nine, he was at the library calling for his sister, and then spent much of the following hour with her. If that were the case, he could not have been here to bother you at the time you named."

"That is ridiculous. Everything happened exactly as I have described. Why would anyone believe anything that sister of his said? That strumpet. And why would anyone believe anything said by a vulgar man who crawled out of a ditch?"

Lord Ingram's pen never faltered, but his breath caught. Livia risked a peep in his direction. His expression was guarded, his lips pressed tight.

"Do you have any guesses as to why Mr. Arkwright hit you with his walking stick, my lady?"

"No." Lady Holmes's voice rose half an octave. She'd had enough of this questioning. "How am I to know why a dog went mad and bit me?"

Inspector Brighton gestured at Lady Holmes. "Did Mr. Arkwright do anything to your hand, my lady? It was red-stained."

Lady Holmes looked down at her right hand, which still bore traces of rouge in the nail beds and the creases of the palm. "Well, he must have."

"But you do not know what he did?"

"No, I haven't the slightest idea what he did. But I'm sure it was reprehensible, whatever it was."

"And did he commit any other reprehensible offenses against you, Lady Holmes?"

Livia recoiled at the implication of the question. For a moment no one spoke, then Lady Holmes sucked in a sharp breath. "Of course not! Is it not terrible enough to be walloped in the head?"

"Indeed, it is most egregious, I agree. But you are certain that nothing worse happened?"

Lady Holmes's cheeks shuddered. "I am very certain."

But Livia was suddenly not so sure. Her mother's strangely deflated-looking skirt when she'd got up from bed earlier—she hadn't been wearing a petticoat! Where had her petticoat gone?

Lord Ingram's pen scratched along, his face unreadable. Norbert, however, blinked a few times rapidly.

"Will you arrest him?" demanded Lady Holmes. "Will you arrest that man Arkwright?"

Inspector Brighton did not answer, but asked instead, "According to your account, Lady Holmes, after you returned from dinner, you did not leave your cabin again?"

Lady Holmes cleared her throat. "No, I did not."

"You are also very certain about this?"

"Y—yes."

"We found this in the pocket of the dress you wore last night, Lady Holmes. Would you care to identify this for me?"

He held out the small silver lid that had Lady Holmes's initials embossed and that Norbert had already identified earlier.

Lady Holmes flattened her lips and waved a dismissive hand. "Some detritus from home, most likely. Norbert, you should have cleared out those pockets better."

Norbert bowed her head. "Yes, my lady."

"But this item does belong to you, Lady Holmes?"

"Probably," answered Lady Holmes, her voice rough with both impatience and a trace of fatigue. "I have many monogrammed items at home."

Inspector Brighton affixed his gaze on Norbert. "Miss Norbert, you said earlier that Lady Holmes's rouge pot is made of glass, with an etched silver lid. Is this that lid?"

"What? I do not use rouge! Norbert, what is this nonsense you spouted?"

Norbert glanced at her mistress and then at the policeman. "Yes, Inspector."

"When did you last see the lid, Miss Norbert?"

"When I helped her ladyship get ready for dinner last night. When we were finished, I put the rouge pot back in the cabin trunk."

"Do you recognize *this?*" Inspector Brighton held out a small round glass container one quarter filled with a red substance.

"That—that appears to be Lady Holmes's rouge pot, but it was full when I saw it last."

"Are you familiar with Lady Holmes's rouge?"

"Yes, Inspector. I made it myself."

"You did not, you stupid woman," cried Lady Holmes.

"My lady, I'm a nobody," said Norbert quietly. "I could be arrested if I didn't answer the inspector's questions properly."

"You could?" echoed Lady Holmes, as if the thought had never occurred to her.

Inspector Brighton beckoned Norbert to approach. "Is this the rouge you made?"

Norbert crossed the cabin, took the pot from him, sniffed it, dug an index finger inside, then rubbed the pads of her thumb and fore-finger together. "This has the same scent and texture. Yes, I would say it is."

Inspector Brighton placed the monogrammed silver lid atop the glass jar. It fit perfectly. "Your rouge pot, my lady."

"I do *not* use rouge," said Lady Holmes between clenched teeth.

"As you say, my lady. You do not use rouge. But a rouge pot with a lid bearing your initials came aboard the *Provence*. And this morn-ing, the container sans the lid was found in Mr. Arkwright's parlor."

Foghorns blared in Livia's head.

Lady Holmes's mouth opened and closed like that of a fish. "Well, how dared he steal my rouge pot after assaulting my person!"

"Indeed, why would he do such a thing, and then use your rouge to write *common*, *vulgar*, and the first five letters of *baseborn* on the wall of his parlor?"

"You—you should ask him!"

"I would very much like to, Lady Holmes, but I cannot. You see, Mr. Arkwright was shot dead last night."

All the women in the room sucked in a breath, but only Lady Holmes said, after that, "Good riddance!"

Livia half rose. She should have leaped across the cabin to slap her hand over Lady Holmes's mouth. But even if she'd managed to briefly muffle Lady Holmes, Lady Holmes would have pushed her aside and repeated herself at twice the volume.

"But good riddance at whose hand?" asked Inspector Brighton silkily.

"Roger Shrewsbury's!" offered Lady Holmes eagerly. "Didn't that baseborn villain Arkwright strike him before the *Provence* sailed?"

Livia winced and wished she could strip all adjectives from her mother's vocabulary. They had just been informed that someone had written half of *baseborn* on Mr. Arkwright's wall and now she deployed the same word against him. And good God, she'd called him vulgar earlier, too, hadn't she, at which point Lord Ingram had all but hissed?

"By that token, do you not have just as much reason to want to rid yourself of Mr. Arkwright, Lady Holmes, you who consider yourself unjustly insulted and impugned by him? Have I mentioned that we also found the key to Mr. Arkwright's cabin in the pocket of your dress? Surely *that* could not be detritus from home."

Inspector Brighton took a few steps forward. He loomed over Lady Holmes on her sickbed. "How did it happen, my lady? He caned you on the head and left. And you, after coming to, found the key that he accidentally dropped and decided to vandalize his cabin? And then he caught you while you defaced his walls? What did he do then, my lady? What was so intolerable that you picked up the revolver he set aside and shot him?"

"What rubbish are you going on about?" cried Lady Holmes, for the first time sounding genuinely worried.

Livia's fingertips shook. Was Inspector Brighton really accusing Lady Holmes of Mr. Arkwright's death? It was unthinkable!

"I speak from evidence, Lady Holmes. You were clearly in his cabins last night. You clearly have a great sense of grievance against him. You—"

"Why would I ask to speak to you about my grievances against that most common man if I'd shot and killed him?" shouted Lady Holmes.

The first reasonable thing she'd said all morning. But dear God, *common*.

"Would you have known, in a dark cabin, that you'd killed him when you were first and foremost bent on escape? You arrived back here shaken and rested your head for a moment against the door, leaving behind a smear of blood. Then you entered and took almost twice your usual amount of laudanum to calm yourself down.

"This morning, after being awakened and cared for, you observed that the ship seemed to be carrying on normally and everyone thought your injury the result of a mishap at night. Was Mr. Arkwright perfectly fine? This did not sit well with your sense of grievance. You must reveal him for the common villain he was. The policeman was speaking to everyone except you? Well, that would not do, would it?"

Lady Holmes blinked. And blinked again.

"I was never inside that man's cabin—the very thought of it!" she erupted. "I only stood outside and—"

"Mother!" Livia screamed.

Lady Holmes started.

"Yes, Lady Holmes? You only stood outside Mr. Arkwright's cabin and . . . ?" said Inspector Brighton, in the tone of a waiting cat who just saw a little white rodent's whiskers emerge from the mouse hole.

Livia rushed to Lady Holmes's bedside. "Mother, you're still not well. Dr. Bhattacharya warned of the possibility of a concussion. You should rest now."

"Olivia Holmes, I do not need you to—"

Livia turned to Inspector Brighton. "Inspector—"

She stumbled—Lady Holmes had shoved her aside with surprising strength.

"Leave my cabin now, Olivia! *I* will say when I am well or not, not you. Get out!"

In desperation Livia sought Lord Ingram. "My lord—"

He looked at her with grave sympathy but said, "Miss Holmes, perhaps it's best if you stepped out."

Why wasn't he helping her? Given free rein, goodness knew how else Lady Holmes would incriminate herself.

"Miss Norbert," Lord Ingram went on, "will you see to it that Miss Holmes has a cup of tea and something to eat? I don't believe she's had time to look after herself today."

"Yes, my lord."

"My lord—" Livia began again.

"Go, Olivia!" Lady Holmes roared.

Livia resisted, hanging on to the doorjamb. Norbert pried her fingers loose. As the cabin door closed, she heard Inspector Brighton murmur, "Now where were we, my dear Lady Holmes?"

Fourteen

The ship's surgery was located near the rear of the saloon deck, separated from and forward of the gentlemen's baths and the menservants' dormitory by a transverse corridor that led outside.

A neat plaque on the door stated the purpose of the room and the name of the resident physician. Charlotte knocked; no one answered. She knocked again, still no sign of Dr. Bhattacharya, but the cabin next door opened.

A man of about thirty peered out. His features were regular and pleasant, rather than handsome, but he did have a thick head of sandy hair that appeared unlikely to fall victim to baldness. That hair also concealed any cuts and bruises Mr. Arkwright might have inflicted on him the day before, at the end of their unproductive exchange.

"Good morning," said Charlotte cheerfully, though it was close to noon. "Did I disturb you with my knocking, Mr. Pratt? Do you remember me? We met the day the *Provence* left Southampton."

Mr. Pratt screwed his face in concentration. "Mrs. Ramsay, is it? No, you didn't disturb me. I wish you a good day."

Charlotte barely managed to utter a reciprocal "good day" before he retreated into the dim interior of his cabin.

Mrs. Ramsay's frank and lively demeanor usually drew a better social response. Failing that, the day's blue skies and blue horizons had put the typical passenger in a lighthearted mood. But Mr. Pratt was not a typical passenger, was he? Fair winds or not, he was still a man whose romantic pursuit was destined to fail.

Charlotte waited a minute, then knocked on Mr. Pratt's door. If he'd had anything to do with the murder of the man who'd stood firmly in his way, he *would* be feeling preoccupied, wouldn't he?

"Who is it?"

"You should be in the dining saloon come luncheon, Mr. Pratt," she said—and walked forward without waiting for him to open the door.

A few doors down she stopped again.

Livia and Norbert stood outside Livia's cabin.

". . . didn't mean it like that," said Norbert. "You know how her ladyship is."

"Yes, I know how she is. Thank you, Norbert," said Livia, looking at nothing in particular, her words as listless as her gaze.

"My dear Miss Holmes!" Charlotte trilled, even though her Mrs. Ramsay voice did not exactly lend itself to trilling. "How lovely to see you. Do come and keep an old woman company. I adore spending time with young people."

She marched up and took Livia by the arm.

"Ma'am—" began Norbert.

"It's quite all right," said Charlotte over her shoulder as she drew Livia along. "It's that mother of hers, isn't it? Trust me, I understand. I was raised by an aunt who was even worse—I still shudder when I think about her, and she's been dead these past thirty years."

"Please, Mrs. Ramsay, you don't need to look after me," said Livia in a small voice, even as she allowed herself to be led away. "I shall be fine if I could sit by myself for a bit."

"I'm sure that is the case. But I'm equally sure that you'll be far better than fine if you'll sit with me and my dear Miss Fenwick for a bit. Come now. There's a good girl."

She unlocked her cabin, maneuvered Livia inside, and closed the door. Then she let out a long breath and said, "It's me. Are you all right?"

———— ∗∕∗ ————

Lord Ingram did not know Holmes's parents very well.

That said, if one measured only time spent together in physical proximity, he'd barely have any association with Holmes herself. The lifeblood of their friendship had always been their correspondence—the reason that their recent separation had been long excruciating weeks without a single line to look forward to.

A correspondent who wasn't fastidious about the quality of her stationery could send three sheets—*and* an envelope—for a single penny stamp. Over the years he'd become intimately acquainted with the weight of her letters, little half-ounce packets of news and musings, the latest one of which he often used as a bookmark until the next one landed on his desk.

For someone who spoke very little, she was much more voluble in writing, everything that had come to her notice set down on those three pages, front and back, sometimes with postscripts written diagonally to the already existing lines, making everything a sore trial to read.

But for all her observational powers, the scope of her life had been severely limited, especially in those years before her London debut, when almost all her time had been spent on her father's small estate, with even the nearest village too far away for daily ventures.

As a result, he'd ingested a great deal of minute yet unsentimental commentary on her family members, as she discussed their speech, actions, and motivations—in an attempt to understand humanity in general and her place in it, he would realize only later.

Her mother had figured prominently in her letters from that era, this unhappy woman who desperately wanted to be important, but always went about it the wrong way.

Lady Holmes could not bear to be trespassed against, yet the one who had trespassed against her the most was her husband, upon whom she must continually depend. Without the strength of mind or soundness of character to handle that perennial anger, her pride had hardened into an obdurate unreasonableness, and her desire for happiness degraded to a reflex to grasp at any pleasure or satisfaction in the moment.

Inside the confines of her daily life, the consequences of her rages, mostly directed at her servants and her children, had resulted in an ill-run household and distant offspring. And her impulses, largely having to do with spending money that she didn't have—a fault that her husband shared in abundance—had brought about a perilous state of finances.

Those were chronic conditions, serious yet not fatal in the short run. But now she was outside the confines of her daily life; now she was in circumstances that would have tested the judgment of the wise.

She didn't fear Inspector Brighton enough: She had deemed him a social inferior. She could not be made to stop talking: Her grievance against Mr. Arkwright had yet to be addressed. And she could not be coached: Her need to be important had, over the years, calcified into an inability to listen to advice.

Lord Ingram fully sympathized with Miss Olivia's desperation, but one did not erect roadblocks to a murder investigation. Inspector Brighton would have his way. And Lady Holmes, in believing her right to justice and redress, would only assist Inspector Brighton in having his way.

There was nothing for it.

He flexed his cramped fingers and made ready to write again.

"Now where were we, my dear Lady Holmes? You said you only stood outside Mr. Arkwright's cabin door and . . ."

Lady Holmes hesitated.

Lord Ingram raised a brow toward his notebook. Was Lady Holmes hesitating because she realized her danger, or had she already forgotten, after Miss Olivia's interruption, what she'd said earlier?

"I understand, my lady, that there was some sort of disagreement between you and Mr. Arkwright during embarkation?" prompted Inspector Brighton.

Lady Holmes's features hardened. "He and that strumpet sister of his blocked my way and refused to apologize."

The air in the cabin smelled of the tarry sweet residue of carbolic acid—and Inspector Brighton's malicious anticipation.

"I understand there was another instance of unpleasantness yesterday morning?" The policeman almost smiled. "I happened to have my window open and overheard a conversation between you and Miss Holmes. Or perhaps I should say it was a monologue on your part, with Miss Holmes trying to remind you that you were still in public, while you thundered that you were already on the other side of the ship from 'that despicable man' and could not care less if he had ears as long as an elephant's snout.

"It took me some time to ascertain what had enraged you so, my lady, but apparently, despite the unpleasantness during embarkation, instead of consigning Mr. Arkwright to a rubbish heap of ineligibility, you encouraged Miss Holmes to befriend his sister, so that Miss Holmes might become Mrs. Arkwright, the wife of a wealthy man. And Mr. Arkwright, who overheard your plan, had unkind things to say about it. And about you, in particular."

Lord Ingram's heart ached for Miss Olivia—she should not have been subject to such distress.

Lady Holmes's face twisted—her vexation against Inspector Brighton darkening into anger. "I will not deign to address that."

"But it must have been infuriating," said Inspector Brighton smoothly, with seeming sympathy.

"Of course it was. My husband is a baronet. That vulgar man should have been on his knees praying that my daughter would condescend to marry him. Yet he—the sheer gall and presumption—"

Her face turned red. Had she a teacup in hand, she might have thrown it against the wall.

"Indeed, most unacceptable of Mr. Arkwright. But I imagine even that would not have compelled you to deface his dwelling. Did something even worse come to pass? What further outrages did he commit?"

Lady Holmes hesitated again.

"How difficult it must have been, my lady, to suffer those provocations," said Inspector Brighton silkily.

Lord Ingram was reminded of what Holmes had once written about her sisters. *Livia may be the most honest person I have ever met: She cannot act contrary to her true sentiments. In that she is the exact opposite of our eldest sister, Henrietta. If anything, Henrietta despises our parents more—she has never once called on them since her marriage. But while she still lived at home, she agreed with everything our mother said, no matter how ridiculous, and was always sympathetic to the slights she experienced, real or imaginary. And by doing that and no more than that, Henrietta obtained everything she wanted from our mother.*

Inspector Brighton read Lady Holmes as accurately as the former Henrietta Holmes had, and now he had adopted the same solicitous affirmation.

Would he also manage to obtain everything he wanted from Lady Holmes, this man who only minutes earlier had accused her of murder?

"Oh, you have no idea," lamented Lady Holmes. "The world isn't the same place it was. The commonest riffraff think they can now claim a place for themselves—and to walk and dine among true ladies and gentlemen. It is intolerable."

Loathing flickered in Inspector Brighton's eyes: In Lady Holmes's view, he was no doubt a member of the "commonest riffraff." But then he smiled and sighed. "Truly, what you have endured at the hands of such riffraff, but especially at the hands of Mr. Arkwright."

"Oh, my life has been a nightmare, Inspector," said Lady Holmes with a catch in her voice.

"But you need not swallow your grievances, my dear Lady Holmes. You need not suffer in silence," murmured Inspector Brighton. "And you may rely on the discretion of those in this room."

One of whom—despite his professed discretion—wishes to pin a murder on you, Lady Holmes.

Lady Holmes wiped at the corners of her eyes with the cuff of her dressing gown. "It was last night. I went to the upper deck to—"

She glanced at Lord Ingram. He pretended not to notice, but braced his abdominal muscles.

"Well, I went up in the hope of speaking to Lord Ingram about my daughter—not the one on this ship, but my youngest."

Who is also on this ship.

Lord Ingram looked up this time, but didn't say anything. He could only wish Lady Holmes wasn't such an inept liar. Why had she bothered to declare that she had not left her cabin after dinner if she was simply going to contradict her own assertion a short while later?

"Lord Ingram and my Charlotte have long been friends. Now that he is once again eligible to marry, I was hoping that, well, he would consider offering his hand to my Charlotte."

She prefers a different part of me.

She probably preferred every other part of him to his hand in marriage.

"But when I reached the upper deck, I became confused as to which cabin was his lordship's. In my disorientation, I stood for a bit in the starboard passage."

Mr. Gregory's cabin was one of the three that lined the upper-deck starboard passage.

Of course.

Of course.

Lord Ingram supposed he ought to be thankful that Lady Holmes had enough sense to say that she meant to see him rather than Mr. Gregory. But all he felt was the icy embrace of imminent disaster.

"While I was hesitating," Lady Holmes went on, "that Arkwright man came out of the cabin next to the one before which I stood. He saw me and—and he said—he said—"

"Yes?"

"He said that Mr. Gregory already had someone else inside—and I immediately knew it had to be that German governess!"

Her words deafened. From the moment Lord Ingram had learned of Lady Holmes's presence aboard the *Provence*, he'd had an unhappy presentiment. Now she'd borne out every foreboding of doom. Now Frau Schmidt had come before Inspector Brighton's attention.

Lady Holmes gritted her teeth. "I mean, I had no idea why that man brought up Mr. Gregory when he saw me but I said that Mr. Gregory would never consort with governesses and such, especially one who was so old. And he said that he didn't know about Mr. Gregory, but he would rather spend a night with Mrs. Ramsay than with me!"

Lord Ingram coughed. He had no idea Arkwright had possessed such excellent taste in women.

"What uncouth and unforgivable utterances," decreed Inspector Brighton. "I am so sorry that you had to see him again, my lady, after he'd already injured you in your cabin."

"But no!" exclaimed Lady Holmes. "This was before my injury."

"Is that so?" Inspector Brighton feigned surprise. "What time was this then?"

"A bit before half past nine."

Inspector Brighton nodded. "I hope, my lady, that you gave Mr. Arkwright what for after his very rude and uncalled-for comment?"

Lady Holmes's jaw worked. "I'd like to tell you that is what I did, Inspector. But unfortunately, by the time I recovered from the sheer stupefaction of having been spoken to thusly, that Arkwright man had disappeared."

"And what did you do, my lady?"

"What could I have done? I returned here, of course."

"But someone as strong-willed and resourceful as you—surely you didn't simply sit and stew in your maltreatment?"

"Well, I did, until I was about to go to the baths. I opened my door and heard his voice! But that was too much, to have demeaned me so and then to come near my cabin to enjoy my humiliation some more?"

This must be what Mrs. Watson, as Miss Fenwick, had mentioned, seeing Mr. Arkwright in this part of the ship about an hour after she'd last encountered him in the library.

Lord Ingram doubted that Mr. Arkwright had come for Lady Holmes, but Lady Holmes was obviously convinced otherwise. She clutched at her bedcover, blue veins standing up on the back of her hand. "Yet what could I do? Somebody ought to publicly proclaim him a villain, but who would do that? It occurred to me after a while that I could do so myself. I had rouge, which I don't use, of course, but I might as well find a purpose for it—in branding *villain* across his door!"

Lady Holmes's tone was both boastful and somehow . . . hungry for praise.

She received no praise.

"So you proceeded, this time with the rouge, back to the upper deck?" asked Inspector Brighton, his words pointed.

Lady Holmes slapped away invisible specks of dust from her bedcover. "Yes, but I wasn't able to do anything. Just as I got ready to write on that man's door, it opened. And closed."

She sounded flat—and disappointed that her cleverness had received no affirmation.

"Was it Mr. Arkwright who opened and closed the door?"

"Of course—who else could it be? I was startled. But then the door opened again and all I saw was this cane headed toward me. And the next thing I knew, it was this morning, and everybody and his brother-in-law was in my cabin!"

Inspector Brighton narrowed his eyes. "You were never inside Mr. Arkwright's cabin?"

"Indeed not! The mere thought of it, going into the accommodation of a man. A stranger at that."

Lord Ingram glanced back at his notes. Was Lady Holmes aware that she had overturned every last one of her previous statements about the night before? Her veracity concerning anything at all was now in doubt. Even he was ready to believe that she'd gone into Mr. Arkwright's room and scribbled on the wall.

"What about what you told me earlier of having been assaulted in your own cabin at nine o'clock?"

Lady Holmes sniffed. "Well, that was merely to simplify things for you, wasn't it?"

"Then at what time were you actually standing outside Mr. Arkwright's cabin?"

Like a child who'd sat too long at her lesson, Lady Holmes fidgeted, pinching and rubbing the fabric of the bedcover between her fingertips. "I can't be sure. A few minutes before ten, maybe. But why are you so interested in that? Mr. Arkwright struck me unprovoked. What did it matter when or where that happened?"

"It matters very much, my lady, when we are in the middle of a murder investigation. And the time you gave puts you as quite possibly the last person to see Mr. Arkwright alive."

Lady Holmes stilled. "But surely you were jesting about that man being dead?"

She was perfectly sincere in her bafflement. Lord Ingram dropped his forehead into his left palm.

Even Inspector Brighton took a moment before he could reply. "Not so, my lady. And in case that is in doubt, I was also completely earnest about your nearly empty rouge pot having been found in his parlor, after having been used to scribble two and a half derogatory words on his wall."

Lady Holmes's incomprehension seemed to grow only thicker, a chronic liar's inability to grasp that while she treated truth as but one ingredient in the dish, to be served up with whatever embellishments or distortions she chose, there existed others who did not do that, and whose words must be taken seriously from the very first.

"But that's—that's——" Her mouth opened wide. "That is *not fair.*"

"What is not fair, my lady?"

"You—you should have told me that you were telling the truth."

Inspector Brighton chuckled humorlessly. "Lady Holmes, I am an officer of the law, entrusted with a murder investigation by the captain himself. What made you think I was playing games? Or that anyone would be lobbing around such claims willy-nilly?"

Lady Holmes pulled her cover up to her chin. "But—but—"

Inspector Brighton gave his necktie a slight adjustment. "I see that you are weary and in need of the tender attentions of your maid and perhaps your daughter. We take our leave of you, my lady, but when you are feeling more yourself, we will be back."

—❖—

Livia held Charlotte tight.

She'd felt exhausted, a traveler crossing the Sahara on foot, with only a mouthful of water left, and her compass lost to bandits. But now, it was as if she'd been helped onto the back of a camel, handed a cluster of juicy, sweet dates, and told that an oasis was within a day's march.

She was still in the middle of a desert, still facing daunting odds, but no longer on the edge of defeat.

She hugged Charlotte tighter before letting her go and wiping at her own eyes. "I'm so glad you're here, Charlotte. So glad."

"I'm glad to see you, too, Livia."

Charlotte gave her a handkerchief that smelled of bergamot. Livia inhaled deeply, the scent of her deliverance.

They talked, Charlotte on a sling stool, Livia on the lower bunk, two sisters in a small cabin with its curtain drawn, a little haven on a ship of dangers. Livia gave a quick account of Lady Holmes's difficulties. Charlotte briefly explained why she was on the *Provence*, who and where the real Mrs. Ramsay was, and what she knew about the murder so far. Several times Livia needed a draught of Mrs. Watson's whisky to steady her nerves, but she hung on to her composure.

"I will know more when I read Lord Ingram's transcripts. But from what you said, it sounds as if the murderer was forced to deal with Mamma when he opened Mr. Arkwright's door to leave and found her standing right in front of him."

Livia shivered. "So the *murderer* rendered her unconscious?"

"With Mr. Arkwright's walking stick, to avoid her raising a hue and cry then and there. Afterwards, the murderer had no choice but to drag her into Mr. Arkwright's parlor, as she couldn't very well be left in the passage. And then, since she was already there, she might as well be the scapegoat."

"Will she be all right?"

Livia only wanted to get away from Lady Holmes, not for her mother to hang.

Charlotte's fingertips smoothed along the side of her sling stool. Livia couldn't look away from her sister's made-up face—so many wrinkles, like a dendritic drainage pattern crisscrossed by gullies. She'd removed her blue spectacles and her eyes, for some reason, did not look at all out of place on this face that wouldn't be hers for at least half a century.

"Inspector Brighton has a difficult task: The murderer did not leave behind any direct evidence to his or her identity. As far as I can tell, there are also no direct witnesses except Mamma, who remains convinced that it was Mr. Arkwright himself who beat her with a walking stick. If Inspector Brighton doesn't uncover anything else, then is the evidence against Mamma compelling enough for her to be charged with murder? It's a possibility."

Livia looked longingly at the silver flask in her hand. It gleamed and, in a feat of attention to detail, bore a large monogrammed R: R for Ramsay and R for when Mrs. Watson had been Johanna Redmayne.

In the end, she did not take another sip. It was far too early in the day for finishing Mrs. Watson's stock of whisky—the dining saloon hadn't even started serving luncheon yet. "So what are we to do?"

They could scarcely stand by and watch while officers from the Gibraltar constabulary led Lady Holmes off the ship. Would their mother make such a scene that the police would be forced to clap her in handcuffs?

"Soon the captain will inform the passengers about Mr. Arkwright's death. In the wake of the announcement, Inspector Brighton might face an influx of witnesses and learn such things as to render Mamma's little peccadillo completely irrelevant to the proceedings."

Charlotte rose—it was nearly time for luncheon. "And if not, don't worry. My own safety hinges on the swift, successful conclusion of this investigation. I will see to it."

Fifteen

Charlotte was late arriving to luncheon.

Lady Holmes, distressed at the end of her inquisition, had begged Lord Ingram to find and send her daughter to her. Lord Ingram, locating Livia in Mrs. Ramsay's cabin, had taken the opportunity to pass along his transcripts to Charlotte. And she had sat down and read them carefully, before leaving them with Mrs. Newell for him to retrieve later.

When she at last entered the dining saloon, it was three-quarters full and humming with conversation. Passengers laughed loudly and often, their collective buoyancy fueled by the smoothness of the *Provence*'s progress, a pleasure keenly appreciated after a night at nature's mercy.

Mr. Arkwright's murder had been handled with calmness and discretion. Neither the blockage of the upper-level starboard passage, which housed the Arkwright siblings and Mr. Gregory, nor the commandeering of the library had caused major complaints.

All the same, unease rippled underneath the apparent gaiety of the meal. It did not affect everyone: Several civil servants headed for India held a lively debate on cricket; the four missionaries were deeply immersed in a discussion on recruiting female physicians who would be allowed to see patients—and evangelize them—inside the *zenana*.

But other passengers whispered to one another, some asking questions of every steward and stewardess who came near.

The soldiers with whom Charlotte had dined earlier welcomed her to their table. At their previous meal, she had lent her wise, ancient ears to the romantic woes of one Lieutenant Younghusband. Now, even the possibility of losing a lovely young lady to a rival didn't prevent him from exclaiming to her, albeit in a low voice, "Have you any idea what's going on, Mrs. Ramsay? It's just been *odd* today, what with half of the upper deck closed. I say someone must have died during the storm."

"You always say someone must have died," pointed out his friend, Lieutenant Wallis.

"I'm bound to be right one of these days, don't you think, ma'am?"

"I think, if speculation has reached such a fever pitch, then the captain needs to address the passengers. Perhaps we will find out very soon."

Charlotte accepted a bowl of soup from a stewardess. After a morning that saw her miss breakfast, then decline perfectly wonderful biscuits—the real Mrs. Ramsay didn't believe in the restorative powers of baked goods—she was ready to eat anything.

She'd been so busy, busier even than when she had her own cases to handle.

They were fortunate. Inspector Brighton, his vertigo exacerbated by a full morning's work, especially by interrogating Lady Holmes while on his feet, needed to take rest. Had he called for Frau Schmidt right after he left Lady Holmes's cabin, the risk to Charlotte would have been that much greater. But the policeman had gone to recuperate in his cabin, and Lord Ingram had spoken to Mr. Gregory. By now Mr. Gregory should have conveyed the message to Frau Schmidt, and the two should have agreed on what they each ought to say concerning their whereabouts the night before.

Mrs. Ramsay's young companions continued their debate about what had truly happened on the ship, all the while demolishing thickly buttered slices of bread without a second thought. Charlotte's mouth watered, but Mrs. Ramsay would never have allowed herself such excesses.

Lieutenant Younghusband's voice suddenly lowered. "Oh, you're right, Mrs. Ramsay. Here comes the captain!"

Captain Pritchard, flanked by his officers, entered the dining saloon. The appearance of so many men in spiffy uniforms caught everyone's attention. Charlotte's gaze, however, landed on her lover, who crossed the threshold in their wake. He, too, had seen her and her new gentlemen friends.

The corners of his lips curved up.

It was interesting that he'd had his moments of doubt on whether her affection would hold true over time, but had never feared that she would transfer it to someone else. As if he'd always viewed himself as an experiment for her, and she might decide abruptly one day that she'd gathered enough data and no longer needed to perform further tests.

He was not entirely wrong. Hadn't it begun that way for her? But now . . .

The passengers fell silent. Through the open window came the swash and ripple of the *Provence* slicing across the Atlantic. The captain closed his eyes briefly, then looked around at all the upturned faces. "Ladies and gentlemen, I regret to inform you that our esteemed fellow passenger Mr. Jacob Arkwright was found dead in his cabin this morning."

A greater silence, followed by an eruption of cries and questions.

The captain raised his hand. "We are fortunate that Inspector Brighton of Scotland Yard is aboard the *Provence*. He has generously agreed to take the case in hand. Given that this is an ongoing investigation, I cannot speak more on the matter except to implore you, ladies and gentlemen, to aid the good inspector by furnishing him any relevant information that you may possess. Thank you, and good afternoon."

The captain and most of his entourage left, leaving behind Mr. Spalding to field inquiries. He had no more to say on the matter than Captain Pritchard, but he repeated his few lines—*We don't know much yet; Inspector Brighton is still making inquiries; I'm afraid I'm not at liberty to discuss that*—calmly and patiently to anyone who wished to hear those bits of nothing directly from his lips.

"I can't believe you were right for once," muttered Lieutenant Wallis.

"I can't believe it either." Lieutenant Younghusband sounded no less shocked. "Is Mr. Arkwright's cabin in the upper level starboard passage? We were right nearby in the smoking room last night, weren't we, Wallis?"

Lieutenant Wallis shivered. "My goodness, so we were."

Charlotte cut into the salmon that had just been set down in front of her. "Oh, did you see or notice anything?"

The two men shook their heads in unison. "We were just trying to be drunk enough not to be afraid," answered Lieutenant Younghusband.

Charlotte chortled. "Think carefully. You never know what you might have seen or heard."

"Aie, I can't really think right now," moaned Lieutenant Younghusband. "My head is still aching from last night."

Charlotte glanced around the dining saloon. None of Inspector Brighton's current main suspects were on hand. Of the rest of the passengers who'd had some entanglements with Mr. Arkwright, Mr. Russell, a known antagonist, appeared outright gleeful. Mr. Pratt sat blinking. And Roger Shrewsbury . . .

Roger Shrewsbury had his hand over his mouth, his one blackened eye less swollen than earlier but even more dramatically discolored, all inky blue and angry purple. His wife tapped him on the shoulder, but he seemed unable to recover from his distress.

Charlotte's gaze connected again with Lord Ingram's. He tilted his chin up a fraction of an inch in salute. He had come as Inspector

Brighton's observer at the captain's announcement and now he, too, was leaving.

Their travail had barely begun.

———— ❊ ————

The clock on the library's wall ticked. Lord Ingram inhaled and exhaled, but his heart would not stop pounding.

One by one, things that should remain secret and hidden would be dragged into the open, subject to Inspector Brighton's scrutiny. He tried to think beyond this afternoon, beyond the next few days—Holmes already had her sight set weeks, months ahead. But anything could happen here. Anything could overturn her grand architecture for the future.

The door opened. Inspector Brighton. He did not look well rested—the fine lines on his face had etched deeper into his skin. But his voice was firm as he spoke to the steward stationed outside. "I would like to see Mr. Gregory and Frau Schmidt."

Lord Ingram's stomach dropped. Surely he wasn't planning to interview those two *together*?

"Inspector! I must speak with you, Inspector!"

The voice did *not* belong to Steward Johnson.

"And you are?" demanded Inspector Brighton.

"Steward Jamison, sir."

"Very well, come inside."

Jamison, as Johnson had before him, chose to remain standing. Inspector Brighton lowered himself into his chair with a grimace. Lord Ingram would have taken heart in his ill health, but alas, vertigo or not, the policeman loved the hunt.

His gaze was certainly keen as he studied Jamison. "Thank you for coming forward, my good fellow. What is it that you wish to tell me?"

Jamison, a small man with sparse yellow brows and a careful demeanor, tugged at his collar. "I—I saw Mr. Shrewsbury last night, and he was holding a revolver."

A muscle leaped at the corner of Lord Ingram's eye.

Inspector Brighton sat up straighter. "What time of the night was this? And you are certain it was Mr. Shrewsbury?"

"Yes, Inspector," said Jamison, his voice growing more assured as he spoke. "It was ten minutes after ten when the summons came—right after electricity was restored to the passenger levels. Mrs. Shrewsbury answered the door when I knocked. She said that her husband left their cabin not long after she returned from dinner and she hadn't seen him since. She'd already checked the public rooms, so she asked me to search inside the gentlemen's baths and, if he wasn't there, have a look on deck."

Inspector Brighton leaned forward. "On deck? She believed he'd be out there in the middle of the storm?"

"Well, I don't think she *believed* that he'd be out there. It was—well, it seemed to me that she'd *rather* he be out there on deck than elsewhere, if you see what I mean, Inspector."

Lord Ingram certainly did, but he thought it was possible Mrs. Shrewsbury was truly concerned for her husband's safety: He was not *that* promiscuous, and had never displayed either the talent or the temperament for skirt-chasing.

"I see," said Inspector Brighton. "Carry on."

"I checked the baths and he wasn't there. I checked the public rooms and the baths again before I went down to the duty room to fetch a lantern and some rain gear. Frankly I thought it would be a fool's errand, but when I got out on deck, I came across a man standing by the starboard bulwark amidships.

"I shouted, 'Are you Mr. Shrewsbury, sir? Mrs. Shrewsbury sent me. She's worried about you!'

"He couldn't hear me at first. We were standing near each other, but between the sea, the wind, the rain, and the *Provence*'s engines, everything howling and growling, it was like trying to talk inside a tornado. So I had to go even closer, and the light of my lantern shone on the revolver in his hand. I had quite a start. 'Sir,' I shouted at the top of my lungs, 'your wife is worried about you! Please go to her!'

"'She is?' he said. 'Poor thing.' He looked odd, all drenched like a wet rabbit—even odder if you remember the revolver. His eyes were bloodshot. He was shaking, especially his hands, and I was terrified he'd do something he'd regret.

"Then all of a sudden he threw the revolver overboard. At that same moment, the ship listed hard to port. The revolver clanged against the side of the ship as it went down.

"'Thank you. I'll go to my wife,' he told me after we'd recovered our balance. He left. I was still standing there, wondering what happened, when he came back and gave me a tip."

"That's it?"

Inspector Brighton's hand settled on the globe. Lord Ingram's gut tightened. But this time the policeman's caress of the brass meridian ring came across not as a prelude to intimidation so much as an expression of absentmindedness.

"If you mean, sir, whether that was the last I saw of Mr. Shrewsbury, then no. I told him he should go back from the stern entrance and head directly to the baths. And I also told him that I'd fetch a change of clothes for him."

"Very kind of you."

A blush crept into the steward's cheeks. "I suppose it was considerate, but I was also looking out for myself, sir. If I didn't steer him directly to the baths, he'd have dripped all over the place and I'd have spent half the night mopping up after him."

Inspector Brighton chuckled. "That's my favorite kind of good deed, good for everyone all around."

"Thank you, sir." Steward Jamison reddened further, this time with pleasure. "Like I said, he was odd, Mr. Shrewsbury. The entire thing was odd. I didn't think that much about it—gentlemen can be a peculiar lot. But when I learned just now that Mr. Arkwright had died, I couldn't help but think of Mr. Shrewsbury's revolver that he threw overboard for no reason at all."

—※—

A terrified-looking Roger Shrewsbury was shown into the library.

"Ash! My lord! Ash, oh, thank goodness you are here," he cried when he spied Lord Ingram. "I had absolutely nothing to do with Mr. Arkwright's death. You must believe me!"

"Mr. Shrewsbury," said Lord Ingram coolly. "May I present Inspector Brighton of the Metropolitan Police? Inspector, Mr. Shrewsbury."

Shrewsbury's lips quivered.

Until Steward Jamison had made the comparison, Lord Ingram had never thought Shrewsbury's appearance particularly leporine. But now that the notion had entered his head, the otherwise classically handsome Shrewsbury did resemble a lost bunny, with big round eyes—one blackened—and a mouth that was slightly too small for his face.

Shrewsbury managed to shake hands with Inspector Brighton and squeak out a "Charmed, I'm sure," but his panicked gaze remained on Lord Ingram, who said nothing.

Even though on the inside, he, too, shook with panic.

Roger Shrewsbury finally turned to Inspector Brighton. "Inspector, please, you must believe me. I'm not the kind to retaliate just because someone beat me up. You can ask his lordship. He'll tell you that."

True. Rather than plotting vengeance against his tormentors, the most Roger Shrewsbury had ever done to better his lot was to hide behind Lord Ingram, who had not been afraid to use his fist.

Inspector Brighton disregarded Shrewsbury's request for character testimony. "Mr. Shrewsbury, Mr. Arkwright died of gunshot wounds, gunshot wounds that we have no reason to believe to be self-inflicted. It has been reported that last night you were seen on deck with a revolver in hand, a revolver that you later threw overboard, in full view of a steward. I would like to hear your account of that."

"Oh, that." Shrewsbury tittered.

He sounded like someone sawing at a pocket violin.

Lord Ingram wanted to throw aside his notebook, open a window, and leap down to the deck below. Or perhaps even into the waves below.

Shrewsbury cleared his throat. "Right-o, the revolver. It was the strangest thing. I was standing there, and the revolver fell at my foot."

"It *fell?*"

Inspector Brighton slid a fingertip along the strip of brass that served as the quadrant of altitude. Lord Ingram felt ill. The policeman's outpouring of skepticism had already begun in earnest.

Shrewsbury, whether he sensed his peril or not, nodded with a simpleton-like vigor. "Yes, just like that. I was lucky it didn't conk me in the head. I mean, the *Provence* was all but flipped on its port side, and I'd lost my balance and hit the deck with my hindquarters. I heard something thud but I didn't see what it was. I had to get myself up and it was difficult, what with a torrent sloshing about. And when I did get upright again, my foot kicked something. When I picked it up, what should it be but a revolver."

"Did you not think it strange?" drawled Inspector Brighton.

Shrewsbury gripped the armrests of his chair with both hands. "Of course I thought it strange. I thought it terrifying."

"Terrifying?"

"Yes, I thought it was a sign from God."

Inspector Brighton looked Roger Shrewsbury up and down. "Mr. Shrewsbury, were you outside in the middle of a tempest looking for signs from God?"

"No, Inspector. Not exactly, I mean. I was . . ." Shrewsbury brought his hands into his lap. He cleared his throat again. "I was wondering whether I ought to throw myself overboard."

Inspector Brighton let out a slow breath. He looked very much like what he was, a man working through ill health who had little strength left to coddle a fop. "You don't strike me as a suicidal man, Mr. Shrewsbury. But perhaps I'm mistaken?"

"You aren't, Inspector." Shrewsbury waved both hands in negation. "I'm not at all suicidal. But when things don't go well, I do have a tendency to think that it would be so much easier if I were no longer on this earth. I wouldn't need to deal with any unpleasant or unhappy consequences then."

Inspector Brighton let out another long breath. Perhaps, under different circumstances, he would have enjoyed pitching Roger Shrewsbury overboard himself.

Abruptly, his attention turned to Lord Ingram. "My lord, if I recall your written statement of time correctly, you held a conversation with Mr. Shrewsbury from about nine to quarter after nine—and again from about half past ten to quarter to eleven."

"That is correct."

Inspector Brighton glanced sideways at Shrewsbury. "Do you also recall both conversations, Mr. Shrewsbury?"

"Yes, I do, Inspector. The first one was the reason I was outside. I was trying to defend what I'd said and done with regard to Miss Arkwright—and a different young lady from an earlier time. Lord Ingram annihilated my defense. I left our chat convinced that I was the most worthless man to have ever spoken the English language."

Inspector Brighton looked toward Lord Ingram again.

"No, his lordship was not at fault," Shrewsbury hastened to clarify. "His words merely drove home how careless and reckless I've always been in my conduct, and I did not want to face that. I felt too restless to go back to my cabin—or remain inside anywhere. But out on deck, the thought came that since I'd been a complete wastrel, I might as well rid the world of my useless person."

He grinned ruefully—Lord Ingram noticed for the first time that his front teeth were ever so slightly oversized. "Of course, being a generally useless person, I couldn't make any decision firmly. I just stood there, getting wetter and wetter, alternately pondering my death and wishing for a hot toddy.

"And then came the revolver, and for a moment I thought God really wanted me to end it all, that not only did He bring me before a tempest, but also provided me a firearm. I was genuinely frightened until the steward came to find me.

"All at once I came to my senses. Of course I wasn't looking at divine judgment. If anything, the revolver must have been temptation from the Devil himself. I threw it away from me as hard as I could, but the ship listed port again and the revolver only barely made it overboard."

Inspector Brighton's hand left the globe, but his tone was outright harsh—he must have realized that it was pointless to practice subtle intimidation on a fool. "I don't suppose it at all crossed your mind, Mr. Shrewsbury, that the revolver might have been used in a crime and therefore needed to be preserved as evidence?"

"My goodness, no! Who would think of such a thing?"

"Very well," said the policeman through gritted teeth. "Given that I cannot possibly examine this weapon myself, dare I hope you noticed something about the revolver, Mr. Shrewsbury, some particulars that might be of use to this investigation? Was it still warm from a recent firing, for example?"

"No, it was not warm. There was a great deal of rain on deck and the revolver was submerged for a good minute or two in all that cold water before I accidentally found it.

"As for particulars, I suppose there was some illumination from the ship's mast light, but it was pouring rain and I could scarcely open my eyes, let alone make out details. I did open the cylinder and feel the chambers. I think there were five chambers, four still loaded, one empty."

Lord Ingram's pen scratched furiously.

"Was . . . was Mr. Arkwright killed with a single shot?" ventured Shrewsbury.

Inspector Bright on did not answer. "Mr. Shrewsbury, tell me what you did afterwards."

He radiated displeasure. Shrewsbury swallowed. "I went back inside, washed, put on the clean clothes the steward brought, and went back to my cabin. There I assured Mrs. Shrewsbury that I was still quite sound in the head, all in all.

"Not long after that she fell asleep—she'd taken some laudanum once she learned from Steward Jamison that I was safe. Instead of sitting in the cabin all by myself, I called on Lord Ingram to tell him that even though I'd stormed out earlier, I'd at last heard his rebuke."

"How so?"

"Oh, I thought—I thought—" Roger Shrewsbury stuttered.

Lord Ingram felt he himself suspended above an abyss, strung up on a rope that had frayed to its last filament.

"I thought I'd already mentioned it," managed Roger Shrewsbury, "when I talked about how I decided to toss the revolver overboard?"

"No." Inspector Brighton ground out the word. "You mentioned that you came to the decision that the Good Lord would not wish to see you dead and that the revolver was a temptation from some devilish quarter."

"Right—you must be right, Inspector. But at the same time, I realized how kind his lordship has always been to me, how helpful. Instead of agonizing over why he didn't think I was right, I should have listened to him. I should have listened to him all along."

"And you went to him to say just that?"

"Yes, yes!" Shrewsbury nodded like a hen pecking at the ground.

Inspector Brighton again examined Lord Ingram's time statement, on which both meetings with Shrewsbury had been plainly recorded. "And after that?"

"After that I went back to my cabin and went to sleep."

Sixteen

THE NIGHT OF THE STORM

The knocks came again, louder, more insistent. "My lord! My lord! Are you at home?"

Shrewsbury. The idiot. What did he want *now?*

Lord Ingram kissed Holmes on her lips, pressed his revolver into her hand, and, on his way out, pulled the door of the sleeping cabin almost but not quite closed.

He opened the front door to a damp-haired Shrewsbury. But he had not come alone. Mr. Russell stood with an elbow braced on the doorjamb, flushed, glassy-eyed, and reeking of whisky.

"You see, Mr. Russell," said Shrewsbury, his tone placating, almost beseeching, "I told you I wasn't calling on any lady. I only wanted to talk to an old friend."

Russell sneered. "You're still a bounder who doesn't deserve Anne."

He looked and smelled drunk, but sounded lucid enough.

"Well, good night, Mr. Russell," said Shrewsbury.

He dashed into the parlor and closed the door. "I met Mr. Russell outside my cabin. He's had a bit to drink and wouldn't take my word for it that I only wanted to see you."

Lord Ingram caught a whiff of the cool sharpness of storms. Had the fool been outside in this weather? "But I've no wish to see *you.*"

"My lord, it's really important."

"It can wait until tomorrow."

"Ash, please!" Shrewsbury gripped his arm. "Please just hear me out, Ash."

After the incident with Holmes, Lord Ingram had addressed his old school chum strictly as Mr. Shrewsbury. Realizing that he had been exiled from Lord Ingram's circle of friends, Roger Shrewsbury had accordingly addressed him by his honorific, rather than Ash, as he had done since they were children.

But his appeal now to their once long-standing friendship, the desperate reliance in his wide, bloodshot eyes . . .

Lord Ingram pulled away from Shrewsbury's grasp, crossed his arms, and waited.

The ship plunged. Shrewsbury grabbed the edge of the writing desk and offered a conciliatory smile—only to wince at the pain the movement caused his still swollen cheek. "After we spoke last, I spent some time on deck. And when I was out there, I came to an epiphany. You were right, Ash. I have acted the fool far too many times."

Lord Ingram debated punching him so that he'd sport an even pair of black eyes. *This* was what couldn't wait until morning? "I am honored that you wish to heed my words."

At his acid tone, Shrewsbury flinched but pushed on. "There's something else I need to tell you, something for which I'll need your advice."

He didn't need to listen to another blabbering word. He could simply toss Shrewsbury out on his rear. But Shrewsbury went on speaking, and sirens began shrilling in Lord Ingram's head.

"When the revolver left my hand, I was filled with a sense of purpose and well-being," said Shrewsbury a few minutes later, his eyes wide and earnest. "That . . . near euphoria, I suppose, carried me to the baths and back to my cabin before it occurred to me just how thoroughly alarming it was that a revolver, of all things, dropped from the sky."

Lord Ingram flexed his fingers but held back from throttling his old schoolmate. How was it possible for anyone to take that long to see the ominous significance of a free-falling firearm?

Shrewsbury prattled on. "So I thought I should speak to someone who would know better than me. I know you suggested Mrs. Newell earlier, but I'm sure you're the better choice in this situation."

The back of Lord Ingram's knees tingled. "You're right—better to talk to me now than to Mrs. Newell. Since you've had time to go to the baths and your cabin, would you say you came back inside about half an hour ago?"

"I looked at my watch after I came back in and it was ten after ten. But I don't wind my watch very well, so it can run a little behind at night."

Lord Ingram checked Shrewsbury's timepiece against his own. Shrewsbury's was seven minutes behind. "Let's say you came back between quarter after and twenty after. When did the revolver materialize? How long before that?"

"Maybe twenty minutes before? I can't be exactly sure."

"Did you hear any shots?"

"No." Shrewsbury screwed up his face, thinking hard. "Ah, I remember now. I think the revolver fell not too long after the *Provence* passed another ship—two ships that pass in the night, eh?"

His attempt at levity received a flat stare. Shrewsbury coughed and went on in a more subdued manner. "The horns blasted a few times—deafened me. That would have drowned out the sound of the shot, if the storm and the creaking of the rivets hadn't."

Lord Ingram picked up on his use of the singular. "*The* shot? How do you know it was only one shot? You opened the cylinder?"

"Yes, and one chamber was empty. One of the five."

"Five?"

"Yes, I think it was a Webley. It felt like a Webley. I opened the action and the ejector popped up right away. And with my fingers I could tell that one of the chambers was empty."

"Were there any initials or other identifying traits?"

"I don't know. The mast light and the sidelight were on, but with the rain and everything, I could hardly see."

And you threw it into the Atlantic, you dunce.

"Well, what do you think happened, Ash?"

Lord Ingram glared at him. "You've already reasoned for yourself what happened. That's why you came to see me, isn't it?"

"So . . . you also think someone was trying to get rid of the revolver—and didn't succeed entirely?"

Lord Ingram made no reply. Shrewsbury covered his lips with his hands. "Come to think of it," he mumbled, as if to himself, "I'm surprised they managed to throw it as far as they did, because the ship listed badly to port at that point. When I got rid of the revolver later, even though I stood with one hand on the gunwale and pitched it with all my strength, because the ship tilted again, it hit the side on the way down."

The Storming of the Bastille raged in Lord Ingram's head, full of screams and an occasionally earsplitting cannon fire. Like a desperate father searching for children caught up in that revolutionary mob, he ran through the list of everyone on the ship he needed to worry about.

"Do you remember the direction from which the revolver fell? Did it plummet from the upper deck or had it come from one of the cabins on the saloon deck?"

"The upper deck. I remember something catching my eye even as I landed on my arse. It definitely came from overhead. That was the reason I thought it dropped straight from heaven."

"And where exactly were you?"

"Near the dining saloon. I was probably next to the aft-most window of the dining saloon."

And he'd mentioned earlier that he'd been on the starboard promenade.

Holmes was safe and sound inside Lord Ingram's suite. His children, in their port cabin, were fine. Mrs. Newell and Miss Olivia's cabins, too, were on this side of the ship. Mr. Gregory dwelt starboard on the upper deck, but he was located far aft of the dining saloon. Besides, when Frau Schmidt had left his cabin, she'd looked too happy for there to have been a gunshot in her vicinity.

Mrs. Watson was starboard on the saloon deck, but he would wager that Holmes had met with and spoken to her before she'd called on him, so Mrs. Watson, too, should be all right.

Shrewsbury's hands crept up on his own face until only his eyes showed. "So . . . someone was trying to get rid of a revolver that's been used. What—what do you think it was used for, Ash?"

Lord Ingram's relief froze into dismay. If the worst had happened, if some unfortunate soul indeed lay dead aboard the *Provence* . . .

He'd endured a murder investigation. He'd seen how everyone who worked for him was questioned and asked to give an account of themselves, and how minute discrepancies or even guilty mannerisms were caught by the shrewd chief inspector and made to yield information.

There were so many moving parts tonight. And Frau Schmidt— what if someone had seen Frau Schmidt going about at a sensitive moment?

Now his head felt as muddy and chaotic as the Grande Armée's fateful retreat in the Russian winter.

"What do you think, Ash?" Shrewsbury repeated himself. "Do you think someone might be hurt? What if they're crying for help but nobody can hear them because of the storm?"

Thunder ripped. The floor tilted. Lord Ingram stumbled back two steps before he caught himself—and Shrewsbury, who had unwisely let go of the desk. "I wouldn't have discarded my weapon before my task was done."

Roger Shrewsbury gulped—he understood what Lord Ingram had implied. "Still—shouldn't we at least inform the captain?"

Now he wanted to do the right thing? Lord Ingram, his hands still on Shrewsbury's upper arms, gave him a shake. "Did you not tell me that a steward saw you throw a revolver overboard?"

"Y-yes?"

"Were there any eyewitnesses to the revolver falling at your foot?"

"Ah, no."

"Do you still want to inform the captain right away that someone on this ship might have been shot?"

Shrewsbury shook his head as if it were a child's rattle.

Lord Ingram desperately wished to consult Holmes—she might have more useful instruction for Shrewsbury—but he didn't want Shrewsbury to infer that he had someone else in his suite.

He let go. "Return to your cabin and stay there the rest of the night. Do not say anything and do not *do* anything. Do you understand, Roger?"

Shrewsbury nodded with a panicky vigor.

"If I need you to know anything else, I'll either come myself or send a note. Don't be afraid, but do use care. Ultimately this should not concern you."

"It wouldn't concern you either, would it, Ash?"

At the sincere concern in his old friend's eyes, Lord Ingram sighed. "No, I'm completely uninvolved in any shenanigans on this ship. Now go."

The door closed behind Shrewsbury. Thunder boomed again, so violent against the eardrums that it might as well serve as the opening volley of the Armageddon. Lord Ingram panted for a moment before he turned around. Holmes, brown-wigged and bespectacled, had already emerged from the sleeping cabin.

She carried the plate of cake he had ordered for her, and, with her usual imperturbable serenity, served herself another forkful. "Well," she said, "that was unexpected."

Seventeen

Lord Ingram's shirt clung to his back. Roger Shrewsbury had at last exited the library and he felt as if *he* had survived an assassination attempt.

The moment he'd heard about the falling revolver, he'd feared that a murder investigation would take place on the *Provence*, headed by the astute and ruthless Inspector Brighton. Having endured a Scotland Yard–led inquiry on his own estate, every dire possibility had occurred to him at once.

All related to Holmes.

The very worst would be the discovery of the rewiring behind the summons panel in the duty room. If it became known that summonses from Frau Schmidt's cabin had all been rerouted to Mrs. Ramsay's, even if Moriarty's agent aboard didn't immediately connect the minor sabotage to Charlotte Holmes, he or she would still realize that something was going on.

Lord Ingram had to restore the original wiring. And for that, he had to retain his freedom of movement, which meant he couldn't let Shrewsbury alert the captain about the revolver, for fear that all passengers would be immediately confined to their cabins or the two passenger levels patrolled for the remainder of the night.

But factoring Roger Shrewsbury into his clandestine mission had been a desperate and possible fateful choice. Sooner or later Shrewsbury's incident with the revolver and his subsequent visit to Lord Ingram would come into the open. He would be questioned. And Lord Ingram would need this man, to whom he wouldn't entrust anything more important than the consumption of a cucumber sandwich, to convince Inspector Brighton that he'd never mentioned the revolver to Lord Ingram.

There was a chance, however slender, that Inspector Brighton would believe Shrewsbury too stupid to understand the right thing to do. But Lord Ingram would instantly come under suspicion were it known that he, too, had learned about the revolver the night before.

He would have despaired if Holmes, who had suffered greatly from Shrewsbury's incompetence, hadn't pointed out that the man's earlier carelessness with herself and Miss Arkwright had arisen from an intuitive awareness that whatever he accidentally did to diminish their reputation, it would not materially damage himself.

This was different. A man who had recently punched him in public lay dead, and he was the one caught pitching a revolver overboard before an eyewitness. Were he charged, he stood a good chance of being convicted in a court of law. And did he really think that Miss Arkwright, whose reputation he'd destroyed, would hesitate in asking the crown to bring charges?

Perhaps Holmes had been right. For once, Shrewsbury had not derailed his errands.

On wobbly knees, Lord Ingram rose and went to the food trolley in the corner to pour himself a glass of carbonated water. The air bubbles bursting upon his tongue felt as chaotic as the inside of his head, but at least this part of the ordeal was behind him. He didn't think Inspector Brighton believed Shrewsbury entirely, but he was coming to the opinion that Inspector Brighton never believed anyone entirely.

As if to underscore his point, behind him Inspector Brighton's voice rose. "Mr. Shrewsbury said nothing to you about the firearm, my lord?"

No, the ordeal was still ongoing—he had been but allowed a minute to breathe. Lord Ingram turned around. "Mr. Shrewsbury only consulted me on what he ought to do about Miss Arkwright."

The policeman's fingers ascended, alpinist-like, up the meridian ring of the globe. "And what did you advise him?"

Lord Ingram enjoyed and admired well-made instruments, but he longed to toss this globe into the great furnaces deep in the ship's bowel. "I advised him to apologize, loudly and publicly, on the ghastly mistake he'd made after a few drinks too many the night before. To declare that now, properly sober, he is horrified that she, in fact, looks nothing like the woman he saw covered in hors d'oeuvres."

Inspector Brighton affixed him with a stare that could cut glass. "I find it difficult to believe that he wouldn't have consulted you about the firearm, my lord."

"I understand perfectly, Inspector," answered Lord Ingram with all the gravitas he could muster. "To be acquainted with Mr. Shrewsbury is to experience such disbelief profoundly and repeatedly, more frequently than one would have thought possible. My old schoolmate, alas, is also in the habit of saying too much when it is not called for, and too little when it is."

He shook his head. "And to think, if only he had said anything, we could have raised the alarm that much sooner."

"And perhaps the culprit would have already been caught, and I could have spent this day abed, waiting for my dizziness to pass," said Inspector Brighton through gritted teeth. He pinched the bridge of his nose. "Very well, nothing we can do about what Mr. Shrewsbury should have done. Let's carry on. At least now we have a much clearer idea of time of death for Mr. Arkwright—the culprit would not have got rid of his firearm before the crime. So by ten o'clock Mr. Arkwright should have been dead."

And Lord Ingram had last seen him scant minutes before!

Inspector Brighton rang a hand bell. One of the stewards stationed outside immediately entered. "Yes, Inspector?"

"Kindly open a few windows. Are Frau Schmidt and Mr. Gregory here?"

"Yes, Inspector." The steward leaped to do the policeman's bidding. "Frau Schmidt is in the ladies' lounge, and Mr. Gregory waiting in the smoking room."

"Mr. Gregory first," said Inspector Brighton.

The stiff breeze that swept the library quite chilled the back of Lord Ingram's neck. The next segment of the ordeal had commenced.

———❄———

"Mrs. Ramsay? Mrs. Ramsay?"

Charlotte, crossing the dining saloon toward Lady Holmes's cabin, looked back. It was Mr. Pratt, who'd been thoroughly uninterested in her earlier in the day. "Yes, Mr. Pratt?"

Mr. Pratt came close and looked around. The dining room had emptied since luncheon. There was only a civil servant playing solitaire in one corner and, in another, a mother reading a book to her daughter.

"I understand you were among those who discovered the body this morning, Mrs. Ramsay?" asked Mr. Pratt, his voice low.

"And where did you hear such a thing, young man?"

"From Mr. Russell. He said he saw you, Miss Arkwright, and Mr. Arkwright's valet congregated outside Mr. Arkwright's cabin this morning. After he learned of Mr. Arkwright's death, he realized you must have been waiting for the doctor or the captain."

Charlotte caressed the lioness head of her cane, its silver mane rugged and sharp against her gloved fingertips. "Have you become friends with Mr. Russell now?"

"Hardly." Mr. Pratt gave a rueful smile. Deep vertical grooves appeared on either side of his mouth, making him look years older. "I wanted to learn more about Mr. Arkwright—I hoped that would help me fathom how to get him to relent so that Miss Arkwright and I could marry. But Mr. Russell wasn't interested in that; he only wished to vituperate against Mr. Arkwright.

"But anyway, as curious as I am about Mr. Arkwright's death, I am still more concerned about Miss Arkwright. I haven't seen her, but I know you have, since you were with her this morning. Was she all right? It must have been a terrible shock."

"Yes, that it was. She was devastated."

Mr. Pratt passed a hand over his face. "That poor woman. I wish there was something I could do."

Charlotte did not say anything.

The silence elongated. The mother droned on pleasantly—she seemed to be reading from *Heidi*. Mr. Pratt's breaths quickened. His chest rose and fell with agitation. When he spoke again, his voice was noticeably louder. "I feel myself in a dilemma, Mrs. Ramsay. I'm not sure what to do."

"With regard to Miss Arkwright?"

"Yes. No! I mean, I don't know. I don't know that it has anything to do with her, but I also don't know—well, I also don't know otherwise. No one knows anything now, do they?"

His gaze held hers, seeking understanding. Charlotte had a fair idea what he wished to convey, but said, "I'm afraid your meaning escapes me, Mr. Pratt."

He bit his lower lip, not a gentle scrape of his teeth, but a near mauling of his own anatomy. "I saw something last night. But I don't know what I saw exactly. If I speak to the police inspector, what if he finds something—adverse to Miss Arkwright?"

"You think Miss Arkwright killed her brother?"

"No! No, I don't!"

His vehemence startled the other passengers. The mother's reading stopped. The solitaire player looked up in surprised disapproval. Mr. Pratt panted, as if he'd run up ten flights of stairs. "I don't know anything," he said, his voice now barely audible. "I found her brother perfectly hateful. How do I know she didn't? How do I know what her life has been truly like after he barged in and took over everything?"

"Well, I have no good advice to give you, young man." Charlotte sighed. "If you think your beloved is innocent, speak to the inspector.

If you think she is guilty, then you might have bigger problems than whether or not you hand a piece of evidence to the police."

Mr. Pratt sank into the nearest chair and gripped fistfuls of his own hair.

"Good luck, young man," murmured Charlotte and moved on.

———— ❈ ————

Mr. Gregory appeared altogether bewildered by the request to appear before Inspector Brighton. But he also exhibited a suitable caution, as anyone with an ounce of sense ought to feel with regard to a murder investigation, as well as a hint of curiosity, the kind of inquisitiveness that only a true bystander could evince.

Lord Ingram was more than satisfied with the legendary lover's demeanor. It was his own that he questioned. What *was* the natural reaction of a passenger who genuinely had no connection to the murder at all, except as deposited by chance on the same ship? Should he show a bit of impatience from time to time? A greater desire to be with his children? Or should he simply continue in his current incarnation, that of a man doing his duty, who occupied his place beside Inspector Brighton solely because he had been appointed by the captain?

The policeman began the interview with his hand on the index of the globe. "Mr. Gregory, can you account for your movements last night after dinner?"

Mr. Gregory glanced at the globe. "Yes, of course, Inspector. I returned to my cabin after dinner, and other than a trip to the baths before bed, I never left. I didn't even open my door, except when Mr. Russell was making a ruckus in the corridor."

"When was that?"

"Somewhere between half past ten and quarter to eleven, I would guess."

So Mr. Russell, after leaving Roger Shrewsbury with Lord Ingram, hadn't returned to his own cabin, but gone to the other side of the boiler casings to make a fool of himself in front of the Arkwrights' cabins? The conditions had been such that Lord Ingram hadn't even heard his drunken racket.

Or had it been something else, something meant to make people think that he couldn't have killed Mr. Arkwright? In any case, it was well done of Mr. Gregory to draw attention to the antics of someone with a known grudge against the victim.

"You are sure it was Mr. Russell?"

"Yes, Inspector. When I summoned a steward to escort him to his cabin, he shouted that he was one of the Lincolnshire Russells."

"I see," said Inspector Brighton. He rested his entire hand against the surface of the globe—and obscured half of the Atlantic Ocean. "I understand you were entertaining a guest in your cabin."

Briefly, Lord Ingram's pen paused in its scratching. He hadn't meant for that to happen, but for a prude such as him, perhaps that was understandable?

Mr. Gregory's spine slammed into the frame of his chair, as if Inspector Brighton's words had been an explosion that had blown him back bodily. His lips parted in bewilderment. "Me? Last night? But who would say such a thing?"

"The late Mr. Arkwright, for one."

The late Mr. Arkwright had *not* named Frau Schmidt. He'd only told Lady Holmes that there was already a woman in Mr. Gregory's cabin and Lady Holmes had immediately—though correctly—leaped to the conclusion that it must have been the governess. As far as Lord Ingram could tell, Arkwright had not been in the upper level starboard passage when Frau Schmidt had knocked on Mr. Gregory's door and could have said what he'd said purely out of mischief, to bludgeon Lady Holmes's romantic aspirations.

If only he had not done that!

Mr. Gregory shook his head, and kept shaking his head. "But why would Mr. Arkwright have said that?"

"To needle someone. Apparently, there is competition for your time and affection on this vessel, Mr. Gregory."

"I'm sure that is the furthest thing from the truth, an old man such as myself," replied Mr. Gregory, pink with embarrassment.

"But Frau Schmidt was in your cabin?"

The great lover stiffened instantly. "Inspector, please, you can make fun of me if you'd like, but I beg you not to repeat any such groundless rumors with regard to Frau Schmidt. She is a respectable woman. And furthermore, the condition of her employment is entirely dependent on that respectability.

"She would never have come into my cabin to . . . be entertained. And even if she had lost her sense and shown up at my door, for her sake I would not have admitted her. I would have escorted her to the library, where we might talk without giving rise to undue whispers."

He spoke with such sincerity—and such innocence—that Lord Ingram could almost believe that he had never committed a greater incursion upon a woman than merely holding her hand and walking across a flower-strewn meadow.

Inspector Brighton turned the globe at a leisurely pace—did he feel godlike, to set a small world in motion at his whim? "So you were saving yourself for Lady Holmes then? Lady Holmes has no employment to worry about and more latitude in such things than Frau Schmidt."

Mr. Gregory shuddered. "Goodness, no. I'm sure Lady Holmes is handsome, but her company is more rigor than I can handle."

Inspector Brighton regarded him.

"Really, Inspector," Mr. Gregory cried in exasperation, "I assure you that I was not conducting an affair last night. It was only our second day at sea—if you trust nothing else, you should trust that there hasn't been enough time for such shenanigans. Besides, does any of this have anything to do with Mr. Arkwright's death?"

Lord Ingram would have liked to know the same. Mr. Gregory and Frau Schmidt were at most incidental to the murder. Was Inspector Brighton merely following up on any and all lines of inquiry or had he, as Moriarty's minion, sensed irregularities that might lead him to Charlotte Holmes?

Or was Lord Ingram thinking too much and too deeply when Inspector Brighton but possessed a voracious appetite for gossip and used the power of his office to satisfy his personal curiosity?

"You will please leave the question of what does and doesn't concern Mr. Arkwright's death to me, Mr. Gregory." The policeman stopped the globe, holding it still under his hand. "Now, setting aside the question of Frau Schmidt and whether the two of you may or may not have enjoyed each other's company last night, can you tell me more of your encounter with Mr. Russell?"

"I'm not sure I can tell you much more than I already have, Inspector. It was late enough that I was beginning to feel weary in spite of the storm. Mr. Russell's tomfoolery outside, though not terribly loud, given all the other noises, was highly tiresome." Mr. Gregory inclined his head, as if apologizing for having been cross enough to take action. "It was one thing if he wished to be combative with Mr. Arkwright, quite another to drag Miss Arkwright into it. So I summoned a steward and had him escorted back to his own cabin."

"Did it not strike you as strange that Mr. Arkwright didn't do so himself, but left it to a stranger to get rid of this irritant before his door?"

Mr. Gregory considered this. "Perhaps I did think for a moment that it was odd, but it was late and I did not dwell on it."

All very good answers. By Lord Ingram's estimate, Inspector Brighton should be nearly finished with Mr. Gregory. The latter had had no dealings at all with the Arkwright siblings, so it would be a waste of time to ask for his thoughts on who could have committed the murder.

As he'd anticipated, Inspector Brighton murmured, "Thank you very much, Mr. Gregory."

Lord Ingram had already begun to prepare himself for what might happen once Frau Schmidt stepped into the library, when the policeman continued, "Will you stay here a bit longer, Mr. Gregory? Have you tried the biscuits?"

He extended a plate to Mr. Gregory. Then he rang the bell and asked for Frau Schmidt to be brought in.

Bloody hell.

Mr. Gregory, to his credit, did not look at Lord Ingram. Or rather, he stared a moment at Inspector Brighton, then at the door, and only then at Lord Ingram, an earnestly baffled man in search of explanations.

And then he reddened, and all of a sudden it was as if Lord Ingram was looking at a shy adolescent whose secret romantic longing had been exposed for the world to see.

He was a marvel, but it was never he who worried Lord Ingram, was it?

Frau Schmidt entered. She looked every bit the implacable German governess, her dress as severe and humorless a blue as the Atlantic of last night, her hair gathered into a bun so tight it was a wonder she could move anything on her face.

Her sternness faltered somewhat when all three men in the library rose. "My apologies, gentlemen," she said, her accent sounding particularly strong. "I was told to come in. Did I interrupt something?"

"Not at all. Are you acquainted with Mr. Gregory, Frau Schmidt?"

Frau Schmidt lowered her face. She hadn't blushed, but the bashfulness in her demeanor echoed that of Mr. Gregory's. "Yes, I am. Mr. Gregory has been very kind to my charges and myself."

Inspector Brighton glanced from Frau Schmidt to Mr. Gregory and back again. Lord Ingram did the same—he couldn't help himself.

He'd been afraid that by setting the two new lovers in close proximity, an unmistakably erotic charge would roil through the room and demonstrate to Inspector Brighton once and for all that, indeed, the governess had paid Mr. Gregory a nocturnal visit.

But as far as he could judge, between Frau Schmidt and Mr. Gregory there was more of an . . . awkwardness than anything else? No, that wasn't entirely on the mark. The tension between the two was gentler and sweeter than the embarrassment of two strangers being thrust together, but most assuredly not the unmistakable carnality that sometimes characterized every interaction between new lovers.

The Frau Schmidt who'd emerged from Mr. Gregory's room last

night had not been bed-rumpled precisely, but she also hadn't appeared anywhere as austere and closed off as she did now.

"You did not interrupt anything, Frau Schmidt," pronounced Inspector Brighton. "We were saying our good-byes to Mr. Gregory. Thank you again for your time, sir."

Mr. Gregory bade good day to everyone, and half bowed to Frau Schmidt. She watched his departure before accepting a seat and a cup of tea from Inspector Brighton.

"You said Mr. Gregory has been kind to you and your charges, Frau Schmidt," said the policeman. "Do you wonder why?"

Lord Ingram had once been asked by an investigator, point blank, whether he was in love with Miss Charlotte Holmes. Compared to that, Inspector Brighton's question barely qualified as blunt.

But then he had been the main suspect, and Chief Inspector Fowler's inquisitiveness, however intrusive, had been germane to the case. Frau Schmidt's involvement in Mr. Arkwright's death, even in the eyes of the most jaundiced police investigator, could only be considered tenuous. Why dig into her motivations then? Why spend any time on her at all?

The fear that had swirled in his head since the middle of the night descended, a murder of crows.

"No, Inspector," answered Frau Schmidt, her tone softened with a trace of wistfulness. "I have not given any particular thoughts as to why Mr. Gregory has been kind. Some people are simply kinder."

"You did not attribute that to perhaps Mr. Gregory harboring some special interest in you?"

At this question, even though her posture was already ramrod straight, Frau Schmidt managed to raise the top of her head another fraction of an inch. "Mr. Gregory is a well-looking man. His attention is extremely gratifying. And it *is* tempting to think that perhaps something about my soul has piqued his interest.

"But I did not live to be my age, Inspector, working in my particular profession, without learning that all such thoughts are to be discarded gently but firmly. Not to say that the fairy tale never comes true—Mrs. Ramsay told me as soon as we met that she'd been a governess, too, for a short while, before she married her employer. But if I were the sort to inspire such good fortune, or if I could bring about such good fortune with my own determination, it would have happened decades ago."

Her words possessed the sheen and the urgency of truth.

Inspector Brighton deviated not an inch from his path of inquiry. "Did you leave your cabin at any point last night, Frau Schmidt?"

But his hand did not approach the globe. He only lifted a cup of tea from the small collapsible table that had been set next to him.

"I did, for the ladies' baths."

Frau Schmidt, like the inspector, stirred her tea. The library chimed with a soft *plink* or two of silver on porcelain.

"Less than optimal conditions for a bath," mused the policeman.

"It wasn't so much for hygiene that I went, Inspector, but rather the clothes that needed to be washed—and they could not wait."

Inspector Brighton took a sip of his tea. "Your employer did not give you an allowance for laundry?"

Echoing his motion again, Frau Schmidt also drank. Lord Ingram hoped the tea did not taste like hemlock on her tongue.

"He did, but that allowance does not take into consideration that a great many more items need to be laundered when a boy is seasick. Besides"—she smiled, her smile lopsided and forlorn—"if I did the laundering myself, then I could keep the allowance. A woman is a governess because she has no other means of support. If she wishes to retire someday, she must hoard every penny that comes her way."

With a pang in his heart, Lord Ingram thought of his beloved Miss Potter, who had once been his governess before coming out of retirement to take his children in hand. What hopes and fears had she concealed beneath her kind, smiling countenance? And what had she thought about spending the best years of her life raising other people's children?

"And your charges, were you not concerned about leaving them alone when you were in the baths?"

"They were asleep, Inspector. Not to mention, at home I would not have been in the same room."

She was not a nursemaid dealing with infants who must be supervised at all times. Rupert Pennington and Georg Bittner were both almost old enough to leave home for preparatory school. Certainly the latter's relations thought him old enough to travel with a stranger.

Inspector Brighton ceded that point. "When were you in the baths?"

"I'm not sure what exact time I left my cabin, but I returned shortly after the lights came back."

"You remained in the baths in the dark?"

Inspector Brighton was so incredulous, he set aside his tea. Frau Schmidt held on to hers and even took another sip. "What could I do? By the time I'd finished with all young Master Rupert's soiled clothing, I was in a state of perspiration. And it seemed a good idea, since I was already in the baths, to launder myself as well.

"I'd just sat down in the tub when the lights went out. With the ship rocking the way it was, it would have been difficult dressing even with the lights on. And I would have had to gather everything in pitch-dark. So I decided to wash, praying that electricity would be restored. God smiled upon the *Provence*—she remained afloat and the children were both sound asleep when I got back."

She gave her answer with great conviction, her eyes wide open, her gaze locked with the policeman's, fighting for her reputation, her livelihood, and her retirement, for which she'd stashed away every spare penny.

"Did you see anyone while you were there?"

Lord Ingram kept peering out of the corner of his eye, but Inspector Brighton still hadn't touched the globe. Surely he didn't believe Frau Schmidt that much. Or was she simply too insignificant?

The governess thought for a moment. "I heard the commodes once or twice—I didn't pay close mind. But there was another passenger taking a bath during the time I was there."

"Did you see who it was?"

"No, but I imagine it must have been someone in a position similar to mine, if she was using the baths during hours when there was no attendant."

So Mr. Gregory had passed on Norbert's claim of also having been in the baths.

This mutual corroboration did not make much of an impact on Inspector Brighton. He picked up his tea again. "Frau Schmidt, did you see anything unusual either on the way to or back from the baths?"

Frau Schmidt, who had been holding her teacup with admirable steadiness a few inches above her lap, now rotated it a half turn on its saucer. Did she sense the end of her interrogation? "On my way back, I saw a cabin steward with a mop and a bucket. But that can hardly be considered unusual, can it, on a wet night?"

That would have been Steward Jamison, who'd brought back Shrewsbury from outside and cleaned up after him. Was that why Frau Schmidt had insisted on the fiction of having been to the baths, because he'd seen her?

"Would it be possible for me to speak to your charges, Frau Schmidt?"

Thunder cracked against Lord Ingram's skull. He kept his head down and his pen moving. Mr. Gregory must have cautioned Frau Schmidt against mentioning the stewardess that she'd summoned, with the excuse that should Inspector Brighton examine the duty room log, he would know exactly how long she'd been away from her cabin—too long by any measure.

But it would be far too risky to ask Georg Bittner to maintain a similar silence on the "stewardess." If the policeman spoke to the boy and subsequently looked into the stewardess who did not exist, Frau Schmidt's problem would become a little worse, but Holmes's problem would become unmanageable.

"Well, I don't know what the children can possibly tell you, Inspector," began Frau Schmidt gamely. "They—"

An urgent voice rose outside. ". . . blood last night. *Blood.* I need to speak to the inspector."

Mr. Pratt. His request was followed by whispers from the stewards stationed by the door.

"Oh, he's speaking to someone?" said Mr. Pratt, sounding embarrassed. "Oh, well. I'll wait, then."

No one spoke inside the library until Frau Schmidt murmured, "They were sleeping, my charges. But I suppose I could bring them to speak to you, Inspector?"

Eighteen

Lady Holmes's roars blew past the door of Cabin Number 9. "Close the window! Close the window! Are you trying to send me into an early grave?"

The murmurs that followed must belong to Norbert—Livia would not remain so calm and reasonable while being accused of malice.

"I most certainly did not tell you to open it earlier!" Lady Holmes bellowed at an even greater volume.

She did not sound concussed.

Charlotte knocked and gave Mrs. Ramsay's name. Inside the cabin, whispered words were exchanged. Or rather, Livia and Norbert whispered. Lady Holmes's *What does that woman want?* carried clearly.

The door had been thoroughly cleaned. No trace of blood or rouge could be seen anywhere; its white paint and bronze handle both gleamed, as if to emphasize the typical order and orderliness aboard the *Provence*.

Charlotte knocked again. "Are you at home, Lady Holmes?"

The door opened, but only a crack. Norbert bobbed a curtsy. "I'm afraid Lady Holmes isn't well enough to receive callers, Mrs. Ramsay."

She kept her voice low, in the tone of a nursemaid trying not to disturb a sleeping patient. Behind her, the lamp was turned off. Despite the occasional fluttering of the curtain, which had been drawn across the still-open window, the interior of the cabin was cavelike, its dimness highly conducive to hibernation.

Charlotte nearly yawned. Last night, instead of sleeping, she had rid herself of everything that could betray her identity, stolen down to the luggage hold to dig through Frau Schmidt's steamer trunks, and helped distract the steward on duty so Lord Ingram could restore the wiring behind the summons panel.

"Oh, I'm not here to inquire about her ladyship's health," she said. "I have news—the situation could turn highly unfavorable to her."

"What?" cried Lady Holmes.

Charlotte was admitted. "Leave us for a bit," she said to Norbert. "And you, too, Miss Holmes. The discussion will not be suitable for your ears."

Once she'd cleared the cabin of everyone except Lady Holmes, Charlotte closed the door.

Lady Holmes stared at her with a mixture of anxiety and hostility. "What is it you want to tell me?"

Charlotte crossed to the window and closed it, and drew the curtain shut again. The airing had swept out the odors of carbolic acid, blood, and night sweat, but the cabin still smelled of too much perfume that had been very recently applied.

"What are you doing, changing the arrangements in this cabin without my permission? Convalescents need fresh air!" cried Lady Holmes, who a minute ago had brayed for the opposite.

"My lady, there are passengers outside. You already had exchanges overheard by others. Do you really wish to have your private particulars known to one and all?"

"What private particulars?" demanded Lady Holmes. Her face was a wall of disdain.

"I have just heard from Mr. Gregory, who is very upset with you, my lady."

"What could he possibly have to be upset with me about?" Lady Holmes looked genuinely baffled.

"He understands that you declared, without any evidence, that Frau Schmidt was in his cabin last night."

"But that man Arkwright—"

"Mr. Gregory recalls that more than once you deemed Mr. Arkwright to be the scum of the earth. Why would you have credited anything he said? And did he ever mention Frau Schmidt by name?"

Lady Holmes blinked.

"You have brought unwelcome police attention on both Mr. Gregory and Frau Schmidt. Worse, anyone who should read transcripts of the case in the future would learn of those groundless assertions. Mr. Gregory has confided to me that because of your thoughtlessness, he no longer considers you a lady."

Lady Holmes's face . . . If ever a vase cracked spontaneously, fissures developing one by one and then engulfing everything in a web of fractures, it would have looked like that.

A scene of ruin, small in scale yet thorough and irreversible.

"You lie," she shouted the next moment, her eyes blazing with anger.

"Quiet!" Charlotte commanded in a low voice.

Lady Holmes acquiesced briefly, before becoming mulish again—she had recalled that she was Mrs. Ramsay's social superior. "How dare you speak to me this way. How—"

"Mr. Gregory is planning to pen a letter to your husband, the baronet. He will detail how you have pursued him relentlessly and warn the baronet that he ought to recall you—or you will plague other men from here to India."

"How—how . . ." Lady Holmes's voice trailed off.

A second later she reared up in a swirl of blanket and dressing gown. "I'm going to shout from the bow about that slut of a governess. I'm going to—"

"And thereby assure that Mr. Gregory will send out his letter the moment the *Provence* sails into Gibraltar? I am sure it would be very satisfying for you to slander Frau Schmidt, but tell me, my lady, will you dare go home again, should Mr. Gregory's note indeed reach Sir Henry?"

Lady Holmes blanched.

At ten, Charlotte had discovered evidence of one of her father's affairs. *I wonder why Mamma doesn't have the equivalent of a Mrs. Gladwell,* she had said to Livia, then twelve. *Do you think she wants to?*

They'd been in their shared room at home, its window giving out to a sky ablaze at sunset. Livia had been sitting on the bed, her head in her hands, and Charlotte's question had made her bolt upright. *Have an affair? I've no idea if she wants to, but I'm sure Papa would be extremely cross if she were to.*

Why? He does it. And he doesn't seem at all ashamed about it.

I can't explain it. I just know he'd be angry, Livia had answered with a certainty that would have seemed groundless, were it not for the trace of fear in her voice.

Now that fear was stark in Lady Holmes's eyes.

She was currently confined to her cabin because of her injury, but there was no telling what she would say about Frau Schmidt once she was able to walk about again. And the last thing Charlotte wanted was for Frau Schmidt to pay the price for Mr. Dannell's scheme.

She had not forgotten what it was like to be alone, without the protection of her respectability.

"He—he wouldn't. Mr. Gregory wouldn't do that to me." Lady Holmes's words had become weak. Hoarse.

"Why wouldn't he? Remember, to him your conduct has disqualified you as a lady."

It gave Charlotte no pleasure to threaten her mother with the same arbitrary standards that had left Charlotte exiled but Roger Shrewsbury mostly unscathed. But while Lady Holmes had been made largely powerless in life, it could not be disputed that she had also roundly abused whatever little power remained to her.

So yes, Charlotte would shut her up, using the only means Lady Holmes understood.

"But—but I am a lady. I can never *not* be a lady. That light-skirt governess deserves to lose everything, not me!"

Lady Holmes's voice choked, then she burst into tears. "Why would he do this to me? Why are *you* doing this to me?"

Charlotte regarded her mother, for whom the Golden Rule was *Do unto others as you would never wish them to do unto you.* "I am only the messenger, and it's no use crying in front of me. You should be offering me reassurances I can take back to Mr. Gregory, to persuade him not to write that letter."

She knocked her cane against the floor. "Remember, Lady Holmes, you could be locked away in an attic for the remainder of your life."

Mr. Pratt, connected to the victim, claimed to have seen blood. Frau Schmidt, with no ties to the dead man, asserted that she hadn't been anywhere near the upper level. For an investigator to continue to dispute her whereabouts, to the extent of interviewing two boys of six who had been asleep at the time, would be an instance of extraordinary insistence, one unsupported by either deductive logic or available evidence.

Inspector Brighton, faced with this obvious choice, expressed his gratitude to Frau Schmidt, let her go, and bade Pratt enter. But he did not immediately begin his questioning. Instead, he turned the globe and regarded the volunteer with suspicion, as if he believed that the latter had deliberately interrupted his session with Frau Schmidt.

The globe creaked every time it completed a revolution. Three times it creaked; three times Lord Ingram felt as if someone had taken a needle to his eardrum. He tried to recall when he and his children had looked up strange and wonderful countries on the globe at home, a time before this instrument of learning had become a tool of torture.

A sheen of perspiration appeared on Pratt's forehead. He breathed with his mouth open. His face was flushed; his hands kept smoothing over his trousers.

"Mr. Pratt, if I recall correctly, you are the gentleman who wishes to marry Miss Arkwright."

Pratt started at Inspector Brighton's voice. He chortled, an unhappy sound. "I *did* wish to marry her. Yes, very much so. But . . . I don't know. I don't know anything anymore."

"Oh? Only hours before Mr. Arkwright's death, Lord Ingram here overheard an exchange between you and Mr. Arkwright. At that time you were still adamant in your desire to wed Miss Arkwright. If rumors about her past did not change your mind, then what did?"

"Mr. Arkwright's death?" answered Pratt with an expression of bitter self-mockery. "I used to think that her brother's disfavor of me was what stood in our way. But now that he's dead—I learned about his death in the dining saloon, by the way, alongside all the passengers who hadn't the least connection to her. And still that wasn't hint enough for me. I had to further humiliate myself by sending a steward to her room with a note. I only saw the truth when the steward came back saying there would be no reply."

He closed his eyes briefly. "She never intended to marry me. Her reserve, which I'd thought maidenly and admirable—well, in any case, none of it matters anymore. She'll go her way, and I mine. I'm only here to discuss what I saw last night."

Was love truly blind or simply tremendously obtuse? Lord Ingram would have thought Pratt a shrewder man. But then again, he'd thought himself astute and failed to perceive that his wife had married him only because of her family's financial distress.

Inspector Brighton paused the spinning globe—Pratt's misery seemed to have made his presence less objectionable to the policeman—but his hand remained on the instrument. "Very well, then. Let's have your account."

Pratt tugged at the cuff of his right sleeve. For all his earlier determination to give testimony, he now peered uncertainly at his interrogator. "I don't sleep very well to begin with, and last night I sat on my bed most of the night, fully dressed, waiting for either the storm to pass or the order to abandon ship to come.

"Around half past twelve I thought I heard something. I have one of the aft-most cabins on the *Provence*, right next to the surgery—and

I thought the noise came from there. As I was about to perish from boredom, I took a look. But there was no one. Since I was already on my feet with my door open, I decided I might as well visit the convenience. But when I walked in, I couldn't help but notice a great deal of water on the floor, water that was faintly red in color."

The row of water closet stalls in the gentlemen's baths was situated across from the row of bath partitions. On an older ship, it might have made sense for a murderer to visit the baths, to wash the blood from his person. But on the *Provence*, every cabin had its own fold-up washstand with a faucet that supplied running water.

Unless . . . the murderer shared a cabin with someone else and didn't wish to be seen by the cabin mate?

"I thought my eyes played tricks on me. But I followed the trail of water into a bath partition and saw reddish water inside, too."

Pratt tugged at his sleeve again. He didn't bother to hide his nerves, but with the half-hopeful expression now on his face, he seemed less a witness under scrutiny and more a suitor standing before a prospective father-in-law for the first time.

Inspector Brighton's eyes were half closed. It was difficult to gauge whether he was considering Pratt or deep in his own thoughts. "Were you not disturbed by the sight?"

"Of course I was. At first I thought it might have been a shaving accident. Then I rationalized that it must be something less alarming: someone washing a garment that was less than colorfast. And a man who used the baths late at night? Probably a servant responsible for his own laundry."

"In any case, I was washing my hands when I heard a noise. Again I thought it was coming from the surgery; again when I went to check, I saw nothing. I shrugged and went back to my cabin—and didn't think it was worth mentioning to anyone until I heard about the murder."

Pratt, finished with his account, let out a breath and leaned back in his chair.

"You are certain about the times you gave, Mr. Pratt?" Inspector Brighton spun the globe, producing that small yet thunderous metallic creak.

Pratt cringed. "Yes, I'm sure, Inspector. I had little to do last night besides checking my watch. I left my room a little after half past twelve and went back at five minutes to one."

He sounded convinced, yet it was plain that Inspector Brighton doubted him. "Did you see anything else unusual, Mr. Pratt, anything from nine o'clock last night onwards?"

Pratt raked his hand along his trousers, producing a scratch of fingernails on wool. Only then did he look up, his expression again that of someone earnestly wishing to be believed. "No, indeed, Inspector, though what I did see was astonishing enough, wasn't it?"

Nineteen

"A re you in need of medical attention, Mrs. Ramsay?" asked Dr. Bhattacharya, a man in his thirties, slender of build with a head of curly black hair.

He was courteously skeptical.

Charlotte smiled. "Not precisely, Doctor. I simply find it a good policy, at my age, to make the acquaintance of the local physician."

This sounded so reasonable that she might, in fact, do just that in her old age. But, in truth, she wanted to see the inside of the surgery. She'd called earlier in the day but the good doctor hadn't been in. This time she caught him.

The surgery was larger than her cabin, but not by much. There was a swing-down berth on one wall, at a height that would serve as an examination table. There were the expected table and chairs. And there were many locked cupboards and cabinets, white-lacquered like the walls. They housed no glass fronts to see through, but labels had been affixed, in neat rows, to show the precise location of supplies and substances.

Dr. Bhattacharya watched her take in his place of work—and his framed diploma from Medical College, Bengal. "Are you here for your health, Mrs. Ramsay, or out of curiosity about Mr. Arkwright? I understand you discovered the body."

Charlotte chortled—the man wasted no time in getting to the

point. "I'm here for a few grains of chloral to help me sleep, but I will be happy to hear what you know about Mr. Arkwright, good sir. If, that is, you haven't been forbidden to speak of it."

"Forbidden, not exactly. But I was asked not to discuss details, except with the captain and the inspector."

"Alas, I thought so. Can you tell me whether you will be performing an autopsy? That isn't a 'detail,' is it?"

"I can answer that, and the answer is no. It has been an age of the world since I practiced dissection. Inspector Brighton and I both feel that it would be better to leave the matter to the Gibraltar constabulary—or perhaps even borrow an experienced surgeon from the garrison, if it comes to that."

"He isn't worried that Mr. Arkwright might have been poisoned in addition to having been shot?"

Her old woman's overactive imagination made the physician grin, revealing two rows of strong white teeth. But he answered without mockery. "The inspector might have had other ideas, but once he saw my surgery, I'm sure he realized that I am unequipped for any kind of chemical analysis, let alone assays as delicate and complicated as the detection of poisons. But I am willing to say, to someone who saw Mr. Arkwright's body as well, that upon visual inspection, I do not suspect him to have been the victim of poisoning."

Charlotte chuckled with the delight of a busybody who felt that her cleverness had earned her an unexpected nugget of information. "Have you dealt with an influx of patients like me, Dr. Bhattacharya, since the news of the murder was made public?"

"I have and I do not object to them—I haven't had too many patients."

And more patients, even the gawking variety, meant more income. "Not even for seasickness?"

He shook his head. "Their own laudanum would work as well as anything I can prescribe, and most passengers know that."

Charlotte inquired into the cases he saw and the kinds of drugs and supplies he carried, given that it was impossible to prepare for every eventuality. Then she took a small vial of chloral, paid his fees, and bade him good-bye.

※

The tea was hot, and strong enough to wake the dead. Lord Ingram touched his tongue to the roof of his mouth, feeling the slight scalding of his taste buds. He didn't mind it, just as he didn't mind the bitterness of the brew. Fatigue was beginning to catch up to him: his head weighed too much for his neck; his temples throbbed; his eyes, dry and scratchy, longed to be closed.

He drained the tea.

Inspector Brighton, who must yearn for rest and recuperation even more than he did, stared at the door through which Mr. Pratt had departed.

"Have I mentioned to you, my lord, that I slept early last night?" he said all of a sudden. "The grain of chloral I took was blessedly helpful. When I woke up somewhere in the middle of the night, the conditions had become much calmer and I was able to totter to the gentlemen's baths."

The policeman turned toward Lord Ingram, his gaze penetrating. "I did not see any water on the floor, my lord, reddish or otherwise. Granted, by that time some hours had passed since Mr. Pratt's visit. But given the damp conditions, it's odd that the floor should have dried so thoroughly."

"Perhaps someone cleaned it?" offered Lord Ingram.

Inspector Brighton pinched the bridge of his nose. "That would seem the only likelihood. But who?"

Lord Ingram latched on to the opportunity. "Are you not feeling well, Inspector? Would it help to have Dr. Bhattacharya come?"

Perhaps a little reminder of his vertigo would encourage the policeman to end the day sooner.

Inspector Brighton waved his fingers in a gesture of negation. "That would be a waste of the good doctor's time. Mine is an old problem. It will take a few days to sort itself out, that's all."

He sounded exceedingly weary. Lord Ingram mentally composed his next line of attack. *It has been a long day. You must not neglect your health.* Or should he be less transparent? *We've already accumulated a great many transcripts—it would take me all night to copy them in longhand.*

"Let's see," said Inspector Brighton, his voice raspy, "which other passengers visited the gentlemen's baths last night in a watery state?"

A nasty jolt shot down Lord Ingram's spine; his lethargy evaporated in an instant. Not Roger Shrewsbury again!

Shrewsbury and Steward Jamison, when they were brought back together, both looked apprehensive, Roger Shrewsbury especially so—he had the panicked eyes of an escaped prisoner on the verge of being caught again. Lord Ingram tried to let him know through a nod that there was nothing to be afraid of, but his own heart pounded like the pistons of an overheated engine.

"Gentlemen," commanded Inspector Brighton. "I'd like to hear in greater detail the time you spent in the baths. We'll start with you, please, Mr. Shrewsbury."

Shrewsbury, who'd declined the offer of a seat and remained on his feet, took a step backward. "I, ah, I stripped off my wet clothes and toweled myself dry. The ship was buckling something fierce, and as much as I was chilled to the core, I didn't want to have a wash then. So I wrapped myself in some towels and waited. Fortunately, Steward Jamison here returned speedily. He said he'd make sure that my clothes went to the laundry, so I changed into the dry clothes he brought me and left."

Inspector Brighton turned his gaze to Jamison.

"That is correct," piped up the steward. "After Mr. Shrewsbury left, I wrung out his clothes and set them aside for the laundry. And then I mopped the floor of the bath partition where he'd changed— I'm not a bath attendant, but if the head steward knew that I'd been there and didn't clean up, he'd have my hide.

"After that, I got a bucket from below to retrieve my mackintosh— I'd stowed it just outside the door to the deck. Then I mopped the parts of the corridor where Mr. Shrewsbury had walked in his wet clothes. When that was all done, I took everything down below where they belonged."

"My goodness," marveled Shrewsbury despite his nervousness. He clapped a hand on Jamison's back. "I had no idea there was so much work involved. Thank you, my good man."

"Well," said Jamison, reddening a little, "it's what's expected of us, sir. We are here for you to have a pleasant and most hygienic voyage."

"Indeed, very admirable, how hard everyone on the *Provence* works," said Inspector Brighton, his voice more cutting than admiring. "Was that the last you saw of the baths, Mr. Jamison?"

"Well, you see, Inspector, I didn't enter the baths again, but after I took everything down below, I did come up to the saloon deck one last time with a few rags, in case I'd missed anything."

"And?"

"There was a fresh trail of water leading from the deck door to the menservants' dormitory," said Jamison, sounding ever so slightly self-pitying. "I wiped it up with my rags, and I checked that there was no similar trail leading to the baths. After that, I was finally able to sit down in the duty room and have a cup of tea."

"Who lives in the menservants' dormitory?" asked Inspector Brighton.

His question, however expected, sounded ominous. The policeman must know as well as Lord Ingram did who occupied that particular cabin.

"That would be Mr. Arkwright's valet, Mr. Fuller. He's the only gentleman's gentleman on this sailing, so he has the menservants' dormitory to himself," said Jamison with a trace of envy. His own dormitory must be cramped.

Inspector Brighton glanced at the deck plans. "And you are sure the trail of water leading from the aft entrance to the menservants' dormitory wasn't there before?"

"I'm sure, Inspector. I wiped that area with a dry mop. There might have been drops and sprinkles I'd missed—the reason I went back with the rags—but not a whole trail of water."

"Anything else you saw that I should know? Or anyone?"

"I caught a glimpse one time of a lady passenger going back into her cabin. I think it was Frau Schmidt. But that was just after I answered Mrs. Shrewsbury's summons, before I found Mr. Shrewsbury on deck."

Inspector Brighton filliped the deck plans. They produced a loud, almost sibilant *thwack*. "Were you on duty all night?"

"No, sir, only until midnight. After that, it was Smith in the duty room by himself until six o'clock in the morning."

Inspector Brighton did not forget Roger Shrewsbury. "And you, Mr. Shrewsbury, anything else you saw that you should tell me?"

Shrewsbury, who had relaxed somewhat while Jamison spoke of cleaning and tidying, stiffened again. "No, no, Inspector. I didn't see anything else of any importance."

"Oh, what did you see of *no* importance?"

"I—I also didn't see anything of no importance." Shrewsbury flushed to his ears. "I went back to my cabin after I called on his lordship, and I didn't see anyone else the rest of the night except my wife, who was sleeping. That is—that is—unless my sleepwalking counted."

Perspiration beaded on the tip of his lobster-hued nose. Lord Ingram felt as if he himself was about to be swept away by an enormous wave. The man had bungled the simple hymen-breaching Holmes had asked of him. Was he going to fail them here in similarly spectacular fashion?

"Sleepwalking?"

"When I woke up in the morning, my wife said that I'd sleepwalked in the middle of the night and she was awakened by a steward—not Mr. Jamison here but the one on overnight duty that he mentioned—when he delivered me back to the cabin."

At least Shrewsbury was a known sleepwalker. Anyone who had gone to school with him could attest to that.

"And what time was that?"

"The small hours of the night, she said. Three or four, I'd guess."

The globe did not spin, but Inspector Brighton's hand obscured not only the coast of Portugal but half of the Mediterranean Sea. Lord Ingram imagined an enormous palm blocking the sky. It suffocated.

"You are sure, Mr. Shrewsbury?" asked the policeman.

More than ever, Roger Shrewsbury resembled a small creature frozen before the open maw of a predator. "Yes!" he squeaked. "I'm sure, Inspector. I really had nothing at all to do with anything. It was just a piece of evil luck that the revolver should fall right in front of me. Really, I can't tell you anything else."

"And I didn't expect you to, Mr. Shrewsbury. I called you back only to be thorough." The policeman narrowed his eyes. "But why are you so nerve-stricken, good sir?"

"I—I—" Shrewsbury glanced at Lord Ingram. He looked as if he could barely hold himself back from launching headlong at Lord Ingram and crying in his arms.

Lord Ingram tamped down his own panic—he, too, wanted to be held safe and not deal with this bloody investigation a moment longer. "Mr. Shrewsbury, I cannot answer any questions for you. If you've a reason for feeling fraught, by all means let Inspector Brighton know."

Shrewsbury looked down at his feet. "I—I don't know whether you've heard, Inspector, but my mother was swept up in a murder investigation last summer."

"Ah, yes, that's right," murmured Inspector Brighton. "The case that brought us Sherlock Holmes."

"When the truth was revealed, she lost her good name posthumously because of something she did decades ago. And my lord Ingram here, he was caught in a murder investigation, too. And well, the outcome was similarly unhappy, wasn't it?"

Lord Ingram said nothing.

Roger Shrewsbury's fingertips shook. The cuffs of his trousers shook, too. "So you see, Inspector, I'm not afraid because I've anything to hide about what I know—everybody knows I know nothing. But you must think I hate Mr. Arkwright and I did sleepwalk last night . . . I'm just afraid that the investigation might pulverize me even though I'm only a bystander."

He fell into the chair that was earlier offered him and went on shaking.

Inspector Brighton's eyes blazed. "No, Mr. Shrewsbury," he said, enunciating every word. "If you truly are only a bystander, then you have absolutely nothing to fear."

Despite that statement, which nearly made Shrewsbury slip from his chair in a faint, Inspector Brighton dismissed Shrewsbury and Jamison and asked for Fuller the valet to be brought.

Lord Ingram wiped his hands on a handkerchief, ostensibly to remove ink stains on his fingertips—his palms had never before perspired in such a manner, not even when his life had been in danger. It was ten times more terrifying to entrust one's fate to a fool, and to watch from the sidelines as said fool bleated, blathered, and all but twisted in the wind.

He weighed down the papers before him and went to one of the windows that the steward had opened, so he could stand for a while with his back to Inspector Brighton. The window faced west, giving onto thousands of miles of open Atlantic.

He'd always loved this about long ocean voyages, the distance from settled lands, the occasional sense that the ship and only the ship had existed since time immemorial. But now the isolation felt oppressive, the danger, inescapable.

"It's almost possible to forget what we're dealing with, isn't it, traversing the vastness of the world?" murmured Inspector Brighton from his chair.

"Precisely," said Lord Ingram. If only he could forget it, even for a moment.

Fuller entered the library, looking tentative, but nowhere near as frightened as Roger Shrewsbury had been.

"Have a seat, Mr. Fuller," said Inspector Brighton, glancing over the record of his earlier interview with the valet.

Before the interviews resumed in the afternoon, Lord Ingram had transcribed his notes from the earliest morning sessions. With that fresh review, he knew that Fuller had not said anything directly contradicting a walk on the deck last night. But given the conditions at the time, few would consider an evening that included a complete soaking to be "uneventful."

Inspector Brighton was direct. "Mr. Fuller, we have report of a trail of water last night that led from the aft deck door to the menservants' dormitory. What were you doing outside in such frightful weather?"

Fuller did not appear too surprised at the question. "There are some who like a good storm, Inspector. I consider myself one of them."

"So do I, while on land," countered Inspector Brighton. "But I can enjoy a storm just fine from the comfort of a parlor or a bedchamber, without thoroughly drenching myself on a cold night."

"It wasn't particularly cold."

"It wasn't the Siberian winter, to be sure. But April on the North Atlantic is no trifling matter."

"We are verging on May, Inspector," Fuller pointed out.

"I am not here to split hairs with you, Mr. Fuller."

Inspector Brighton did not raise his voice, but Fuller recoiled. The policeman's hand was on the globe again, and the valet had not forgotten the menace he'd experienced in the morning, while his interrogator gently stroked the brass rings that encircled the instrument.

The corners of Fuller's lips turned down in a petulant, almost childish expression. "Very well, I was outside because I was unhappy and I couldn't stand another moment in my bunk. Is *that* an acceptable answer?"

It was more an outburst than an answer.

Inspector Brighton traced the outline of Australia. "And why were you unhappy, Mr. Fuller?"

The valet's jaw moved. "Because I wanted to stay in London. In

Britain. The queen's Golden Jubilee is coming up this summer, for goodness sake. I wanted to dress Mr. Arkwright for all the dinners and balls. And maybe even his wedding. I didn't want to go back to Sydney so soon, I didn't want to be on this ship, and I especially didn't want to be in the middle of that stupid storm.

"That's why I was at the aft rail, howling into the night. Because nothing was going my way. Who would have thought . . ." His eyes filled with tears. "We should have stayed behind in Britain. Then none of this would have happened. Mr. Arkwright, Miss Arkwright, myself—we would all have been much better off, Mr. Arkwright most of all."

Inspector Brighton snorted. "So you just stood at the aft rail and screamed?"

Fuller looked down at his hands. "You see why I didn't wish to admit it earlier, Inspector. But yes, that was what I did. Doesn't everyone do stupid things sometimes?"

"And then?"

"Then, once I realized I was frozen and very likely to catch my death, I went back to the menservants' dormitory."

"Did you go anywhere else after that?"

"No."

"What about the baths? You didn't go to warm yourself up?"

"I had my doubts about the supply of hot water—even the electricity was gone for a bit, wasn't it? So I wrung out my wet clothes in the washstand, took a few swallows of whisky, and went to bed."

"Is there anything else I should know about your night, Mr. Fuller? Anything that would help me find out who killed Mr. Arkwright?"

Inspector Brighton took hold of the index atop the globe and twisted, as if he aimed to remove the decorative finial. Fuller's hands tightened around the armrests of his chair.

"I've racked my brains, Inspector, trying to think of something, anything, that would help. But I've come up empty-handed. It feels as if Evil itself struck down Mr. Arkwright."

Inspector Brighton's eyebrows shot up, and it seemed to Lord Ingram that he barely restrained himself from rolling his eyes at this metaphysical interpretation of events. "You no longer suspect Mr. Russell?"

"I do, but he's the sort to whisper rumors and half truths in people's ears. I don't know that he had the guts to confront Mr. Arkwright face-to-face, as the murderer seemed to have done."

"Was there any particular reason for Mr. Russell's antagonism toward your late employer, besides the general resentment of a man of higher birth toward one who came from nothing and yet was far more successful?"

"Before we left Australia, Mr. Arkwright instructed his lawyers to negotiate with Mr. Russell's senior partner. He wished to acquire the senior partner's stake in the venture. It was a business decision that had nothing to do with Mr. Russell, but trust Mr. Russell to see it as a personal vendetta."

A light came into Fuller's eyes. His voice, too, carried better. Did he realize how different he looked and sounded when he spoke the undiluted truth? When he wasn't busy cutting and stitching together answers that would pass muster?

Certainly Inspector Brighton knew—he lifted his hand from the globe. "What will happen to those plans concerning Mr. Russell's senior partner, now that Mr. Arkwright is no more?"

Fuller shook his head. "I don't know. No one knows until we hear Mr. Arkwright's will. And then whoever inherits his estate would need to want the same thing. So perhaps that deal would proceed no further."

If that were indeed the case, then Mr. Russell had strong motivation to be rid of Mr. Arkwright. Perhaps the strongest of everyone aboard.

Inspector Brighton dismissed Fuller—and in the same breath asked for Norbert to be brought back.

A vein jumped at the back of Lord Ingram's head. A muted

reaction—after the untrammeled fright that had been Roger Shrews-bury's encore interview, he could summon up only a flutter of appre-hension at Inspector Brighton's renewed interest in Norbert.

The lady's maid arrived looking as trim and put together as ever. Her attitude remained as respectful as ever.

"How is Lady Holmes, Miss Norbert?" began Inspector Brighton.

"Today has been trying for her, Inspector. But Dr. Bhattacharya came by to see her again and said that she appeared fine. She is resting right now."

"I'm glad to hear that. Now, Miss Norbert, would you mind tell-ing me in some greater detail about your trip to the baths last night?"

Norbert cocked her head. "Certainly, Inspector. Is there anything specific you'd like to know?"

There it was again, her insouciance bubbling up to the surface— she was sincerely unconcerned that the investigation would cause her any harm. Or even inconvenience.

"Was anyone else there the same time as you were?"

"Yes, there was another woman in the bath. She was there before I got there and still there when I left."

"Did you see who it was?"

"No, but I'm almost certain it was Frau Schmidt. She was croon-ing to herself in a foreign tongue."

Frau Schmidt had not been in the baths, except perhaps for a few minutes, to wrap up her hair and make herself look as if she'd spent copious time washing. What game was Norbert playing, exactly? On the surface, it appeared that she was helping Frau Schmidt—and inadvertently helping Holmes, too. But what if she wasn't?

"What do you think of the case so far, my lord?"

Inspector Brighton had been silent for some time. Lord Ingram had taken to transcribing another interview to look busy—and so that his own silence would not convey too much tension.

The ship advanced with the soothing rhythm of a gently rocking cradle. From the open windows, came the equally soothing sounds of the sea foaming around the hull. Inspector Brighton's question was soft, yet in its wake Lord Ingram could no longer hear the waves or feel the motion of the ship.

Was it remotely likely that the policeman valued his opinion? No. But he still had to give a well-reasoned answer, one that contained only what he would know from his work today as the case's official stenographer.

"I confess myself perplexed," he said. "As the investigation stands now, Lady Holmes and Mr. Shrewsbury are the greatest suspects, as they are the ones for whom we hold physical evidence, the revolver that Mr. Shrewsbury threw overboard in view of Steward Jamison, and in Lady Holmes's case, her rouge pot that was found in Mr. Arkwright's cabin, as well as his cabin key that was later discovered in the pocket of her dress."

"That is correct," said Inspector Brighton. "But I sense that you are not satisfied with our current crop of likely culprits, my lord?"

"I have known Mr. Shrewsbury for most of my life. I cannot heap praise on him, but I have a difficult time believing that he would kill Mr. Arkwright over a pair of punches. Certainly during our conversation yesterday evening, shortly before the murder took place, he evinced no animosity toward the Arkwrights.

"As for Lady Holmes, she is assertive only before the powerless. It is unlikely that if she had indeed been subject to physical abuse by Mr. Arkwright, she'd have found the wherewithal to retaliate by shooting him with his own firearm. I'd have expected her to cower and snivel—and accomplish no more than that."

Inspector Brighton did not appear either pleased or displeased. "What about the others? Mr. Russell, Mr. Pratt, Fuller, and Miss Arkwright?"

Lord Ingram weighed his words. "I am puzzled as to why anyone would choose to commit murder in a milieu from which they themselves cannot escape. Mr. Russell faces the sale of his senior partner's shares to Mr. Arkwright, but that imperilment dates from before Mr.

Arkwright left Australia for Britain. As for Mr. Pratt, whether his pursuit of Miss Arkwright is for herself or her brother's money, his greatest opportunity would arise *after* the Arkwright siblings step onto Australian soil, not before. The situation in Sydney could become so intolerable for Miss Arkwright that Mr. Arkwright would have no choice but to give his blessing to Mr. Pratt's suit.

"With regard to Miss Arkwright . . . if her brother greatly minded Roger Shrewsbury's revelations, would it not be more profitable for her to persuade him that she was the wronged party rather than to kill him, whose protection she needed now more than ever?"

"And yet he lies dead. So something must have happened to force someone's hand," murmured Inspector Brighton. "But what?"

Lord Ingram offered no suggestions.

"As for motives," continued the policeman, "were we on land, or if ship-based telegraphy were already practicable, we'd be able to learn the contents of Mr. Arkwright's will, as well as a number of other things that require independent verification. But until we reach Gibraltar, we've no way of knowing, for example, what Miss Arkwright stands to gain in the event of her brother's death."

The journey from Southampton to Gibraltar typically took around five days, though a newer, faster ship such as the *Provence* could cover the distance in four and a half days.

They were two days and four hours into the sailing, which meant at least another fifty-some hours before cables could be sent out. Another fifty-some hours in which Inspector Brighton could tear the ship apart in search of the phantom stewardess who had played with Georg Bittner the night of the storm.

The policeman reached for the bell, grimaced, and abandoned the effort. "No, I'm afraid my head spins too much. Shall we stop now and resume our work tomorrow morning, my lord?"

Twenty

"Have you heard of the bloody water Mr. Pratt saw in the gentlemen's baths, ladies?" whispered Lieutenant Younghusband.

The somewhat overbright lamps of the dining saloon shone on an assemblage of huddled passengers. The passengers spoke in low voices, looked tense and worried, and threw many a surreptitious glance over their shoulders with the air of a theatrical but haphazard conspiracy in progress.

If her stomach wasn't the size and weight of a Mons Meg cannonball, Mrs. Watson would have relished the company of the young soldiers—that of the mischievous Lieutenant Younghusband, especially. But it had been a long day, and she felt no safer—and no more knowledgeable—than when she'd first learned of the murder.

Her lamb tasted like sawdust and was even less fun to swallow. Miss Charlotte beside her, however, had the opposite problem. Before they'd traveled to Southampton, Mrs. Watson had undertaken a trip to the vicinity of Mrs. Ramsay's house outside Cambridge. And there, under the guise of a visitor interested in purchasing a nice, quiet property, she'd learned a good deal from enthusiastic locals about the modernization of Mrs. Ramsay's house—and about Mrs. Ramsay herself. And unfortunately for Miss Charlotte, the real Mrs. Ramsay was well-known for her dainty appetite.

The aroma of Mrs. Watson's lightly seared and butter-drenched lamb chop, too rich and meaty for her current state of nerves and her clenched digestive system, must be a seductive siren song for Miss Charlotte, who had to content herself with a fillet of fish poached in water. But if Miss Charlotte salivated, she showed no sign of it.

She leaned forward. "Well, tell me everything!"

They occupied the port table nearest the aft entrance, the ladies on the sofa, the young men on chairs with their backs to the rest of the saloon. Lieutenant Younghusband turned around halfway and looked to where Mr. Pratt stood, beside the missionaries' table on the starboard side.

In a room full of weary, nervous diners, Mr. Pratt alone radiated energy and confidence. He spoke, his eyes lit; the missionaries listened in horrified fascination.

Lieutenant Younghusband reported to Miss Charlotte and Mrs. Watson what Mr. Pratt had told them about an hour ago, when the young officers had come across him on deck: hearing something in the middle of the night, leaving his cabin to use the convenience, and seeing the possibly bloody water in the baths.

Lieutenant Wallis also glanced in Mr. Pratt's direction. "It was thrilling to have his account, all right. But now I'm not so sure that it was entirely appropriate for him to tell us."

Lieutenant Younghusband flicked his fingers in dismissal. "Come, come, old fellow. What's the harm, as long as the inspector didn't tell him that he must keep everything a secret? Besides, if Mr. Arkwright had been murdered in England, the details would be splashed all over the papers."

Inspector Brighton, after declaring himself unequal to further investigative endeavors for the day, had not granted Lord Ingram a similar rest. Instead, he'd requested Lord Ingram to make his excuses to the captain, arrange for a copy of the duty room summons record for the night of the murder, and transcribe as many of the interviews as possible for him to review before work started on the morrow.

And Lord Ingram, between complying with Inspector Brighton's requests and seeing to his children, had contrived to pass the transcripts of the afternoon sessions to Miss Charlotte, who, after reading them, had given a brief encapsulation to Mrs. Watson and Miss Livia. Poor Miss Livia, after spending an entire afternoon at her irascible mother's bedside, had listened with her head on Mrs. Watson's shoulder, too worn out to speak.

So this was the second time Mrs. Watson had heard the account, and her reaction was unchanged. "But . . . that's it? That's all Mr. Pratt saw?"

At the failure of his tale to elicit a greater reaction, Lieutenant Younghusband, instead of being disappointed, beamed with approval. "My sentiments exactly, Miss Fenwick. I find Mr. Pratt's tale hair-raising and yet, well, rather empty. It tells us nothing."

"Perhaps not nothing," mused his friend. "But it would take a mind more astute than mine to make sense of it."

Across the dining saloon, Mr. Pratt, now finished with his narrative, inclined his head at the missionaries and sauntered toward the aft entrance. But en route he was stopped by Mr. Russell, who signaled Mr. Pratt to take a seat at the table he occupied by himself.

Mr. Pratt declined. Mr. Russell's expression turned petulant.

They did speak, their exchange brief and less than friendly. Mr. Pratt resumed his departure. Mr. Russell stared after him, his gaze sharp with contempt and speculation.

Mrs. Watson cast a glance at Miss Charlotte, who must have witnessed the same interaction. Miss Charlotte signaled for service. A stewardess materialized quickly. Miss Charlotte indicated for her half-eaten fillet of flounder to be taken away.

"Any pudding for you, ma'am?" the stewardess asked solicitously. "We've a very nice trifle, a coffee custard, and some dessert ices."

"Everything sounds delicious, but alas, at my age, rich foods have become anathema. Some fruits will do nicely."

Mrs. Watson resolved to swamp the girl in pudding and cake as soon as they got off the ship—provided, that is, they could do so safely.

The stewardess soon returned with a dish of cut pears and another of French plums.

"Thank you, my dear," said Miss Charlotte, her voice even more gravelly than usual for Mrs. Ramsay, as if the old lady had trouble staving off her fatigue. "Quite a sailing this has been. I hope it isn't always this exciting for you to be at work."

"No, indeed, ma'am," answered the stewardess. "Sometimes we have unruly passengers and whatnot, but this is the first time that anything like *this* has happened—for me at least."

Earlier Miss Charlotte had been careful not to make too many inquiries—she hadn't wanted to bring unnecessary attention to Mrs. Ramsay. But now, with heated speculation all around, it would be strange if the sociable and curious Mrs. Ramsay didn't take a greater interest in the proceedings. "Has it upset the crew? I know the captain must be disturbed, but what about the rank-and-file members?"

The stewardess looked around and lowered her voice. "Well, I don't know about the firemen or the deck crew, but for the victualing crew, we were all mighty sad about Mr. Arkwright."

"Oh, has he sailed on this vessel before?"

"No, I don't believe so. But the afternoon before he was found dead, he came down and toured the galley, the duty room, and even had a look inside the stewards' dormitories. He said he grew up on the docks and had worked his way to Australia on a steamer and knew how hard the work was for all of us. And he tipped us all, too, everyone who happened to be on hand. I was there to help move some fruits to decorate the dining saloon, and even I got a florin."

"Good for you, my girl."

"I thought so—it was really good luck, that. My brother is a greaser, and he said that when Mr. Arkwright toured the engines, he tipped everyone, too. Not arrogant-like, throwing coins about and expecting everyone to pick them up and be grateful. He had a good word for everyone and thanked them for their labor."

The stewardess nodded. "Respectful, he was. Real respectful."

A lady missionary wanted service; the stewardess bobbed a curtsy and hurried off.

As soon as she was out of earshot, Lieutenant Younghusband leaned forward and whispered, "Did everyone hear what I heard? Did it not sound as if Mr. Arkwright was looking for someone?"

"I agree," said Mrs. Watson, her heart beating faster. "It did sound that way."

"I wonder who that was," murmured Lieutenant Younghusband.

Miss Charlotte set down her fork after only three pear slices. "I wonder whether he succeeded in finding that someone."

The table fell silent. The ship rose and fell gently, as if it rode upon the heartbeat of the sea. Beyond the starboard windows, the sun had largely disappeared beneath the western horizon. A deep coral pink suffused the sky; the sea was wine dark, as Homer had once said of the Aegean.

The storm now seemed impossibly remote, an event from a lifetime ago.

"Come to think of it . . ." Lieutenant Wallis rubbed his chin. "I don't know that this is related to anything at all, but yesterday morning I was taking a bath. My faucet was running and I was pouring water over my hair when I vaguely heard someone whistle, and then there was this scream that sounded like 'Flowers!' I was so startled, I sloshed water out of the tub.

"There were running footsteps. Then that same scream came again—it came from a—a—"

He stopped and turned red.

"A commode stall, yes, we have those in the ladies' baths as well," said Miss Charlotte. "No need to be embarrassed, young man. Carry on, a scream originated from a commode stall, someone ran off, the scream came again, and then?"

Lieutenant Wallis smiled sheepishly. "And then a few seconds later I heard a—a flush, a door bursting open, and someone else sprinting out."

"That's it?" asked Lieutenant Younghusband, his skeptical tone reminiscent of Mrs. Watson's from earlier.

"That's it." Lieutenant Wallis shrugged. "I had to finish my bath and make myself halfway decent before I could stick my head out of the bath partition for a look. By the time I did that, the baths were quiet and peaceful, and it was as if I'd conjured the whole thing in my head."

Lieutenant Younghusband took a plum from the dish that had been brought for Mrs. Ramsay. "At first I was going to denounce you, Wallis, for not having told me sooner, but I see now why you didn't. Your story is even worse than Mr. Pratt's. At least his had the spine-tingling aspect of blood in the baths, perhaps. But yours . . ."

He shook his head.

"I did say that it probably had nothing to do with anything." Lieutenant Wallis shrugged again. "Now I know not to plague anyone else with this useless tale."

A quarter moon hung overhead, a marble-pale, near-perfect semicircle. It painted an avenue of silver on the surface of the sea, one that quivered and gleamed from the edge of the *Provence* all the way to the edge of the sky.

Wind cut across Charlotte's path and filled her ears. She leaned forward to advance along the starboard promenade. But who was that standing outside Frau Schmidt's window?

Norbert.

The two women greeted the elderly Mrs. Ramsay respectfully as she passed. The next time she walked down the starboard promenade, however, Frau Schmidt's window was dark and closed and Norbert nowhere to be found.

At least when Charlotte had been on the other side of the ship, she'd seen the light of Lord Ingram's parlor come on.

He'd passed along his cabin key to her earlier. It had been meant as a safety measure, so that she would be less likely to be seen knocking and waiting outside his cabin. But still, one could interpret it as an overt invitation, and she very much enjoyed an overt invitation from him.

She took another round on deck before she headed inside, sneaked upstairs, and unlocked his door. He was at the writing desk, transcribing his notes. As soon as she closed the door behind her, he rose and went to the door to peer out.

"No one was about," she reassured him when he'd shut the door again.

Norbert was the only person she saw outside. Inside, too, the passages had stood empty, all the public rooms unoccupied except for Mr. Gregory, puffing absentmindedly on a cigar in the smoking room.

He embraced her briefly and tilted his head toward the sleeping cabin. "I've some food for you."

His loot came from the library, the biscuits pilfered while Inspector Brighton was at his noontime rest and the small sandwiches after the policeman retired for the day. Charlotte ate three sandwiches and two biscuits and fell sideways on the bed—because of course he'd placed the plates on the bed again.

"Did you take a nap?" she murmured, propping her head up on her elbow rather slowly. Now that she was full, she was suddenly sleepy.

And he'd had a more grueling night than she and a far more grueling day.

Her lover removed the plates and lay down crosswise on the bed, facing her. "I slept for an hour before dinner."

He still looked tired. She plunged her fingers into his thick, dark hair, then touched the tiny lines at the corner of one eye. His bathing soap was made by his valet, and this close she inhaled notes of cedar and cloves on his skin, that barest hint of warm wood and spice. "How are your children?"

"Saddened and a little disturbed, but not devastated," he sighed.

"I always worry that they will be devastated by life's various misfortunes, but they understand—and accept—the vicissitudes of the world better than I give them credit for."

After the former Lady Ingram's departure, he'd been so worried about not being able to provide his children a perfect childhood that sometimes he failed to see everything he'd already given them.

"They have strength in their hearts," she said. "And you are a good father."

He looked curiously and a little warily at her: She had never commented on his parenting before. He cupped her face with one hand. "Thank you."

She still had her makeup on and felt his touch—and the warmth of his palm—as if through a woolen muffler. "How does it feel, my face?"

"Somewhat hard, somewhat rubbery, and somewhat sticky, too, like nothing I've ever felt before."

"Is it strange to look at me behind someone else's face?"

He continued to explore her "face." "Believe me, after the baptism by fire that was Sherrinford Holmes, I have accepted all your other guises with ease."

Her lips quirked slightly. "I hope I live to be old enough to have this many wrinkles."

"I hope to be half as good-looking as Mr. Gregory when I reach his age."

"I'm convinced that in thirty years you'll be at least three quarters as handsome as he is right now.

He snorted. "Since I'm still young and relatively prepossessing, I'll let that pass. But in thirty years, you had better tell me that Mr. Gregory of yesteryear couldn't hold a candle to me."

"I can do that."

"In person or by post?"

Before she could answer, he shook his head. "No, never mind, it's a stupid question. Thirty years is too far in the future."

"I can do it in person," she told him. She didn't see why not, if they were both alive three decades from now.

He didn't jump back and respond with *Don't say things like that*, as he had last night, before their peace was shattered by Roger Shrewsbury's knocks, but he did regard her a long moment.

Since the de facto end of his marriage last summer, they'd become closer. Or rather, they'd become assuredly closer physically and tentatively closer . . . on some other level. For a while he had been the one making the greater strides, but now it seemed that she, pleased with how things were going, conducted herself in a manner that unnerved him.

He was a romantic, a romantic who had been deeply disappointed in love. It had made him cautious, fearful, perhaps, of being closer . . . on some other level. She did not find his reactions remotely exasperating or incomprehensible, but fascinating in the way of the sea, the tides, and the wheeling of the stars, ever changing, ever constant, and always rewarding for the observer.

Her hand settled on his lapel. He wore a cheviot dressing gown in midnight blue, the wool fine and soft beneath her fingertips. Under that, his pajama shirt had three buttons undone. She was tempted to caress the skin exposed by that opening but in the end laid her palm over his heart to feel its strong, steady beat.

He kept gazing at her. The wariness in his eyes gradually faded, replaced by a profound concern. Slowly he sat up. "Did you read that Inspector Brighton wanted to speak to Frau Schmidt's charges?"

She pulled him back down—there was no reason they couldn't discuss Mr. Arkwright's murder while lying comfortably on their sides. To that end, she gave him a pillow and took another for herself.

"You're wondering whether Inspector Brighton's fixation on Frau Schmidt marks him as Moriarty's minion? On its own, not necessarily. I've seen him interrogating Mrs. Treadles. I believe he can sense when he's being lied to. And he does not care to be lied to—he kept on questioning my mother until she surrendered the true version of events.

"Here he kept questioning Frau Schmidt and Mr. Gregory, and kept receiving elaborate answers, even a corroboration out of nowhere from Norbert. Were you him, would you have been reassured or would the entire situation have appeared even odder to you?"

Her lover filliped his pillow and produced a surprisingly solid *thwack*. "I wonder what Norbert wants. Not only did she lie to cover up for Frau Schmidt, but she did it in such a way that I, at least, would realize exactly what she'd done. And of course, there's the part she must have played in getting Lady Holmes to come aboard the *Provence*."

Charlotte told him about seeing Norbert at Frau Schmidt's window just now. "Norbert has purposes of her own. But I do not believe she is particularly interested in unmasking Mrs. Ramsay, so for the moment let's not worry about her."

He touched her face again. Indeed, that was where their chief worry lay. "How is your skin feeling?"

"Still holding up." It was not beneficial to wear the makeup continuously. But having flushed most of the solution she'd brought down the commode, she had to keep on her current layer until tomorrow. And then, she had only enough for one more application.

Disquiet shadowed his eyes. They'd had to rely on Inspector Brighton to do most of the information gathering for them. The man might have made an unnecessary detour with Miss Fenwick and sniffed too hard at Frau Schmidt, but overall his pace and effectiveness could not be faulted. And yet, today's investigation hadn't yielded compelling evidence of guilt except for Lady Holmes and Roger Shrewsbury.

"Don't worry," she told him. "We still have time."

He leaned forward, kissed her on her lips, and smiled. "I do worry, but that's by nature. You are a queen upon this board, Holmes, and my faith in you is unbroken."

❧

In the morning, Inspector Brighton did not look particularly well rested. In fact, he appeared grey, his eyes bloodshot. But he brushed aside Lord Ingram's expressions of concern. "There is nothing to be done. I slept well enough. But perhaps I shouldn't have studied the transcripts as closely."

The sea, too, had become choppier again. Nothing alarming—it remained sunny and the barometric pressure held steady—merely the Atlantic being its ceaseless self. A seasoned and hardy traveler would still consider the conditions favorable, but to someone already suffering from vertigo, the interminable motion underfoot must prove challenging at every turn.

As much as he wanted Inspector Brighton unable to concentrate, Lord Ingram felt an instinctive upswelling of sympathy.

"And although as a policeman I have my qualms, as a man I must command your gallantry," continued Inspector Brighton, inclining his head with some difficulty.

He would be referring to the selective redaction Lord Ingram had performed in his transcription of the interviews, omitting all mentions of Frau Schmidt's visit to Mr. Gregory's room. Lord Ingram had attached a note, explaining that he'd recorded everything verbatim in the shorthand version, but felt Lady Holmes's charges against Frau Schmidt to be unsubstantiated and did not want them repeated in longhand versions that could easily be read by others. Inspector Brighton, in any case, had been there in the library and knew exactly what the excisions entailed.

"Thank you for permitting a measure of gallantry in this investigation, Inspector," said Lord Ingram.

This honorable and harmonious moment, however, did not last very long. "I should like to speak to Mr. Pratt again," said Inspector Brighton, rubbing at his right temple. "But we'd best catch Mr. Smith, the steward on overnight duty, before he goes to bed."

Lord Ingram braced his feet more firmly against the floor. "Mr. Smith, was he also on duty the night of the murder?"

"Correct," came the inexorable answer. "I hope it's not too late for a man who has worked all night."

The man who had worked all night arrived quickly and appeared alert enough: Half past seven in the morning probably amounted to early evening for him, and not the middle of the night. He was in his twenties, with a lean face and close-cropped brown hair—and seemed more curious than apprehensive. Like the other stewards, he remained standing while he answered questions about himself and his work.

Having established that Smith had been a steward on the ship for several voyages between London and Wellington, New Zealand, and had served as the overnight duty steward since the day the ship sailed from Southampton, Inspector Brighton took out the summons log he'd requested the previous afternoon via Lord Ingram and pointed at a few entries.

"Mr. Smith, on the night of the murder, at quarter after three you recorded three summonses that came at the exact same time."

"Yes, Inspector. Actually, two came at very nearly the same time and the third a minute later, while I was still recording the other two."

"Is that not unusual? Three summonses on top of one another?"

"Not in and of itself, sir. Summonses don't come at regular intervals. They either happen in a spate—everyone wanting a cup of tea before the dining saloon opens for breakfast, or everyone wanting a drink before bed—or they come irregularly. It was a bit unusual that I got several summonses at once in the middle of the night, but given that the sea was all roiled up and passengers were awake and worrying, even that was to be expected."

He gave his answer gladly, but unlike his colleague Johnson, whose willingness as a witness had a whiff of ingratiation, Smith seemed simply happy to talk about his work to an attentive audience.

"I see," mused Inspector Brighton. "I notice that although you registered cabin numbers and passenger names, you did not put down any reasons for the summonses except in the case of Mrs. Ramsay's cabin, and listed a fall for Miss Fenwick."

"There is a reason for that, sir," Smith explained patiently. "We aren't required to note down the reasons passengers request service, unless someone is ill—or in Miss Fenwick's case, potentially hurt—or if they request beverages that aren't included in the price of the passage."

"I see. Can you elaborate for me how you handled these three summonses, Mr. Smith?"

"Yes, sir. Of course, sir," said Smith, his eyes bright at the prospect of further discussion. "Summonses from Mrs. Ramsay and Mr. Gregory's cabins came at about the same time. And then there was also a summons from the smoking room. So I decided to first go to Mrs. Ramsay's cabin, since hers was on a lower deck, and since one answers a lady's summons first.

"When I got there, it was rather extraordinary, as Miss Fenwick was fast asleep *on the floor.* Apparently she normally stayed away from sleeping draughts but had a few drops of Mrs. Ramsay's laudanum and went out like a light. Mrs. Ramsay explained that she'd heard a thud, and when she got up to look, she almost stepped on Miss Fenwick, who must have rolled off her bunk.

"I was worried and thought we should call Dr. Bhattacharya. But Mrs. Ramsay said Miss Fenwick wouldn't wish to be poked and prodded in the middle of the night. She sounded sure, so I didn't insist.

"It took us a bit of time to raise Miss Fenwick to the lower bunk because Mrs. Ramsay didn't want me to be the one holding Miss Fenwick under her arms." Smith demonstrated on his own torso where his hands would have been, right under the armpits. "She said that Miss Fenwick was very particular and wouldn't have appreciated a man touching her in that manner, even if it was in aid.

"She's very nice, Mrs. Ramsay, but she's old and frail. We tried a few times, she took some rest in between, but still in the end I took Miss Fenwick under the arms and Mrs. Ramsay took her by the feet and we got Miss Fenwick back into the bunk again.

"Then I went to see Mr. Gregory. He'd tripped when he got up to drink water and spilled most of the water in his cup on his bed. I fetched some fresh linens, remade his bed, and went to the smoking room to answer the third summons.

"Mr. Shrewsbury stood inside, near a window. But when I spoke to him, he didn't respond. He didn't even look at me as he turned around and walked to the other side of the room.

"His eyes were open but he had a glassy look. I waved my hand before his face and still he didn't respond. Occasionally passengers sleepwalk, so I tried to guide him to where he ought to be, but he kept turning around to walk in the opposite direction. It must have taken me at least a quarter hour to return him to his own cabin."

Smith let out a long sigh, as if he'd again spent the better part of eternity shepherding Roger Shrewsbury. "And that would be all three summonses."

Lord Ingram wrote furiously, trying to keep up with the voluble Steward Smith. Even so, he felt Inspector Brighton glance in his direction, a look that froze him to the spleen.

"According to the log, Mr. Smith," said Inspector Brighton after a long minute, "there were no other summonses during your time on duty by yourself?"

"Indeed not, Inspector. The storm quieted down around that time. Passengers must have finally dozed off, and I didn't get the usual requests for tea and whatnot before the end of my shift."

After Smith left, Inspector Brighton turned to Lord Ingram. "How interesting. The passengers who made the requests at the same time, they are all your friends, my lord."

A glacier ground across Lord Ingram's back, an iciness with serrated teeth. At the time his friends and allies had mounted their various antics, he'd been in the duty room, frantically readjusting the wires behind the summons panel, praying that he would finish and be gone before Smith's return. But he would do that ten times over, rather than subject himself to one more second of Inspector Brighton's scrutiny.

"Of the passengers Mr. Smith mentioned," he said, forcing his hand not to clench around his pen, "only Mr. Shrewsbury is an old friend—and our friendship has suffered of late because of his conduct. Mr. Gregory and Mrs. Ramsay are Mrs. Newell's acquaintances, and I never met either before setting foot on the *Provence*."

Inspector Brighton did not argue the point, but instructed an attending steward to see whether Pratt was in the dining saloon, having his breakfast. "If he's not there, bring Mr. Russell. But I want to see Mr. Pratt."

Russell arrived a few minutes later and sat down without a word of greeting to anyone and before a seat was ever offered—it was an efficient way to convey contempt and displeasure.

Inspector Brighton studied him for a moment and got to the point. "Mr. Russell, you were observed disturbing the peace outside Mr. Arkwright's cabin on the night he died. Do you care to explain yourself?"

"What's there to explain? I had a little too much to drink, that's all."

"According to the duty room log, you were not provided with any potent beverages. Did you bring some aboard with you?"

"No, I drank Pratt's whisky. He brought some with him."

"I did not realize you and Mr. Pratt were comrades."

Russell snorted. "Comrades, hardly. Not me, not with a sniveling little man like that. But one had to pass time somehow and he hated Jacob Arkwright, so we had something in common."

"This is not the best time to profess your hatred of Mr. Arkwright, Mr. Russell," Inspector Brighton reminded him.

Russell made a phlegm-y sound in the back of his throat. "If I stopped now, would you think I didn't hate the man? I thought not. So why bother?"

He rose, went to the refreshment cart at the rear of the library, and poured himself a cup of tea. "I might have to speak to the captain. Clearly refreshments have been provided and clearly I've not been offered any. The courtesy of your investigation is greatly wanting, Inspector."

Lord Ingram almost heard the gnashing of Inspector Brighton's teeth.

In a way, Russell was the obverse of Mrs. Ramsay. She had her age and respectability to counterbalance Inspector Brighton's authority, and he his landed gentry arrogance. His nonchalance also reminded Lord Ingram of Norbert. Norbert disguised her blitheness with a deferent, cooperative demeanor; Russell could not be more blatant in his indifference.

Inspector Brighton's voice emerged sharper than usual. "Mr. Russell, where were you between the end of dinner and when you showed up outside Mr. Arkwright's door?"

Russell, now back in his chair, gave a leisurely stir to his tea. "After dinner, I escorted my cousin Mrs. Shrewsbury back to her cabin. Afterwards, in the corridors I encountered Mr. Pratt, who said he heard that I despised Mr. Arkwright. I said I did. He invited me for a drink in his cabin. I was in the mood for a drink and I went."

"What did you discuss?"

"Why would I discuss anything with that man?" Russell tapped a teaspoon on the edge of his teacup, the sound not as alarming as the creaking of the globe, but no less abrupt. "I was there to drink his whisky, which was very middling, by the way. No, he talked. He talked and talked and talked about how sincerely he wished to marry the sister and how shocked and disoriented he was, and how he wished the brother would just let them marry. Mewling, really. Endless, tiresome mewling. On land I'd never be caught in such company."

"How long did you stay?"

"I was drinking. Why would I look at my watch? I left when I couldn't take his whingeing a moment longer. Or was it when I'd finished his whisky—I can't remember now."

"To hurl abuses at Mr. Arkwright outside his door?" The terseness of Inspector Brighton's questions was a clue to his short mood.

Russell shrugged. "I'd have preferred to have another few drinks with Shrewsbury—he's a stupid man, but even he would have been an improvement over Pratt. But Shrewsbury was intent on visiting Lord Ingram, so I entertained myself as best as I could."

Lord Ingram glanced at the globe. Inspector Brighton had yet to set his hand on it. Did he sense that Russell's cavalier attitude hid not fear but an absolute confidence that the investigation could not touch him?

"And then?"

"And then I was in my cabin, sleeping off the whisky for the rest of the night."

"Were I to speak to Mr. Pratt, would he bear out your statement that you were in his cabin until half past ten?"

"If he was paying attention to the minute and the hour, then yes, he should."

Russell left. Inspector Brighton's fingers at last landed on the globe. "Very interesting," he murmured, as if to himself. "Two passengers who have reason to want Mr. Arkwright out of the way form each other's best alibi—or at least that is the case according to Mr. Russell. If memory serves, Mr. Pratt said nothing about Mr. Russell in his account of his evening. I wonder what he would say now."

Lord Ingram glanced at the door. Going by Inspector Brighton's patterns of the day before, he would ring for an attending steward to open the windows and bring a fresh pot of tea, and then, in a few more minutes, call Pratt inside.

Inspector Brighton rang. An attendant came and opened the windows. A short while later he came back with hot water.

"I will see Mr. Pratt now," said the policeman.

The attendant hesitated. "I don't think Welder has located Mr. Pratt yet, Inspector. Shall I also go look for him?"

Pratt had been the one Inspector Brighton wanted to see before Russell. Welder the steward must have been looking for him for a good twenty minutes then, if not close to half an hour. There were only two passenger levels and a few public areas. Since the murder, the captain hadn't allowed tours of the engines or any other areas below deck. It shouldn't take this long to find a passenger, unless he was hiding.

Or unless . . .

Inspector Brighton rose—and swayed as the *Provence* encountered a larger wave. He gripped the top of the globe for balance. "Has anyone checked Mr. Pratt's cabin?"

Twenty-one

B y the time Inspector Brighton and Lord Ingram arrived on the saloon level, a number of passengers had already joined Welder in his search, as he'd made no secret that he was having trouble finding Mr. Pratt. At the detective inspector's request, the head steward, his hand shaking, opened Pratt's door to a neat, empty cabin. No blood, no carnage, no dead man with his eyes still wide open.

This being the hour for breakfast and morning walks, the news that Mr. Pratt could not be found spread with the speed of fire and pestilence. After looking through Pratt's cabin, a wan-looking Inspector Brighton delegated the next step. The master-at-arms and Lord Ingram, the back of his neck prickling, peered into every cupboard and coal bunker below deck, the captain in tow. Captain Pritchard, already in a state of anxiety, was beside himself at Pratt's disappearance.

"If only Sherlock Holmes had come on the *Provence*, too," he lamented. "If only. Will things get any worse, my lord?"

The hairs on Lord Ingram's forearms rose. Was the captain a little too interested in Sherlock Holmes? He'd directed a great deal of wariness against Inspector Brighton, in case the police officer also served as Moriarty's minion. Yet here was Captain Pritchard, Sherlock Holmes's name on his lips at every turn—had he been suspecting the wrong man?

"With regard to how the situation will develop—your guess is as good as mine, Captain. But as for the prowess of Sherlock Holmes . . . These are unusual circumstances. Even Sherlock Holmes needs a working telegraph line to verify information and ascertain motives. At the moment our best policy would be to arrive in Gibraltar posthaste, so that these inquiries can be made."

"Speed, I see." Captain Pritchard inhaled deeply. "We must make haste."

Lord Ingram let out a long breath when the man left for the bridge.

Once the corners and recesses of the ship, likely and unlikely, had been looked into, Inspector Brighton, with Captain Pritchard's permission, ordered a search of all passenger cabins. This engendered a certain amount of grumbling, but given that two lives had been lost and the culprit was still loose, the complaints were neither loud nor sustained.

The search unearthed a pair of service revolvers that belonged to the young lieutenants. Russell, too, had a pistol among his possessions. The missing Mr. Pratt, however, had a set of lock-picking tools stashed deep in his cabin trunk.

Did this overthrow Inspector Brighton's initial theory that only those Mr. Arkwright would have invited into his parlor could have committed the murder?

"I wish, very sincerely, that I'd taken a different steamer." Inspector Brighton rubbed his chin wearily. "On second thought, now that I know I fare no better on ocean voyages than I do on trains, I wish I'd simply taken the overland route all the way to the south of Italy, and only there boarded a seagoing vessel to Malta."

It was not yet four o'clock in the afternoon, and already he looked haggard. Lord Ingram withheld his sympathy and calculated. They'd been at sea for more than seventy-two hours. At latest, day after tomorrow they should reach Gibraltar. And from there, Holmes and

Mrs. Watson could find some excuse, any excuse, to walk ashore and never return.

If anyone would be permitted to disembark, that is.

Inspector Brighton asked for Russell to be brought into the library. Russell arrived in a state of obvious ill humor. Inspector Brighton, the corners of his eyes drooping, his face lined with fatigue, was no more charitably disposed.

"You do realize, Mr. Russell, that your alibi has disappeared. You said you were drinking with Mr. Pratt in his cabin. But it is unlikely Mr. Pratt would ever be able to confirm that."

"And that's too bad," retorted Russell.

"You feel nothing for Mr. Pratt's possible end in a watery grave?"

Russell rolled his eyes. "It's inconvenient for me, certainly. But it wasn't as if I felt anything for the man other than a mild revulsion."

"Do you have any alibi for your whereabouts *last* night?"

Mr. Russell at first frowned, then his jaw clenched with understanding. "No. I slept."

Inspector Brighton crossed his arms before his chest. "I imagine, with Mr. Arkwright dead, you no longer need to fear becoming his very junior partner in your Australian venture."

"Sometimes a stroke of good fortune happens. Why shouldn't I enjoy it?"

"Mr. Russell, why did you bring aboard a pistol?"

"It is a long way from Southampton to Sydney. Who knows what kind of ruffians I might encounter?"

"Do you know how to pick locks, Mr. Russell?"

"What? Of course not. What gentleman would know that sort of thing?"

Lord Ingram, who excelled at lock picking, did not look up.

"You never know what skills any individual might possess, however unlikely on the surface," said Inspector Brighton. "My lord, from what I read of the Stern Hollow case, you have mastered several different styles of penmanship, is that not so?"

Lord Ingram did look up briefly this time. "A personal hobby, yes."

"But not exactly a common competence among people who are not forgers."

"No."

Inspector Brighton, satisfied, turned back to Mr. Russell. "You see, Mr. Russell, there is no reason for you not to be conversant with lock picking."

Mr. Russell snorted. "Nevertheless, I have no idea how to pick a lock. I would kick down a door or shoot a lock before I would pick it."

Inspector Brighton smiled, as if amused by the thought of Mr. Russell violently breaking and entering. The next moment, all mirth disappeared from his face. "One could make the argument that you killed Mr. Arkwright, Mr. Russell. You had clear motives. You have a firearm. You had no alibi for the time he was killed, and the lock-picking tools in Mr. Pratt's cabin could very well be yours.

"You picked the lock on Mr. Arkwright's door so you could ambush him in his own cabin. You thought you'd got away with it, but Mr. Pratt saw something. With his babble about blood in the bath he was signaling you, wasn't he?

"To those in the know, you may be in for a highly uncertain financial future. But Mr. Pratt didn't know. To him, you looked wealthy enough. And with Miss Arkwright unlikely to marry him, why shouldn't he take advantage of what he'd seen and bilk you for some funds?

"But he played a dangerous game. Too dangerous. You, not being able to afford a bloodsucking leech, decided to get rid of him instead. What could be easier than setting up a little rendezvous last night and pitching him overboard? And then this morning you conveniently used him as your alibi, knowing that he would not contradict you, not anymore."

At first, Russell listened with a sneer on his face. Gradually the sneer disappeared. "Maybe one could make an argument of that ilk. But one could also argue that you, Inspector, are a vainglorious copper who resorts to the most outlandish claims in order to call a case solved. You are just that, aren't you?"

Inspector Brighton tapped his fingers on the globe, once, twice, three times. "Insult me all you care, Mr. Russell. But the law applies even to those who disdain it. Perhaps you have nothing to fear; perhaps you have everything to fear. We will know soon enough."

Twenty-two

THE NIGHT OF THE MURDER

"Well, that was unexpected," said Charlotte, after Roger Shrewsbury's departure.

Her lover let loose a string of expletives. They looked at each other. Something terrible had taken place. There was a Scotland Yard inspector traveling aboard the *Provence*. And they had been at something illicit tonight, which they would need to conceal from this expert investigator.

"If Roger Shrewsbury was correct about where he'd stood, he'd have been almost directly underneath the window of Mr. Arkwright's parlor," said Lord Ingram.

She walked to the sofa and set down the plate in her hand. "Do you have your lock-picking tools?"

Before they could formulate a plan on how to protect themselves, they needed to know what had happened.

His eyes widened in astonishment, but only for a moment. "We came aboard with theft in mind—of course I have my lock-picking tools."

They checked the library first, because it was also possible that the revolver had been thrown out from one of its windows. The library was empty and undisturbed. As soon as they neared Mr. Arkwright's door, however, Lord Ingram sank to one knee on the floor. Here the varnished, amber-hued surface was marred with a thin, inch-long smear of a dark red substance.

"Blood?" Charlotte murmured.

"Blood."

There were two other small streaks of blood, everything located within a few feet of Mr. Arkwright's door. They found no visible traces toward the library or aft in the direction of Miss Arkwright's cabin. The way to the stairs was also clean.

Charlotte knelt down and looked closely at the smears of blood. They seemed to convey . . . contradictory information. Then again, maybe not. The marks stretched toward the door, as if a bleeding person had been pulled into the cabin. But at a later point, when the stains had largely but not entirely dried, they'd been acted on by some force that tugged toward the staircase, erasing them partially in the process.

Could the victim have been shot in the corridor and then dragged inside? Setting aside the fact the gunshot had produced too little blood, would that not have been loud enough to alert the other passengers, even if the foghorn had been braying at the same time?

How far and at what strength sound traveled depended not only on the force of the original noise but on atmospheric and other conditions. The storm would have dampened a shot on deck. But a shot in the passages, the bang echoed and magnified by the smooth teak floor and the equally smooth white wall paneling—someone should have heard.

Lord Ingram rose and knocked on Mr. Arkwright's door. When he received no response, he picked the lock—not the easiest task with the ship rolling and buckling. Charlotte kept watch for him. It was not the best idea for her to be abroad, barely disguised. But with Shrewsbury back in his own cabin and ordered to stay there, she didn't anticipate running into anyone else who would raise a hue-and-cry upon seeing her real face.

Her lover put away his tools—he'd succeeded then. He turned around and indicated that she should wait for him between the boiler casings, where she would be less likely to be seen.

Be careful, she mouthed.

He nodded, entered the cabin, and closed the door behind him.

She listened, one hand braced on a boiler casing, cold metal vibrating beneath her palm. With her other hand she held her pocket watch. The second hand must have developed a phobia of time itself: It quivered in place, refusing to advance.

A very long four minutes later, the door opened a crack; she peered around, then crossed the passage and slipped inside. The parlor was dark—the entire suite thick with night. The air smelled fresher than she'd expected, cold and damp.

"The place is empty," murmured her lover, opening the shutter on his pocket lantern. She'd have preferred to use the cabin's electric lamp, but its intense luminosity might attract unwanted attention, especially if anyone, like Shrewsbury, happened to venture out to the starboard promenade.

The light from the pocket lantern swung to the right. "There is Mr. Arkwright, dead."

A bulky shape cast a low shadow against the wall. Charlotte exhaled.

The feeble ray of light now alit on a puddle deep in the parlor. "There's water by the window, possibly from when the window was opened to eject the revolver," Lord Ingram continued, his voice tight but even.

The light traveled left. "And then there's *that*."

Large scarlet letters had been scribbled on the wall, defacing not only the white paneling but the entirety of a painting. COMMON. VULGAR. BASEB—which likely would have been BASEBORN, had the writer not decided to stop scrawling for whatever reason.

"The accusations sound like my mother," she said, "giving vent to her feelings about heiresses who keep pocketing our impecunious noblemen."

"I hope not to encounter Lady Holmes in a homicidal mood. But as for the words themselves, I don't believe they are written in blood. The substance didn't drip and smelled faintly sweet."

Curious. "Is that a revolver on the floor under the painting?"

"Yes, and a monogrammed walking stick, too. The firearm is quite clean. I had a look at it. Webley. Five chambers. Three empty."

"Do I need to watch where I put my feet?"

"I would encourage you to, but other than a puddle of blood under Mr. Arkwright, the floor seems clean—or at least with this dim illumination it seems clean."

Sidestepping the blood puddle, she inched closer to Mr. Arkwright and crouched down. She didn't want to disturb the body or betray their presence. Once the murder was discovered in the morning, a great many people would come trooping through this cabin, the killer among them, perhaps.

A rough observation revealed that Mr. Arkwright had been shot once in the shoulder. But he would have died of a head wound. That made for two bullets fired.

Roger Shrewsbury had been sure that only one chamber had been emptied in the revolver he'd thrown overboard.

She moved to the revolver on the other side of the parlor and opened the action. As Lord Ingram had said, five chambers, three empty.

"Whoever shot Mr. Arkwright did so from near the window," she deemed. "Mr. Arkwright would have stood near the door."

Under normal circumstances he might have fallen on his back, but it was possible that he'd already been stumbling forward from the ship's motion.

She closed the revolver, set it back on the floor, took the lantern from Lord Ingram, and scanned the wall opposite the window. "There. That might be a bullet hole."

Lord Ingram moved to examine the aperture near the doorjamb. "You're right. The bullet is still inside."

If the revolver on the floor had killed Mr. Arkwright, why was that not the weapon thrown away? Shrewsbury had mentioned that the revolver he'd found had five chambers and might have been a Webley. This one also had five chambers and was a Webley. Had the killer been confused in the moment?

She inspected the parlor in greater detail, beginning at the window. The puddle. The rain-dampened sofa under the window. The floor. The walls. Mr. Arkwright's lifeless form. More floor. More walls. The walking stick. The bullet hole. The desk by the door with the cabin key thrown on top.

Silently, patiently, Lord Ingram held the lantern for her.

"Is your arm not tired?"

"For you, no. Otherwise, a bit."

She smiled a little and sank to her knees. She only had the floor under the desk left to scrutinize.

Thunder cracked. The *Provence* listed hard to port. Her head almost hit the desk. Lord Ingram's shoulder banged into the wall. She took the pocket lantern from him so she could see better into the darkest recess. Something gleamed in the feeble light.

"Who are you and what are you doing here in my brother's parlor?" demanded a woman's voice. "Where is my brother?"

Charlotte froze. When she looked back, Lord Ingram was already in front of her, his revolver drawn. With one hand on the desk, she pulled herself upright and shone her lantern in the direction of the sleeping cabin.

Its door had been shut earlier, but now in the doorframe stood Miss Arkwright, ghostly in her loose hair and her voluminous white nightgown.

Her brother lay less than ten feet from where she stood, but with the pocket lantern the only illumination in the entire suite, it was possible that she hadn't seen his body, a shadow among shadows.

If she was telling the truth about not knowing where he was, that is.

Time slowed. Charlotte sorted through potential answers and their ramifications—she wasan explorer of hedge mazes, testing the turns to see which ones led to viable paths, and which ones blind alleys.

"What are *you* doing here, Miss Arkwright?"

Her question was serious, her tone firm, without the least awkwardness at having been caught trespassing. Someone had been shot dead. She knew herself to be innocent. She could not say the same about Miss Arkwright.

"I—" Miss Arkwright stared at Charlotte, incredulity sweeping across her face. "I'd taken some wine and gone to bed. But just now, Mr. Russell was outside shouting, saying far worse things than Mr. Shrewsbury ever did. I worried that my brother might begin another altercation, but then he didn't, and I realized that the light in the connecting bath had gone dark. He'd specifically told me not to turn it off at night, so—"

Lord Ingram held up a hand. Charlotte heard it, too, minute scratches at the lock. Lord Ingram took her by the arm and steered her toward where Miss Arkwright stood. Charlotte placed a finger over her lips to signal for silence. Miss Arkwright shook as Charlotte took her by the wrist, but allowed herself to be led into the sleeping cabin.

Lord Ingram closed the door. They continued to retreat until they stood at the connecting door between the en-suite bath and Miss Arkwright's cabin. Charlotte extinguished the pocket lantern in her hand. At almost that exact moment, the electric lamp came on in Mr. Arkwright's parlor, the light seeping through under the door.

Outside, the sea still lashed, wind still howled, and rain still pounded the *Provence*. Would they have heard sobs of disbelief and horror if the intruder had made such sounds?

Charlotte had barely counted to five when Lord Ingram guided the women into Miss Arkwright's cabin and latched the door.

She had no idea how long they waited, her hand in her lover's, perhaps only a minute, perhaps fifteen.

And then the connecting door latched on the other side, the small sound that should have been drowned out by the storm explosive in her ears.

Charlotte let go of her lover's hand and took Miss Arkwright by the arm. Like that for Lord Ingram's children, Miss Arkwright's accommodation was a parlor cabin that boasted both a sleeping cabin and a parlor. From the connecting bath they had entered her sleeping cabin, now Charlotte walked her to her parlor. There she lit her pocket lantern again.

A pea-sized flame flickered to life.

"Would you like to have a seat, Miss Arkwright?"

The meager reddish light cast shadows across Miss Arkwright's face; the shadows quivered with the thrashing of the ship. "Would someone please tell me what's going on? And who are you two?"

"This is Lord Ingram Ashburton, and I am his lover," Charlotte answered.

Behind her, her lover shifted.

Miss Arkwright blinked. "Lord Ingram's—wait, why are you in a stewardess uniform?"

"Oh, the uniform. It's but a costume, to add a little piquancy to what would otherwise be a long, uncomfortable night. Lord Ingram's children are traveling with him. So you understand, Miss Arkwright, that of course he hasn't brought a lover. I am not on this voyage at all."

"No, of course not." Miss Arkwright's incomprehension became only thicker. "I—I understand."

"I'm glad you do. As for what is going on—are you sure you wouldn't prefer to sit down first?"

"My God, Jacob!" Miss Arkwright was still whispering, but her voice suddenly pierced. "*Jacob.*"

"I'm very sorry to inform you that your brother has been slain."

Miss Arkwright stared at Charlotte with the kind of disbelief that was, in fact, a desperate hope that she had not heard what she had heard—that if she concentrated hard enough on the strangeness of the messenger, she didn't have to truly understand the message.

"He—you—"

"It was not our doing. We were alerted to the fact that something might be amiss when Mr. Shrewsbury—yes, that Mr. Shrewsbury—called on his lordship. Mr. Shrewsbury had been standing on the saloon deck, below the window of your brother's parlor, when a revolver fell from above and very nearly struck him."

"Lord Ingram and I decided to investigate. We saw some traces of blood outside Mr. Arkwright's cabin, which alarmed us. We were able to enter, and what greeted us was death."

Miss Arkwright panted. "Jacob, I need to see him. I need to see him."

"I would not advise it. That was most likely his killer who had come back. We don't know whether he has left, and we don't know whether he might return again during the night. It won't be safe for you to see your brother until morning—and it also won't make a difference to him whether you sought him now or later."

Miss Arkwright spread her fingers over her face, only to ball them into fists, her knuckles against her jaw. "My God, he was just telling me about it this evening. I always thought there was something strange about our departure from England. He'd commissioned an entire wardrobe, hired a house in London until the end of July, and was in the middle of looking for a place in the country, a place with its own grouse population, so that he could treat guests to some good shooting.

"And then all of a sudden he asked me if I was willing to come with him to Australia. Obviously I said yes in the end, but I'd thought I wouldn't have to make that decision for months.

"He never did answer my question on what prompted him to leave—until this evening, when he told me that he was more or less ordered to go, by someone who threatened to reveal his true identity and the reason he'd had to run halfway across the world."

"Did he kill anyone? Was that why he'd fled all those years ago?"

Lord Ingram's hand settled on Charlotte's lower back. Was he worried that her question had been too blunt?

But Miss Arkwright only swallowed. "Before he ran away, he swore to me he didn't do it. This time, he swore again, not only on his life but on his entire fortune, that he was innocent. That he'd indeed been framed."

Charlotte leaned back slightly, enjoying the contact with her lover. "The person who framed him was the one who'd committed the crime in the first place?"

"And the one who'd threatened exposure to force him to leave Britain." Miss Arkwright's voice thickened. She trembled, too, though she seemed not to realize it. "He said he got scared. Everything had been coming up roses for him, and we even became reunited. And then this threat. The thought of losing it all terrified him, and he believed he had no choice but to leave as soon as possible.

"But after I explained to him how I was powerless before the kind of rumors Mr. Shrewsbury spread, he became angry and ashamed at his earlier reaction. He'd run, too, even though he was no longer powerless and hadn't been for a long time. Why hadn't he stayed and fought? And why had he believed he would be any safer in Australia when the man already knew his current identity? No, it was the other way. He was the innocent party. It was the other man who ought to be afraid.

"And then this morning he heard the whistling of an odd tune in the gentlemen's baths, a tune he'd only ever heard from that man. And when he'd shouted the man's name, the whistler fled. Since then, Jacob had been trying to see if that had been him indeed."

Lord Ingram took a step back—he must have determined that tonight at least Miss Arkwright posed no threat. Charlotte hadn't been cold earlier, but now she missed the warmth of his protective touch. "Did Mr. Arkwright tell you the man's name?"

"Yes, Ned Plowers, but he couldn't find the name on either the passenger list or the crew list, so he suspected that Plowers had also changed his name." Miss Arkwright glanced in the direction of her brother's suite. "Before we parted ways this evening, Jacob showed me a list of names that he'd made—he'd struck off everyone he'd seen on board. That's part of the reason I chose to believe you and Lord Ingram, because he had crossed off his lordship—whatever the former Ned Plowers had become, he could never have turned into a wellborn gentleman."

"Do you remember the names that still remained on the list?"

Miss Arkwright shook her head, her cheeks tight with frustration. "Jacob wanted me to know and to beware; he didn't want me involved in the search—or anywhere near Ned Plowers. So I only saw the list for a second."

"Where is that list, Miss Arkwright?" Lord Ingram spoke for the first time since their flight into Miss Arkwright's cabin.

Miss Arkwright started, as if she'd forgotten that there was a man in their midst. "It—it was on the writing desk in his parlor."

Charlotte exchanged a look with her lover. The list, if it existed, was no longer there.

"Looks like Plowers took it," she said. "Your brother was right about not wanting you near the man—he is indeed dangerous."

Miss Arkwright chewed her lower lip. The parlor fell silent. Outside, waves pummeled the ship. Underfoot, the floor leaped and shuddered. Seconds fled, a loss of time that Charlotte could ill afford.

"At the moment there's nothing more you can do for your brother, Miss Arkwright," she said. "But you must think of yourself. Are you prepared for what's coming? A murder investigation grinds up all privacy in its path. Mr. Arkwright's recent conflict with Mr. Shrewsbury would be brought up. You would be questioned concerning details that might be distasteful to you."

"I see," mumbled Miss Arkwright.

"But that is not the worst. A good investigator does not eliminate anyone from suspicion. Are you a beneficiary of your brother's will, Miss Arkwright?"

Miss Arkwright gazed again in the direction of her brother's suite. The shadows on her face seemed to lengthen and grow darker. "Yes. He made me his sole heir."

"As his sole heir—and as someone who is of age and can control that fortune from the moment you inherit it—you have as much motive as anyone else."

The dead man's sister jerked. For the first time, she looked truly fearful. "Then—what should I do?"

Twenty-three

The cabin search had been announced while most passengers were at luncheon. Passengers who lingered elsewhere were rounded up. Those who had ordered meals sent to their cabins were also cordially requested to make their way—trays in hand, if they so wished—to the dining saloon.

Miss Arkwright appeared in the venue for the first time since the *Provence* weighed anchor. Eyes followed her, a curiosity that was less than friendly. Charlotte took advantage of the distraction she created and stole a piece of chipped potato from Mrs. Watson's plate. The potato, fried golden, was crispy on the exterior, soft inside, and salted just enough to make her taste buds rage for more.

She licked the back of her teeth in futile longing and pushed away her own plate.

Next to her, Mrs. Watson lifted a hand in greeting to Miss Arkwright. Miss Arkwright returned a grim smile and walked past. Perhaps she chose not to sit with them because Livia and Mrs. Newell shared their table, or perhaps that would not have swayed her decision one way or the other. Fuller stood in a corner and stared at Miss Arkwright. He looked pinched, his gaze both worried and resentful.

Livia, who had been largely silent, hissed, a sharp intake of air through clenched teeth. "Anne Shrewsbury is looking at me. How dare she?"

Charlotte, who was already turned halfway around in her chair, glanced toward the table Mrs. Shrewsbury and Mr. Russell usually occupied by the starboard windows. Mr. Russell, for once, did not sit with Mrs. Shrewsbury. Roger Shrewsbury had his head lowered almost to his chest. His wife tested the struts of her open French fan one by one, pale fingertips creeping across painted blue silk.

"Now she pretends she didn't," came Livia's irate comment.

Frau Schmidt and Miss Potter entered from the aft, herding their four charges. The party of six sat down at the same table. Norbert, who had been standing near the forward entrance, rushed over full of solicitous inquiries. Soon she was seated next to Frau Schmidt, her arm around Rupert Pennington's shoulder. She tried to pull Georg Bittner to her lap, but the boy wriggled away to rub elbows with the Ashburton children.

After luncheon, the gentlemen were taken elsewhere and the ladies and their handbags searched. For the first time in her life Charlotte had a pair of women lift her skirt to expose the structure of her bustle, to make sure nothing had been hidden there. They also, apologetically, ran their hands over her body.

But of course the vial that contained what remained of her cosmetic solution was inserted somewhere the stewardesses would *not* think to check.

Once she had emerged from behind the privacy screen set up in a corner of the dining saloon, Charlotte happily proceeded to the central table presided over by the head stewardess and handed over her handbag, with its supply of bonbons, cough drops, and suppositories. But her attention was again on Norbert.

Mr. Gregory had kept his distance from Frau Schmidt for obvious reasons. He would have passed on the message that he and his friends would try their utmost so that no malicious gossip about her gained a toehold on board, but Frau Schmidt, understandably, was anxious.

The glow Charlotte had witnessed post-rendezvous had disappeared. She did not look haggard but rather exactly who she was, a governess decades past her first bloom, a woman who questioned herself and feared for her future.

Into this fraught scenario Norbert had entered seamlessly with her concern and solidarity. She had not been present when Lady Holmes had brought Frau Schmidt into her testimony, but Charlotte was certain she knew of the governess's difficult straits. Had she proposed to help Frau Schmidt defend her reputation—or at least outlast the police interrogation?

Soon it became Frau Schmidt's turn to have her handbag searched. The head stewardess, stationed at one of the dining saloon's long central tables, looked through the contents of her satchel, placing everything on the table. Next to her another stewardess took notes.

Norbert did not limit herself to this proper look at everything in Frau Schmidt's satchel. As her own handbag was being rummaged through, she got the governess to open her repacked satchel and take out a few items so Norbert could look at them up close.

The search of the ladies' persons and handbags, as far as Charlotte could tell, turned up nothing except five pounds that thrilled Mrs. Newell, as she'd thought she'd lost the banknote.

The search of the cabins similarly failed to advance the investigation.

Charlotte spent the rest of her afternoon chatting to her fellow passengers, only to find out that Mr. Pratt had told his story to just about everyone. Inspector Brighton used his time to question those members of the crew who had met the victim. When he was done for the day, Lord Ingram compiled a list of everyone who had *not* seen Mr. Arkwright—and in return had also not been seen by him. But who was to say that the murderer, should he or she number among the crew, wouldn't have lied about it?

At half past nine that evening, Charlotte met Norbert in Livia's cabin. Or rather, Livia summoned Norbert, saying that she wished to hold a private conversation. But when Norbert arrived, only Charlotte was waiting.

Charlotte, her skin now smarting under her disguise, which had been plastered to her face for more than forty hours, indicated for Norbert to take a seat on the bed. *"Him þæs liffrea, wuldres wealdend, woroldare forgeaf."*

Norbert sighed. *"Beowulf wæs breme blæd wide sprang, Scyldes eafera Scedelandum in."*

The lines from *Beowulf* were meant to identify Lord Remington's subordinates. It made sense for him to station someone inside the Holmes household, to deny Moriarty that opportunity, if nothing else.

The password had been how Mr. Gregory had revealed himself to Charlotte and Lord Ingram. Norbert, on the other hand, had opted *not* to let Charlotte know that she was, theoretically, on her side.

Charlotte poured whisky into a travel cup, amber liquid splashing against bright silver, and handed it to Norbert.

Norbert cleared her throat and accepted, not quite looking at Charlotte. Charlotte studied her without wavering. Not staring at people had been something she'd had to practice; staring at someone at length had never presented any difficulties.

Norbert took a sip of whisky and again cleared her throat. "May I say that your disguise is very good, Miss Holmes?"

Charlotte had not been content to settle for Lord Remington's aegis of protection—frankly she hadn't been too certain of its strength and potency. What she really wanted was his agents loaned to her: Her talents as a budding mastermind would be wasted if she didn't have enough capable individuals to carry out her plans.

Next time, however, if she desired such outcomes, she would bargain with Remington directly, and not through an intermediary. His emissary Mr. Dannell, who relayed the terms of her demands to his overlord, had not wanted to become her subordinate, however temporarily. And Norbert, unless she was very much mistaken, had come because Dannell wanted one of his own, someone other than Charlotte, to obtain the dossier.

"And let me not forget to apologize." Norbert rose and inclined her head. "If I'd known that Lady Holmes would be so . . . feisty away from home, I would not have brought her on board. As it was, when Mr. Dannell sent word, it seemed a good idea for me not to leave my position abruptly, not before we had a candidate ready to take my place."

Every cabin Charlotte had seen aboard had a sofa under the window, and Livia's was no exception. Charlotte walked over and sat down on it. "You arranged for her to find the tickets, I take it?"

"Yes, miss. She was feeling restless in London and it wasn't difficult to persuade her to use those tickets that she 'found.'"

Lord Ingram had mentioned that Norbert's obliging attitude hid a great indifference—where Inspector Brighton was concerned, at least. Here Norbert was equally deferential, a pleasant smile on her face, her replies prompt and unforced. But was she going to prove just as much of a stumbling block for Charlotte?

Livia had been thoughtful enough to arrange for biscuits in her cabin. Charlotte took one. Hmm, a lemon biscuit, its sweetness bright and tangy on her tongue. "Miss Norbert, I'd like to know the contents of Frau Schmidt's satchel."

"Let me see," murmured Norbert.

And proceeded to knit her brows in concentration.

"Mr. Dannell fears being under my authority," said Charlotte, "so much so that he arranged for you to work at cross-purposes. I see no reason to conceal this from Lord Remington. In fact, I plan to let him know as soon as possible."

Norbert's expression stiffened.

"There is, however, no reason I cannot put in a good word for you, Miss Norbert," continued Charlotte. "After all, you are the—relatively—innocent party in this."

But keep working at cross-purposes and there would be no good word for you. There might be the opposite.

Norbert hesitated a moment, and only a moment. "Do you know, miss, I almost forgot, but I actually wrote down a list of what was in Frau Schmidt's satchel."

She took out a small notebook from a hidden pocket in her skirt, opened it to a page in the back, and came forward and offered it to Charlotte.

The list read:

A stack of handkerchiefs, four in all
Notebook and pencil (The notebook contains only progress on R. Pennington's
lessons)
One package of sticking plasters
One multipurpose pocket knife
One jar of ointment
One shawl
One spare pair of gloves
One sewing pouch and a small bag of buttons
One paper pouch of phenacetin pills
One package of perforated tissue paper
One box of safety matches
Two family letters
An abridged volume of The Count of Monte Cristo *by A. Dumas*

So the governess at least had a book for herself.

"That's everything set down by the investigation," said Norbert. "But naturally one also finds the usual detritus at the bottom of the satchel—a match or two that had escaped the box, a few farthings, a few safety pins, and the sort."

"What did you think?"

Norbert shook her head. "At the moment I would say whatever it is we are looking for must be in Frau Schmidt's steamer trunks in the luggage hold."

"The night of the storm Lord Ingram and I already searched trunks in the hold belonging to everyone in her cabin."

"Oh! You must not have slept a wink that night."

Charlotte waved her hand—such unspeakable suffering; best not to speak of it again. "I imagine you searched her house, too, while you were in London?"

"Yes, I did."

For the first time, Norbert's voice betrayed a hint of frustration. Charlotte read the list again. She was beginning to believe that she would be able to identify Mr. Arkwright's murderer fairly soon. But would she also find the dossier before she was forced to disembark the *Provence*?

The night was bright and clear. Livia's hat ribbons danced, held aloft by fresh, bracing currents. A trail of bluish froth churned and splashed in the ship's wake, a sound almost as soothing and silence-like as that of soft waves lapping at the edge of a shingle beach.

The first time Livia had been on a steamer—a night crossing of the English Channel—it had been fiercely cold. And there had been no moon, no stars, only thick clouds hanging from horizon to horizon. But she had been full of a rare exuberance. For freedom, for adventure, for love.

Her dear Mr. Marbleton had stood beside her, smiling, and it had been wonderful. Everything had been wonderful.

She moved from the aft rail to the port promenade and tried to make out the stony silhouette of Portugal in the distance. Sometime in the night the *Provence* would round Cape St. Vincent, the southwesternmost point of the Iberian Peninsula, indeed of entire mainland Europe. And she would be as close as she had ever been to Andalusia in the south of Spain, where he had spent some of the happiest days of his life.

But he, in his caged-songbird imprisonment, had never been farther away.

"Miss Holmes, may I have a word?"

Livia whipped around. Anne Shrewsbury stood erect, her cape streaming, her features stark in the moonlight.

Livia suddenly understood how the late Mr. Arkwright must have felt that morning in the hotel foyer. A hot rage. A surge of wild energy. A fist hurtling forward as if it had been launched by heavy artillery.

Had she more experience in the punching of others—or any at all—Anne Shrewsbury would have crumpled to the deck, yowling. As it was, Livia's nails dug into the center of her palm, but her hand remained by her side and her violence remained imaginary.

"I don't wish to hear anything from you unless it is an abject apology to my sister," she said coldly.

Mrs. Shrewsbury laughed, a soft, insubstantial *ha* that quickly disappeared into the night. "No, that you will not have."

"Then you may leave."

Without waiting for a response, Livia turned back and set her hands on the top rail. To her surprise Anne Shrewsbury, too, approached the rail. She looked down. "I will not apologize, but I will tell you this, Miss Holmes. I believed that bringing down a scarlet woman would make me feel vindicated, if nothing else. But it didn't. It has made me think about your sister morning and night, in a way that I have never bothered with anyone else."

Livia, too, stared down at the line of foam where the hull met the sea. Anne Shrewsbury was right, this was not an apology. But it was an admission. Of guilt, misery, and perhaps even concern.

You stupid woman.

That was not an unfair judgment: Everyone involved in Charlotte's downfall had displayed astonishing asininity, Charlotte herself most of all.

"I am more than happy to see you wretched," Livia said, "you and your husband."

Anne Shrewsbury flinched but said nothing.

"But for reasons I do not understand, my sister has never blamed you—either of you. As far as I can tell, she does not miss Society at all. And she has prospered since last summer."

"Is that so?" Anne Shrewsbury's sentence, full of self-mockery, floated away on a gust of wind.

She slipped away, only to turn around and cry, "Good. Maybe now I won't need to think about her ever again!"

—❧—

The rising sun parted a bank of clouds and stained the horizon red and gold.

Lord Ingram stood at the bow as the ship sailed directly into that sunrise. During the night the *Provence* had rounded the Iberian Peninsula and was now headed east.

They should reach Gibraltar tonight.

He braced his hands on the cap rail and closed his eyes. Wind ruffled his hair and reverberated in his ears. A few droplets landed on his hand, a cool, damp touch from the waves.

He exhaled, turned, and headed for the library, now exhibiting all the charms of a Château d'If prison cell. He loathed the thought of crossing its threshold, loathed the sensations of its walls and shelves closing in, loathed the sight of the squeaky globe, which he longed to lubricate and to smash with equal intensity.

He found Inspector Brighton already seated in the library. The policeman sported a pair of bloodshot eyes again. His jacket was rumpled, his necktie skewed noticeably to the left, as if he had not looked in the mirror before he left his cabin.

After a simple greeting, Inspector Brighton drank two cups of black tea in complete silence. A rich, bitter aroma wafted. Lord Ingram, his heartbeat accelerating with every passing minute, looked out of the forward-facing windows. A sliver of brown-and-green landmass showed in the narrow gap between the bridge and the upper deck.

Gibraltar tonight, he repeated to himself. Gibraltar tonight, deliverance tomorrow?

But first, he must get through this day.

He was beginning to perspire when Inspector Brighton called for Mr. Russell to be brought in again. He bit his lower lip so as not to exhale too obviously.

Russell was warier this morning, a fox sniffing for a trap. He did not attempt any antagonistic action, but sat down and waited.

"Mr. Russell, do you know of a Miss Corwin in Sydney that Mr. Arkwright might have wished to marry?"

Lord Ingram looked up at this unexpected question.

Russell blinked. "No, I don't. Mr. Arkwright wasn't known to possess any interest in matrimony. Last I heard, his mistress was a wealthy widow named Mrs. Saunders. There was never any Miss Corwin linked with him. And believe me, I kept abreast of his news."

This last was said with a lip twist of self-disdain.

"You are sure about that, Mr. Russell?"

"Yes, I'm absolutely certain."

"Thank you, Mr. Russell. You may leave."

Lord Ingram vaguely recalled, and only because he'd transcribed his initial notes into longhand, that Fuller, Mr. Arkwright's valet, had, in the course of his first interview, referred to Miss Arkwright as Miss Cor—before catching himself and explaining that he'd accidentally called her by the name belonging to an Australian young lady.

"You've been reading over the notes again, Inspector?"

One had to admire the policeman's persistence.

Inspector Brighton rubbed both temples. "Only in the hope of nabbing the culprit sooner. Or at least to hand everything over to the Gibraltar Police Force in good order."

Fuller arrived not long after.

The policeman ate a biscuit and made him wait. The valet managed not to fidget, but he blinked more and more rapidly.

Inspector Brighton finished his biscuit, wiped his fingertips with a napkin, and tapped the top of the globe. "My lord, would you read back what Mr. Fuller said concerning Miss Corwin?"

Lord Ingram found the spot in Mr. Fuller's interview and recited the exchange word for word.

The valet's Adam's apple bobbed. "Did I say all that? I'm afraid I recall very little of that morning, Inspector."

"Do you stand by your original statement?"

Fuller shot a dark look at Lord Ingram, as if it were Lord Ingram's fault that he now had to answer questions on what he himself had said. "I—ah—why wouldn't I stand by it, Inspector?"

"Think carefully, Mr. Fuller. Soon it will be possible to verify your statements via cable."

"But what does it matter whether that particular statement is true?"

"I will decide whether the truth of any particular statement matters, Mr. Fuller. From you, I only require a simple answer. Do you stand by your original statement?"

Fuller gripped his hands together. He swallowed again. "Yes, I do."

Inspector Brighton set his palm against the middle of the globe and rotated it a few degrees in one direction, then the other. This did not produce any creaks, but invoked an instinctive discomfort in Lord Ingram, as if the policeman had done something unnatural.

"You are sure about it, Mr. Fuller? You would not wish to be caught lying openly to an officer of the law."

Fuller bit down on his lower lip. "Yes, I'm sure about it."

The door opened and in walked Miss Arkwright. Fuller rose and bowed to his late employer's sister, Miss Arkwright inclined her head, but neither looked the other in the eye.

Inspector Brighton, rising with a grimace, dismissed Fuller and invited Miss Arkwright to take a seat. Once everyone had settled down, he said, "Miss Arkwright, describe for me, if you would, your childhood."

Miss Arkwright shifted, the layers of her starched petticoats shushing. "It was an ordinary childhood on the Liverpool waterfront."

"Is such a thing possible?" Inspector Brighton's question was conversational. He might have been at a dinner party and just learned of the ground-breaking of the Eiffel Tower. "I may not know Liverpool's waterfront intimately, but in my line of work I've met a great many criminals from that particular environs. By 'ordinary,' Miss Arkwright, do you mean destitute and desperate?"

It almost looked as if Miss Arkwright would not reply, then she said, "It was not easy."

"No, indeed. Sometimes it's a wonder anyone survives such a childhood. Yet many do. I must congratulate you on not only surviving but somehow thriving, even before your brother returned with his millions."

Inspector Brighton's tone was soft, almost kindly, yet Miss Arkwright's jaw clenched.

"I don't know much about handkerchief-embroidering operations, especially ones that cater to Savile Row shops," continued the policeman, "but even supposing your employees all worked from home, Miss Arkwright, saving you the expense of a shop front, you still needed to buy silk and linen handkerchiefs in bulk and supply needles and threads. Not to mention you must obtain presentable garments for yourself, and be willing to invest years to establish your reputation with those hoity-toity tailors that serve the cream of the crop."

He gazed at her, his expression quizzical. "Where did an orphan girl from the waterfront of Liverpool, whose brother ran away from home well before she reached majority, obtain the funding for such a respectable undertaking?"

Miss Arkwright, whose face grew more shuttered the more Inspector Brighton analyzed the difficulties that she must have faced, said only, "I had a benefactor."

"A benefactor who helped you out of the sheer goodness of his heart?"

"No, I worked for him, of course."

"What kind of work?"

"Chores and errands."

Inspector Brighton picked up a pencil from the collapsible table beside his chair and spun it between his fingers. "What types of chores and errands paid well enough for you to establish, while still a very young woman, this independent venture of your own? No, don't look offended, Miss Arkwright. I've come across many prostitutes in my professional life and I do not think you are one—at least not habitually, whatever Mr. Shrewsbury may think. Which makes me wonder, what *did* you do for this benefactor of yours?"

Miss Arkwright returned the blind gaze of a stone statue. "Nothing unusual. He was simply generous and I simply lucky."

"Nobody from such a background is that lucky. And whatever luck they obtain must come at considerable cost." The policeman set the pencil back down with a soft yet ominous click. "What was your cost, Miss Arkwright?"

<hr>

"A valid question—Miss Arkwright's story does sound too good to be true," murmured Holmes.

From within Lord Ingram's embrace. Her hair tickled his cheek. Her hand, very mobile for someone who was so good at being completely still, trailed down the center of his spine, not roaming but methodically exploring, vertebra by vertebra.

The moment she stopped, he loosened his hold on her: She did not like to be held overlong. Even if she now openly said she missed him—after an absence of a few hours—*and* initiated embraces—this one, for example—her instinctual preferences hadn't changed. And he wanted to make sure that he always heeded them.

He took half a step back, but she remained in place at the center of his parlor, her still-short hair a golden halo around her still-reddened face. He lifted his hand but stopped short of touching her.

"Does it hurt?"

"There's a smarting sensation, but it's tolerable."

She'd worn her makeup for almost two entire days, not taking that layer off until she came into his cabin last night, after her meeting with Norbert. She hadn't left since. What little remained of the solution had to be saved for when Mrs. Ramsay absolutely must make an appearance in public, and his private bath made it easier for her undisguised person to stay away from prying eyes.

Her attention finally shifted to the interrogation food he'd brought back from the library. She imprinted a quick kiss on his palm, which still hovered beside her face, then rounded him to reach for the plate on the desk.

The prickling of heat hadn't yet faded from the center of his palm when he told her, "After Inspector Brighton dismissed Miss Arkwright, he questioned those passengers to whom Mr. Pratt had told his story of bloody water in the baths."

There's nothing more to be learned here, the policeman had said wearily after he'd ended his last session. *We must now place our faith in the technological marvels of this century.*

"I think he has decided on the identity of the culprit," Lord Ingram went on. "And is only waiting on the remainder of his suspicions to be borne out by what he can learn overnight."

Holmes selected a biscuit. "It's about time he settled on someone. I did."

He trusted her deductions. But to actually prove the murderer's guilt, they still had much work to do. "Let me go arrange that tour for my children."

He'd promised them that together they would marvel at the engines and the boilers that powered the *Provence*, accompanied by the captain himself. Captain Pritchard, naturally, needed to be kept apprised of the latest developments in the investigation. But also, he had requests to make of the man.

With Holmes temporarily restricted in her movement—not to mention, having no authority to conduct inquiries in the case—he would serve as her sword arm. They'd discussed the matter at length the night before and formulated their plans accordingly. All that was left was to execute those plans.

He leaned down to kiss her good-bye, but she did not notice his approach, her gaze on the blank wall beyond the desk. "Holmes?"

She looked up and tapped the edge of her biscuit against her lower lip. "I should have paid attention to the matter sooner, but perhaps it's still not too late."

He tensed. "What is it?"

———❖———

Roger Shrewsbury arrived with the left side of his face veined with purple-black bruises—and pink cheeks and bright eyes, thrilled to be invited to Lord Ingram's suite. "Hullo, Ash. You wanted to see me?"

Lord Ingram closed the door behind him. "Tell me about the occasion during which you saw Miss Arkwright in hors d'oeuvres."

Shrewsbury's gaze dimmed instantly. His lips trembled. "Why— why do you want to know?"

"It might be relevant to the investigation."

"Thank goodness." Shrewsbury slapped his chest a few times, in relief that he was not about to be castigated again. Then a thick confusion blanketed his face. "How? How can that matter to what happened on this ship?"

"It's best for you not to know that right now, Roger. Just trust me," said Lord Ingram.

He had asked Roger Shrewsbury repeatedly to trust him, but did Shrewsbury understand how much desperate hope they had placed in *him*? As much as Lord Ingram had feared Inspector Brighton learning that he'd known about the thrown-away revolver since the night of the murder, he'd been even more terrified of Shrewsbury blurting out that he hadn't sleepwalked in truth, but had only pretended to do so at Lord Ingram's behest.

"You know I do trust you, Ash. You told me to bring up my mother and the Stern Hollow case if I got too afraid in front of Inspector Brighton, and that worked." Shrewsbury nodded, and nodded again in emphasis. "And about that gathering, it was Richard Sutton's stag party in the country."

"Richard Sutton, your second cousin's brother-in-law?"

"That's right."

Lord Ingram frowned. "And when was this party again?"

"September before last."

It was spring 1887. *September before last* put the party in the autumn of 1885.

"Richard Sutton lost his wife six or seven years ago, didn't he?"

asked Lord Ingram. "He didn't become engaged again until this past winter. Why would he have thrown a stag party a good fifteen months before he had a fiancée, let alone a wedding date?"

Roger Shrewsbury blinked. "You know, I did wonder about that when I heard about his engagement—I thought maybe the stag party was so egregious that a previous fiancée cried off. Come to think of it, I never did see him at that party. A friend took me and he mentioned Richard Sutton, so I thought it was Richard Sutton's party."

Lord Ingram sighed inwardly. Shrewsbury was not dishonest, but sometimes it was just as toilsome to extract useful information from the scatterbrained as it was from the mendacious. "Was there no host?"

"I remember plenty of servants—and more scantily clad young women in one place than I could imagine." Shrewsbury scrunched up his face, deep in recollection. "But how odd, I don't recall anyone acting the part of the host."

Uneasiness plucked at Lord Ingram. "What were guests doing at the party, besides ogling the centerpieces?"

Shrewsbury flushed. "There was some card playing. Tables full of food. And grouse shooting, too, I think—but I don't know for certain. I was—my mother was still alive at the time, and as soon as I walked in, I thought she'd have my hide if she only knew I'd been to such a place.

"So I decided I'd just stay close to the buffet, as surely I couldn't get into trouble that way. Almost dropped my plate when I saw Miss Arkwright on the buffet table. She looked so angry and so—stuck."

"Did you ask her anything about the party? Did she say anything to you besides that she wanted some water?"

"No and no. I was desperate to leave. Fortunately, that was when my friend came back. He was completely unsettled by the place, too, and we left together."

Lord Ingram's unease hardened into a sense of foreboding. "Where was this party?"

"Somewhere in the Kentish countryside. We got off near the end of a branch line, and waiting carriages took us to the house. And when we left, we returned to the same railway station and got on the next train out."

"So you didn't know where you were exactly?"

"Not precisely. But the estate is new. The fittings in the cloak rooms, my goodness. I thought it was built within the past twenty years. My friend said ten, at most."

"Who else were there?"

Shrewsbury shuddered, reliving the dread that he wouldn't be able to get away from the place before someone informed his mother. "I was mainly trying *not* to be seen, you understand. My friend said as we were leaving that he saw a few people he recognized, but he didn't say who, and I didn't want to know."

Lord Ingram asked a few more questions, but it soon became apparent that there was no more to be learned. He showed Shrewsbury out and held on to the door handle for a while, his forehead on the doorjamb.

They were far south of England now, approaching the Mediterranean, and the sun had been shining all day, yet the cold crept up his limbs, a reptilian slither.

Footsteps approached. A warm hand settled on his shoulder.

He took the hand, held it tight, and forced himself to ask, "Are you thinking of Château Vaudrieu?"

Château Vaudrieu, Moriarty's stronghold in the outskirts of Paris, hosted a yearly yuletide ball that was also an art auction. Unbeknownst to most attendees, those who committed indiscretions in the château on the night of the ball risked having their photographs taken by cameras that had been secretly placed for just such a purpose.

The photographs were then used for blackmail and extortion.

This supposed "stag party" Roger Shrewsbury had stumbled into lacked the sophistication and the tradition of the yuletide ball at Château Vaudrieu. It appeared more an impatient imitation, an unsubtle enticement to sin in the here and now.

"Whoever organized the party seemed to have misread the mood of his intended audience," answered Holmes. "A transparent orgy thrown by an anonymous host—Roger Shrewsbury ran off, that ought to tell you everything."

"Roger Shrewsbury is useless, not a wastrel."

"And wastrels hardly make for useful targets. One needs apparently upstanding pillars of society caught in acts of immorality." Her arms wrapped around him. "But yes, however shoddy and misguided the imitation, I was indeed thinking of Château Vaudrieu."

He leaned against her and breathed through his fear. "All this time, I thought it would be Inspector Brighton or perhaps Captain Pritchard working for Moriarty. When it's Miss Arkwright . . . *and she saw you*. She saw you that night, without any disguises."

They had submitted a photograph of Holmes taken with Miss Moriarty during Sherlock Holmes's previous investigation, to prove to Moriarty that his daughter was alive and well. While Mrs. Watson had not been in that particular picture, she had once been on stage, and with some digging, one could find old photographs. He was almost certain that Miss Arkwright had recognized her, too.

Holmes held him tighter, her warmth and strength replenishing his. "Don't worry too much. In any case, I need to speak to Miss Arkwright. You have your tasks, too. Let's concentrate on what we need to do."

The night of the murder, after they'd done everything they could, he'd remained convinced that their efforts would prove inadequate. But instead of allowing his mind to construct ever more outlandish worst-case scenarios, he'd told Holmes that he would find a way to take part in the investigation, probably by bringing up before Captain Pritchard his proficiency in shorthand writing. Her disguise as Mrs. Ramsay did not lend itself to too active a role, but she needed to know everything Inspector Brighton learned, in order to bring the matter to a quick solution.

And those fraught hours spent in the library had not been in vain: The transcripts he'd brought back had enabled her to spy the discrepancy that pointed to the identity of the killer.

In concentrating on what they needed to do, they'd come far. But much still needed to be done before they could unmask the murderer, and this was no time for him to panic.

He turned around and kissed her. Then, smoothing his thumb over her lower lip, he murmured, "I'm headed out. Look after yourself, Holmes."

Twenty-four

The *Provence*, upon reaching Gibraltar, had not entered the harbor, nor berthed itself at one of the manmade breakwaters that marked the harbor's boundaries. Instead, the vessel was moored in the middle of the horseshoe-shaped Bay of Gibraltar. The bay opened almost directly due south, and Livia, on the aft deck, was spoiled for views.

To the east lay the sharp ridge and great bulk of the Rock of Gibraltar, rising thirteen hundred feet high, its abrupt rock faces bare white limestone, its gentler shoulders thick with vegetation. To the south, not even ten miles away, reared the northernmost spur of the Atlas Mountains on the coast of Morocco, its peaks almost as blue as the sea and the sky. And to the west, situated almost directly across the bay from the town of Gibraltar, sat a pretty little Spanish settlement, with red-roofed villas and sections of old fortified walls, nestled against the green hills of Andalusia.

But Livia, like everyone else gathered on deck, had eyes only for the tugboat steaming toward the *Provence*. Representatives of the Civil Police Force of Gibraltar were arriving. And once they did, there would be an assembly of law enforcement and material witnesses, with Captain Pritchard and Dr. Bhattacharya also in attendance.

Lady Holmes had been excused from the meeting due to her head injury, but Livia insisted that she be there in her mother's stead. Norbert could testify that Lady Holmes never left her cabin on the night Mr. Pratt apparently met his end, but Livia still didn't trust Inspector Brighton not to pin Mr. Arkwright's murder on Lady Holmes.

The assembly didn't take place immediately. After the welcome and the introductions, Inspector Brighton and Gibraltar's chief of police sequestered themselves in the library. A great many passengers thronged the upper deck passages and even the stairs, trying to get a look.

Livia's eyes twitched when those who were deemed relevant to the case were finally asked to gather. Roger Shrewsbury, the dark blue bruises on his face now flecked with bits of pus yellow, looked terrified. Even Captain Pritchard kept rubbing his chest, as if his heart were beating too fast.

They filed into the dining saloon. The space had been cleared of other passengers and crew members, but still smelled faintly of bacon from breakfast service. Witnesses were placed around a long table at the center. Charlotte, back to being Mrs. Ramsay for the day with the last of her cosmetic solution, sat on the starboard side, near the aft end of the table. Mr. Russell occupied the seat next to her, Fuller and Livia farther to the fore. On the port side were Roger Shrewsbury, Lord Ingram, and Miss Arkwright. The members of the Gibraltar constabulary observed from a starboard sofa table, the captain and the ship's surgeon, a port one.

Inspector Brighton stood between Charlotte and Roger Shrewsbury, his hands braced on the back of a chair. The Bay of Gibraltar was sheltered and the ship barely bobbed, but his jaw remained clenched. Or perhaps he wasn't so much gritting his teeth against dizziness and nausea, but only in grim determination.

In a scratchy voice, the detective inspector expressed his gratitude to Captain Pritchard and the entire crew, conveyed his indebtedness to Chief Inspector Morris of the Gibraltar Police Force and his two uniformed officers, and did not forget to thank the passengers for their cooperation, especially Lord Ingram, without whose assistance he could not have conducted as efficient an investigation.

One of the uniformed police officers took notes of the proceedings. Lord Ingram, at last freed from stenographic duties, inclined his head at Inspector Brighton's acknowledgment.

Finished with the courtesies, Inspector Brighton went on to narrate the events leading up to Mr. Arkwright's murder, beginning with the millionaire's decision to leave England. He minced no words in rendering the incident in the hotel foyer. Roger Shrewsbury flushed scarlet; Miss Arkwright listened blankly, as if those repeated claims had nothing to do with her, as if the first time she'd heard them she had not fled in despair.

But Livia had only a quick glance to spare Miss Arkwright. Under the table her knees would not stop knocking. Would Inspector Brighton lay bare the obnoxious yet pitiable inner workings of Lady Holmes's mind, and to what degree?

To her astonishment, he allotted Lady Holmes only a quick line, painting her as the unintended victim of a murderer bent on getting away from Mr. Arkwright's cabin. Frau Schmidt and Mr. Gregory, who had not been asked to attend the conclave, weren't even mentioned.

This was . . . excellent, was it not? For Charlotte, at least?

From where Livia sat, unless she stuck out her neck, she couldn't see much of Charlotte except her cane. But across the table, Lord Ingram did not look elated or even relaxed. In fact, the longer Inspector Brighton spoke, the graver his expression became.

The policeman's own countenance turned troubled as he reached Mr. Pratt's disappearance. "We are clearly dealing with a dangerous and ruthless mind here, a mind that cares little for the rules of civilized conduct. I greatly hope that today will be the last day that our culprit breathes free."

Livia's pulse accelerated. The morning was cool, yet with the dining saloon's windows and doors closed, she was stifled and on the verge of perspiration.

"After the ship dropped anchor last night," continued Inspector Brighton, "thanks to the captain's expeditious support, we were able to connect with the gentlemen of the Gibraltar Police Force and send cables to four corners of the globe. And this morning, Chief Inspector Morris brought me the replies that had come."

Livia swallowed. Charlotte had not wanted her to be here this morning. Charlotte had also warned her last night, via a note, to sleep fully dressed and with a chair wedged against the cabin door. *I don't think anything will happen,* her note had said. *The murderer is likely feeling confident that blame would go to someone else. But in any case, err on the side of caution.*

Except for the *Provence's* arrival in Gibraltar, nothing had happened during the night. The new day had dawned fiercely clear, the sky a blue that Livia had never before seen in her life, the blue of warmer climes, the blue of the Mediterranean. And she had decided that she would not let Charlotte face any danger alone.

But now, with the moment of truth drawing near, she was afraid for Charlotte. She glanced around the table. Lord Ingram was the only person she trusted not to harm Charlotte. As for the rest of the, well, suspects—she almost wished it were Roger Shrewsbury, too useless to be a menace to anyone.

Inspector Brighton extracted a stack of cables from his pocket and smoothed them. "It is human to misbehave—otherwise, my honorable profession would not exist. It is also human to dissemble and lie, to protect oneself from the consequences of one's misconduct.

"A murder investigation compels—or at least it seeks to compel— the truth from everyone about a particular hour. Very few people commit murders, but many may be in the midst of misdemeanors at any given moment in time.

"So an investigator must pare back a forest of lies. Most lies prove minor, innocuous. But it takes time to separate the minor fibs from the major falsehoods that attempt not to cover up ordinary indiscretion but homicidal action.

"It was only night before last, as I read over the transcripts yet again and reflected upon the case, that I saw what I'd overlooked earlier. The merest slip of the tongue by Mr. Fuller."

Livia's gaze swung to the valet, seated to her immediate left. He looked as if he were holding his breath, his hands fisted on his lap, his lips sealed together.

Inspector Brighton, too, slanted a look his way. "During our interview, Mr. Fuller had called Miss Arkwright 'Miss Cor—' before correcting himself. When inquired, he said that there was an Australian woman named Miss Corwin that Mr. Arkwright almost married and he'd simply called Miss Arkwright by the wrong name.

"Mr. Russell, who knows something of Sydney society, firmly denied the existence of such a woman in Mr. Arkwright's orbit. But Mr. Russell may not be as knowledgeable as he thinks he is and he may have his own reasons not to answer truthfully . . ."

Inspector Brighton paused, as if giving room to Mr. Russell to object. But the latter said nothing. He didn't even snort with disdain.

"So we had the Sydney constabulary pose the question to Mr. Arkwright's housekeeper," Inspector Brighton carried on. "Her answer concurred with Mr. Russell's, that there was no one named Miss Corwin among Mr. Arkwright's acquaintances, nor had he seriously considered marrying anyone.

"But that was not the only question I entrusted my esteemed Australian colleagues to ask. I also wished to know whether Mr. Fuller has ever corresponded with anyone whose name begins with that syllable. And to that the housekeeper answered in the affirmative. She recalled letters to and from a Miss W. Corbett."

W? Wasn't Miss Arkwright named Willa?

Miss Arkwright, who kept an empty chair between herself and Lord Ingram, sat directly opposite Livia. She had been listening with her gaze downcast, but at the mention of the name, her eyelids lifted a fraction of an inch.

Inspector Brighton spoke now with his gaze fixed on Miss Arkwright. "As it so happens, there were also cables dispatched to the Metropolitan Police in London, requesting their help. From the papers Mr. Arkwright had left behind in his cabin, I was able to ascertain the identity of his English solicitors. My Scotland Yard colleagues were able to speak to them—in particular, the one who handled Mr. Arkwright's last will and testament.

"Or perhaps I should say, his last wills and testaments, for he made two before he left England, one dealing strictly with the disposal of his Australian properties—the executor was to convert everything into fungible funds and transmit the sum total to the executor of his English will. And his English will bequeathed everything that would be received from Australia to one Miss Willa Corbett.

"It was noted at the time that Miss Willa Corbett planned to change her surname to Arkwright in Australia, and in due time, a newer will would be drawn up to reflect that. The solicitor also stated that Miss Willa Corbett had accompanied Mr. Arkwright on the occasion and was perfectly conversant with the terms of the two wills."

Everyone stared at Miss Arkwright, including Lord Ingram, who was usually too well-mannered to engage in such discourtesy, however minor.

Inspector Brighton at last left his spot at the head of the table, only to take up position directly behind Livia. The hairs on the back of Livia's neck rose. She forced her knees to stop knocking.

"You assured me that you knew nothing of the contents of your brother's will, Miss Arkwright."

Livia's heart pounded, as if she herself had been caught in an egregious lie.

Miss Arkwright said nothing. And did not look up.

Inspector Brighton seemed unsurprised by her lack of a response. "So here we have an interesting story. Mr. Jacob Arkwright—born Jacob Corbett, I would imagine—ran away from home at an early age. His much younger sister, being of a resilient and enterprising temperament, not only survived her childhood near the docks of Liverpool but prospered enough that she became the proprietor of a shop that produced quality embroidered handkerchiefs."

At last the policeman moved away from Livia—to stop by Fuller, Mr. Russell, and Charlotte. Now he rounded the table to stand behind a wide-eyed Roger Shrewsbury. "The handkerchief shop operated on a small scale, but it turned a profit and allowed the sister to be self-sufficient, an admirable accomplishment for a young woman who'd had only herself to rely on."

He walked on, bypassing Lord Ingram. But he didn't take up position behind Miss Arkwright. Instead, he set his hands on the back of the empty chair between the two. "But this young woman, beneath her apparent success, had a problem. She was being black-mailed. The amount she was forced to pay would not be considered jaw-dropping, five pounds here, ten pounds there. But a handkerchief shop was not a gold mine, and the demands of this blackmailer felt like a noose around her neck.

"And then one day, out of the blue, she received a letter from Australia. I would be speculating if I said I knew the degree of acquaintance between the young woman and the letter writer; suffice to say he took the trouble to inform her that he now worked for a gentleman who bore a remarkable resemblance to her. Was there any chance she knew this gentleman?"

The empty chair faced Fuller, and so did Inspector Brighton. "I imagine that a photograph had been sent along, something not terribly difficult to obtain for a man who worked as the subject's valet, with access to his employer's private rooms and personal items."

Where the policeman could not see, Fuller's hands gripped the apron piece under the tabletop.

Inspector Brighton turned his head toward Miss Arkwright. "Our young woman recognized not only her long-lost brother—but her salvation. She could now disappear off the face of the earth, and be sure of a warm welcome in the Antipodes.

"Alas, the blackmailer had drained her financially and she could not afford to travel to Australia, not even a third-class ticket, let alone passage on ships that carried only first-class passengers. But soon she had even better news. Her brother was on his way to England. Now all she needed was to contrive a meeting with him, not a difficult task as she already had a friend on his staff.

"And what a joyous reunion. The fly in the ointment? Her blackmailer, having learned of this development, latched even more tightly on to her. Leeched on, one might say. He was not going to let her get away, not without exacting a heavy toll for his silence.

"But then something most unexpected happened. Another man came along, one with no intention of blackmailing anyone, and spoke in public of an episode in her past that she would prefer to forget."

Heads around the table swiveled in Roger Shrewsbury's direction, but Livia glanced from Fuller to Miss Arkwright and back, trying to decide which of the two would prove more dangerous when cornered.

Miss Arkwright. Without a doubt, Miss Arkwright.

Inspector Brighton spoke again. "Mr. Shrewsbury's conduct, however lamentable, neutralized to a degree the threat of the blackmailer—our young woman no longer needed to keep her past a secret from her brother. But she now faced an even thornier problem. Her brother had been so overjoyed to find her that he willed to her the entirety of his fortune. Would he still be pleased when he had learned the truth behind her success, *all* the truths?

"The answer was no. He was so ashamed that he could not attend the dinner to which the captain had invited him. So ashamed that on the one occasion she left her cabin, he came himself to drag her back.

"And what intense and unhappy conversations did they hold in private? Easy to imagine, isn't it? All the fervent hopes our young woman had experienced, all her wonderful sense of renewal, wilted under the onslaught of her brother's anger and displeasure. Leave everything to her? What was he thinking? Once they reached Australia, he would make a new will.

"In fact, he didn't need to wait that long. As soon as it was possible to go ashore in Gibraltar, he intended to cable his solicitors in London, to invalidate the ones he'd just signed.

"And what would our young woman do, she who had suddenly risen high in the world, only to be told that she was about to be thrown down from that great summit?"

Inspector Brighton's voice was almost sympathetic, almost a caress. Livia, who'd felt too warm only a minute ago, shivered. It seemed to her that Miss Arkwright, too, shuddered and grew smaller.

"She did not get to be where she was without being willing to do just about anything. As the crisis loomed, she recognized a tremendous opportunity. Given that technology has not yet advanced enough to allow ship-to-land communication, she had a little time left, a few days before the *Provence* reached port and her name was irreversibly struck from a most lucrative document.

"But only a very little time. In his anger—and he had never been a subtle man, even when he wasn't angry—her brother might publicly disavow her on the morrow. Should he die after such a pronouncement, suspicion would fall upon her that much more easily. There was no time to lose.

"In her endeavor, she had some help. Mr. Fuller, who had been a good enough friend to report on her long-lost brother, was now again proving his loyalty and dependability."

Livia glanced to her left. Fuller's chin jutted out in his effort to keep himself still. He did not look once at Miss Arkwright, nor she him.

"It was easy enough to shoot Mr. Arkwright in the dark—she had, after all, access to his cabin via the en-suite bath that he had been generous enough to share with her. But complications arose, first among which being Lady Holmes, who, angry at Mr. Arkwright's slights against her, had come before his cabin to write uncivil words on the door.

"Miss Arkwright again recognized an opportunity. Why not throw suspicion on this foolhardy woman instead? Lady Holmes was incapacitated and dragged into the parlor, her rouge used to scrawl exactly such words as she would have written on the door."

Inspector Brighton was an excellent raconteur, forceful and persuasive. But a lesser narrator would still have done the story justice. There was nothing here *not* to believe. Miss Arkwright had too much to lose and too much to gain. How could anyone—no, how could *she*, who had struggled so mightily in her life—accept a verdict that would make her nothing and no one again?

"But even as Miss Arkwright and Mr. Fuller vandalized the wall with Lady Holmes's rouge, they faced yet another problem. What to do with the woman? Leaving her inside Mr. Arkwright's parlor was out of the question—she would come to and start screaming. Leaving her outside in the starboard passage would also arouse unwanted attention.

"They had a stroke of luck: The electric lamps went out. The ship's officer who came around let them know that they would have approximately a quarter hour of darkness. Abandoning their last, half-written word, they took a risk and dragged Lady Holmes back to her own cabin. They further left Mr. Arkwright's cabin key in her pocket in order to better incriminate the hapless lady, and marked her door so that she would come to the attention of this investigation.

"But things still did not go smoothly after that. Somebody saw something. And this somebody was none other than Mr. Pratt, our blackmailer. This is a notebook I found in Mr. Pratt's cabin, on which he'd recorded payments he received from a W. Corbett, among others."

His statement was addressed to the Gibraltar police. A uniformed officer came and took the notebook from him. A crease formed between Lord Ingram's brows. Had he, a vital member of the investigation, not been informed of this notebook?

"Mr. Pratt must have thought himself the luckiest man in the world. Just when he'd lost you, Miss Arkwright, as a subject of blackmail because your past conduct became known to the public, he regained you as an even better subject of extortion because now he could hold your brother's murder over you.

"He told his tale to a number of different people aboard—with the precise intention that it should get back to you. But he did not count on your determination, more fool he, and now he is lying at the bottom of the Atlantic."

Inspector Brighton sighed with weariness, but also with great satisfaction. "Superintendent Morris, I recommend you arrest Miss Arkwright and Mr. Fuller for the murder of Mr. Jacob Arkwright."

———— ❧ ————

Silence rippled and expanded endlessly. Fuller trembled. Across the table from Livia, Miss Arkwright remained utterly still. It could be the stillness of concentration or, just as likely, the petrified fear of a small creature facing a predator it could not possibly escape.

The uniformed policeman who was not taking notes approached the long table. Fuller shook harder. Miss Arkwright rose slowly. She wore a double-breasted beige reefer jacket trimmed with muted gold braids. The jacket-and-skirt ensemble didn't overwhelm her, per se, but its confident masculine construction was nevertheless at odds with her tentative demeanor.

Was she planning to surrender herself to avoid the humiliation of being dragged away?

Inspector Brighton, from his close vantage point, studied her. Lord Ingram, in the next chair over, peered at both, his expression betraying only a profound watchfulness. Livia dared a glimpse toward Charlotte, but with Fuller and Mr. Russell in her way, again she only caught sight of Charlotte's cane.

Miss Arkwright straightened. "Captain Pritchard, Chief Inspector Morris, may I—may I have a moment to defend Mr. Fuller and myself against these very serious charges that Inspector Brighton has leveled against us?"

Inspector Brighton's eyes narrowed. The uniformed policeman, already rounding the table, stopped and glanced toward Chief Inspector Morris. But it was Captain Pritchard who cleared his throat. "If you wish, Miss Arkwright, certainly."

The uniformed policeman took several steps back. Inspector Brighton raised a brow, but shuffled to the head of the table and lowered himself into a chair. "Please, Miss Arkwright, tell everyone what you should have already told the investigation."

Miss Arkwright took a deep breath and looked about the dining saloon. Now that she was on her feet, she must have a good view of

Chief Inspector Morris. And indeed she looked in his direction, but then her gaze came to settle on Livia.

"Inspector Brighton laid out a convincing scenario," she said, her eyes holding Livia's, "so convincing that even I came close to believing him. After all, some of the things he learned were damning, and everything he speculated sounded eminently reasonable. Why would a brother not be furious with a sister who had lived as I had? Why would he not wish to dispossess me of everything with which he had endowed me? And why wouldn't I wish to take vengeance upon him to preserve all my hard-won gains?"

Livia's heart thudded. Why was Miss Arkwright addressing those questions directly to her? Even if Livia believed her, her opinion would not sway anyone. Or had Miss Arkwright strategically chosen to speak to the person most likely to be sympathetic?

Miss Arkwright shifted her gaze a few degrees toward Fuller. "Mr. Fuller and I met in London, before he left on that trip around the world which saw him stranded in Australia. He had done for some fussy gentlemen, and was strict about fashionable accessories he presented to his masters. He heard about my handkerchiefs and decided to investigate my shop, a very small place off Oxford Street but one that I was extremely proud of.

"He knew fabric. He knew embroidery. But he also recognized quality work. He was the one who helped me get my wares into some of the Savile Row shops—a very good friend he has been from the very beginning."

She spoke softly and with apparent fondness, yet Fuller jerked as if she'd whipped him—her admission chained them together like a pair of prisoners, with no escape for either.

Her eyes met Livia's again. "Alas, Mr. Fuller left for that ill-fated trip, and my own evil fortune began when Mr. Pratt moved into a residential hotel near mine. He recognized me from a compromising moment and decided to use that to extort money. I was caught in a bind. I needed my respectability to run my respectable business. But my business would suffer and ultimately flounder if I kept paying Mr. Pratt for his silence.

"But then a miracle happened. Mr. Fuller's letter came, my brother returned to England, and I was no longer alone in the world."

At those words she glowed, an incandescent light at last connected to electricity. She even smiled faintly. "Jacob was stunned. When he'd made enough money, he'd hired men to find me. But our mother had died years before and I'd long ago left Liverpool. To those in our old neighborhood, I'd disappeared off the face of the earth. His men looked in London, too, in the sort of seedy places that one would expect a girl like me to end up. Where they did not find me, of course.

"He couldn't believe I'd escaped the fate common to so many. He couldn't understand how I'd accumulated enough capital for a shop of my own, however modest. I asked him then what he would have done if he'd found me working as a prostitute in a rookery slum. And his answer I would never forget."

The rims of her eyes turned red. Her voice caught. "'I'd make it up to you, Willa,' he said. 'I'd spend the rest of my life to make it up to you.'

"So I told him then and there that while I'd never had to earn a living on my back, I was pressured into being a human centerpiece on one unfortunate occasion and was seen by a man who practiced blackmail."

She stared into the distance and wept silently, her tears collecting at the tip of her chin before falling to the table with tiny, yet all too audible splashes. And then, as if waking up from a trance, she started, pulled out a handkerchief, and wiped at her eyes.

"I'm sorry. Where was I? Oh, right, I told Jacob that I was being blackmailed. At first he wanted to beat Mr. Pratt to a pulp, but then he calmed down. He could not leave for Australia immediately because he had many plans for Britain. Not to mention, such sums as Mr. Pratt wanted were nothing to him. I would continue to pay those sums until our departure to Australia, at which point Mr. Pratt would never be able to find me again—certainly he would not consider it worthwhile to chase me to the other side of the globe for what little funds he could squeeze out of me.

"Unfortunately, Mr. Pratt happened upon me and Jacob together on one occasion. And when he learned that Jacob was a very rich man, he immediately presented himself as my sincere suitor, taking for granted that I would never dare breathe a word of any past scandal to my long-lost brother, not knowing that Jacob already despised him because he knew exactly what he was, a fortune hunter who was not above a bit of extortion on the side, while he waited for a foolish heiress to fall into his lap.

"When Jacob changed his mind about the length of his stay in Britain, we couldn't get rid of Mr. Pratt. He followed us to Southampton, still intent on his ruse as my suitor. And even after Mr. Shrewsbury made a scene in the hotel foyer, he kept up his pretenses."

With her face patted dry, Miss Arkwright used the handkerchief to soak up the puddle of tears on the table. She then refolded the cloth into a neat square. "The incident at the hotel upset me greatly. I'd worked very hard not to sell myself or depend on any man, yet that one moment of disadvantage kept haunting me. I was all fury and self-pity, until the night of the storm. First, I encountered Miss Fenwick, whose kindness restored a bit of my faith in humanity. And then Jacob spoke to me, and his problem took on an urgency greater than mine."

Roger Shrewsbury, who'd sat with his head hung since he first took his seat, now darted her a furtive look. Inspector Brighton reordered the stack of cables that had come overnight, cables that testified to her dishonesty and murderous motives.

Miss Arkwright glanced out of the corner of her eye—at those very cables? Or was it at Charlotte? But then her attention returned to Livia, a weight like a pair of hands pressing down on Livia's shoulders.

"When my brother first arrived in England, he'd intended a long stay. But he abruptly changed his mind. At the time, he did not tell me why and I, eager to get away from Mr. Pratt, chose not to look a gift horse in the mouth.

"But the night of the storm, as the ship tilted drunkenly, he told me the truth. He had been forced to leave by the same person who'd framed him for murder years ago: The man sent a note that ordered him to get out of England or risk being revealed as a fugitive. Even worse, the man, whom he knew as Ned Plowers, was also sailing on the *Provence*."

Livia sucked in a breath. Miss Arkwright's gaze was clear and sincere, but her story was much too convenient. Inspector Brighton sat on ironclad evidence that she knew about a will that would endow her with unimaginable wealth. What proof could she provide, besides her own avowal, that her brother's nemesis had indeed boarded this vessel?

"My brother began to search the ship. He made a list and struck off everyone who couldn't be Ned Plowers. But by the time he spoke to me the night of—of his murder, he'd begun to regret his haste.

"Jacob was a smart man. But to hear him tell it, this Ned Plowers was by far the superior schemer. He wondered whether he hadn't tipped his hand too soon. If Plowers realized that Jacob sought him on the *Provence*, and that he aimed to expose his criminal, murderous past to the world, well, Plowers had much to lose.

"Jacob didn't fear for his own safety. He was more worried about me—he thought I would be the means Ned Plowers sought to threaten him, if it came to that. He told me to keep my doors locked and not to answer for anyone unless I heard his special knock, the same one that he'd used when we were children."

Tears rolled down Miss Arkwright's cheeks again. "I said good night to him, and that was the last time I saw him."

"I find it suspect, Miss Arkwright, that you failed to mentioned this Ned Plowers, among other things, in your interviews," said Inspector Brighton acidly.

For the first time Miss Arkwright looked him in the eye—and smiled ruefully. "It was pointed out to me that in a murder investigation, I would quickly become a suspect. I had access to my brother's cabin. I was named in his will. And in the eyes of the world, he must be angry with me and therefore I must stand in danger of losing an enormous inheritance, giving me a most plausible motive.

"It was also pointed out to me that to save myself, the best thing to do would be to continue my brother's work and find out whom he had and hadn't seen on this ship. Those he had seen could presumably be eliminated from consideration as they are not Ned Plowers. Those he had not seen, however, I must keep in mind.

"Such as, for example . . ." Her gaze swept the gathering and landed on one man. "You, Captain Pritchard."

Twenty-five

I'm sorry I have no tea to offer you," said Charlotte.

Mrs. Watson, who liked to think of everything, had packed an Etna stove, but it was in her steamer trunk in the luggage hold. And it would not do to order tea to Lord Ingram's cabin—or even his children's—since they were all out.

"That is quite all right," murmured Miss Arkwright.

Arranging a meeting with her had been easier said than done, but here she was in Lord Ingram's parlor, seated on the sofa beneath the window. Charlotte occupied the writing desk chair near the door, her cane at her side.

"You understand the reason I've asked to see you, I hope, Miss Arkwright?"

"But I'm afraid I don't. Not really." Miss Arkwright set her hands on her lap, a most decorous gesture. "Unless . . . unless as Lord Ingram's mistress, you think we might have something to talk about because of my unorthodox past?"

"I am Lord Ingram's lover, not his mistress. And I have little interest in your unorthodox past—I am only concerned, Miss Arkwright, with your current endeavors as a member of Moriarty's organization."

After the *Provence* rounded Cape St. Vincent, the window in Lord Ingram's parlor faced north and did not receive a great deal of light at this time of the day, with the sun lowering toward the western horizon. Miss Arkwright's face, already half in shadows, seemed to fade even more into the background.

After a while, she said, "But my current endeavors are not detrimental to you, Miss Holmes."

Ah, the admission that she knew exactly who Charlotte was. That was the reason she'd been so forthcoming that night, telling Charlotte all about her brother's will and Ned Plowers. She'd been speaking to Sherlock Holmes, consulting detective.

"Is that so? Not at all detrimental to me?"

"Mrs. Watson was most kind to me. And you, too, in your own way." Now that she'd made the decision to be at least somewhat truthful, Miss Arkwright's voice rang with sincerity. "I haven't been the recipient of much generosity in my life, but I've never not repaid a debt of kindness. I promise you, Miss Holmes, that no news of your whereabouts would pass my lips. On this voyage, I've only met Mrs. Ramsay of Cambridgeshire and her companion, Miss Fenwick—and I would do my best to omit them, too, as far as possible, from any accounts I must give."

"Thank you, Miss Arkwright," Charlotte answered coolly. "I assume you've worked with Mr. de Lacey—several Mr. de Laceys, most likely. What did you do for him?"

The man who assumed the position of Moriarty's chief lieutenant in Britain was always called de Lacey.

"I was a thief—an excellent thief." Miss Arkwright smiled halfheartedly. "Later, after I came of age, I worked less in the field, so to speak, but oversaw those who did."

That sounded about right. For someone who looked as she did, with features that should at least be memorable, if nothing else, her lack of presence could very well have been cultivated over years—decades—of illicit activities.

"And what happened at the bacchanal? Were they short a center-piece?"

"We were short two centerpieces—two girls who had been hired did not come." Miss Arkwright's smile became bitter. "I wasn't even in charge of that."

And yet she'd been pressured into taking off her clothes and serving in a capacity she'd found demeaning, by the organization to which she'd devoted her entire life.

"I'm sorry," said Charlotte.

Miss Arkwright made a sound that approximated laughter. "So am I. But let's speak of more pressing matters."

"Before we do that, I'd like to know what Mr. Fuller was doing out on deck that night."

"Sulking, as he said." Miss Arkwright briefly sucked in her cheeks. "We knew each other since before he left for Australia, and he helped me find my brother. You would think we should have remained reasonably good friends. But the proximity we were thrust into turned out to be too much for us.

"He was in love with Jacob and sometimes overstepped his bounds—not in *that* way, but in certain other ways, trying to influence my brother's decisions in a manner unbefitting his office. I did not like that. And he was already unhappy with me when Mr. Shrewsbury shouted for the entire world to hear that I was once naked in public.

"The evening of the storm, he knocked on Jacob's door. When he got no answer, he knocked on mine. Our exchange became heated, I'm afraid. When he left, I was upset enough to venture out of my cabin for the first time since the ship sailed—into the library, where I met Mrs. Watson. And he chose to drench himself at some point during the night, instead of stewing in his dormitory another moment longer."

Friendship, it could be just as fragile and inconstant as love.

Charlotte doubted that such a prosaic explanation for Fuller's venture outside would satisfy Inspector Brighton, but that could not be helped now. "After Lord Ingram and I left that night, did you go back into your brother's cabin again?"

For her safety, they had asked Miss Arkwright to stay put. But concerns over one's own safety were not always the strongest deterrent.

"I wanted to heed your advice—I really did. But in the small hours of the night, the urge came upon me to see his body for myself. I'd almost left my lock-picking tools behind in England, but put them in my handbag at the last minute. Since I had them, I let myself in to his parlor."

Her eyes dimmed. Had she allowed herself to hope, however improbably, that Charlotte and Lord Ingram had been mistaken about the identity of the victim? "When I was in his parlor, I heard some sounds in the passage. I was afraid it might be the murderer coming back again, so I went back to my cabin via the connecting door."

The sounds might have been made by Steward Smith, fetching new beddings for Mr. Gregory or trying to get Roger Shrewsbury to go back to his cabin.

The barrel bolt on the connecting door had been latched earlier in the night by the murderer. Miss Arkwright, who wouldn't have wanted to leave an unlatched device in the wake of her exit, must have performed a minor sleight of hand to relatch it from her side, with either a string or a rubber band and a matchstick.

In either case, something would be left behind on the barrel bolt, which she would then need to remove before anyone else saw it in the morning. Ergo, her dash to the bath, not to vomit but to erase evidence.

"Another point of disfavor with Inspector Brighton," said Charlotte. "He might not know exactly what you did in the bath that morning, but he is sure you did something."

"He's right about that. And when we reach Gibraltar tonight, he would find out very quickly that all along I've known about my brother's will, too."

Miss Arkwright emitted a dry cackle. But that facsimile of mirth quickly drained from her face. In her lap, her fingers knotted together. "What should I do?"

When she'd asked that question on the night of the storm, Charlotte had told her, among other things, that whatever she did, it would be best to have Fuller's support—they should not undermine each other before Inspector Brighton. And she'd directed Miss Arkwright to find Miss Fenwick in the morning so Charlotte could inspect Mr. Arkwright's suite again, at the first opportunity, to see what the murderer might have done when he'd revisited the scene.

Now, however, Charlotte only leaned back in her chair. "Miss Arkwright, earlier, out of gallantry, I gave you what I hoped to be helpful suggestions. But you are no damsel-in-distress. In fact, you might be more self-possessed and competent than anyone else on this vessel. I see no reason that I or anyone else need to rush to your rescue."

"But I am in peril. Tomorrow this time I might very well be led off in handcuffs for something I didn't do."

To Miss Arkwright's plea, Charlotte returned a blank gaze. Some mistook the typical lack of expression on her face as a look of wide-eyed innocence, but Miss Arkwright, she was sure, recognized ruthlessness for what it was. "Are you seeking my help, Miss Arkwright? I charge for my work."

"But I already told you I wouldn't reveal your whereabouts to my superiors."

"And you said that was in repayment for Mrs. Watson's and my kindness to you. Saving you from a likely indictment of murder—murders, that is—requires its own separate remuneration."

Miss Arkwright's throat moved—she'd realized that Charlotte was perfectly serious. That not only would she not help Miss Arkwright out of the goodness of her heart, she wouldn't even lift a finger in exchange for only a promise of continued anonymity. "How much? I might not have enough on me, but I can wire you the rest later."

"I am not interested in taking money from you, Miss Arkwright,"

Charlotte said lightly. "Allow me to repeat myself: I am only concerned with your current endeavors. I want to know what you are doing on this vessel for Moriarty."

Moriarty, too, faced his share of difficulties, one of which was a shortage of personnel in the wake of an internal coup. Charlotte did not believe that de Lacey had enough staff to spare someone for the *Provence*, solely in the hope of locating Charlotte Holmes on board. What, then, was important enough for an experienced underling to be dispatched?

"Can I not simply be traveling to Australia because my brother asked me to accompany him?"

Miss Arkwright spoke with just the right degree of weariness and torment, a woman on the verge of desperation. Charlotte remained unmoved. "You could. But I found it odd that according to Mr. Fuller's testimony, you bought the tickets, not he, the manservant who presumably, in the ordinary course of events, took care of such mundane details. Not to mention, when you realized that Mr. Pratt had also purchased passage for the same sailing, you could have shaken him loose by boarding a vessel that departed sooner. You'd have been free of his vile company for the duration of the voyage—no small prize, that. But you did not do so, which tells me that you—or someone from Moriarty's organization, at least—had to be on this particular boat. What is the reason?"

Miss Arkwright's jaw worked. "And if I choose not to part with that information?"

"Then as you predict, you would be led off the *Provence* in handcuffs—or at least in a blaze of ignominy."

Inspector Brighton hadn't even bothered to summon Mrs. Watson back to ask whether Miss Fenwick, in using the ladies' baths at about twenty minutes to ten the night of the murder, had seen or heard anyone else in the baths: He had abandoned Frau Schmidt as a line of inquiry to focus on the prize, and that prize was Miss Arkwright.

"I'm sure that in exchange for your loyalty," she added, "Mr. de Lacey would see to it that you are exonerated in time."

The peeling back of Miss Arkwright's lips expressed eloquently what she thought of the likelihood of that.

Silence ensued. Briefly, Charlotte considered everything that could still go wrong. But because she'd already considered that earlier and nothing had changed, she chose instead to enjoy the subtle teetering of the ship, advancing with the breaths of the waves.

"Very well," came the abrupt words of Moriarty's minion. "I will tell you what you want to know. And in return?"

Charlotte grazed a finger against the sharp teeth of the silver lioness atop her cane. "In return, Miss Arkwright, I will spare you from the gallows."

"I can spare myself from the gallows—I may not convince a jury of my innocence, but I should be able to arrange for an escape," replied Miss Arkwright. "What I need, Miss Holmes, is for you to avenge my brother."

Her eyes bored into Charlotte. "Can you do that?"

Twenty-six

L ivia's jaw fell.

By pointing out that Captain Pritchard had not come face-to-face with Mr. Arkwright, was Miss Arkwright insinuating that—that—

"What?" exclaimed Mr. Russell.

Roger Shrewsbury twisted around in his chair to stare at the captain. Even Lord Ingram turned his head. Inspector Brighton's gaze, however, remained fixed on Miss Arkwright.

Captain Pritchard leaped to his feet. "It's true I didn't meet Mr. Arkwright before his unfortunate demise. But I very much wished to—I invited you both to dinner!"

"And how providential for you, sir, that we did not attend," replied Miss Arkwright calmly. "Or there would have been a scene."

"Miss Arkwright, really—"

Miss Arkwright lifted her handkerchief from the table and tucked it into her sleeve, leaving a cascade of lacy edges to drape around her wrist. "You mustn't take offense, Captain. I am not accusing you of having murdered my brother. I only brought you up because yours was one of the few names I remembered from a cursory glance at my brother's list."

At those words ostensibly meant to soothe, the captain only grew red-faced and frantic. "I have never framed anyone for murder—I have never committed a single crime in my life! And a half-dozen men of honor and rectitude can attest to my presence on the bridge the night of the murder from before dinner to when the storm at last abated in the middle of the night!"

Miss Arkwright gave a slight yank to her other sleeve. "In that case we can remove you from suspicion altogether, Captain."

Captain Pritchard blinked, having trouble deciding whether she was serious or whether he ought to advocate more vociferously for his innocence.

But she had already turned away to address Chief Inspector Morris, on the other side of the dining saloon. "Inspector Brighton, in his summary, mentioned Mr. Pratt's rather cryptic story about seeing bloody water in the gentlemen's bath. He also mentioned that no other witness saw such a sight in the baths that night. Chief Inspector, Captain Pritchard, with your permission, I would like to hear the interview transcripts of those passengers who had heard Mr. Pratt's story in person."

Captain Pritchard appeared at a loss. The two uniformed policemen both looked toward Chief Inspector Morris, who indicated for them to stay put. He pulled out a pair of spectacles from his pocket, set them on the bridge of his nose, and turned the dossier that had been set on the table before him.

When he found what he was looking for, he glanced through the pages, then read aloud three rather repetitive interviews. To a one, the passengers who had spoken to Mr. Pratt on this matter mentioned the bloody water in the gentlemen's baths, and then various of Mr. Pratt's speculations on how that could have come about.

"There are still more of such interviews," said Chief Inspector Morris, peering over his glasses, "but I do not believe they would add to our understanding of the case."

"Indeed, Chief Inspector, I believe you're right. Would you be so kind as to also read aloud what Mr. Pratt had said, when he'd volunteered the information to Inspector Brighton?"

Chief Inspector Morris looked nonplussed.

"Are you wasting everyone's time, Miss Arkwright?" said Inspector Brighton, his soft voice sending a chill down Livia's arms. "You are only delaying the inevitable."

Miss Arkwright's hands gripped the edge of the table, but she spoke evenly, once again addressing her words to the Gibraltar police. "Chief Inspector, I assure you that I am not playing tricks. I have a serious inquiry to make."

Chief Inspector Morris said nothing. The uniformed policeman hovering behind Inspector Brighton took a step toward Miss Arkwright.

A chair scraped against the floor—Charlotte, silent and still until now, had turned around. "Chief Inspector," rose her Mrs. Ramsay voice, "pray read the account so we can hear what Miss Arkwright wants us to hear."

Lord Ingram reached inside his jacket, and Livia was suddenly of the belief that he carried with him another copy of the transcript and that if Chief Inspector Morris did not honor Miss Arkwright's request, he would see to it that everyone in the dining saloon would still hear, word for word, Mr. Pratt's original testimony.

"Very well," said Chief Inspector Morris. "Let me find it."

Lord Ingram pulled his fingertips back from inside his jacket and gave his lapel a light brush. Inspector Brighton shot a hooded glance at Charlotte. Chief Inspector Morris pushed his spectacles higher up the ridge of his nose and read from Mr. Pratt's interview.

When he'd finished, Miss Arkwright again scanned the assembly. "I believe, after hearing three very similar accounts in a row, some of you have detected the difference in this particular version.

"To the other passengers, Mr. Pratt broached only the subject of the water in the baths. But in his own interview with the police, he mentioned repeatedly that his cabin was right next to the surgery and that he'd heard noises coming from there."

Livia had caught the difference, but it was only at Miss Arkwright's reiteration that it began to seem ominous. The surgery, the noises, Mr. Pratt poking his head out in the middle of the night . . .

"The success of blackmail depends on the exploitable knowledge being a secret known only to the blackmailer and the person being extorted. Clearly, the water in the baths cannot be the crucial piece of information here—in fact, I would argue that it is irrelevant and might be altogether made up to act as a distraction.

"Instead, it must be the seemingly unimportant bit about the location of Mr. Pratt's cabin and the noises he'd overheard which signaled to the murderer that he had been seen that night."

"Preposterous," said Inspector Brighton coldly.

Miss Arkwright ignored him. "But what was the murderer doing in that part of the ship? One thing the investigation failed to take note of was the firearm thrown away that night. According to Mr. Shrewsbury, in front of whom the revolver landed, one round was missing from the cylinder.

"Three shots had been fired by the weapon left behind at the scene. As for why the murderer wanted everyone to think only three shots were fired, and only by him, I propose it's because my brother's bullet had injured him and he did not want anyone to inquire in that direction.

"Knowing that a body would be found in the morning, the murderer, of course, could not present a gunshot wound to the ship's surgeon. But he still needed bandaging and antiseptic, which he could only steal from the surgery.

"At the moment the breaking-and-entering occurred, Mr. Pratt would not have realized the significance of the burglary. But with a blackmailer's instinct, he took note. The next day, when my brother's death became known, he put two and two together."

Miss Arkwright looked around the dining saloon. "I see much doubt, but that is why I have come prepared. Dr. Bhattacharya, please relay what you discovered when you were asked to inventory your place of work yesterday."

Dr. Bhattacharya's brows shot up—clearly he had not expected to be called on to speak. But he rose gamely. "Well, when Captain Pritchard put the request to me, I did as he asked. I took stock and discovered two rolls of bandaging gone, as well as a bottle of carbolic acid, and a bottle of absolute alcohol—all from locked supply cabinets. The thief had been clever and pilfered items from the back of the cabinets, so that from the front nothing would appear to be missing. Unless I emptied everything and counted, as I did, I would have continued in my belief that the surgery had remained undisturbed."

Murmurs rippled. Livia's breaths came in short. But on Miss Arkwright's face there was no rising triumph, only a greater wariness.

"Did you discover any contraband bandaging in your search of the ship, Inspector Brighton?" she asked.

"No, I did not," replied Inspector Brighton, stone-faced.

"I believe you did not search the captain's quarters?"

Captain Pritchard, who had only recently retaken his seat, sprang up once again. "Miss Arkwright—"

"Please, Captain, a moment of patience. I would like to hear the inspector's answer."

Inspector Brighton's fingers tightened around the stack of cables before him. "No, we did not search the captain's quarters, as he was on the bridge that night and I had no reason to suspect him."

"So not every place aboard this ship was searched?"

"You could say so, if you wish."

Miss Arkwright looked across the dining saloon. "Chief Inspector Morris, please note—again—that I do not believe the captain to be involved in my brother's murder. I merely wished to establish the incomplete nature of the search. But the captain's quarters was not the only place exempted from the search. There is at least one more cabin that was not subject to scrutiny, and that cabin belongs to Inspector Brighton."

Fuller and Roger Shrewsbury gasped. Livia's jaw dropped. Inspector Brighton rose, his height formidable, his countenance dark with anger. "May I remind you, Miss Arkwright, that I am an officer of the law, and you are very much under suspicion for murder."

Miss Arkwright raised her chin a fraction of an inch. Suddenly, in her gold-braided jacket, she looked as forceful as any general marching to war. "Inspector, everyone on this ship is under suspicion for murder—two murders, in fact. There can be no exceptions, not even for you. This morning, while you conferred with Chief Inspector Morris in the library, a search was carried out of your cabin. Captain, will you show us what was found?"

The captain exhaled and nodded at Dr. Bhattacharya. The ship's surgeon opened his bag and took out a roll of bandaging, and half a bottle each of alcohol and carbolic acid. "The search was conducted by Captain Pritchard, Second Officer Spalding, the head steward, and myself."

Miss Arkwright looked back at Inspector Brighton. The latter snorted. "If the murderer is, as you say, capable of entering the surgery in the middle of the night, then he must be able to pick locks. He placed those items in my cabin, hoping to frame me."

"The murderer is perhaps capable of doing that, but can he also give you a wound that would require all these supplies? It is easy to prove your innocence, Inspector. Have Dr. Bhattacharya perform an inspection of your person. And if you do not have an injury consistent with that of having been grazed by a bullet, then you have nothing to fear. If you do not agree to it, then you are Ned Plowers, and—"

Inspector Brighton lunged—at Charlotte. He yanked her to her feet with his left hand. A revolver had materialized in his right hand. A cry tore from Livia's throat. He would threaten Charlotte's safety and try to get away. But the life of a very old woman might not matter so much to the Gibraltar police. They might—

Charlotte's cane whipped up, lightning-quick, and slammed toward his skull. He jerked back, letting go of her. Freed from his grip, she brought her cane down and smacked his right hand. He yowled and the gun fell.

Charlotte's cane swung back and struck him again, this time across his right thigh. He screamed at a much higher pitch and staggered sideways, but immediately threw himself toward the fallen revolver. Livia sprang up. She was vaguely aware of others scattering, but she rushed forward and smashed her reticule on Inspector Brighton's head—she'd pilfered a saucer from breakfast service, and it produced a most satisfying *thunk* against his skull.

Lord Ingram leaped clear across the table, grabbed the revolver, and pointed it at the policeman. "Surrender yourself," he said coldly. "I will not hesitate to shoot. And I will not hesitate to kill."

Twenty-seven

There was no reason for you to write that threatening note, Inspector. You were respectable and successful; you stood every chance of rising higher in your profession. But you couldn't bear the thought, could you, that the nobody who had taken the blame for you all those years ago was now a millionaire and moved in rarefied circles? You couldn't help the evil inside you that had been hidden all these years, but never eradicated."

Miss Arkwright spoke those words just after the uniformed policemen handcuffed Inspector Brighton. As he was frog-marched out of the dining saloon, she called out, "And you wanted me to hang for your crime because you were afraid that I would find Ned Plowers and avenge my brother. How right you were, Inspector!"

By the time Livia exited the dining saloon herself, news had spread, and the entire vessel was a buzzing beehive of astonished if barely coherent discourse on the identity of the true culprit.

"No wonder he kept asking us to open windows between interviews!" exclaimed a steward whom Livia recognized as having been stationed outside the library for several days. "He must have been worried about the smell of blood and antiseptic and whatnot on himself."

"I'll bet the lock-picking set he 'found' in Mr. Pratt's room wasn't Mr. Pratt's but his own," concluded a missionary sagely.

Livia and Charlotte repaired to Charlotte's cabin and ordered a plentiful tea, now that Charlotte no longer needed to conceal how much she ate. Watching Charlotte eat always spurred Livia's appetite. She laughed—for a moment it felt as if the sisters were fighting over a plate of sandwiches, which had never happened.

Livia was able to put together some details of the case for herself. For example, Inspector Brighton, upon learning of Mr. Arkwright's presence on the *Provence* at his dinner with Captain Pritchard and Lord Ingram, must have immediately decided to give himself a condition of vertigo, so that in subsequent days he could hide in his cabin to avoid accidentally running into the man he had forced out of Britain not once but twice. And after he'd murdered Mr. Arkwright, having no choice but to investigate his own crime, he'd continued to feign dizziness and imbalance, symptoms commonly associated with vertigo, to disguise the fact that he was moving about with a wounded limb.

For another example, it also became clear what must have happened to her mother's missing petticoat: It had been used as bandaging and also to mop up any blood drops in Mr. Arkwright's parlor that might hint at the injury of another person.

Other facets, however, continued to puzzle her. How had the two nemeses run into each other after all? Charlotte theorized that the policeman had probably not wanted to use a chamber pot for days on end and had believed he would be safe in the gentlemen's baths, since Mr. Arkwright had his own en-suite facility. But of course, if Mr. Arkwright had to heed a call of nature while his sister was in their private bath, off to the public convenience he went.

Then there were aspects of the case Livia hadn't known at all, because they were mentioned in neither Inspector Brighton's summary nor Miss Arkwright's. Charlotte told her how, after Inspector Brighton had dragged Lady Holmes back to her cabin and poured enough laudanum down her throat to keep her unconscious the rest of the night, he had gone back to Mr. Arkwright's suite.

"Whatever for?" exclaimed Livia, feeling a chill at this fresh information even though the danger had passed.

"He wiped clean the few smears of blood in the passage and put

Mother's rouge pot in a corner of the parlor. But it was more about retrieving the bullet that had injured him."

Mr. Arkwright had confided to his sister the night of the storm that perhaps he had been too hasty in going after Ned Plowers. Yet afterward he'd patrolled the passenger levels once again, unable to rein in his compulsion to find his archenemy. When Mrs. Watson encountered him near the ladies' baths, the policeman, who had the port cabin closest to the ladies' baths, was likely eavesdropping on their exchange.

With his foe closing in, Inspector Brighton also abandoned the wiser course of continuing to remain in his cabin. He didn't care to hide, and he didn't care to avoid confrontations. He was a man who thrived on dominating others, for goodness' sake.

When Mr. Arkwright left, he followed. Mr. Arkwright went into the smoking room; Inspector Brighton let himself into Mr. Arkwright's suite. Perhaps he'd only meant for a parley, but given his domineering ways, not to mention Mr. Arkwright's deep-seated anger, explosive temper, *and* strong intention to expose Inspector Brighton's past crimes to the world, it was hardly surprising that everything went awry.

"Inspector Brighton did not think through things with extreme clarity in the wake of the killing. He was injured, in pain, and reeling from the enormity of potential consequences. That he was able to immediately latch onto our mother as a scapegoat rather testified to his cleverness, but in doing so he took on a bit too much.

"It was probably only after he'd returned to his own cabin that he remembered the bullet that had grazed him. If Mr. Arkwright had been shot only twice, then how to explain the presence of an extra bullet, one that very well might be bloodstained. So, he took a risk, went back, found the bullet under the desk, put the rouge pot in its place, and pilfered Mr. Arkwright's cabin key to better implicate Mother.

"But I saw the bullet that night. And by swapping it out, he allowed me to deduce that the murderer had been injured and did not wish anyone to know."

Charlotte bit into another sandwich. "It would seem that once

Inspector Brighton gave in to the impulse to take Mr. Arkwright down a notch, everything else he did led step by step to his own downfall."

———※———

"Oh, you should have seen her, Mrs. Newell." Livia swished her parasol in demonstration. "She went like this, then like this, and his firearm went flying. And then, *whack*, and he lost his balance."

"Oh my," exclaimed Mrs. Newell, who loved a good exciting story.

"It looked easy, as if a child could have done it. But when I think about it, I'm amazed at the speed and precision of her strikes—the whole thing took no more than a second. Every other time she wrote me last autumn she moaned about how her entire body ached from *canne de combat* sessions with Mrs. Watson and how she never seemed to improve. But she improved. She is skilled now."

Livia hugged the parasol to her chest, bursting with both pride and aspiration. "I'd like to learn *canne de combat*, too, Mrs. Newell. I—"

A knock came at the door. "Are you there, Miss Holmes?"

Oh no. Norbert. What did Lady Holmes want *now*?

Norbert was apologetic. "Miss, her ladyship has decided that it would be best for her to disembark right here in Gibraltar and head back to Britain. And she is of the firm opinion that you should come with her."

The gentleness of Norbert's delivery did little to lessen the blow of Lady Holmes's command. Livia had been feeling breathlessly alive and triumphant. But after Norbert's departure, she could only stumble to the edge of the bed and clutch her head.

She felt buried.

Mrs. Newell came to sit next to her, her hand on Livia's back. "My dear, I don't know whether anyone has told you this, but all your life you have been a most dutiful child."

Tears rushed into Livia's eyes. "Thank you, Mrs. Newell."

"Unfortunately, your parents would not say the same thing." Mrs. Newell sighed. "Your dutifulness, to them, is their due. They expect your utmost, return little, and are convinced you ought to be grateful for this state of affairs."

It was an all-too-accurate description of Sir Henry and Lady Holmes as parents. Livia's eyes stung even more painfully.

"By this point, I'm sure you have realized that whatever you do for your mother would never be enough. So you must ask yourself, do you wish to continue as before, or do you wish to make a different decision?"

Mrs. Newell left. Livia sat with her head buried in her lap for a long time. Then she rose, washed her face, placed the moonstone cabochon Mr. Marbleton had given her inside her bodice, next to her heart, and headed out.

When she arrived in her mother's cabin, Norbert bustled about, with Lady Holmes issuing orders and picking faults from her bed. Her head wound was coming along, and she no longer needed to be bed-bound, but there she remained out of bile.

"What took you so long, Olivia?" she groused. "Are you packed? Have you told the stewards that you need your steamer trunk retrieved from the luggage hold?"

Livia turned to the maid. "Norbert, will you give us a moment?"

"Certainly." Norbert lost no time in slipping out.

Lady Holmes rolled her eyes. "What's this? What is it you can't say in front of Norbert?"

Livia's calves shook. When she'd left her cabin, she'd been enveloped in a martyr-like calm, but now that false serenity had splintered completely.

She *had* been a very dutiful child. No matter how much she had grumbled—and sometimes raged—on the inside, the vast majority of times, she had obeyed her parents. She hid much from them, did not trust them, and constantly plotted her escape, but she had rarely defied them and certainly never practiced defiance on this scale.

Now the muscles of her calves bunched painfully. She welcomed the pain—it speared through her incipient panic. "Mamma, it would not be a good idea for me to return home with you."

Her words emerged as if they'd been glued together, and then tossed in a heap. But they'd been spoken at last. The beginning of dissent.

"What?" cried Lady Holmes. "I was injured and you would let me travel alone?"

"You won't be alone, Mamma. Norbert will accompany you."

"And how will that look to the neighbors?"

"The neighbors would not know that we were on the same ship unless you tell them. Would you tell them? Would you let word get back to Papa that, without informing him, you were headed for Bombay?"

Lady Holmes's jaw set. "Olivia, enough. You are coming home with me and that is that."

Only a few exchanges, and Livia already felt as if she'd thrown herself repeatedly at a brick wall. But even brick walls gave way before large enough sledgehammers, and she hadn't even swung hers yet.

"No, Mamma. It really would not be a good idea—for you. You see, I know how much you admired Mr. Gregory. You are leaving today precisely because you don't want that to become common knowledge. But Mrs. Ramsay has told me everything, including your attempted nocturnal visit to Mr. Gregory's cabin. Why would you wish to drag me home? Aren't you worried that I might let something slip before Papa?"

The inside of her mouth burned. She could not believe what she'd said to the petty despot who had ruled over her for twenty-eight years.

Lady Holmes's eyes bulged. "Are you threatening me, Olivia?"

Yes, I am. My God, I am. And I am not threatening you just to sail on to Port Said.

She could almost touch the precipitous cliffs of the Rock of Gibraltar, on the other side of the cabin's window. There was so much of the world left to see, so many new things to experience. And she would take this very small opportunity and shove through a whole new life for herself.

Her cheeks trembled with the effort, but she smiled. "I've been thinking a lot about your welfare lately, Mamma. I've been a constant source of frustration and embarrassment; it would be a great relief to you if I took up permanent residence at Mrs. Newell's."

And when you are not looking, that permanent residence at Mrs. Newell's could easily become permanent residence at Mrs. Watson's, with Charlotte.

"Not only would I be out of your hair, Mamma, with me gone there would be almost no chance of Papa accidentally learning anything detrimental to you."

"You—you—"

Livia smiled wider. Her calves still hurt; her cheeks now hurt, too. But she felt nothing except six inches of air under the soles of her feet. "We're agreed then, I'm glad to see. I'll tell Norbert to come back inside, Mamma. I'm sure you two still have much to do before you can disembark."

—◆—

Mrs. Watson tried hard not to stare at Georg Bittner.

The boy gazed, with a hesitant happiness, at the spread of cakes, sandwiches, and fritters before him. Mrs. Watson had wanted to dazzle the children at this afternoon tea prepared especially for them, and she seemed to have succeeded very well.

"Lemonade or ginger beer? We also have limeade and pineapple water," she said, sweeping her hand along the row of glass pitchers, their contents vibrant and beautiful.

"Ginger beer," said Georg Bittner without hesitation.

"A man of taste, I see." She poured him a full cup. "Save some room in your stomach. We are going to have ice cream, too."

"I'm going to save at least half the room in my stomach for ice cream," enthused Rupert Pennington.

"This is so lovely," murmured Frau Schmidt. "Thank you for doing this for the children."

"It couldn't have been easy for them the past few days," said Miss Charlotte, still in disguise as Mrs. Ramsay, "but at least everyone seems to be having a good time in Gibraltar."

The ship had docked hours ago. After the passengers were allowed to go ashore, Frau Schmidt's charges had already climbed to the top of the great rock formation. The Ashburton children had only walked around town because their father was even now assisting Chief Inspector Morris with the case, but he'd promised that he would take them on the ascent tomorrow.

Mrs. Watson asked the children about their day and suggested that they play games while they waited for the ice cream to arrive. As the children debated which game to play, Miss Charlotte pulled out a twenty-pound banknote, so crisp it might as well have left the mint only hours ago, and said, "I will put this up as a prize, if you win at my game."

The children were agog; even the grown-ups around the table were surprised—one seldom saw twenty-pound banknotes in circulation.

"Really? You'll really give it to us if we win?" cried Rupert Pennington.

"Yes. And the game is simple. Does anyone have some coins? I want to give each of the children six pennies—they'll use those to play."

Aboard the ship there were few daily financial transactions—those passengers who ordered beverages and services not included in the price of the passage could settle their accounts all at once before disembarkation. So Miss Charlotte and Mrs. Watson, still disguised as Miss Fenwick, had a perfectly good excuse for not having brought their handbags.

The mother-and-daughter duo who had joined the tea party contributed a few pennies. Miss Potter, who had also left her handbag behind, turned up her palms in resignation. Frau Schmidt fished a coin purse from her satchel and found a few pennies inside, but they were still far short of the thirty Charlotte wanted.

"What about at the bottom of your handbags? Any coins there?" Mrs. Watson, her heart thumping, suggested.

"I have a handful here," said Frau Schmidt, reaching deep into her satchel. "But they are farthings—oh, look, I even have a pfennig."

The pfennig looked dark and ancient, even though it couldn't be

older than the founding of the German Empire in the early eighteen
seventies.

"Anything will help, but the pfennig might be a bit confusing, as
it doesn't have an obvious 'head' side," said Miss Charlotte. "I'll hold
on to it and see if we couldn't get some more pennies."

They didn't. Mrs. Watson, as Miss Fenwick, was obliged to go
back to their cabin to unearth more pennies, which she did. And
when she returned, the children learned a hard lesson in probability:
It was practically impossible, while blindfolded, to line up six coins
all heads up or tails up.

Mrs. Ramsay, with a smile, put away her twenty-pound banknote.

———✺———

"That child is—that child is—"

The deck was empty—passengers were either still ashore or in
their cabins with their feet up. But still Livia slapped a hand over her
mouth, so that she wouldn't blurt out loud what Mrs. Watson had
carefully whispered into her ear.

Georg Bittner, Frau Schmidt's temporary charge, was none other
than the son Miss Moriarty and Mr. Finch had been desperately trying to find—and the reason that Miss Arkwright had sailed on the
Provence instead of a different vessel: Since she was anyway headed
east, she'd been tasked to make sure that an unwitting Frau Schmidt
delivered the child safely to his "father."

But Mr. Finch, the boy's real father, was Livia and Charlotte's half
brother, which made him their nephew.

Livia did not form strong, instant bonds to others simply because
they were related to her by blood—too many of her close relations
were people she'd rather not have known. But for this child, all but
assured of a difficult life, she felt an enormous sympathy.

Alas, Mrs. Watson went on to inform Livia that as part of the
agreement between Charlotte and Miss Arkwright, Charlotte could
not simply abduct Georg Bittner to return him to his parents.

Miss Arkwright had already disembarked alongside her brother's
body—the police might still keep it for some time, but afterward,

the late Mr. Arkwright's will stipulated his burial in England. Before her departure, she had asked that Charlotte and, in turn, Miss Moriarty, not make any move until Georg Bittner had been handed off, so that his disappearance would not be blamed on either Frau Schmidt or herself.

But still, now that they knew where the boy was and where he was headed, there was a possibility, however slender, that soon he would be reunited with his anxious parents. And perhaps, if they were lucky, and if *he* was lucky, he could grow up to be someone as remarkable as Mr. Marbleton, someone whose travails in life had forged in him only a greater, purer joie de vivre.

She gazed across the Bay of Gibraltar to its western shore. Andalusia, that was Andalusia. She hadn't wanted to go ashore earlier because she'd wanted to spend as much time as possible with Charlotte and Mrs. Watson. But tomorrow, when they were gone, she would find a boat to ferry her across, and set foot where her dear Mr. Marbleton had once been so happy.

"Here's something else we want to tell you, my dear Miss Livia, before we parted ways," murmured Mrs. Watson, the fringes of her white lace parasol dancing in the wind. "We have news of Mr. Marbleton's whereabouts. And we plan to take advantage of that."

It felt a little odd to be back on land, where nothing moved underfoot. But Charlotte and Mrs. Watson would not remain on land for long—Mrs. Watson had already booked passages on a local steamer headed for Málaga, about to weigh anchor any moment.

Their luggage had been transferred, their good-byes said to the passengers of the *Provence,* who were sorry to see them go, especially the young lieutenants who thought Mrs. Ramsay brilliant company. But they understood that two murders had been too much for an elderly lady and of course she would wish to carry out the remainder of her travels on some other vessel, and possibly along a very different route.

Now Charlotte waited only to see Lord Ingram, who had been at the police station since the *Provence* docked.

She saw the Shrewsburys first. Husband and wife were awkward with each other. There was no great hatred between them, merely a great deal of unsuitability. Charlotte, as Mrs. Ramsay, smiled and waved. Perhaps Australia might mark a new beginning for them. Or, perhaps, in a territory where divorces were more common, they would go their separate ways.

Mr. Gregory returned next. He and Charlotte chatted briefly before wishing each other farewell and bon voyage. Lord Ingram, in the end, had asked Mr. Gregory about that night. And as it turned out, nothing had transpired between him and Frau Schmidt. The great lover had understood that even when Frau Schmidt had sought him in his cabin, what she had desired had been more of the same, his undivided, sympathetic attention. And her slight dishevelment that Lord Ingram had witnessed had been caused not by any passionate kisses, but because the first time she'd got up to leave, the lights had gone out, causing her to stumble, knocking her coiffure askew.

Charlotte watched Mr. Gregory amble up the *Provence*'s gangplank. It hadn't been only for his rare misprinted stamp that the late Mr. Newell had chased him all over the Continent but for love. In the end, however, Mr. Newell's pursuit had failed precisely because of its fervency: When he wasn't working, Mr. Gregory preferred to be alone.

Charlotte, too, very much enjoyed being alone. But she was fortunate: Those who loved her never saw her inclination toward solitude as something that needed to be overturned to make room for them.

The sun dipped closer to the horizon. She was beginning to feel conspicuous, standing on the quay, when at last her lover returned, leaping out of a carriage. Upon spying her, he schooled his expression into a polite smile and approached at a sedate pace. For the grave business with the police, he'd donned a black day coat and striped trousers. She'd forgotten how well suited he was to such formal attire, like a beautifully packaged present ready for her to unwrap.

"My dear Mrs. Ramsay, how sorry I am to hear of your departure. We've only just met," he murmured, briefly taking her hand in his, his eyes dark with a lupine carnality that might give actual old ladies apoplectic attacks.

Or awaken in them such an energetic lust that he would find himself overwhelmed and begging for mercy—one never knew with such things.

She tapped his shoulder not with her cane, which had already been packed away, but with a folded-up silk fan. "I know. But when we meet next we shall be old friends, and I shall permit *much* familiarity on your part, my lord."

His lips quivered with suppressed mirth, but his expression turned serious when he looked down at the small envelope she'd pressed into his palm during their handhold. It contained the pfennig she'd taken from Frau Schmidt, which was not a real coin but a tiny case with microphotographic film pellicules concealed inside. Lord Remington's emissary had been right about one thing: The dossier would be something recognizably German. And it had been slipped into Frau Schmidt's satchel along with an offer of German biscuits.

"So . . . my lord Remington's aegis of protection would be yours soon." He glanced back at her, his gaze now wistful. "I shall expect letters, lavishly discursive letters, ten pages front and back."

He still looked under-rested, her lover who had done so much for her. Without his successful persuasion of the captain, who had been astounded at the idea that one could suspect the investigator in a murder case—in fact, without everything he had undertaken since the night of the murder—she would not be feeling as confident about their next step.

"Why, I might even compose the next installment of my very mildly erotic story," she promised extravagantly.

"I had best prepare a purification ritual for myself then," he answered in mock horror.

"Or there may not be time for my sophomore authorial effort. I believe we'll meet again very soon."

They rarely parted with avowals of swift reunions—there was

often no telling when they'd see each other again. But this time she knew it would not be long—pieces were already moving.

He lowered his face a few degrees, then peered at her from beneath long, dark lashes. "Will you miss me—or would we be apart for too short a time for that?"

Her chest constricted with a bittersweet pleasure. "I will miss you. I already miss you."

"Then I will miss you, too."

Carefully, he placed the envelope she'd given him in a hidden pocket of his day coat. The westering sun gilded the brim of his hat and cast his features in a golden glow. He lifted his head and looked her in the eye, his gaze so luminous that her heart missed a beat.

"I miss you all the time, Holmes," he said. "I have missed you for years upon years. And I will always, always miss you."

ACKNOWLEDGMENTS

Kerry Donovan and the team at Berkley, for making the publication process almost zen with their cheerfulness and dedication.

Kristin Nelson, the GOAT.

Janine Ballard, who makes sure that I produce my best work time after time.

Srinadh Madhavapeddi, for always being a font of knowledge when I need it.

Kate Reading, who could not be more marvelous in her narration.

The ladies of the Turtle Enclave, Liz Essex and Tracy Brogan, for making it fun to be a slow writer—or at least more fun.

My family and friends, so many great people in my life.

My brain, still amazingly intact considering how many times it exploded in the course of writing this book.

And you, if you are reading this, thank you. Thank you for everything.

USA Today bestselling author Sherry Thomas is one of the most acclaimed historical fiction authors writing today, winning the RITA Award two years running and appearing on innumerable "Best of the Year" lists, including those of *Publishers Weekly, Kirkus Reviews, Library Journal,* Dear Author, and All About Romance. Her novels include *A Study in Scarlet Women, A Conspiracy in Belgravia, The Hollow of Fear, The Art of Theft, Murder on Cold Street,* and *Miss Moriarty, I Presume?,* the first six books in the Lady Sherlock series; *My Beautiful Enemy;* and *The Luckiest Lady in London.* She lives in Austin, Texas, with her husband and sons.

CONNECT ONLINE

SherryThomas.com

Ready to find
your next great read?

Let us help.

Visit prh.com/nextread

Penguin
Random
House